Caffeine Ni

# When A Killer Strikes

## RC Bridgestock

Fiction aimed at the heart
and the head..

Published by Caffeine Nights Publishing 2017

CONDITIONS OF SALE

Published in Great Britain by
Caffeine Nights Publishing
4 Eton Close
Walderslade
Chatham
Kent
ME5 9AT
www. caffeinenights com

Also available as an eBook

British Library Cataloguing in Publication Data.
A CIP catalogue record for this book is available from the British Library

ISBN: 978-1-910720-85-1

Cover design by
Mark (Wills) Williams

Everything else by
Default, Luck and Accident

Also by RC Bridgestock

The D.I. Dylan Series

Deadly Focus
Consequences
White Lilies
Snow Kills
Reprobates
Killer Smile
When The Killing Starts

All available in paperback and eBook

Deadly Focus is available on MP3 CD audiobook and as a downloadable audiobook

Consequences is available to download as an audiobook

White Lilies is available to download as an audiobook

# Acknowledgement

We are tremendously grateful to the many kind, dedicated and professional individuals that work within the emergency services and who keep us updated as to how it is, in the 'real world' nowadays... This helps us give our readers the most realistic experience possible in our factual tales.

Our special thanks to our publisher Darren Laws and everyone at Caffeine Nights Publishing, our literary agent David H. Headley, Emily Glenister and all at DHH Literary Agency for their continued support and encouragement.

Thanks too, to West Yorkshire's vehicle recovery experts Colin Exley and Shane Coach, Stoneywood Limited. As always the 'devil' for us was in the detail.

To those who bid at charity auctions, to name a character in this book, we want to thank you from the bottom of our hearts. We sincerely hope you have enjoyed the experience, and how we have utilised the information you supplied for your character. We know how important the money donated means to the charities involved.

We will be forever grateful for the love and support of our family - you all mean the world to us.

Last, but by no means least thanks to #TeamDylan - we really couldn't do it without you!

To:

Our families, friends, police colleagues, emergency service personnel, charity workers, volunteers and fundraisers who gave us the heart, blood and bones for this book.

And, to emergency service personnel and first responders around the world for putting us all before themselves to make the world a safer place.

A special mention here to the charities that we support, in the hope that this raises public awareness, and much needed funds.

We are proud Patrons for :-

B.A.S.H Local - www.bashwy.co.uk
B.A.S.H provides an outreach service that connects those in need with the charities and services they may not have otherwise known about whilst offering food, clothing and friendly faces, located in Brighouse, West Yorkshire.

Isle of Wight Society for the Blind - www.iwsightconcern.org.uk
The Isle of Wight Society for the Blind provides information, practical help and emotional support to approximately 1,000 people living on the Isle of Wight, located in Newport.

The Red Lipstick Foundation - www.theredlipstickfoundation.org
The Red lipstick Foundation offers support and links for those whose lives have been affected by suicide, located in Southampton

Ambassadors for:

Bethany Smile - http://www.bethanyssmile.org
Bethany's Smile - aim to raise a minimum of £300,000 to build Smile Cottage – a holiday/respite home, in Yorkshire, where families can go and spend quality time plus build happy memories,

when they are faced with the news that their child has a very short life expectancy.

The Yorkshire Down Syndrome Group - www.ydsg.co.uk @YorkshireDownSyndromeGroup

The Yorkshire Down Syndrome Group is a group based in Batley, West Yorkshire that holds a fortnightly meeting for families and people who care for children with Down Syndrome. All ages welcome.

Last but not least a charity that is close to our hearts. Forget Me Not Children's Hospice, Huddersfield is a special place that supports children with life shortening conditions and their families throughout West Yorkshire. www.forgetmenotchild.co.uk

# When A Killer Strikes

# Chapter One

Colonial House didn't warrant a second glance. The red brick, detached Georgian home blended harmoniously with its surroundings. At its front a bowling green lawn ran the breadth of the residence. It faced a tree-lined avenue set in an orderly manner and was surrounded by a trim privet hedge, behind white painted railings and an ornamental gate. However, situated in a quiet, semi-rural neighbourhood on the outskirts of Harrowfield town, behind its solid, locked, glossy blood red door the house held a macabre mystery.

Detective Inspector Jack Dylan, a middle-aged man, father to four-year-old Maisy and a seasoned detective was house-hunting with his wife Jen when his mobile phone rang. Used to Dylan's sudden departures when summoned the pair's eyes locked.

'What makes you think it's suspicious?' he said earnestly to the caller as he turned away and walked to a more private place to speak, near the window. 'Has someone pronounced life extinct?' Dylan nodded twice. 'Okay. Tell those present I'll be with them shortly.'

Dylan's eyes were drawn to an elderly couple across the road who stood looking in the toyshop window with a young girl who was pointing out something that had taken her eye. She looked up at the older woman and put the palms of her hands together, as if in prayer. The old man walked away. The old lady tugged at the young girl's hand. She let it go and the young girl turned to face the window once more, her arms crossed. A silver-haired man dressed in a caramel-coloured Crombie coat and hat stood a few yards away obviously taking an interest in the altercation. He was hesitant, as if about to intervene at one point, then thought the better of it. As the young girl turned and chased after the old man and the old woman he got into the back of a chauffeur driven car.

Phone still in hand Dylan kissed Jen on the cheek. 'I'll be in touch,' he said softly. She gave him a tight-lipped smile and he moved swiftly towards Maisy. 'Be good for Mummy,' he continued, patting Maisy on the top of her fair head. At the door he raised an apologetic hand to the estate agent sat at her desk – his mind already running through the many questions he needed answering from those at the crime scene. When he left the estate agents the older couple and little girl was crossing the road towards him.

'Detective Inspector Dylan,' said the old man, reaching out to shake his hand.

'That can't be Gemma,' Dylan said. The little girl gripped her grandmother's hand shyly and pulled her into the sweet shop.

'It certainly is,' said Ken. 'No word on the whereabouts of her good-for-nothing father yet? Drug baron status, apparently now. What an accolade; it's five years since her mother was burned to death, and your colleague Larry Banks got murdered?'

Dylan nodded his head. 'Life goes on. We get bits of intelligence now and again about Malcolm Reynolds. Last we heard he was in Spain. But, we'll never give up in our search.'

\*\*\*

Once Dylan had been notified of an incident the responsibility for what happened from then on fell firmly at his feet. Briskly, he headed towards his car – a man on a mission.

Jen continued to scour the glossy property pamphlets. The midsummer sun shone directly onto her back through a wall of plated glass that showed her the hustle and bustle of the high street. Inside the shop was by contrast quiet and peaceful.

'Seen anything of interest?' said Natalie, sliding from behind her desk and stifling a yawn. At the sight of the solemn shake of Jen's head she settled herself on the warm carpet next to Maisy. Her outstretched hand reached into the toy box where she instantly found what she was looking for; sections of railway track for Thomas the Tank Engine and his friends the little girl was happily pushing too and fro.

Head down, Jen screwed up her nose. 'I want something different...' she said, turning the loose-leaf plastic sleeves over one by one – unwittingly dismissing each box-like house with a little sigh.

'Would you consider something that needs work doing?' Natalie asked, tentatively.

Jen's eyes shot upwards in the estate agents direction. 'What do you mean by work?'

Natalie raised an eyebrow. A smile touched the corners of her mouth and her face lit up.

'Maybe...' said Jen her eyes narrowing.

'Then I have just the one for you!' Eagerly she jumped up from the floor with the ease of a twenty year-old.

Jen raised her shoulders. She smiled at Maisy who fleetingly observed the interaction with interest, before hurriedly sticking her hand back in the toy box to retrieve a fuzzy-haired doll that caught her attention.

Hearing the metal filing cabinet clunk-click open and shut Jen's head turned to see Natalie carrying a yellowing sheet of paper towards her; it was quite clear this was not a glossy brochure of the day.

At that very moment Maisy threw her arms in the air with a squeal of delight and she held a figurine high above her head. 'Joe's here Mummy!'

Natalie giggled at Maisy's excitement. Seeing Jen's face blanch, the smile dropped from her face. 'You okay?'

Jen put her hand directly to her beating heart. 'Yes, yes,' she said stumbling on her words. Blindly, she reached for the paper Natalie held out for her taking. Tears that had sprung into her eyes over-spilled down her face. Natalie sat down on the chair next to Jen with a look of concern. 'Are you sure?' she said putting a hand over Jen's, to feel her shaking.

Jen took a deep breath. 'Joe is the name of my husband's late father. He was a stationmaster,' Jen said, by way of an explanation for her random behaviour. She swallowed hard. 'Maisy and Dylan call the Thin Controller Joe, after him.' Jen leant forward in her chair and plucked a tissue from her handbag.

'Oh, I see.' Natalie watched her dry her eyes. 'Has he passed over recently?' she said in a hushed tone.

Jen chin wobbled. She shook her head and swallowed hard. 'No, no, he died a long time ago... I never met him.'

Natalie looked puzzled.

'We recently buried our stillborn son who we named after him.'

The tree-lined avenue that led to Colonial House was awash with crime scene vehicles, police cars and an ambulance. Dylan noted each one in turn on his approach. He knew that the scene would be secured with uniformed police officers as he had instructed en route. The blue and white 'DO NOT CROSS' police tape was a simple barrier command for people to adhere to, allowing the crime scene to remain sterile. There was only ever one chance at a crime scene and no one knew that better than Inspector Jack Dylan.

The local officers watched out for his arrival. Dylan was in charge, and they knew it. Him being responsible for the investigation from now on was somewhat a relief to the most senior officers in attendance at the scene.

He parked his car and walked towards the rendezvous point. He was pleased; it had been chosen wisely as the gated entrance that led into the driveway. He could feel the concealed eyes of the neighbouring householders upon him. When he looked upwards he saw one occupant peering at him from behind a curtain, a mobile phone against the streaky glass, unashamedly filming the police activity. A sign of the times he knew, and he was in no doubt that the ongoing action would be on social media prior to related family members knowing that anything at the address was untoward. He shook his head.

Detective Sergeant Vicky Hardacre walked towards him.

'What've we got?' asked Dylan.

'What've you been told?' she said, tucking a soft, blonde tendril of hair behind her ear. Her eyes were upturned in a serious face.

'Suspicious death of a teenage girl and that you're at the scene, just about sums it up.'

The two stood still for a moment observing the house and its surroundings.

Vicky broke the silence. 'Our deceased is a Patti Heinz, fourteen years old and apparently a talented gymnast, competing at national level.'

He turned to her, his eyes narrowed. 'I read an article about her recently in the local press. Wasn't she destined for the Olympics?'

Vicky nodded. 'Apparently so; first impressions suggest that she's been strangled with her bra, and she's naked – there's blood... in a way which suggests to me that she may also have been subjected to rape.'

'Who found her?' Dylan's eyes wandered to the gate considering his approach. The windows sparkled in the afternoon sun and the white painted walls looked fresh and new. Seasonal flowers were strategically placed with precision up the pathway.

'Mum's partner, Elliot Black. He's lived with them since Patti was eleven. Sandra Heinz's first husband died when Patti was little.'

'Have the couple any other children?'

'No.'

'Where's Mr Black now?'

'I've had him taken to the nick. You should know there was blood on his trousers.'

Dylan's eyebrows rose. 'Make sure the car transporting him is valeted before it's used again. I don't want the suggestion of contamination to be an issue in court.'

Vicky regarded his comment with a brief nod.

'Who've you got with him?'

'Detective Constable Donna Frost and Michelle Robinson; they've been instructed to seize all his clothing and record the circumstances surrounding him finding her.'

'And his initial explanation?'

'He popped home to get his phone charger that he keeps on the bedside table. Obviously he got a shock to see Patti laid on the landing.'

'What did he say he did then?'

'Checked for signs of life – his explanation for the blood on his trousers, and immediately after rang three nines.'

'From his mobile?' Dylan was quick in responding.

'Landline.'

Dylan looked at her questioningly. 'But?'

Vicky cocked her head to one side and looked up at him. 'But, I'm having that verified.'

'Good. And?'

'Paramedics have confirmed life extinct. I've made arrangements for statements to be taken from them later today.'

Dylan took a step closer to the entrance. 'By the way,' Vicky continued, 'the vomit at the side of her body – it's his.'

'Thanks for that,' Dylan grimaced. 'Does Mr Black work nearby?'

Vicky looked puzzled.

'No, car in the driveway?' he said. His eyes followed the neatly cut hedge and beyond up the driveway.

'Apparently he cycles. He works down the road at the Spar shop.'

Dylan scanned the front of the house. 'Where's the bike?'

'Out back. It appears he's a bit of a fitness freak. He's recently turned their garage into a gym for himself, and Patti apparently.'

'What's your first impression of Mr Black?'

'Seems to be coping a little too well for my liking... Then again he could be in shock.'

Dylan frowned. 'And where's mum? Is she aware?'

'DC Jaene Booth has gone round to the local bookies where Patti's mum works. Jaene's family liaison trained so she's been given the task of breaking the news to her, take her to the nick, and keeping her away from her partner until we've got their independent initial accounts of their last contact with Patti.'

'I want any known business premises, or private CCTV in the area checked and seized. Especially those covering the route from where Mr Black works to here.'

The uniformed police officer nodded her head in acknowledgement as they reached the rendezvous point. 'I've shown you on the Log as arriving at three thirty-five pm, Sir,' she said to Dylan.

'Thanks Rachael.'

'Who's Crime Scene Investigator?' He stood on the roadside with his back to the garden wall. 'I need a suit.'

'Tony's here,' Vicky said, rolling her eyes. Dylan turned and raised his hand in acknowledgement to the man who was laying the footplates in the grounds.

'That's not very nice,' he said giving a half-hearted laugh.

'Well, he walks around like the grim reaper. As if crime scenes aren't bad enough without seeing his miserable bloody face.'

Dylan looked past Vicky, shrugged his shoulders at Rachael and both smiling at the DS they were united in shaking their heads. 'As long as he does his job,' he said, raising an eyebrow at his number two. He lifted his chin in the direction of the neatly cut lawn where the path now had footplates in situ. 'And, he looks to be cracking on.'

'That's thanks to David Funk, thankfully he was on call Crime Scene Manager.'

As if mentioning the six foot two, brown haired man's name conjured him up Dylan saw David confidently walking towards them. Vicky saw Rachael's eyes looking in his direction approvingly; his right wrist instantly went into his pocket.

'David!' Dylan said enthusiastically as he took a few steps towards him. He took the coveralls he offered him and happy to see him energetically shook his hand.

'Good to see you. How's Eccles?'

David's smile was wide. 'Always showing off, like most border terriers.'

Dylan and David talked about the crime scene as the Detective Inspector bent down to slip on the overshoes. He reached out and touched the wall for support.

'Who's that?' Rachael whispered to Vicky as she nodded in the Crime Manager's direction. 'Is he married? Got a girlfriend? What do you know about him?'

It was Vicky's turn to shake her head at the younger woman. 'God, you make me feel old.' A puzzled look crossed Rachael's face as she studied David more closely.

'Is he left handed? I've never been out with a guy who's left handed,' she said.

The young women watched David hand Dylan gloves and a mask from his pocket.

'David? No, he lost his fingers and thumb on his right hand, just below his wrist in an accident when he was younger. Actually he's one of the nicest men I've met... He's kind, generous, hardworking. He does loads for charity... In fact...' she said, with a wink and a smile.

'Hands off,' said Rachael. 'He's mine.'

The Detective Inspector was more than aware of how much information a crime scene could hold but it was up to them, the investigators to uncover it. Personally, he desperately needed to get a feel of how the deceased had lived, which in turn ultimately gave him some indication usually, of how they died.

Via the footplates to the door Dylan took the lead down the path. The walkway was free of debris and litter. Detective Sergeant Vicky Hardacre, David, CSI Tony Oswald and DC Emily Scotcher, nominated Exhibits Officer, walked behind him. He stopped at the entrance and turned to see Tony Oswald's droopy eyes in his solemn face looking at him mournfully.

'Smile Tony, it could be worse.'

'How's that?' he mumbled.

'Well, it could be raining.'

Tony scowled at Dylan and put his head down showing a saggy, protruding bottom lip. Dylan looked over his head at David, raised his eyebrows and gave a tight-lipped smile.

Led by Dylan the five entered the semi-detached home via the front door, which had been the chosen-route by the emergency services, them being the first in attendance. Instantly, Colonial House felt invitingly warm, smelt lemon fresh and looked exceptionally tidy. Dotted around the lounge an occasional vase of seasonal flowers. Family pictures mostly depicted the growing-up of an auburn-haired girl. There were no knick-knacks, as Dylan's mum would have said, no clutter. Due to the care taken on the exterior of the house, the neat and tidiness of the interior wasn't unexpected. However, this was the exception rather than the rule in houses he attended, in his role as a police officer; houses where he felt the need to wipe his feet on his way out due to the garbage, rotting food and animal and human waste on the floors inside.

As he stood looking at the plain cream walls that merged into a plain cream carpet, for a moment he was taken back to being a young copper on the beat. The particular house he had been called to had been stripped on the interior – floorboards were missing, the odd wooden step from the stairs gone. The internal doors non-existent, just so the inhabitants could burn the wood in the fireplace to keep them warm. He was offered a drink from an old jam jar on that occasion. The lady of the house apologised for having no crockery due to it being sold, the results of a family struggling to survive – best they knew how, with the hand that life had dealt them. In those days there were no cash machines, no credit cards... just human kindness, that a neighbour might show in the giving another a cup of sugar, or a jug of milk when times were hard.

'Before we go upstairs,' said Dylan, conscious that all eyes were on him for direction. 'I know she was allegedly discovered by her stepdad, but have we checked down here to see if there's an insecure window or door?'

'All downstairs windows and doors checked sir,' said Emily. 'Patio door not secure, but I am reliably informed that nothing appears to be out of place, or taken.'

Dylan sighed, 'Let's see where she is then...' he said, striding onto the footplates that had been positioned on the highly polished floor. The house was eerily silent and the peeling of his plastic shoes could be heard. It felt like Colonial House was holding its breath to reveal the dead body to Dylan – the man in charge of finding out who had killed Patti Heinz.

The marble-coloured body of a young girl was naked except for a white bra, which was wrapped tightly around her neck. She was flat to the floor, her distorted face resting to one side, her mouth open wide as if gasping for air. The teenager's legs were wide apart, her left knee bent slightly. The tip of her thick, plaited, auburn hair rested at her elbow.

'Is this where the attack had taken place?' Dylan wondered.

'Every scene tells a story,' said Emily pointing to the indentations in the carpet. 'Fascinating...'

'Scuff marks where she struggled Sherlock Scotcher,' mumbled Tony under his breath. 'It's not a dump-site.'

Dylan stood quietly taking in the scene unfolding before him.

'No furniture upturned, no open drawers, no discarded purse or wallet to suggest a burglary,' said Vicky. 'This scene tells us naff-all.'

Before he instructed for the body to be turned, Dylan knelt down to see at close quarters the victims face in situ. She clearly had a wound to the top of her forehead and her nose was bloody.

Tony huffed and puffed. 'I don't know why folks are afraid of a dead body. They can't hurt you.'

Dylan's face was but a few inches from the young girl's. What no amount of training prepared him for was the image of the body, that he knew, like any other dead body he had seen, would remain with him forever.

'Not unless they're diseased,' said Emily with a grimace.

'Or fall on you from a great bloody height,' said Vicky.

'Obviously!' said Emily stifling a laugh.

'Poor kid.' Dylan inhaled deeply as he stood.

A smear of blood was clear to see on the top of Patti's thigh.

'School gym kit do you think?' He nodded towards a pair of Nike trainers that were positioned neatly next to the door jamb under dark blue shorts. A green T-shirt lay haphazardly close by on the landing.

'Where's her knickers?' said Emily.

Vicky frowned, 'Yes, where are her knickers?'

'Tony, make sure we get tapings from the carpet and a sample,' said David. 'We might be lucky enough to find fibres stuck on the offender's shoes.'

'And I know we will be seizing her trainers, but let's have an impression of the sole. You never know, she may have kicked her attacker,' said Dylan.

Dylan moved slowly around the deceased, careful to disturb nothing. He was quiet; he looked thoughtful. As previously warned he noted the patch of vomit, to the side of the body. 'Confirming what the stepdad told you?' said Dylan to Vicky. Vicky nodded. 'An understandable reaction.' He turned to David. 'We've got the scene captured on video?'

'Yes sir, and numerous digital photographs have been taken, and will continue to be taken when the discarded clothing is collected and the body is moved.'

'Ready to bag and tag as soon as your ready sir,' said Emily.

'I want the bra left on the body until the post-mortem.'

'Of course.' Emily stood, pensively waiting further instructions.

'Bag both her hands, just in case she made contact with her killer,' said Dylan. 'Our priority has got to be securing the evidence. The last thing we want is to lose evidence in transit either.' Dylan's instructions continued. Vicky noted them all.

'Check the walls and the banister for finger prints,' he said to David.

When Dylan was at a murder scene it was as if time stood still. No matter what the external demands or desires were, there was no rushing him at this stage of the enquiry. The available evidence had to be secured and that task was much easier when the body was found inside – unlike a recent body he'd dealt with where the incoming tide was lapping at the dead man's feet. Within minutes that scene was gone, and he knew with it valuable evidence had been lost to the elements. And bodies found outdoors needed protection from inclement weather conditions as well as from zoom lenses of the cameras used by observers.

Ten minutes later and the scene surrounding Patti had been digested to Dylan's satisfaction and it was time to move her body. With those in attendance assisting, very slowly and carefully the dead girl was turned on her back. Near where her head had rested a patch of blood could now be seen. Closer examination revealed a partial yet very distinctive footmark in it, and a sideways glance at David brought about a nod of understanding as to what the SIO expected of the CSI. Dylan's eyes went upwards to see three sets of eyes staring back at him over their masks; the same thought on the tip of their tongues. 'Was the impression left by the sole of footwear, that of the killers?'

Experience of murder scenes over his CID-led police career told Dylan that scene examination was about recovering evidence and recording facts. He also knew that compliance with data protection was essential. This meant that investigators had to record, retain and reveal all potential evidence to any subsequent defence team whether the police thought it was relevant or not. The defence team would make their own decision, having been made aware that the evidence existed whether it was important or not. Evidence seized at the crime scene also eliminated people just as efficiently as it connected people to a crime.

It was time to visually check Patti's body from head to toe. 'Any sign of bruising or discolouration of the skin?' said David.

'Upper torso there appears to be bruising,' Emily pointed out with her gloved hand.

Dylan nodded. 'That'll be looked at in more detail at the post-mortem.'

Patti's staring, heavily blood shot eyes, bulging, cold and unseeing in her distorted face.

Dylan went down on his haunches again, to get a closer look. Patti's lifeless eyes bid him to do what she could not – bring her killer to justice. It sent a shiver down his spine. Whoever said you got used to seeing a dead body, was lying.

'Her face, it's like something you'd see in a horror movie,' said Vicky, her forehead buckled as she frowned. As she turned to Emily there lurked a flash of mischief in her eyes, 'Or round town on a Saturday night when they're off their heads on summat or other.'

Emily eyes turned towards her colleague. She had an unbelieving look upon her face. 'Because that's smart.'

Dylan concentrated, his face inches away from Patti's. 'We can't fast forward past this bit, as much as we'd like to though, can we?' he said as he reared his head for a second and his eyes caught Vicky's.

'No. 'The bastard who did this to her should bloody hang.'

'Don't mince your words,' Tony said giving Vicky an eyebrow flash.

'That's out of our control and you know it. But, hopefully with the evidence we gather, and put to CPS, they'll be able to put the perpetrator before the court and then it's up to judge and jury,' said Dylan.

'It'd do the do-gooders who oppose bringing back the death penalty good, to see this,' she said with a slight nod of her head towards the body of the young girl.

Dylan was more than aware that rarely, if at all, did you get a second chance at gathering evidence at a murder scene. This initial team of five had begun piecing together the jigsaw of the crime puzzle. It was of paramount importance to ensure nothing was missed at this stage and the anticipation and eagerness of the small group was palpable. All aware that there would be plenty of 'pieces of blue sky' that didn't move things forward, but were all required to be collected, to achieve the full picture.

Dylan as the Detective Inspector was the senior investigating officer, the SIO, the man in charge. His experience, leadership and decision making would be tested to influence the outcome of the case; the pursuit of the killer was driven by him and he pulled on all his experience, knowledge, training and expertise – more than ever at this crucial stage of the investigation. All that was done during the enquiry and why, was being recorded in his policy log. This book was his, in which he would time, date and sign for his actions. And when it came to the court case some eighteen months later, and he stood in the witness box giving his evidence to the Crown, the chronologically process of the investigation could be followed by the judge and jury, as to why certain actions were carried out, and others weren't, to achieve the end result of the perpetrator being stood before them in the dock – on trial for Patti's murder.

Dylan turned to Vicky. 'Make arrangement for her body to be removed to the mortuary,' he said in the knowledge that the next time he saw Patti she would be laid on an examination table at the forensic post-mortem.

Dylan and Vicky stood side-by-side at the entrance to the dead girl's bedroom. The room was bright and warm being south-facing. The sun sparkled on the glass of Patti's framed certificates, photographs and highly polished trophies within; a shrine to her gymnastic career.

'We will never know what she could have achieved.' Vicky sighed.

Emily looked over Vicky's shoulder and admired the model like images. 'Wow, she looked older than fourteen didn't she?' She didn't wait for a reply as her eyes went to the duvet on the single bed. 'Looks like there may have been a tussle.'

'I don't think so. Nothing else appears to have been disturbed?' said Vicky.

'You're right. She probably threw her duvet over her bed in haste before she left for school this morning.'

Dylan's eyes narrowed. 'I don't want to leave anything to chance. Seize the sheets and the bedding Emily.'

'Maybe she knew her attacker; invited them in?' said Vicky.

'Or perhaps her attacker was waiting for her?' said Dylan. 'Imagine it. She steps out of the bedroom, is hit where we're stood, takes one step – and collapses on to her knees.'

'David, when you check the walls and ceiling for marks will you also look for even the slightest bit of blood distribution. Let's face it, we know she was physically fit. I'd have expected there to be more evidence of a struggle if she wasn't taken by surprise.'

Those that knew Dylan also knew that he encouraged views from others. He would be the first to admit he didn't know everything, far from it, being a detective meant you were constantly learning – never knowing what you would deal with next, was one of the attractions of the job. At every suspicious death Dylan had learnt, or seen something new. His past experience, his apprenticeship, schooling that had been invaluable to him allowed him to make quick and positive decisions at scenes now. If the circumstances of a death he was called to turned out not to be suspicious, Dylan was known to give those protecting the outer scenes an opportunity to see the scene close up, by inviting them inside the inner cordon to try to understand for themselves what had taken place. In fact, that's how he had first set his eyes upon Vicky Hardacre – now a detective sergeant on his team.

Dylan's trained eyes scanned Patti's bedroom. A closed laptop sat on her bedside table.

'What you hoping to find sir?' said Emily. 'The room will be searched soon. Won't the outcome of that tell you all you need to know?'

'There is nothing like being in the victim's home environment to get an impression of how the victim lived.' There was fire in Dylan's eyes. 'In the coming hours we'll gather information on her daily routine and her lifestyle choices, which at present appear to revolve around gymnastics. I wonder if she'd normally be home at this time of day?'

'We'll check with her school principal when we inform them of what's happened,' said Vicky.

'Check if any of her clothing has been ripped Emily. If not we could think that the blow to her head disabled her to such an extent that her attacker had full control over her actions.'

Vicky raised her eyebrows. 'Ah, but we never assume though do we boss?'

Dylan's smile reached his eyes. 'Never Vicky, we can be totally misled by what we see, talking of which,' Dylan's eyes looked directly at the floor and then looked about him. 'Whatever she was hit with has either been put back in its original place or her attacker has taken it.' His eyes met Vicky's. 'Have you got a pen? We need a detailed timeline of her movements. I want to know if there has been any issues at school, any gossip involving her, and background intelligence. We need a dedicated team of officers to go to the school and liaise direct with the principal, teachers and Patti's school friends. Nev Duke is Detective Sergeant on lates – get him in early. Let him break the news. We'll also need house-to-house enquiries carrying out as soon as possible. See what the neighbours know about the family, and if they saw anything.'

'There were enough watching what was happening from behind their curtains when we arrived. Let's hope they were just as curious earlier,' said Emily.

'Did Patti have a boyfriend do you know?' asked Dylan.

Vicky shrugged her shoulders. 'No idea.'

'Find out.'

'I'll speak to Connie in the press office and let her know a murder enquiry is underway. We need to stress the fact that relatives have yet to be informed, and make sure the girls identity isn't released, or confirmed, until we are sure that all family and friends have been notified.' Dylan took a deep breath. 'Time to speak to mum and stepdad now I think. They will be desperate to know what's happening.'

'Clear the ground beneath our feet...' Vicky said out of the corner of her mouth to Emily.

'And hopefully they'll share with us anything else that has been going on in Patti's life that they think we need to be aware of,' said Dylan.

'Ahh...That depends what she's told them? Teenagers are not known for being open with their parents.' Emily tapped her nose.

'I don't think I did more than grunt at my parents when I was a teenager,' said Vicky.

Dylan looked perplexed. 'Well, we'll just have to hope Patti isn't another Vicky Hardacre, won't we?'

Emily groaned. 'Heaven forbid.'

Vicky flashed her colleague her middle finger and Emily showed her the tip of her tongue.

'Did you notice her mobile anywhere?' said Dylan. 'I can't imagine a fourteen year old girl hasn't got her phone attached to her person.'

His question was met with shaking heads.

'Make it a priority for the POLSA search. That'll no doubt hold valuable information at this stage of the enquiry for us.'

'Will do,' said Vicky.

'Before I leave I want to take a look at that downstairs patio door,' Dylan said as he turned for the stairs.' He waved Vicky and Emily to go before him.

Vicky pointed to a canvas bag behind the open front door as she reached the bottom. She looked over her shoulder and raised an eyebrow at Dylan. 'Patti's?' She stooped over it, with her gloved hand, she opened it wide and peered inside. 'It's hers...' she said on retrieving a notepad with her name upon the cover. 'And... We have her mobile. It's switched off,' she said, eyes down as she examined the phone in the palm of her hand. She passed it to Emily. 'Lots of other bits and bobs, and a purse...'

'Exhibit each item, Emily. If it's anything like Jen's handbag we'll be here for a month of Sundays if we wait for you to go through it now. But it'll be worthwhile, as it might reveal more about her.'

Dylan's eyes wandered to the patio doors. 'They were only locked at the central lock, you say?' David yanked them with his gloved hand and they glided opened with ease. He gave the handle a shove and they closed back together with a soft click. Entry of the perpetrator, exit, maybe both; or could it simply be the case that the last time one of the family members used the door they didn't put the deadbolts on?

'Interesting,' said Dylan with a frown. 'Vicky, I'll leave you to oversee the movement of her body to the mortuary when we've done that and scenes of crime have finished I want the house secured and guarded. I'll get back to the nick, get the incident room up and running, speak to Detective Sergeant Duke, and then speak to mum and stepdad. I'll see you back at the nick in a while. Keep in touch.' As Dylan walked towards the door the Coroner's Officer, Jim Duggan had just reached the front door. The two men acknowledged each other. 'Do your best to get the pathologist to do a post-mortem as soon as possible will you, due to the age of the victim?' Dylan said.

Vicky stepped out of the front door with Dylan. 'I wonder how mum's coping?' she said as she removed her coverall's hood from her head and wiped her sweating forehead with the back of her hand.

'I'm going to find out very shortly' he said.

# Chapter Two

Press officer Connie Seabourne was sat in the CID office on his arrival. Her big, blue round eyes saw him before he saw her, and making a beeline for him she briskly followed him into his office.

'I was on a course this morning upstairs when I got the call. I am told the press is onto it. What can we tell them?'

Dylan sat down behind his desk and hastily she sat down opposite him – pink pen poised above a blank page in her notepad.

'Nothing yet,' Dylan gave her a brief smile.

Connie puckered her lips. 'Nothing?' she asked.

Dylan shook his head. 'I'm just about to speak to the dead girl's mum and stepdad. I don't want any details of her, or anything that is likely to identify her to be given to the media until we have confirmation that all her family members have been notified.'

Connie shrugged her cashmere sweater-clad shoulders. 'No worries,' she said. I'll get back to the office. You just let me know what and when you want me to do the press release.'

'It might be after five.'

'I'm doing a double shift. There's no one to cover holiday's due to the cuts.' Connie raised her perfectly groomed eyebrows that framed her impeccable eye make-up and ran her sparkly painted nails through her long blonde hair. She stood. 'Good job I love my job!' she said.

'Trouble is that's what they rely on, people loving their jobs. It shouldn't be the case.'

'The world will be run with volunteers in the future my mum says. But, what happens when the volunteers that we have put so much cost and effort to train up decide to move on?'

The skirt on her floral dress swished to and fro as she left Dylan's office. Dylan shook his head. 'God knows,' he muttered under his breath. 'No one will have thought about that.'

Detective Constables Donna Frost and Michelle Robinson weren't hard to find. Dylan spoke briefly with them outside the room where they had been talking to Elliot Black. It was the first time Dylan had seen him, and for now it was through a window in the door. He would introduce himself shortly, but not just now. Donna told Dylan that Elliot had maintained his original account of what had happened that morning.

'Mr Black's partner Sandra is here,' Dylan told the officers in a hushed tone. 'If you give me a couple of minutes to speak to her first, then we'll all sit down together. That way they'll be able to support each other. I'll get someone to message you with our location in the building once I know where Mrs Heinz is being looked after.'

In a private office on the first floor of the building he met up with DC Jaene Booth and Patti's mum. Sandra Heinz held a mug in both hands, at arm's length in her lap. She stared right through the officer sat in front of her who attempted to coax her to take a sip of the warm drink. Patti's mum was shaking, her eyes red rimmed and her pale face tear-stained. She didn't speak, she didn't blink. Dylan walked into the room and Sandra turned to him, her puffy eyes followed him when he sat down and introduced himself to her. Putting his hands together as if in prayer Dylan leaned forward. 'Your partner Elliot is here at the station and we will be joining him in a few minutes. 'Sandra there is no easy way of breaking this news to you, and I need to tell you what we know so far. I promise you I won't keep anything from you and anything you don't understand or want to know please ask me or Jaene. It is Jaene's job, as part of our team to give you constant support as your family liaison officer and I'm sure she has already explained that to you.'

Sandra Heinz held Dylan's gaze. After a moment or two she swallowed hard. Her grip on the cup became tighter. So much so that Dylan could see her knuckles turn white. Dylan went on. 'Earlier this afternoon Elliot discovered Patti's body at the top of the steps, on the landing of your home.'

Sandra gasped. Dylan continued. 'He immediately telephoned the emergency services, the police and ambulance responded. Sadly there was nothing the paramedics could do. She was dead.'

The cry emanating from Sandra's lips was like an injured animal's. After a few minutes she managed to compose herself, her voice quivered. 'How did she...?

'We think from an injury to her head but, a post-mortem will ascertain if that is the case.'

'She fell?' Sandra interrupted Dylan – her expression one of confusion. 'Where did she fall?'

'Please let me finish.' Dylan lowered his eyes, he paused for an instant. When he continued he purposefully spoke slowly, choosing his words carefully. 'She has an injury to her head which is unexplained at this moment in time. Patti was naked when she was found Sandra, except for her bra which appears to have been used to strangle her. We also believe she was raped.'

'Christ almighty!' Sandra's body jerked forward. 'Not an accident?' With presence of mind Jaene swiftly took the cup from Sandra's flailing hand. 'No!' she screamed. She fell backwards in the chair with a thud. 'No! No! No! I can't...' she sobbed, covering her eyes with clawed, ridged fingers.

Just then the door was opened by Donna, and in walked Elliot Black. Sandra looked up at the officers greeting each other, jumped up and threw herself at him, clinging to his shoulders to keep her upright, then to his waist as her crying subsided. Looking physically shaken Elliot helped her back to her seat. He held her hand as he sat down beside her. Dylan gave them a moment before introducing himself to Elliot. Sandra watched the unspoken exchange of words in their eyes and her eyes finally rested on Elliot Black's face. As she did so her eyebrows knitted together and she looked at him as if seeing him for the first time. 'Why are you dressed in that?' she asked him. 'Why is he dressed like that?' she asked Dylan. She turned her head back to Mr Black. 'Are you under arrest?' Her voice rose. 'Do they think you...?' Her eyes widened and she leant as far away from her partner as the chair would allow. 'Oh my god! Tell me no?' she said to Jaene.

Dylan spoke first. 'The reason that Elliot is dressed in one of our paper suits is that we had to take possession of his clothing because he was the one who found Patti, and there was blood on them. Nothing more.'

Sandra reached out for Elliot's hand and begged his forgiveness, crying uncontrollably when he took her in his arms.

'Can we get some more drinks Jaene and arrange for a doctor?' Dylan said, softly.

Jaene moved swiftly and quietly towards the door. As she did so she nodded at Dylan, her face full of concern.

Sandra's sobs were intermittent and Elliot comforted her. 'Where's Patti now? Can I see her? I want to see her. Is she still at home?'

'She's in a private ambulance en route to St Martin's Hospital. And, of course you will be able to see her. I need you to understand that there will have to be a post-mortem examination carried out by a Home Office pathologist though.'

Sandra looked puzzled. 'Why?'

'To find out exactly how she died.'

'I thought you said she was murdered, strangled, raped?' She shook her head. 'When I find out who did this to her I'll...' Sandra's eyes were searing. 'Why does she, have to have a post-mortem? I don't want her to have a post-mortem. I don't want anyone touching her ever again. Don't you think she's suffered enough,' she cried.

'I'm sorry Sandra. I know you're upset but that isn't your decision. I'm sure you want us to secure as much evidence as we can to catch Patti's killer, don't you?'

'Will you be there?'

'At the post-mortem?' Dylan nodded. 'Yes.'

'Thank you,' she said softly before her face crumpled and fresh tears fell unchecked upon her cheeks.

Dylan could almost physically feel her pain. 'We have to prove exactly how Patti died Sandra, and we can only do that with the help of a Home Office pathologist. Although we believe she was sexually assaulted we need to find out beyond doubt that she was, and if so secure the evidence so that when we catch the person or persons who did this to her, we can put them away. At this stage of the enquiry we also need to understand what caused her injuries, and what killed her if that's possible. The post-mortem will hopefully be able to help us.' Dylan was aware he was repeating himself but he would do that as many times as necessary to ensure Sandra understood what was happening and why.

'I just want to hold her... I'm her mother. I should have protected her... I've let her down.'

'No, you haven't let her down. She has been murdered, in her home, a place where she should have been safe. As yet we don't know who is responsible. Now, I need you both to try and think about any recent events, boyfriends, major upsets that may have occurred in her life, anything that you think may help us find her killer.'

Sandra scoffed. 'She's fourteen. She didn't have boyfriends. All her spare time was spent at the gym. She ate, drank and slept gymnastics. Round the house, where other kids slob about in jeans, she wore her a leotard. She was forever stretching, exercising or dancing. Don't you understand she lived for gymnastics? Her coach told us she'd represent her country one day. Tell him Elliot,' she said turning to look at her partner.

Elliot Black had been quiet. He nodded. His eyes briefly closing. He sighed, heavily, looked down at his knotted hands. 'She's right, she loved gymnastics. It's all she ever wanted to do.'

'We will be speaking to anyone and everyone who knows or has had contact with Patti. We'll be digging deep. Starting from today, we will work backwards mapping out her daily routine. For instance, what time did she normally return home from school? And, would she normally be home at any point during the school day?'

Elliot and Sandra looked at each other and then back at Dylan. 'No,' they replied in unison.

Sandra appeared thoughtful. 'Hold on. It's Tuesday. Maybe she forgot her swimming stuff. There's a class after school that her coach encourages her to attend.' She turned to Elliot. A frown appeared on her brow. 'How come you were at home?'

'I've already explained to the police. I nipped home for my phone charger.'

'Where do you work?' said Dylan.

'Spar shop, Church Street, I'm deputy manager.' Elliot straightened his back and instantly his chest rose. 'Takes me literally five minutes on my bike.'

'Would Patti normally pass the shop to get to school?' Dylan held Elliot's gaze. 'I want you to know that we have to confirm everything you say.'

'Yes,' said Elliot.

Sandra's hooded eyelids instantly rose to show bloodshot eyes. Her mouth opened and she turned to her husband.

'It's routine,' Dylan said, as he slowly turned to face her.

Elliot looked down. Reached for her limp hand and lifted it into his. He squeezed it tight. 'It's okay. Everyone is a suspect until proven otherwise. I've heard them say that on the telly.'

Dylan leant in towards the pair. 'What I really need from you, as soon as you feel able, is a list of Patti's friends, acquaintances, anyone you know who knew Patti.' There was a spark of life in Patti's mother's flat, dead eyes. Dylan fixed upon the flicker and spoke softly to her. 'Sandra, who's your daughter's best friend, the person she might confide in? You see shortly our experts will be examining her laptop, her mobile phone. They'll be looking for contacts, any contacts, all contacts but, that takes time. I promise you we will be working around the clock to find Patti's killer but what you can give us, in the meantime to quicken up that process, would be like gold dust to me right now.' The light Dylan had seen in Sandra's eyes faded and two black granite holes stared right past him to the blank wall beyond. 'Patti maybe only fourteen,' he tried again to cut through the pain, 'but she was an attractive girl and she will no doubt have had her admirers. Who were the regular callers at your home?' Dylan continued, unperturbed by the blank, jaded face. 'I know I'm asking a lot of you and truly I don't expect immediate answers but maybe Jaene, here, could help?'

Sandra's head started to shake in short jerky, side-to-side movements. 'My daughter didn't have a boyfriend.' Her reply cut him short, and sharp. She glared at Dylan. 'She didn't have time, did she?' she spoke to Elliot.

'She was beautiful, the image of her mother.' Elliot looked down at his wife's hand and stroked it gently with his thumb.

Dylan shifted in his seat and glanced at Jaene, who had returned with fresh drinks, then back to Patti's mother.

'You will need to inform family about Patti's death. Who do you need to tell?' Blank faces looked back at him. 'If there is anything we can do to help you with that, let Jaene know.'

There was silence.

'One of the reasons I ask is that is that I haven't revealed any details yet to the press, but at some stage I will have to and you might want to identify somewhere, where you can seek some solitude. We have a lot of specialised people at our disposal but in my experience the ability of the media, to spread the word and ask for help from the general pubic, is one I am eternally grateful for. Do you have a photograph of Patti that we can use? Again experience tells me that if we give the media a picture, they won't go seeking another elsewhere. You're going to see a picture of Patti on the television and on the front page of every newspaper in the next few days and beyond, so it makes sense to provide a picture you are fond of, rather than letting them get hold of one by other means – such as social media.'

Uninvited tears once again sprung into Sandra's eyes and she dabbed them with a clean tissue Jaene handed to her. 'She's just had one taken with her medals around her neck at the regional championships. She looks happy, and proud.'

'Good, thank-you,' Dylan's eyes found Jaene's and nodded. 'We'll arrange to take you to see Patti.' Sandra's lips parted and she took an audible intake of air.

'When will the examination take place?' said Elliot.

'I'm hoping later today. I'm awaiting a call from the Coroner's Officer to confirm that the Home Office pathologist is available and what time he or she will be attending. But, remember any questions it's Jaene's role in our dedicated team to keep you updated at all times – that's why she's here, for you.'

'Will I be able to see Patti before I go to bed tonight, please?' said Sandra her eyes pleading.

'I'll make sure so,' said Dylan. 'I know just how important it is for you both to see her. I appreciate it's a big ask for you to be patient but we want the best opportunity to secure any evidence her body may be able to give us to help us catch her killer. Now,' he said as he rose out of his chair, 'I need to chase people to secure a time for the post-mortem. He looked down at three sets of expectant eyes. 'Jaene will stay with you. Please try to focus on the questions she will be asking you about your family history, details of Patti's friends and her routine. Anything you can tell us will be really helpful.'

Sandra looked at Jaene as she moved to sit beside her and Jaene gave her hand a reassuring pat.

'Can you think of anywhere you could stay this evening?' Dylan said. Sandra looked up at him and then quickly back at Jaene, her eyes filled with panic.

Jaene squeezed her hand tightly. 'Your house, it's being examined by our experts. Nothing for you to worry about but you don't need to be upset by it. Better you're out of the way that's all.'

'Your Joan's?' said Elliot. 'She's got a spare room.'

Sandra's hand flew to her open mouth. 'She's going to be heartbroken. I need to inform work – they'll have to get cover for me tomorrow.'

Dylan put a hand on Sandra's shoulder. 'Remember Jaene is here to help you with those kind of jobs, just ask her. One more question,' Dylan said as he reached the door. 'I know Patti has had a lot of publicity recently. Do you know if your address was printed in the media?'

'I think the area where we live might have been mentioned but not the name of the house, as far as I'm aware,' said Elliot.

'No, it's just a matter of trying to think where someone might have got your address.'

\*\*\*

The incident room was in the process of being set up and the relevant staffing sourced. Dylan couldn't quite believe his luck when he was given the news that the Home Office pathologist would be available within the hour. 'Apparently she's in the area for a meeting which has just concluded far earlier than expected,' said Sergeant Cracker Craze, a grin as always on his friendly face. He extended his hand and rattled a tin.

'What we raising funds for this time?' said Dylan digging deep in his pockets.

'A shelter for the homeless,' he said, unapologetically. 'Didn't David Funk tell you?'

Within the hour Dylan was stood in a car park. Vicky Hardacre at his side. She kicked off her heels and threw them on the back seat, replacing them with something more suitable for a visit to the mortuary. She locked her car door.

'We'll have to stop meeting like this,' she said with a cock of her eyebrow as they walked together towards the austere building. Her blonde, shoulder-length hair had been recently cut short and bleached, it made her look older than her thirty years and harsher, Dylan thought. Today her bonny face was full of freckles from the sun and her blue eyes were somehow a mixture of the usual mischief, and sadness.

Dylan shook his head. 'You're insufferable. Jaene needs notifying after the post-mortem to update parents, and we need to arrange a visit for them.' Arriving at the entrance Dylan stepped forward and opened the door to allow her to go before him. 'Get in.'

Vicky shivered.

'You cold?' Dylan asked as he followed her down the windowless corridor. Their footsteps echoed and the noise seemed to bounce off the grey, shiny, newly painted walls.

'No, this place... It gives me the friggin' heebie-jeebies.'

'Just remember, luckily for us we get to walk out,' said Dylan.

'True,' she said, pushing open the door to the examination rooms. She took a deep breath.

'Post-mortem is about to commence,' said the lady who greeted them, clipboard in hand. She wore half moon glasses and a no-nonsense expression. The pathologist on the other hand was Mary Morris. A smiley, slim lady in her forties with short dark hair. The police officers acknowledged her. Her assistant was tying her plastic apron. Suited and booted, the face-mask hanging around their necks and plastic gloves in their hands, the police officers were seated at the door, ready to go into the post-mortem. Dylan saw Vicky's nostrils flare, her breathing become shallow and her lips turn pale. This part of the job was the worse for her, but she was so very proud that unlike some she never turned down the chance to see for herself the injuries that had been inflicted on the victim, by the murderer, and therefore get the chance to learn what she could from the experts first hand. Dylan was on the edge of his seat. On his mind the circumstances of the incident that he would relay to the pathologist once in the examination room.

The lifeless, naked body of Patti Heinz lay on her back on the stainless-steel table. Her bra still around her neck, as instructed by Dylan at the scene.

'Well, perhaps the wrong words to use because she's here, but she certainly looks like she was a very healthy girl young girl.' Mary's eyes flew up to look in the police officer's direction. 'A gymnast you say Detective Inspector Dylan?'

'Yes, and a very good one from what we're told.' Recalling the circumstances of the discovery of Patti's body to the pathologist was easy for Dylan. Having attended the scene, spoken to the family and listened to what fellow officers and the CSI experts told him, Dylan was about to find out how she had died.

Mary Morris took tapings from the body. She swabbed around the breast area and Patti's mouth before moving on to take samples of head and pubic hair, both cut and pulled. She scrutinised the bruising around her shoulders.

Dylan took several sideways glances at Vicky. Her anxiety visibly less, as her interest grew. With bated breath her eyes were focused on the pathologists next move.

'In relation to the bra I want to swab the inside of the knot after it is photographed.' Mary stopped whilst the CSI took the images she required. 'As I remove it,' she continued, 'I'll swab beneath it,' she said carrying out the act. 'If our attacker hasn't worn gloves we may get bits of skin off the hands here.'

The item of clothing was passed very carefully to the exhibits officer and immediately bagged. At the conclusion of the examination the pathologist would sign the label on each article and sample she had taken.

Next came the detailed inspection of the body from head to toe. Mary took the vaginal and anal swabs as gently as if the young girl was still alive. Held with the precision of a surgeon's knife the earbud-like sticks helped her in the collection of blood from her legs. She hovered, pausing for a moment or two periodically over bruises and marks on the shoulders and breasts.

'Likely to have been caused by a firm grip,' she said pointing to the bruise at the top of her arm.' She stepped to the side and moved her gloved hand above the vagina, 'and there's bruising here too,' she said pointing a finger. 'Everything I see appears to be consistent with her having had intercourse – prior to this event what is also evident is that she was a virgin. There is evidence of the presence of the hymen.' Mary's eyes turned upwards. Her attention turned to the head and neck. Patti's eyes were heavily bloodshot with petechiae present. Bruising around her neck was visible. 'Here we have a thumb mark. Which indicates to me that manual strangulation took place as well as the use of her bra as a ligature. I suggest this caused the blood vessels in her eyes to pop. We may know more when we open her up, and look at the carotid arteries.'

'Is it true that a normal individual compressing a single carotid artery will have no effect?' said Vicky, her restlessness had now disappeared and she was enthralled.

'Little,' said Mary. 'The two carotid arteries lie in the front of the neck on either side of the windpipe and carry blood from the heart to the brain.' The pathologists gloved finger pointed to the position of the arteries in the neck. 'They carry around ninety per cent of the brain's blood, with the rest coming from two small vertebral arteries that travel along the spine to the back of the brain. Compressing both carotid arteries can cause the loss of consciousness within fifteen to twenty seconds and death in around two to four minutes. The general rule of thumb is that if the heart stops, the victim will lose consciousness in about four seconds if standing, eight if sitting and twelve if lying down.'

'Reflecting the effects of gravity on the blood flow...' said Vicky.

'That's correct. This is mostly true if both carotid arteries are suddenly pressed shut. But, that's not so easy to do.'

'To the brain, the complete interruption of blood flow through the carotids would look the same as it would if the heart had stopped.' Vicky was thoughtful. 'Either way, the brain wouldn't receive a blood supply, and the brain needs a continuous blood supply to function.'

'Absolutely! Dizziness, loss of consciousness, and sudden death are simply graduations along the same scale. That is, what makes you dizzy can also make you lose consciousness, and the longer the loss of blood supply to the brain would eventually cause death. One of the things that can do this is a compression of the carotid arteries.'

'So it depends on how much the arteries are compressed?'

'Yes, brief compression can cause dizziness, longer compression can cause loss of consciousness, and even longer compression can cause death.'

'If the carotid arteries are only partially compressed though the victim may have no problems at all.'

'A major significance here is most definitely how severely the arteries are compressed.'

'Significant compression can cause death more quickly?'

'Deadly compression can result from strangulation, either manual or ligature – hanging, or an aggressive choke hold.'

'So, let me get this right, depending upon the nature, force and duration of the compression to the carotid arteries, the victim could have no symptoms, become dizzy, lose consciousness or die?'

Mary nodded emphatically. 'And this action can progressively move very quickly from one stage to the next.'

'If the victim struggled, the perpetrator could intermittently release the compression and this would prolong the ordeal though.'

'Yes, and by overpowering the victim, the killer could render them unconscious in twenty seconds, and kill them in two minutes...'

Dylan's phone rang, making Vicky jump, such was her concentration. She turned to face Dylan and her brow held a frown. Dylan turned away to listen to the caller. Permission was being sought to retrieve clothing from the scene for Elliot Black. 'I haven't an issue with that,' he said, his voice sounding muffled through is mask. 'Liaise with the uniform duty inspector, and remind them that I want the scene protecting overnight – from the outside.' As he put his mobile phone back in his pocket and turned to face the team preparations were being made to take the plastic evidence bags from her hands that had been placed over them at the scene to preserve any evidence they might hold.

'I'll do individual scrapings of each finger,' Mary said raising one finger of the right hand, 'and take clippings from the nails.'

Dylan rummaged in his pocket for his mints a few minutes later, and popped one in his mouth before offering them around. Vicky took a sip of her water. The body was about to be opened up.

Nothing could prepare even a seasoned detective for this distasteful act, as necessary as it was.

The examination took two hours and on conclusion Mary Morris confirmed what they suspected.

'One of the most common misconceptions in forensic science concerns the ability to specify an exact time of death,' she said as she slid behind the desk in an adjoining office and offered the seats in front to the officers. Trevor the mortuary attendant hovered in the background. Trevor had been there as long as Dylan could remember. What made a person want to be a mortuary assistant he wondered? 'Another, revolves around the presumed ability of us, as forensic pathologists to definitively differentiate between antemortem injuries and post-mortem changes in a body, depending on the degree of decomposition and character of the post-mortem artefacts, such differentiation may not be possible. Wounds inflicted immediately before or immediately after death, the perimortem interval, are particularly problematic. However, in this case I can confirm, in simple terms, this poor young girl has been raped and strangled to death. Hopefully, the swabs I have taken will contain DNA sufficient to identify the offender. All relevant samples have now been taken and retained for further examination, so my job here is done.' Mary laid her hands flat on the desk as she concluded. 'The cause of death for the Coroner is one of strangulation – confirmed to me by the condition of the carotid artery. The head wound she sustained, whilst it broke the skin, didn't damage her skull. But I would suggest the blow was with such force to have likely rendered her unconscious or at the very least, she'd be dazed. This being the case I would suggest that the attacker would have had immediate control over her before she knew what was happening to her. There are no marks to assist me as to what instrument was used by the attacker, but it split the skin, and it caused external bleeding.'

'The bruising to her nose?' said Dylan.

'Her nose isn't broken. However, it is possible that she was hit in the face, or the injury could have been sustained whilst laid face down on the floor. If her head was pushed into the carpet, that would also account for some of the bruising to her shoulders.

There is also reddening to her knees... We have to consider that she may have been raped from behind.'

The Coroner's Officer Jim Duggan was stood on the corridor. His half smile flaccid. The atmosphere was sombre. Dylan and Vicky stepped out. 'Liaise with Jaene will you,' said Dylan. 'The family can view their daughter's body as they wish now.'

'The body is about to be taken to the viewing room,' said Jim. 'I'll give Jaene a ring.'

The viewing room was dimly lit – an attempt to hide the bruising and lesson the trauma? It was a similar size to the small bedroom at home, with an entry and an exit to enable loved ones to pass through. The room was minimalistic, it housed the trolley upon which Patti's body lay, covered in a starched white sheet, her face and arms exposed – the smell of potpourri wafted in the air. Dylan stood alone by her side as he waited to hear from Vicky that Jaene and the family had arrived at the mortuary. It was quiet, peaceful, still. 'I promise I'll find out who did this to you,' he said in a whisper. The words went around and around in his head as he stared at her young face – she looked at peace. Patti's eyes had been closed and a little make-up applied to conceal the bruising, and the cut at the front of her head. Contrary to the pictures of her in her stage make-up for gymnastic events she looked, as she was, but a child. He turned his head to see that the curtains to the narrow outer corridor where the parents would be brought were closed. The family would see their loved one in the first instance through that window, before moving inside where they would be able to touch her.

'Are you ready?' said the assistant a few minutes later, his hand firmly on the pull cord that would pull back the curtains to allow them to see the body, much like the unveiling of a plaque. Sandra reluctantly nodded. Her chest rose and fell in quick time. Elliot's face was impassive. His jawbone twitched, the only indication of his inner turmoil.

Dylan prepared himself, inhaling deeply, aware of what was to happen. The corridor was narrow and stuffy and the tension tangible. The Coroner's Officer and Vicky exchanged a quick knowing look. Jaene's attention was on Sandra and Elliot. The curtains were very slowly drawn back – but nothing could lessen the shock of what Patti's parents were about to see.

'Oh, my god!' Sandra gasped, on the wave of a sharp intake of breath. The raised flat palm of her hand instantly flew out towards the glass window, stopped and lingered mid-air before reaching its intended destination as a white knuckled fist on the wall. The scream that emanated from her lips was inhuman to Dylan's ears. Jaene put her arm out and grasped Patti's mum's hand in hers. Without further ado she led Sandra gently to the viewing room door. As Elliot reached the entrance he hesitated and turned to look back at Dylan, who urged him to go on, with a nod of his head. Vicky moved to stand next to Dylan and they observed. She knew him well enough to know that his calm exterior masked his emotions as he watched Sandra wail uncontrollably, taking her daughter's cold hand in hers. Instantly she fell to her knees.

'I don't want you to be frightened,' she said to Patti, in a whisper. 'I'm here. You're not alone.' She started to sing a child's lullaby, then stopped – because her tears wouldn't allow her to go on. When she regained her composure she repeated the Lord's Prayer over and over again, amongst telling Patti how much she loved her until Elliot put his hands under her arms and helped her to her feet. A few moments passed in silence. She didn't turn to look at her partner but sniffed, wiped her eyes with the handkerchief he offered, kissed Patti's hand and sobbed into his chest as if her heart would break.

'Her hand was icy.' Dylan heard her say to Jaene. Elliot's body started to shake, his face buckled and he broke down. He wiped his tears away the moment they hit his cheeks with the back of his hand, corrected his posture and stood tall.

Dylan glanced across at Vicky. He could see pity in her watery eyes. He had to remain strong, stand back from what was happening, close his mind to the emotion and focus on the investigation. There was only one thing that he could do for Patti and her family now and that was to find the killer. It wouldn't give them closure as a lot of people hoped, or thought. Their lives would never be the same from this day on. He also knew there was a high percentage of couples who broke up after the loss of a child, to murder. What finding the killer would do, was answer some of the many questions that at this time they had no answers for, and stop them wondering if everyone they met in the future could potentially be Patti's murderer. Dylan knew the statistics were high for the victim knowing their killer – hence the detective's mantra to 'cover the ground beneath your feet'. But, first impressions were that there was no indication of who was responsible for Patti's murder.

Dylan's mind was back on the family. There was no time limit placed on this reuniting but he knew it was time to leave...

'But she might wake up!' Sandra looked distressed at the detective's beckoning. 'Look! She's fine! It's just a scratch on her head, that can't have killed her. Please, please don't make me leave her here...'

Slowly but surely Jaene and Elliot shepherded Sandra out of the viewing room and as the curtains closed to the corridor Sandra swayed, 'She needs a blanket, she's cold,' she said. Her voiced sounded as if she had been drugged. All hands went out to steady her as she collapsed in Dylan's expectant arms. Swiftly, she was taken to Accident and Emergency. A doctor and a nurse watched over her as she came to.

'Tell me, do you have any pain?' said the doctor. Her look of wonderment was a brief respite before the reality of her situation came to mind. Then she turned her head on the pillow, screwed up her eyes and cried, tears of pain, real pain that no one could take away.

'We'll get something that will help,' said the doctor laying a gentle hand upon her arm. He spoke quietly to the nurse who swiftly led the curtained area no doubt in search of the prescribed medication.

Dylan walked out of the hospital with Vicky at his side. 'I don't know about you but I need a drink,' she said.

'Has the necessary staffing been arranged for tomorrow morning's briefing?'

Vicky nodded.

'Scene secure and protected. Incident room fired up.'

'It has.'

'After what we've witnessed today I think we deserve a bottle.' Dylan looked at his watch, found his mobile in his pocket and rang Jen. The cool breeze that blew softly on his face was welcome as he stood waiting for her to pick up. He opened the car door. Vicky flopped into the passenger side. He saw her close her eyes and she lay her head back on the headrest. Her cheeks puffed out. She exhaled slowly.

'Was Jen okay with it?' she said, as Dylan slid into the driving seat a few minutes later.

'Went to answering machine,' he said as he started the engine. 'She'll be fine.'

'I guess she's no choice.' She took a sideways glance at Dylan who was preoccupied manoeuvring the car out of the car park. 'Some people haven't the sense they were born with,' Dylan said under his breath as a woman on her mobile phone let her children run around the parked cars.

Dylan stopped the car abruptly at the junction to the main road. He looked quickly right and left before he steered it out onto the busy road. They drove in silence for a while before becoming gridlocked in the rush hour traffic.

'Patti's mother and Elliot are going to be subjected to independent interviews tomorrow regarding Patti's background and their own movements – it won't be easy for either of them,' he told Vicky.

'For now they need time to come to terms with their daughter's death – as if a few sleepless hours is enough.' Vicky turned to look out of her window and watch the cars pass by in the opposite direction.

'Sadly we can't afford them longer.' Dylan's jaw was set. He looked impatiently at his watch.

'The Anchor, that'll do,' said Vicky, pointing to the pub entrance, two cars ahead.

The two detectives sat together in a quiet, dark corner of the snug. There was a rushing sound of vehicles outside giving the impression that the traffic was moving more freely. Vicky picked up the empty bottle. 'Shall I get another?' Dylan's phone bleeped.

'Jen sends her love,' he said, before tossing his phone back on the table. He handed her his empty glass. 'I'll have a pint of Coke.'

'It seems ages since I've seen Jen. How is she?' she said as she stood. Her voice was more cheery, in an obvious attempt to lighten the mood. Dylan eyes found hers. They were bleak.

'It's not easy, but she's coping, some days are better than others.' He sat up and changed the subject quickly to the lesser painful of the two for him. 'Am I right in thinking that Elliot Black said he thought no one was in the house when he went upstairs to get his phone charger?'

'You're thinking that he would have seen Patti's bag at the bottom of the aren't you? But we didn't see it immediately either,' she said.

'Mmm...'

'Crisps or nuts?' she asked. 'I haven't eaten today.'

'Me neither. Tell you what the steak house is open shall we head over there?'

'Sounds good to me. I've no one waiting for me at home.'

# Chapter Three

When Dylan arrived home the house was in darkness Jen was in bed, sound asleep. He looked at the clock, it was one thirty am. Alarm set, he felt his way in the darkness to the en suite. He shouldn't have gone in for coffee at Vicky's but she'd insisted and she could hardly stand. He felt responsible. He snuck into bed and snuggled up to Jen. She felt lovely and warm to his touch and he dared to put his cold feet tentatively, next to hers. Both mumbled an acknowledgment before he instantly felt himself falling into the bottomless pit of sleep.

The beeping of his alarm, under his pillow, woke him. He could see Jen in the semi-darkness as he stumbled out of bed and opened his sock drawer as quietly as he could.

'What time is it?' said Jen, sleepily.

'Five-thirty. I was trying not to wake you. Go back to sleep,' he said in a hushed tone.

'I've seen a house,' she said, in a muffled tone as she attempted to prop herself up on one elbow and dropped back onto the pillow.

'Can we afford it?' Dylan said, his voice sounding more awake than he felt.

'Yes.' Jen rubbed her eyes.

'Arrange a viewing then if you like the look of it.' Dylan was concentrating on tying the knot of his tie.

'Really? When for?'

'Whenever.' Dylan put his arms in the sleeves of his jacket and pulled the cuffs of his shirt down to reveal his cufflinks.

'And you'll be there?' She looked at him through narrowed eyes as he came towards her.

'Promise! See you later,' he said, planting a fleeting kiss upon her forehead.

'Whatever,' she said in a whisper but, she afforded herself a smile and snuggled under the duvet. She heard the sound of his feet running down the steps. 'Dylan,' she called hurriedly, in a soft voice, as loud as she dared. He stopped. 'What?'

'Don't slam the door.'

'I won't!' he replied.

The front door slammed, Jen held her breath. A few minutes later Maisy shouted. Jen pulled the duvet over her head. 'Grrr... Dylan!'

As early as it was, Harrowfield Police Station was wide awake and buzzing with people. The briefing for the Patti Heinz murder was due to take place in a specially adapted area, near the allotted incident room. Vicky brought Dylan coffee. 'Thanks for last night,' she said, softly. A few heads turned. Dylan shook his head at her, and smiled.

David Funk the Crime Scene Manager stood beside Dylan and Vicky helping to outline the discovery of Patti's body. Photographs, a video and street map were the aids they used. A brief family history of the victim was given to those assembled and a picture of Patti and what they had gleaned so far in the investigation was shared. Priority lines of enquiry, yesterday's post-mortem results and a forensic update were given in detail.

'The press conference is arranged for ten-thirty,' said Connie. 'Are you ready Mr Dylan?'

Connie accompanied Dylan and Vicky down the corridor to the news teams waiting for him.

'I'd considered doing the conference with Patti's parents but I've had a word with Jaene and they're not up to it,' he said.

'It's a big ask, so soon,' said Connie. 'We'll use them at a later date, if necessary to try and keep the investigation headline news.'

'That's if it makes the headline news... It's not a certainty these days,' said Vicky.

'Sadly, it's not,' said Connie.

The television cameras were in place and the desk at the front of the room where they would sit covered from back to front in microphones – tall ones, wide ones, small ones big ones, some snake-like meandering across the great expanse. Dylan walked into the room before the others.

Vicky held a cupped hand over her mouth when she whispered to Connie. 'I don't know how he does it. He doesn't even look nervous. My knees are bloody shaking.'

'Just don't fart,' said Connie with a raising of her eyebrow.

'You mean those microphones are that good? Jesus Christ!'

'He can't help you,' said Connie, her face emotionless. 'Take a seat.' Connie pulled out her own chair at the end of the line and indicated for Dylan and Vicky to do likewise.

As soon as Dylan sat the talking stopped. All eyes were upon him. 'Good morning ladies and gents, for those of you who don't know me I am Detective Inspector Jack Dylan from Harrowfield Police Station, the senior investigating officer for this enquiry. On my left, this my deputy Detective Sergeant Vicky Hardacre and to her left Connie Seabourne, press officer.' Pens scurried across blank pages, in the journalist's notebooks. 'As usual, I'll give you all the details and there will be a chance for questions or one-to-one interviews at the end of this press conference. It was my intention this morning to bring the parents with us but they are too distraught at this time. In the future however, I am sure they will want to say a few words. In the meantime, I ask that you respect their privacy. I am able to release to you this morning the personal details of the victim, as her family have been informed of yesterday's tragic events. Thank you for your attendance.' Dylan paused, briefly looked up, and saw the eagerness in the sea of faces. 'Moving onto these events. Yesterday afternoon the emergency services, by that I mean Ambulance and Police responded to a three-nines call to a house situated in Burford Avenue. This was made by mum's long-time partner of the deceased who had returned home at approximately two fifteen p.m. and discovered the lifeless and almost naked body of the fourteen year old, on the first floor landing of their home. Patti Heinz was a well-known and accomplished local gymnast. She had been attacked inside her own home and we also believe that she had been subjected to a serious and violent sexual assault. A post-mortem was carried out by the Home Office pathologist Mary Morris late last night. The cause of death has been identified as strangulation. We have a major investigation underway to find Patti's killer. That's all I can tell you at this moment in time.'

'Sandra Mangan, Daily Express: Are you saying she was raped?'

'I said she was subjected to a violent sexual assault. We have to wait for test results to confirm what took place.'

'Pamela McNaulty, Daily Mail: Do we have a photograph of the young girl?'

'Yes, we do. Copies of it will be handed to you by the press officer.'

'Virginia Mason, Editor, Harrowfield Courier: I interviewed Patti recently for a feature in the paper. She was in no doubt a very talented young girl, and lovely with it. Can you tell us if there a break-in at the house? And, did she have a boyfriend?'

'Good morning Virginia! I read your article about her. There is no obvious evidence of a break-in. As for her having a boyfriend, that will be one of numerous lines of enquiry. We do have a dedicated team speaking with her family, friends and her teachers etcetera.'

As one journalist sat, another stood and the questions flowed. Everyone had a deadline to make. After fifteen minutes Dylan lifted the palm of his hand up to the crowd. 'Ladies and gents, I'm going to have to bring this to a halt. As you're aware this major investigation is in its infancy and there's a lot of work to be done. So once again, thank you for your attendance and assistance. You can be assured one of my team, or I will update you, as we make progress.'

Dylan stood. Vicky and Connie took his lead. Virginia caught his eye with the raising of her hand.

'I'll call you later with some background info that we obtained when we did the article.'

Dylan gave her a brief nod of his head. 'Thank you.'

Dylan strode along the corridor back to the incident room at a pace. Vicky had to run to keep up with him. 'Connie said them microphones pick up a fart,' she said matter-of-factly. 'And if you're nervous... God my head hurts when I run.'

Dylan spoke over his shoulder. 'Only you Vicky, only you...' He walked on. 'You shouldn't drink so much and why would you be nervous? Apart from the killer we are the only people who know what happened so who's going to challenge you? Have confidence.'

'Easy to say...' Her mouth held a grimace towards Dylan as he turned at the door. He stopped.

'Never, ever be afraid of talking to the media. They have a job to do – just like you and me. Support them, and they'll support you. Look at it this way. They're going to find answers to their questions somehow. And, those answers might as well come from you, as the SIO, because if the information they get isn't accurate then it could lead to all sorts of problems, and detract the public's attention from what's important – catching the killer.'

The incident room was a hive of industry as the pair walked through it to Dylan's office within.

'You didn't get an ear bending off Jen for being late last night then?'

'No, she was asleep.' Dylan was distracted as he read notes that had been left for him on his desk.

'Oh good, the last thing I want to do is cause you hassle.'

Dylan turned his computer screen to face him. 'You won't.' His telephone rang. 'Jack Dylan.'

'It's Sam the photographer from the Courier. Virginia, said to ring you.'

'Go on Sam.' Dylan's eyes rose to see Vicky looking questioningly at him.

'I was wondering if you've had chance to look at Elliot Black?'

'Why, should we?' Dylan's forehead held a frown.

'It's just something that made me a little uneasy when we were working on the feature about her.'

'Go on.'

'He said he had hundreds, thousands of photos of her and was reluctant to let us take our own. Eventually he agreed, but he took some persuading and still insisted on showing me his vast collection. And it was just the way... Like I said, it's probably nothing.'

'I guess we're all guilty of taking lots of photos of our children, but what're you trying to say Sam? Spit it out.'

'Yeah, being a photographer I must be the biggest culprit. But, some were... let's say a little suggestive and it wasn't just that, when we were there he was forever putting his arm around the lass and saying how attractive she was. It left me feeling a little uneasy, you know?'

'Thanks for that. He will be going under the microscope, don't worry.'

'I knew he would be, but the boss thought I should mention it.'

'Absolutely! If he made you feel uneasy when you were at the house with Patti then it's good we know.' Dylan replaced the phone on its cradle. He was thoughtful.

Vicky's expression was searching. Her fingers lay idle on the keyboard. 'All's not what it seems in the Heinz, Black household?'

'I'll type up the contents of the call and pass it into the incident room for recording. Time will tell. Does Elliot Black have any previous do we know?'

'I was just doing some research. Elliot Black came to our attention about three years ago, he got a caution for theft.'

'He's no major criminal then?'

'Maybe not, but you might be interested to know that it was for stealing knickers? And Patti's knickers - were they missing?'

Dylan's eyes were wide. 'You're winding me up?' He gave a little laugh. His mobile rang.

'I'm not. God's honest truth, read it for yourself.' As she spoke she turned the computer screen to face Dylan. Dylan shook his head and put his phone to his ear.

'I'm sorry love, I can't get away this afternoon,' Dylan said to Jen. 'I know you want to view the house as soon as ... Look, you go, if you like it then I'll go as soon as...' There was silence. 'Is that okay with you?' Again silence. 'Okay, see you later.' He put the phone back in his pocket. Dylan's face was set when he turned his attention back to the computer screen. 'Okay, let's see what they say about him at his place of work place, and if he said anything to them about why he was nipping home that day?'

'For his charger... Or other,' she said raising an eyebrow. 'The elimination of the person discovering a body with blood on their clothes is always going to be the starting point. But, it will be interesting to see what he says in interview about his relationship with Patti.'

'Has some grooming been going on, or is that just our suspicious minds?'

'Investigative minds Vicky.'

# Chapter Four

Brelland railway station had served the village in Yorkshire well for near on one hundred years. It was on the Harrowfield and Brelland Junction Railway, and closed in 1976. Because of its locality the powers-that-be had not thought it important enough to have a stone build at the time, so it was built of timber. However, what was built at the same time, of Yorkshire stone, was The Station House.

The property details in front of Jen did this property no favours. Jen stood looking up at the magnificently unique building, dilapidated in principle, and instantly fell in love. Natalie, the estate agent, waited anxiously – The Station House had been on their books for as long as she had been at the estate agents.

Jen turned to face her and her smile was wide.

'You look like the cat that got the cream.' Her eyes narrowed. 'But, you haven't seen inside yet,' she said dangling a set of old keys that hung on a scorched paper fob in front of her. 'Shall we?' she said taking a step towards the door.

'Do you mind if we take a look around the outside first?' Jen said tentatively, reaching out. 'Oh look, there's still coal soot on these walls,' she said excitedly. 'And wow...' Her fingers stroked the graffiti, some of which dated back to Victorian times.

The timber station building remained, as did a platform with a set of waiting rooms. In the gap where the train tracks used to be someone had made a bizarre attempt to install a swimming pool but this had never been completed and what remained was a nasty black puddle. Natalie hurried her inside.

On the sitting room floor of the stationmaster's house marks of his hobnail boot remained, and there were grooves where he had pushed his chair around.

'Its perfect...' said Jen. 'Just perfect.'

Natalie was hesitant. 'You sure?' she said screwing up her nose.

'I've never felt so sure about anything more in my life.'

'Let's wait to see what your husband has to say about it, shall we?'

'Oh, I know he'll just love it too,' said Jen.

***

Today the family of Patti Heinz would be scrutinised. It was a necessity to eliminate any involvement or knowledge of the murder before moving the enquiry forward and outside of the home.

The school, St Martin's, would be another place that would be a hive of police activity, as well as enquiries at the gym Patti used and there would be an in-depth interview with her trainer.

'Make sure you check to see if she had a locker at either of these locations, and if so search and seize any items therein,' Dylan told officers going to the school, and the gym.

He also told Detective Sergeant Nev Duke to remind his team to seize any of Patti's personal property that they may discover.

House to house was continuing around Burford Avenue.

'I want to know who calls at Colonial House, and that includes the postman, the milkman, a regular marketing company... Ask around... Someone must know something. Has there been any cold calling lately, Jehovah's Witnesses?... I'm stating the obvious, I know but I don't want anyone to be overlooked if they've been to the house recently, for whatever reason.'

It was to be an industrious day on all fronts and Dylan first job was to prioritise exhibits that needed to go to go to Forensic. Emily stood beside him and touched her nose, a habit he was beginning to see happened when she was thinking. She sighed as she looked at the pile of seized objects. 'How the hell do we start to prioritise from that lot?'

'Best guess?' said Dylan.

Emily laughed. 'Really?'

'We send the exhibits that will hopefully yield evidence.'

'Why not send them all?'

'Like most things it comes down to money. I have a budget and boy do I know about it if I overspend – which I usually do, but there you go. How do you put a cost on catching a murderer?'

Dylan pulled various exhibits bags out of the cupboard. 'The swabs obviously need to be in this first batch. If they come back with a DNA profile that's going to give the enquiry a massive boost in these early stages which will allow the team to quickly and positively eliminate any potential suspects.'

Emily looked overwhelmed. 'It's just... the amount of... I wonder if the partial bloodied footprint we found at the side of the body belongs to Elliot Black's footwear?' She pointed to a large brown paper exhibits bag with a see-through line down its centre to reveal its contents.

'We'll get the answers in due course to all the questions that will come into an investigation of this magnitude – but we have to wait for Forensic to do their bit. And in the meantime we pray.'

Dylan could almost see Emily's brain ticking. 'So, let me get this right. Exhibits are filtered before going to be examined. Prioritised by way of what you think might reveal best evidential results, and then drip-fed in a continuing stream to Forensic.'

Detective Sergeant Vicky Hardacre being Dylan's deputy senior investigator on the enquiry, and Detective Ned Granger had been given the task to interview Elliot Black. This wasn't a formal interview but it was decided that they would do it away from Sandra Heinz, at Harrowfield Police Station, which also allowed Jaene Booth quality time to talk to her alone.

'This way Dylan says we'll be assured of independent responses Ned,' said Vicky as she stood with her hand on the handle outside the interview room door. 'Assure him that he isn't under arrest and the interview isn't being recorded. He can leave any time he likes. Ready?'

Ned gave Vicky a nod of the head. 'I'm not a complete numpty.'

'That's debatable,' she said as she opened the door and walked in to see Elliot Black sat back in a chair opposite a uniform constable who had escorted him from the front desk. The tiredness showed on Elliot Black's face and so absorbed in his own thoughts he appeared oblivious to the detective's entrance until they spoke to the officer, who left and they sat down and spoke directly to him. Although his red, dark circled eyes were open he looked haunted.

'We'd just like to clarify your account with regard to the finding of Patti's body,' said Ned.

The only movement he made was with his eyes, which wandered slowly from one detective's face, to the other. 'Not again...' they said.

'Its routine Mr Black. Witnesses have been known to remember something they didn't mention when they are spoken to initially – hence us going over things with them again, and again...' said Vicky.

His response was laboured. He sighed several times before answering their questions, as if he was building up energy to speak. 'It's being going around and around my mind all night,' he stopped, and before he began again his eyes found the wall between the detectives and he focused on it, as if seeing the event played out before him. 'I cycled home. I put my bike at the back of the house, so I didn't have to lock it up. I used the front door, headed straight up the steps, because I knew my mobile phone charger was on the bedside table, and when I got to the top of the steps, she was just... there!' His eyes widened and he turned his head slightly, to look directly at Vicky. 'I don't know what I thought. She was so young, so beautiful.' Tears spilled onto his cheeks, unchecked. 'I felt dizzy, I felt sick... I was sick… I ran to the bedroom to the nearest phone, I had to pass her... The sight of the blood and her eyes, her eyes... that sight will stay with me all the days of my life.'

'What happened then?'

'I sat down on the bed. I felt like someone had punched me in the stomach. I dialled 999. A man, he asked me all sorts of questions. I don't even know what I said to him. I felt helpless, useless. There was absolutely nothing I could do for her.'

'Is there anything else you remember?' asked Vicky.

Mr Black shook his head very slowly.

'Did you notice anyone else on your approach to the house?'

There was a spark. He tilted his head and moved to the edge of his seat. 'Come to think of it, yes, yes I did. There were a couple of young lads, a few hundred yards from the house. They had green bags over their shoulders, and leaflets in their hands. They were larking around. One pushed the other onto the road.'

'And did you have a leaflet through your letter box?' asked Vicky.

Elliot looked puzzled. 'No, no, I don't think we had, had we? You probably know better than me – all our post was taken by your officers.'


The officers continued to get background information from Elliot Black and slowly and surely he appeared to relax in their company, and open up. However, he didn't volunteer his previous involvement with the Police.

Vicky dropped it on his toes. 'We have found on our records that some years ago you were cautioned for theft? Is that right?'

'I wondered when you were going to come round to that.' His lip turned up at one corner and he looked down at this hands that were clasped in front of him. 'It was a just a prank.'

'What did you steal?'

Elliot Black's colour instantly returned to his face in all its glory. 'Look, it was just a stupid... I got a caution.' He appeared agitated but in a curious kind of half-pleasurable way.

The detectives paused.

'Why are we talking about that? You should be out searching for Patti's killer.'

'We can assure you Elliot we are. But, we have to be thorough in our approach. I'm sure you understand that?'

Grudgingly it seemed he did, nodding his head in agreement.

'What age would you be when the crime was committed, thirty-one?'

Again he nodded his head.

'Tell us. What did you steal?'

'You know what I stole. I stole knickers off washing lines.' Elliot's shoulder's rose and fell. He lifted his hands towards the ceiling. 'For Christ's sake it was a bloody prank.'

'Does Sandra know?' said Ned.

He gave the detective a sideways glance. 'Does Sandra know what?'

'You have a police caution for stealing knickers?'

Elliot shook his bowed head, 'No,' he said in all but a whisper. 'It was a prank.'

Vicky put her hand on top of the paperwork that sat upon the table in between them. 'Okay, we've got the clothing and footwear you were wearing at the time you found Patti's body but we also need a DNA sample from you, and your fingerprints for eliminations purposes.'

Elliot's mobile phone vibrated in his shirt pocket. Swiftly, he retrieved it and read the type on the screen. 'Sandra, I'm sorry,' he said, looking up. 'I have to go.' He stood, whipped his coat from the back of his chair and headed for the door. Vicky followed him. 'Reporters,' he said, as he hurried to the main entrance, 'they've found out where we're staying and won't leave.'

'We'll postpone until tomorrow,' said Vicky. 'You go.'

'Tomorrow? I'm telling you it's a waste of time. Yours and mine...'

'Nevertheless we need a sample from you and we'll get one, one way or another.'

Vicky opened the door and he was gone in an instant.

Vicky joined Ned and they sat back in their chairs looking at each other, in silence. Vicky's bottom lip was out. 'Well, what do you think?'

'I'm thinking would you expect your bloke to tell you if he had a caution for thieving knickers off washing lines?'

Vicky nodded. 'Why not, if it was a prank, like he says?'

'Yeah, I thought so.'

Vicky gathered the paperwork together, picked it up and cradled it in her arms. 'Dig into the theft he got cautioned for will you?' Her eyes narrowed. 'In fact ring the station and speak to the bobbies; see what they say. He might have side stepped the DNA sample and fingerprint taking for a reason. In the meantime I'll give Jaene a ring – she should be with Sandra.'

The house-to-house team were making good progress although the list was getting longer by the minute, for callbacks.

Dylan was looking forward to the debrief. There would be a vast amount of information to be shared, and it was his job to decide what needed following up as a priority – he needed to be alert.

He took a moment to text Jen. 'Missing you – next briefing is at six. Don't wait for me to eat. x'

Directly there was a response. 'Have you a minute? I could do with a quick chat. I'm on the way back from the seeing the house... I love it! You need to see it asap. x'

'Sorry, you know what it's like when a job breaks – I'm meeting myself coming back. We'll talk later. x'

The briefing room was packed, leaving quite a few people standing. The audience fell silent as Dylan and Vicky walked in, and took up their position at the front to face the crowd.

'Initially we will be working twelve hour shifts,' Dylan said. A rumble of approval travelled like a wave across the room. 'If anyone has an appointment or pre-planned event they need to attend, I am not asking you to cancel it, but I am asking you to make your respective Sergeant aware.'

'Who the hell is going to turn down overtime?' whispered Vicky, out of the corner of her mouth, as the volume of the conversation in the room escalated and they sat on the chairs provided. 'I'm planning on getting a new car out of this one.'

'Ladies and gents please. We have a lot to get through. Please speak out if you have something to say, remember we work as a team, on my shout.' Dylan opened the top button of his shirt and loosed his tie. 'We'll go clock wise around the room.' Dylan pointed at Sergeant Duke. 'So do you want to kick us off Nev? For everyone's benefit DS Duke took a team to Patti's school, St Martin's today.'

Nev, always the gent was already standing. 'To summarise boss, Patti appears to be well thought of by staff and pupils alike. There are no incidents to report and her tutor Mrs Jennifer Van-Cliffe highlighted those pupils that she spent time with. Her best friends are named as Debbie Francis and Gail Carpenter. We managed a brief word with them both in the presence of the head teacher and they will be subject of a home visit this evening so we can speak to them in the presence of their parents.'

'Did either of them give you a reason to be concerned?'

'Gail told us that Patti enjoyed teasing Elliot Black. She didn't go into detail but that's something we'll pursue this evening.'

Dylan nodded.

'We were also told that Patti was the Gym teacher's pet. He's named as a Gary Bale, 28 years old and who was not available for us to speak to today as he was away at a conference in London; early days as yet.'

'Thanks. So, moving on.'

'Sergeant Clegg sir, operational police support unit. We were tasked with the house-to-house and pleased to say we've had approximately sixty per cent success rate. My team is back tonight on the callbacks. Everyone on the Avenue appears to know Patti, or at the very least knows about her, mainly due to the media attention surrounding her gymnastics. Saying that, sadly we haven't found anyone yet who saw her on the day she died. One of the things I was made aware of is that at the house opposite to Colonial House there is a telescope visible at the bedroom window. She may have had an admirer.'

'That address is being visited this evening, I presume?'

'It is sir, yes.'

Dylan made a note in his notebook. 'Let me know what transpires.'

'Did anyone happen to mention seeing a couple of individuals doing a leaflet drop?' asked Vicky.

'Yes, a couple, but no one remembers seeing them yesterday. We were however handed a window cleaning enterprise leaflet that had been posted into a neighbouring property previously. And I've fed that information into the system,' said Simon.

'Patti's mum's partner, Elliot Black, tells us he saw two lads doing a leaflet drop on his way home. We'll check with Sandra and Elliot to find out if they have a window cleaner and likewise any other callers at the house will be traced and seen, as a priority.'

'DC Wormald you were tracking down her Coach, any joy?' asked Dylan.

'On his way home from London today sir, apparently at the same conference as her gym teacher. His name is Malcolm Parkes, he's thirty years of age and I've arranged for him to come in to see me tomorrow. I'm also going to the sports centre where she trains straight after this briefing.'

'Our FLO as you are probably aware is Jaene Booth.' Dylan nodded in the direction of Jaene who lifted her arm to identify her presence to him, and the others.

'We are in possession of Patti's mobile phone and her laptop. The information that these two devices hold, I am hoping, will give us more information about her contacts and lifestyle to open up new lines of enquiry,' said Dylan.

'DC Granger and myself have had an initial interview with Elliot Black, in which he was consistent with the first account he gave to us,' said Vicky. 'However, since yesterday it has come to our attention that he has a caution for the theft of knickers from washing lines, and he wasn't forthcoming with this information in interview, until he was asked. When asked, he didn't deny it. His wife is apparently, according to him unaware.'

The few people in the room that weren't already hanging on Vicky's every word before, were now.

'In fact since interview we have learned that eight pairs of knickers, from three different washing lines were proved to be taken by Mr Black over a period of a week. This is his only previous conviction but there were three separate victims of crime. According to the local police there were also allegations of him being a peeping tom at one time, but we had no evidence to support the claims.'

'Have we now got his DNA?' asked DS Rajinder Uppal.

'We have an appointment to take it tomorrow.'

Raj, the older and more experience detective sergeant frowned.

'He got a telephone call from his wife, who was at home. Apparently, and Jaene will be able to confirm this to us, Sandra was asking for him to return. She was apparently upset.'

Jaene nodded.

'So, he's a knicker nicker,' muttered DC Ned Granger, which triggered off a certain amount of tittering from those around him.

'What do they have to say about Elliot Black at his place of work?' said Dylan.

Raj raised her eyebrows. 'The member of staff who was working with him at the time said he'd told her he was nipping home, but not what for. She tells us that she considered him to be a good boss. He's firm but fair – although he has gained the nickname of Randy.'

DC Andy Wormald confirmed. 'Flirts constantly with the female customers, especially young girls and apparently he's forever making suggestive remarks to the staff. But, what they were quick to point out is that he was all talk.'

'A bit like you Ned old boy,' said Vicky, with an elbow in DC Granger's side. 'But, seriously,' she said. 'It's another day gone... '

# Chapter Five

'So, can I make an appointment to view the house again with you later today, yes?' Jen asked excitedly. When no answer was forthcoming, she turned away from the sink, tea towel in hand and proceeded to dry the utensils, watching Dylan, at the dining table, drain his coffee cup as he checked his mobile phone.

'I've no idea what time I'll get finished,' he said eventually, without looking up. He stood, smiled at Jen, put his cup on the draining board next to her, kissed her cheek and reached out to grab his suit jacket he'd hung on the cereal cupboard doorknob.

'So when then?' Jen noisily threw the kitchen utensils in the drawer one by one. 'Tell me, have you looked at the details of the property?'

Dylan looked sheepish. 'Course.'

Her eyes darted down the hallway to see the brown A4 envelope that contained the information about The Station House still in the same position she'd left it.

'Really?' Her eyebrows remained raised for a moment or two. 'And, what do you think?'

Dylan shrugged his shoulders. 'If you like it, I like it!'

Jen slammed the kitchen drawer shut with a flick of her hip, and looked into a familiar face that, told her she had lost him, for now, to the murder enquiry.

'It's not just a house. This is just a house that I chose before we met. I thought this time we were buying a home, together?'

He turned quickly from her stare and stumbled as he tripped over Max, who yelped, and scuttled under the table. 'Why on earth do you have to sit there you daft dog?' he said, in a raised, agitated voice.

Maisy looked up from the bowl of Weetabix. Her face held a look of concern. Max belly-crawled to lay under Maisy's swinging legs and made a loud disconcerted moan. The little girl leaned over and stroked his soft, solid, Retriever head.

Dylan's eyes were pained. 'Look, I'm sorry love, I have to go.' He sidestepped Jen to reach Maisy and his lips found her head, on which he planted a kiss. His exit was swift and fast but when she looked again the A4 envelope was gone.

Jen sat down next to Maisy and tried to encourage her to finish her breakfast. The room was very quiet, warm and all of a sudden felt calm with Dylan gone. 'Come on you, or you'll be late for school,' she said eventually with more enthusiasm than she felt. 'And, I'll be late for work, and then that nasty Avril Summerfield-Preston will have my guts for garters!' Jen tickled her daughter and she wriggled and chuckled in her arms.

'She's like a witch...' Maisy said pulling her best witch face.

'She is...' said Jen with a laugh.

'Why is daddy grumpy?' Maisy said as they walked to school.

'He's just busy. And tired.'

'Catching bad people?'

'Yes, catching bad people.'

'I don't like it when he's grumpy, it makes me sad,' said Maisy showing her lip.

'I know. Neither do I.'

Maisy looked up at Jen and squeezed her hand. 'I could come and look at the house with you,' she said. 'That'd be fun wouldn't it?'

Jen's grin was broad. 'That sounds like a plan to me!'

\*\*\*

Dylan was keen to hear the update from the previous evenings enquiries.

It transpired that living opposite the scene was a nineteen-year-old male, by the name of Stuart Sykes. 'He fully admitted that the telescope in his bedroom was his – for stargazing, he said. The house being slightly elevated means that his bedroom window looks directly into Patti's, and if she failed to close her curtains... well,' said Simon Clegg.

'And what more can you tell me about Sykes?' said Dylan.

'He's unemployed. He told us that he was out walking alone, on the day of the murder and couldn't give us any evidence to corroborate where he said he'd been,' said Simon.

'And do we believe him?'

'He was nervous and vague in the presence of his parents,' said Simon. 'So, we've invited him into the station to speak to us alone.'

The next update was from those officers who had been to see Patti's friends.

'Gail Carpenter told us, in the presence of her mum, that Patti had lots of admirers but was sure she didn't have a boyfriend. Her older brother had taken Patti's refusal for a date with him, badly – nobody apparently refused a date with Mark Carpenter,' said Vicky.

'Their nickname for Patti's stepdad was Eyeball, according to her friend Debbie – because he never took his eyes off her. And, in the presence of her dad she showed us a picture of a lad at swimming club who Patti liked,' said Ned.

'Did you take the statements last night?' said Dylan.

'No sir, we thought it best to give them chance overnight, to see if they remembered anything else that might assist us so, we have arranged to get them today.'

'Have we got anything from the mobile service provider?' said Dylan.

'We only logged the enquiry yesterday,' said Raj.

'I don't care. Chase them up, and Forensic. We haven't been able to eliminate one male that has been brought into the enquiry yet, with confidence. Everyone therefore remains a suspect. I'll see you all again at debrief.' Dylan looked at his watch. He appeared restless and agitated. 'Make it six-thirty, and don't be late.'

Dylan walked to his office and Vicky followed. Distracted, he didn't see her stood at the door and she watched him sit behind his desk and ease a document out of an unfamiliar type of brown envelope. Dylan appeared pleasantly surprised by the envelope's contents and briefly she saw a softening of the lines around his tired eyes. She tapped on the window of his open door and walked in.

'Elliot Black is coming in to have his DNA taken. Thoughts on this Eyeball and Randy tag people give him?'

He turned his attention to his second in command. 'Why? What you thinking?'

'Well, we've been told by her mum that Patti was forever dressed in her leotard around the house, so he could hardly ignore her? But, it wasn't that long ago he was stealing knickers off, of washing lines. And, I've not managed to prove either way if she had been wearing knickers on the day of her murder, or if they'd been taken from the scene.'

Dylan looked thoughtful. 'The photographs Black showed the journalist... If they haven't been seized, make sure they are.'

Vicky's eyes narrowed. 'Are you thinking that he might have tried it on with her and she rejected him? Maybe, even threatening to tell her mother?'

'It's a possibility. I wonder; did he see her pass the shop on her way home and follow her? What time is he coming in, he's got a few questions we need answers to and now.'

She lifted her arm, and pulled at the sleeve of her jumper to reveal the face of her watch. 'Supposedly, within the next half an hour.'

'I want you to drop it on his toes about Patti's nickname for him. Let's see what his reaction is. We need to put Elliot Black in, or out of the enquiry as quickly as possible.'

Vicky walked towards the door and Dylan stopped her in her tracks. 'Tell you what, give me a shout when he arrives. I'll join you.' She looked over her shoulder to see him picking up the document that he had been reading when she arrived.

'I'm glad something can make you smile.

Dylan looked bemused. 'It's the details for a house Jen went to view.'

'Any good?'

'I haven't been to see... Well, not recently I haven't been to see...'

Vicky scowled. 'You're not making any sense.'

DC Ned Granger appeared in the doorway. 'Just for your info boss. Stuart Sykes, the neighbour with telescope, he's not turned up for his appointment. We've been to his house and there is no reply.'

'Keep me updated,' said Dylan.

'Jaene tells me Elliot Black set off well over an hour ago too,' said Vicky.

Ned ran his hand through is thick, curly hair. 'He should be here by now. We left Burford Road half an hour ago and we've also driven around the park where Sykes hangs out to see if we could locate him.'

'And no joy?' said Dylan.

'No,' he said flopping down on his chair. He swivelled around to face Vicky. 'Get us a sarnie when you go out will you? I'm ravenous.'

Her eyes flared. 'And, tell me, what did your last slave die of, a crack round the bloody head, or a punch on the nose?'

Jen was sat in the office two floors above Dylan. The click, click, clicking of the keyboards, ring, ring, ringing of the phones and chat, chat, chatting of the officers walking in and out, made it a normal day. Avril Summerfield-Preston was doing her best impression of Hyacinth Bucket, the standard bearer of middle class snobbery, as she hosted the Administrators' monthly meeting. Jen's mobile phone rang as Avril was leading them out of her office. Rita raised her eyebrows and grinned. Jen grimaced.

'Jennifer!' Avril called. Her eyes were like steel. 'We are ready for you now dear, if you could kindly show the ladies and gentlemen where their lunch will be served. Jen fumbled frantically in her bag and stopped the ringtone wail. 'I will do anything for you,' Meatloaf sang out in all his glory. 'It was the estate agent,' she hissed at Rita as she passed behind her chair.

Dylan was sat in his office going through the enquiries paper trail when Vicky reappeared at his office door. 'Is he here?'

She nodded. Dylan's phone rang. 'I'll be with you in a minute. It's the estate agent returning my call.' She smiled knowingly and closed the door behind her.

Elliot Black didn't appear to be taken aback by the Detective Inspector's presence in the interview room. Had he expected that a senior officer, the man in charge of the murder investigation would be there?

'How are you? How's Sandra?' asked Vicky.

'Not good.' Elliot coughed into his balled fist. 'I'm not sleeping. Terrible nightmares... I keep seeing her... our Patti... on the landing.' He stared down at the table that stood between them.

Vicky stood from her seating position. A sealed package in her hand. 'I guess that's understandable Elliot,' she said, moving to stand beside him. 'As you know we need to take the DNA sample swab from you today, so we might as well get that over and done with.'

'It's really not necessary...' he said raising his hand. He turned his head and coughed again as he showed her his palm. 'I've got this...' he coughed again, took a handkerchief out of his pocket and spat. 'This terribly sore throat.' Elliot Black looked at the officers as though he had a bad smell under his nose.

'But it is.' Dylan leant across the table towards him. 'You see, for some unknown reason, your DNA was not taken after your caution for theft.' His eyes were set, cold, dark and focused.

Vicky smiled at Elliot. 'Don't worry about me. I'm constantly in the cold zone. I've got young nephews and nieces and they've always got something or other going on.'

She saw what looked like fear in his eyes.

'It doesn't hurt. There's nothing to worry about,' she said pulling a pair of plastic gloves out of the paper handkerchief looking box. 'We just need to formally eliminate you from the enquiry like anyone else. Its standard practice.' Gloves on her hands she picked up a clear tube, a swab visible within. 'This, won't take a minute, open wide,' she said standing over him. Elliot Black's hair was all of a sudden wet at the temples with beaded sweat.

However, looking up at the ceiling Elliot Black duly did as he was told and Vicky gently swabbed the inside of his mouth. 'Thank you! All done,' she said a moment later as she popped the swab in the tube and secured the cap. She sat back down next to Dylan and busied herself writing on the paperwork she later attached.

Elliot Black shuffled in his seat. 'I think I should tell you. I wasn't totally truthful the other day...'

Dylan sat in silence. 'Why's that Elliot?'

'I've got previous for traffic offences.'

'Traffic offences?' Dylan nodded.

When there wasn't the reaction on the faces of the officers that he expected Elliot Black sat in silence, put his elbows on his knees and his head in his hands; concentrating on the floor between his legs.

Vicky's voice was clear and precise. 'Okay, we appreciate your honesty. Anything else we should be aware of?'

'No.'

'So, we need to clarify one or two things that have come to our attention in the early stages of the enquiry, which you maybe able to assist us with.'

Mr Black sat up straight, leant back in this chair and gave a resigned sort of sigh. 'I'll try. How long will this take? I don't want to leave Sandra too long at the moment. She's on the verge of a breakdown the doctor said.' His voice was appealing, tears sprung into his eyes.

'I fully understand,' Vicky said, compassion in her tone.

'Did you know that Patti had a nickname for you.'

'No! Did she? I guess it's wasn't very flattering.' He closed his eyes and he let his head loll back. He sighed again. Opened his eyes and looked up at the ceiling. 'Go on, what was it?'

'Eyeball.'

'Why do you think that was?'

Elliot looked genuinely shocked. 'I've no idea.'

'Her friends tell us it was because you were always watching her.'

'I don't deny it. She was a pretty girl. What man wouldn't try to protect his daughter... stepdaughter.'

'We are also led to believe you have an unusual amount of photographs of Patti?' Dylan said.

'No more, than any other proud parent I wouldn't think.' Elliot bit his lip and held back the threatening tears.

'So you won't mind us looking at them?'

'Why should I Mr Dylan? They're on my laptop which your guys have already seized.' He shrugged his shoulders. 'Feel free!'

'Do you know what your nickname is at work?'

Elliot Black looked skywards and his gaze found the corner of the room. 'I'm the boss,' he said with no apparent interest. 'I've no idea what they call me behind my back.' He turned his attention to Dylan. 'What the hell do nicknames have to do with the murder of Patti?'

'Randy?' Vicky said. 'Your colleagues at work nicknamed you Randy.'

He managed a brief smile and shook his head slowly. 'Look this is absolute nonsense. At work its banter, and at home Patti was Patti. I was, am proud of her. She was beautiful. I'd be blind not to notice how lovely she was. She was always in her gym stuff doing flip-flops and rolls in front of us. I built a gym for her so she didn't have to go out to train any more than necessary. But be assured I am not the person you are looking for. I did not attack and kill Patti. I found her, just like I said I did. That image of her is going to remain with me for the rest of my life. I loved Patti like a daughter, nothing more.'

'It's obvious that the attack on Patti was sexually driven so, you can understand why we are asking you these questions when we are being given information about you that's linked to sexual innuendoes.'

Elliot put his hand to his sweating brow. 'Oh come on, this is bloody ridiculous. I didn't kill her. Am I under arrest?'

'No,' said Dylan. 'No, you're free to go whenever you please.'

Elliot stood to leave and the detectives remained seated.

'But, it would be very unprofessional of us not to eliminate you from the enquiry. It's routine like we said that we do these simple tests and ask the questions. It would be negligent of us not to,' Dylan said.

'Well, I'm sorry. I've had enough of your questions. I find them distasteful to say the least. If I go then you might concentrate on looking for her real killer.' He went to the door and placed his hand on the doorknob.

Vicky stood and walked towards him. 'I'll show you out.'

Vicky led him down the corridor to the exit. She opened the door that led into the police station reception area.

'I'm sorry for kicking off like that, but it's not me. Find her killer and then you'll know I'm telling the truth.'

Dylan was waiting for Vicky in the incident room. 'Do you believe him?'

'He says it's not him. But, we certainly touched a nerve when he heard about the nickname Patti gave him. We haven't enough evidence to arrest him. But, one thing he did say that we know is not true and that is that he didn't like leaving Sandra any longer than he had too, because of course we know he must have gone somewhere else before he came here. I don't know. I just hope they find semen on the swabs that the pathologist took at the post-mortem and then at least we will have DNA for elimination, which of course will make our job easier.'

'I'm sure we'll get a Forensic update before long and I've arranged to have his collection of photographs viewed as a priority. Until then, don't sit on the fence Hardacre, what's your gut feeling?'

'My gut feeling is that you'd better have made an appointment to go and look at that house or you're dead meat sir!'

# Chapter Six

Dylan stood at the top of the driveway that was two tyre tracks with grass growing down the middle. The rickety five bar gate he had stood upon many-a-time waiting for the ice cream van to arrive was tied to the Sycamore tree that met him, as it did when he was but a boy. He stood under the tree and looked up. The limp remnants of old rope told the story of several tree swings of yesteryear and he was taken back to happy, carefree, summer days. Which of his brothers, Ronnie or Charlie, had fallen off the swing and broken his arm, he wondered. His recollection of that day morphed into another when one of them came hurtling down the hill on a go-cart headfirst into that gatepost. Both occasions resulted in a trip to the hospital and a few strong words from his former regimental sergeant major father. A few more steps and he could see The Station House, the grace and favour home that his dad had been given when he worked on the railway. The ivy that he remembered to have framed the wooden porch alongside his mother's favourite climbing rose had now consumed even the chimney, and the roof tiles appeared to be growing hair.

The estate agent leant with her back to her car, her mobile phone to her ear. 'Can I ring you back I'm at the property now with a client,' she said, rolling her eyes and acknowledging Dylan's presence 'Go on then...' She appeared to frown at the news being imparted. Dylan walked on past her and down past the outbuildings.

Broken, rusted chicken wire partly edged an area where his brother had kept chickens, and beyond the remnants of a coal hole led to the outside toilet. Dylan chuckled. Him and his siblings were always glad when mum bought teacakes from Thomas's bakery as they were wrapped in tissue paper – a darn sight softer than the damp squares of newspaper, that was the norm.

Up on the hillside beyond the house a vegetable patch he'd worked on as a child still showed him the outline. Many a meal had been made from the produce the family had grown on that small piece of land.

Natalie came up behind him, unheard. 'Penny for them?' she said noting his eyes labouring on the house. 'The former owner died some years ago we're told, and the house has remained empty ever since,' she said by way of an explanation for the ivy bulging out of the partly open upstairs sash window. A thick tree branch was embedded in the roof. He nodded. His eyes left the building.

'I've dug many a potato from up there in my time,' he said in a quiet, detached voice. 'That was my job, growing the potatoes.'

'Really?' she said, her expression one of surprise. 'Your wife never said you had a connection to the property.'

His reply was laboured. 'My wife doesn't know,' he said, raising an eyebrow at her.

'God, that's spooky... Jen loves it.'

'She might love the idea but in all honesty there's no way we could take on a project like this at this moment in time.'

The smile that she had on her face dropped away. 'Looks like your luck's in then because that phone call I've just taken was to tell me we've just received a blind offer from a local builder who wants the land to develop it. Jen never needs to know...'

Dylan turned sharply. 'He wants to knock it down?'

Natalie nodded.

***

'You're the boss,' said Vicky popping her head to the side as she put her pen to her lips.

Dylan put his hands behind his head and leant back in his chair. 'Like I said before, we've not enough evidence to arrest. I can't deny Elliot Black is a possible suspect. When we've got his DNA profile it'll be automatically checked against the DNA recovered from the scene and Patti. Did we seize his footwear?'

'Yes, already gone to the lab to be checked against the partial bloodied footprint.'

Dylan looked thoughtful. 'Have a word with Jaene will you and ask her to monitor Elliot Black's mood now that we've spoken to him.'

Vicky's elbow was rested on her chair arm. She tapped her pen on her chin. 'Do you think we should be asking Sandra if she's aware of the photographs he's got of Patti, and his nicknames?'

Dylan puffed out his cheeks and blew a long breath. 'If she didn't know it's going to go down like a lead balloon right now isn't it?'

Vicky scowled. 'What do you mean?'

Dylan sat up straight and leant forward – he looked otherwise distracted as he wrote a few words on his blotter. He looked up. 'What do I always tell you, never assume. I've dealt with incest cases where the mum has known full well what was going on but chose to turn a blind eye, or was even involved.'

'That's sick.'

'Too right it is. But sadly, it also happens. For some families it's the norm – it's life as they know it, as they've always known it.' Dylan appeared to ponder. 'Let's wait until we've run the checks on Elliot Black's DNA profile before we consider mentioning it to Sandra. That way we will have put him in, or out of the frame. We don't need to create them any more problems... I suspect their relationship is under a tremendous strain as it is, don't you?'

'And she doesn't need to know about him nicking knickers right?' Vicky asked, tentatively.

'Not for now, but she is going to have to know about that at some point... you can bet your bottom dollar that everything a defence barrister can find on him, if need be, will come out in court,' Dylan looked at her questioningly. Vicky looked sad. 'Talking makes me incredibly thirsty, doesn't it you?' he said. 'Do you consider yourself a good detective?'

Vicky frowned. 'How come you're asking me that?'

'Well, a good Detective would pick up on a subtle hint, especially a Detective with your sensitivity and intuition.'

'Come again?'

'Well, around about now, a coffee wouldn't go amiss.'

Vicky's brows rose as the penny dropped. 'You're about as subtle as a bloody brick.'

Ned Granger could be seen heading towards Dylan's office through the window that showed Dylan his other officers working diligently at their desks. 'Forensic say they'll have an update first thing tomorrow morning with regard to the examination of the vaginal swab boss,' he said on entering.

Vicky turned to Dylan. 'We asked for it to be treated as a priority.'

'So now we know it's only a matter of hours... In the meantime continue to trace others that have been brought into the enquiry,' he said matter-of-fact.

Ned sidled into the chair next to Vicky. He spoke in a hushed tone. 'I've been thinking about people pinching knickers from washing lines. Why do you think it's something we don't come across much these days?'

'Probably because people don't bother to report it to be fair,' said Vicky.

'It's mostly downloading obscene images, or shoplifting kegs...'

'That's right Yorkshire slang if ever I heard it. My gran used to call 'em kegs.'

'Wouldn't you report it if you had your knickers stolen off the line then?'

Vicky showed her bottom lip. 'Now, you're assuming I wear 'em.'

Ned instantly put his hand up to his collar and opened the top button of his shirt and pulled at the knot of his tie. 'You know what I mean?' he said with a huff.

Her wink was for Dylan.

'Stop winding him up,' Dylan said as Ned scuttled out of the office.

Jen appeared at the office door. 'I have in my possession a large takeaway pizza and Costa coffees, and I also have a little girl who would like to see her daddy.' Maisy giggled as she peeped around the door.

Vicky stood and smiled at Jen. 'I'll leave you guys to it I've got to liaise with Emily, and look at the next phase of exhibits to make sure we have them ready to go to Forensic. I'll let you have the paperwork later so you can agree the priority,' she said to Dylan.

Maisy jumped up on Dylan's knee, took the pen from Dylan's hand and began writing her name on his blotter. Dylan whipped the top page off his notepad.

'Thanks Vicky, I've some policy that needs writing up. If you get chance, and they're available, have a quick look at Elliot Black's photos of Patti will you, see what you think?'

Maisy was now quietly drawing and the three had eaten. Dylan noticed Jen was unusually quiet. 'You okay?'

'I checked the estate agent's website. The house, it's under offer,' she said. 'I feel incredibly sad because I could see us living there...'

Dylan's face wore the detective's mask. 'And what makes you think we won't?'

# Chapter Seven

There was little new intelligence to report at the briefing but Dylan informed the team he was waiting for a call from Forensic. Meanwhile, he prepared an arrest and interview strategy should the result be positive in respect of Elliot Black. This preparation meant they could act immediately.

The administration work kept his mind occupied and he waited patiently for the call. Every now and then he would look into the outer office and could see Vicky pacing the incident room floor. Every time his phone rang she looked across at him for confirmation, or not that it was the call they were waiting for: the call that would put Elliot Black in the frame for his stepdaughter's murder or not.

At ten-thirty am the call came. Semen had been found on the vaginal swab taken at Patti's post-mortem and a full DNA sample was being run through the national database. Dylan waved Vicky into the office as he continued to listen intently to what the caller had to say. Vicky sat quietly, her hands gripped in her lap, her face eager and expectant.

Immediately the phone went down Dylan was eager to move forward. 'Full DNA profile from the vaginal swab.'

Vicky moved to the edge of her seat. 'We can start to eliminate.'

'Black's DNA is being checked and Forensic are continuing working on other exhibits to see if anything can be gleaned from them.'

'We need to know if the footprint is his,' said Vicky.

'Give them a call. It's not going to be the same person working on the DNA.'

Vicky left the Dylan's office to be met by the expectant faces of those working in the main office. Not a word was said as she walked to her desk and sat down. Eyes lowered, as they returned to their work.

Dylan constantly checked his mobile and his inbox. The silent telephone he willed to ring, an update, news, hoping and praying for a quick resolution. When it did ring he had to check himself from snatching it off its cradle.

The news that the bloodied footprint was Elliot Black's was not surprising and the confirmation came quickly. Another piece in the jigsaw and confirmation of what Patti's stepfather had told them but, not evidence that would prove he was the murderer. The following update from Forensic was a blow. The DNA profile that they had from the rapist, Patti's murderer was not anyone that was recorded on the national database – Elliot Black was out of the frame.

Dylan stood at his door and shook his head. 'No match on the database,' he said turning back into his office to answer the ringing phone.

'Boss, DC Donna Frost, just to let you know we have located Stuart Sykes in Burford Park. He's sat on his own on a bench next to the playground. His presence was a concern to the parents whose children were playing on the swings. Rachael attended, and notified me. We've persuaded him to come back to the nick for a chat.'

'Did he say why he hadn't turned up for his appointment for his DNA taking?'

'He said his dad had told him that he wasn't obliged to.'

Dylan raised his eyebrows. 'That's helpful!'

Stuart Sykes had no previous convictions and whilst he answered the questions put to him, his responses were somewhat vague.

When asked if they could take his DNA by means of a simple swab and the process explained to him, the officers were taken aback by his negative response. Even telling him that it was a quick and easy way of eliminating him from the murder enquiry, which in turn meant they wouldn't have to trouble him again didn't work. They offered him a hot drink. He declined, but instead asked for a glass of water.

'We haven't sufficient evidence to arrest him. We can't force him to give us a sample,' said Dylan.

'Don't you think the refusal in itself may suggest he might be involved?' said Donna. 'He lives opposite the scene, he has binoculars on the windowsill, a telescope in his room, a straight chair positioned where he can see into Patti's...'

'What else is he saying?' Dylan frowned.

'He's cooperative in his own weird way but he's refusing to let us swab him for no other reason he says but that his dad says he doesn't have to. He's still in the station. What do you want me to do sir?'

'He's had a drink of water?'

Donna nodded.

'Seize the glass. We should get his DNA and fingerprints from it. We can have him checked without him knowing it.'

'And then release him?'

'For now.'


DS Mike Scott was busy creating a database on the HOLMES system for DNA processing and submission.

'In the first instance they'll call you but you'll get the confirmation through from Forensic. This will be our only elimination factor for all suspects now we have a full DNA profile,' said Dylan.

'Elimination for males by DNA sample only,' said Ned Granger.

'You going deaf?' Vicky Hardacre clipped him around his curly head, as she walked past.

'No,' he said rubbing his ear frantically. 'I'll have you for assault!' he said with a scowl.

'You'll have me for assault what?'

'Boss,' he said sulkily swinging his legs back under his desk. He held his hand up to the sky. 'For god's sake why doesn't some member of parliament do something good for a change, and lobby for a compulsory national database, and every child born, or person entering the country should go on it automatically. Think how much easier catching a criminal would be?'

'True,' said Dylan. 'And, if we had no match we would instantly know it was someone who was in the UK illegally too.'

'Let's face it, compulsory DNA is never going to happen is it?' said Vicky.

'Sadly no, because of legislations within the Human Rights Act nineteen ninety eight.' Dylan ran his hands through his hair. He stopped for a moment. 'But, why the hell they don't they see it's about protecting the masses. Being able to identify, locate and arrest the murderers before they had chance to strike again or exit the country would save hundreds of lives.'

Vicky followed Dylan into his office.

'Sykes has refused to have his DNA taken,' he said over his shoulder. He sat behind his desk and she sat facing him. Dylan's concentration was on his computer screen.

Her eyes narrowed and she screwed up her face. 'He's a wanker.'

'Vicky!'

'No, really! Not long after he left here apparently uniform patrol officers responded to a call. Someone acting indecently in the park. Guess who they've found?' Her eyes were wide, head cocked to one side and her lips formed a pout.

'Really?'

Vicky nodded. 'A double unit attended and he was still there laid on his back, on the grass, masturbating. Apparently the officers had to shout at him to stop!' Vicky bit her lip and her eyes sparkled before she burst out laughing. 'Shelagh got out her baton to hit it apparently.'

Dylan put his head in his hands. 'Tell me she didn't?'

'No, no,' she chuckled. 'He got up when he saw the baton, fled and her and Rachael gave chase, floored him and had him in handcuffs before he knew it.'

'Well done them. And what did he, have to say for himself?'

'He told them his parents wouldn't let him do it at home so he had to do it outside.'

'I've heard of parents being blamed for a lot of things, but that takes the biscuit.'

'Shelagh's booking him in as we speak and then she'll be coming to speak to me whilst the cells arrange a solicitor for him.'

'He's got to be a priority to eliminate.' Dylan's computer beeped an incoming message and his concentrated on the screen. 'Since Donna Frost and Michelle Robinson were speaking to him earlier, update them.'

Dylan looked up from the documents he was signing when he heard laughter. Three women stood around Vicky's desk – Ned Granger was hovering. By weight the DC was worth the three ladies put together. Dylan paused and threaded his pen slowly through his fingers – something he did when he was thinking. There was a serious side to this. Sex offenders were addicts just like drug users, looking for their next fix and taking things to the next level to achieve the desired result. They were dangerous predators who were a menace to society and should, in his opinion never be under estimated as to what lengths they would go to to satisfy themselves. Stuart Sykes at the age of nineteen was a name Dylan wouldn't forget – he had already shown to Dylan that he had no self-control. 'Was he the person that raped and killed Patti?' he asked himself.

# Chapter Eight

The autumnal sun was shining through the window. It was as warm and as comforting as a blanket thrown around her shoulders. Jen didn't notice her feet were as cold as ice but read on, reading about the history of the Queensbury railway lines.

\*\*\*

It was debrief time and the team had all gathered to hear the good news that the vaginal swab taken at Patti's post-mortem had indeed given the detectives a full DNA profile of her killer, and the results that had been put through the national database were in. Dylan broke the following news quickly to the momentarily euphoric team.

'This is indeed the news we could have only wished for. However, I can confirm that our offender is not on the system,' said Dylan. 'It is therefore imperative that any male coming into this enquiry be subjected to a DNA test, to eliminate them as soon as possible. No matter what our thoughts about Elliot Black, he is not our man.'

It was apparent from the look of the sea of faces in front of him how many had believed him to be responsible. There was a wave of whispers that continued to ebb and flow for a couple of minutes, then silence ensued with Dylan's raised voice. 'We will come across what appear to us good suspects during the course of any enquiry, and this is no different. There will be people who we think are capable of rape, even murder and ultimately to be responsible for Patti's death. If we do not leave our personal thoughts behind, and deal with the evidence put before us, then we will continue to be bitterly disappointed, and our hopes dashed time and time again. Our strength is in our persistence, which will ultimately lead us to her killer. This DNA profile is a gift, and we must treat it as such, as this allows us to eliminate people very quickly and easily.'

Detective Sergeant Hardacre told those present about the arrest of Stuart Sykes. There were a few titters, and elbow nudges. Her theatrical performance regarding the details of his arrest had the team laughing. She closed on a more sombre note by telling them that his DNA was on its way to the forensic lab.

Because of Dylan's experience he knew that investigations had their peaks and troughs. It was the worst, and the best, roller coaster ride you'd ever wish to travel; even more so if you were the person in charge. Keeping morale up was important, and there was nothing better than laughter to lift the spirit, other than locating and arresting the perpetrator.

'I've briefly met Patti's gym teacher Bale at the gym,' said Ned. All eyes turned to see his bright red face and sweat sitting like bubbles on his brow. He has an abscess and was on his way to an emergency dental appointment when I caught up with him just now. A low moan of a mumble echoed around the room. Followed by a gale of laughter as he described his attempt to keep up with him on the running machine.

'First impressions?' said Dylan.

'Unmarried. Loves himself. Muscles on muscles. But,' he said, tilting his head one way and then the other, 'we all know looks can be deceiving. I've made another appointment to see him tomorrow, and get his DNA sample.'

'I'll join you,' said Donna, laying an arm around Ned's shoulder and squeezing him tight.

'I'll join you Donna,' said Vicky, with mischief in abundance on her face. 'Privilege of rank Ned.'

'And Patti's Coach is also being swabbed tomorrow,' said Dylan, shaking his head at the girls.

'Ned, that's yours?' said Vicky. She looked down at her notes that lay in her lap. 'I thought the action to see Patti's Coach was down to be carried out today?'

'Apparently, due to the train strike, his return from London was delayed. In his absence however I've also been able to show he was out of the area at the time of her death. I'll still be taking his DNA though,' said Ned.

All eyes were back on Dylan. The troops were getting restless. 'Any more information on the two lads that were seen dropping leaflets in the area?'

There was the unanimous show of bowed, slow shaking heads.

'Okay, Nev what have you got for us in respect of enquiries at Patti's school?'

'Presently compiling a list of all boys in Patti's year sir, the year below, and above, as a starting point. The number is likely to take us over a hundred, so we will prioritise those closest to her before moving onto the others.'

'This investigation is still in its infancy and we're making great progress. Remember we are still awaiting numerous results from Forensic and with regard to Patti's mobile, and laptop. I'm confident we'll find her killer.'

Back in the office Vicky stared intently at Dylan across his desk.

'If I had been a gambler I'd have lost money betting that Black was responsible,' she said.

'Understandable, a lot of things pointed to him but now we have to look forward, the good thing is we know we can positively eliminate people.'

'So Stuart Sykes becomes the front runner?' suggested Vicky.

'Him, and the rest...'

Vicky stood. 'A few of us are wandering over the road to the Red Lion if you fancy a drink?'

Dylan was otherwise distracted as he scanned the computer for emails that might update him on the enquiry. 'I'll take a rain check. I've a house to go and look around with Jen and Maisy.' Creases were visible at the corners of his eyes, such was his smile.

'And tomorrow I'll go and see Sandra Heinz and Elliot Black and let them know we have eliminated him.' Vicky smacked her lips together and leant forward on seeing DC Granger approach Dylan's office door. 'You coming for a pint mucker?'

Ned stopped at the opening, rummaged in his pocket for his phone. 'Give me a minute.'

Dylan saw him put the handset to his ear and heard the one-sided conversation that subsequently followed, which was one he had heard many times before. 'Sorry sweetheart, yes, it's gonna be a late one; again, yeah.' Ned turned away from Vicky's mocking.

She raised her eyebrow at Dylan and pretended to put her fingers down her throat. 'He needs to grow some balls.'

'Vicky,' Dylan growled in a warning tone as she walked up behind Ned, her hands threatening to grab his rear end. She turned to look at Dylan over her shoulder, mischief written all over her face. 'Behave, and don't encourage him. You'll both need all your wits about you tomorrow.'

'Don't worry about me sir,' she said with a wave of her hand. 'I'll be here all bright eyed and bushy tailed.'

'It's not you I'm worried about.'

\*\*\*

The darkness was so total it was disorientating. The route around the house nothing more than a cinder path surrounded by dandelions and thistles that flourished in the fissures. The sound of his footwear instantly took him back to his youth. He stood at the foot of the cast iron drainpipe and looked skywards. A titter escaped his lips as he recalled shimmying up the soot-covered wall to the broken window above; the one the tree branch poked through. Headlights from the passing vehicles on the main road cast a web of flickering light and shadow onto the roof tiles above and the puddles below. It would take a team of men working around the clock for the next year to restore the place to its original beauty, but they had all the time in the world if it was to be their forever home.

He sheltered under the front porch his dad had built, when the rain started to fall. As if his arm was lifted by an unseen hand his outstretched finger found the spot on the wooden joists where Joe had carved his initials besides Jack's mothers, in a heart with an arrow going through. Young and childless, him just back from the war they'd enjoyed his coming home in this house. On turning with his back to the door Dylan felt strangely at peace, until slipping on the moss covered paving slab he stumbled. The loud crack that followed announced his unceremonious entering of the house. A deep base rumbling followed by a BOOM and for a few minutes the sound of gushing water; then by silence, an eerie, cavernous silence punctuated only by an echoing drip, drip and the whistling of the wind.

Dylan put his hand to the wall searching for a light switch he knew should be there. With relief he found it – but no light appeared as if by magic, as he had hoped. His eyes becoming accustomed to the dark enabled him to move tentatively forward into the kitchen area. The crunch of his footsteps on entering was followed by scurrying, which ceased so abruptly when he stood still that he wondered if he had imagined it. He expected at the very least puddles, but at the shuffling of his feet the floor appeared dry.

A shivering of apprehension flowed through his body as he recalled his older brother's haunting words, and the stories of the grey figure with blurred features that followed them around Siding No. 4. His heart beat faster. Panic grabbed at his legs and threatened to pull him down. His head turned at the rumble in the distance and ghosts of the past swirled at his feet.

In front of him suddenly a chipped and dirty butler sink could be seen lurking beneath rusty taps. The wire hung curtain below the sink promised behind it a cupboard, or at least shelves. He blinked continually for a moment or two to try focus in the darkness, familiarise himself with his surroundings and he meanwhile wiped the perspiration from his brow with the back of his hand.

A lonely breeze wandered in through the open door to the living room. The floorboards bare, as were the walls. There was dirt in every corner of the room. Rotted fragments of old paper and faded veneer of paint thereon. Dust lay thick on the windowsills where a little light was welcomed. There was no furniture in the room for him to see but the old wooden fireplace stood bold as brass opposite the door, a mass of ash still in the hearth. The door to the stairs swung open at his touch, presenting him with the staircase every bit as abandoned. He didn't dare lean on the banister, which looked as though it would snap off at his touch. Every stair step he trod upon protesting his weight, yet he climbed them anyway. At the top he reached a landing, and the three rooms that he knew to be there opened up to him. Each door had the same cast-iron lock, each with rusted hinges. The first two bedrooms were empty but not the third. The third had been the brothers' room and looked out onto the railway line. Here the built in cupboard where their clothes, toys and drawers, in which the youngest of the Dylan children had slept, still stood rooted to the floor. The built-in wardrobe door's hinges were unforgiving and refused to budge, no matter how hard he tried the pulling of the small wooden knobs. At which point he admitted to himself the house was all but derelict he didn't know. What the hell was he thinking when he had agreed to the asking price to seal the deal?

The pitter-patter of footsteps brought him the much-coveted blanket of light. He walked quickly to the window at the shrieking to see the most welcome sight of his wife and daughter heading towards the front door. 'Daddy! Daddy!' Maisy squealed, as he crept quicker up the stairs than he had come. He welcomed her all encompassing arms around his neck. Her McDonald's Happy Meal bag wafted the aroma of fries under his nose.

'How'd you get in here?' said Jen, dangling the keys on a cardboard fob in front of him. 'Natalie couldn't make it, I had to call in the office for the keys.' He saw a scowl on her face as she switched on the light.

'And what are you doing in the dark?'

\*\*\*

Maisy didn't need rocking that night. Downstairs Max lay in front of a roaring fire and Jen was lighting the candles on the hearth when Dylan joined them. He carried two glasses of wine and placing them on the coffee table in front of the settee he sat beside Jen on the sofa, her laptop on her knee.

The crackling of the fire and the dancing of the flames was the only distraction as Dylan reread the particulars that the estate agent had provided about The Station House. 'I'd forgotten about the attic.' He chuckled.

Jen smiled softly, reading quietly the information she had come across about the house on the Internet. 'It must be surreal to be returning to live in the house where you spent your childhood.'

'Mmm...' Dylan looked thoughtful. 'In all honesty Jen, do you think we may be taking on too much?'

Jen's look was determined.

Dylan looked at the pictures and took a gulp of his wine. Jen's eyes flew up from her computer, her eyes wide, her mouth hung open.

'What?' he said.

'It's the station,' she said. 'Did you know it was haunted?'

Dylan smiled. 'So they say,' he said, leaning back, his head on the cushion. He raised his feet onto the footstool and closed his eyes. The smile remained on his face – the deal was done.

'You knew?' Jen pulled herself up to sit on the edge of her seat. She turned to face him. Her voice rose. 'You knew and you never told me?'

'I know the ghost stories our Ronnie and Charlie used to tell me.' His eyes were now open and full of laughter.

'Well, this newspaper article says the last owner had to call in someone to get rid of a ghost who didn't realise he was dead! It goes on to say...' Jen scrolled down the piece muttering through the text as she did so. 'She believed it was the ghost of a train driver who she claimed walked amongst the sheds, specifically around the Siding No.4. Apparently he was killed when a water boiler exploded...'

Dylan pulled the computer from her lap – it was his turn to question his experience at the house that night.

# Chapter Nine

Detective Inspector Jack Dylan headed to see Patti's mum and her partner Elliot Black directly after the morning briefing. This gave him not only the opportunity to update them but also a chance to speak to, and thank the family liaison officer Jaene Booth. Her role was a difficult one, a role that could be very isolated, because of their caring responsibilities.

The grieving couple remained at Patti's Auntie Joan's house, and it was becoming increasingly obvious to the FLO that they had no immediate desire to return home. Elliot answered the door to Dylan, as if it were his own, and invited him into the lounge where Jaene Booth and Sandra were seated. He extended his arm towards the armchair under the bay window inviting as he did the SIO to be seated.

'Good news, at last, I hope,' said Elliot sitting down next to Sandra who was slumped in between two soft cushions. He reached for her flaccid hand and transported it into his lap, fait accompli. Sitting on the edge of his seat he raised an eyebrow at Dylan that demanded a reply.

'It's still early days, but I do have an update, and I wanted to come in person to reassure you, we are doing our utmost to catch Patti's killer.'

Sandra gave a grunt. Her eyelids looked heavy. 'The medication... It's stopping me from going out of my mind,' she slurred, when he asked how she was feeling.

'I have some good news, as far as the enquiry goes.'

Sandra's actions were laboured but with Elliot's help she pulled herself into a sitting position. Desperately, it seemed she tried to focus her eyes on Dylan's face, his lips, and what he was about to say.

'We have a full DNA profile.'

Sandra held her breath for a moment. Closing her eyes she swayed from side to side, falling eventually into Elliot. 'Oh, what does that mean?' she said, in a sing-song voice, her head coming to rest on his shoulder.

Elliot cocked his head to one side. He tapped the back of Sandra's hand. 'It means my love that people will be eliminated by being subjected to one of their tests. Isn't that right Mr Dylan?'

Dylan nodded silently.

Elliot's voice was softer and held a tinge of bitterness. 'They made me do it...'

Sandra looked up from Elliot to Dylan. There was a moment of panic in her eyes, then confusion. 'You a suspect? Was he a suspect?' Sandra lunged forward towards Dylan and Elliot caught her with his outstretched arm.

Dylan lifted his hand, quick to reassure her. 'We know it was a man that raped Patti so any male coming into the investigation has to be eliminated. I don't apologise for that because I won't leave anything to chance in finding Patti's killer.'

She nodded slowly. 'Ah, I understand.'

The mantle clock gave a Westminster chime that broke the following silence. Sandra snatched her hand from Elliot's grasp. Head bowed, she shook it slowly from side to side. 'No, no I don't understand. You'll think I'm stupid Mr Dylan,' Sandra's pale cheeks had turned a more colourful shade of pink. She was hesitant. 'What the hell is this DNA?'

'I don't think you're stupid at all.' Dylan gave her a reassuring smile. 'DNA is an abbreviation for Deoxyribonucleic Acid. It stores the biological information of an individual. Nearly every cell in the body has the same DNA. It's the hereditary materials in human beings, and almost all other living organisms. It's what makes us different from one another, and although other people in the family may have similar DNA it will not be an exact match. Without confusing you that would be Familiar DNA. The DNA for each person is stored as a code made up of four base chemicals and they create what is typically like a bar code, to you and me. The only exception to this is potentially identical twins. DNA can be obtained from sweat, saliva, urine, faeces, hair follicles, bone, semen, blood, teeth. It can even be found in a place where a person has touched... but in this case it's the semen found on Patti that has given us the full profile. All you really need to understand is once we get a match for the DNA we have found, we will know who the man responsible is for raping and murdering your daughter.'

'He can't deny it then?'

'He can always deny it. He can protest his innocence till he's blue in the face but, the DNA profile we have will convict him and prove beyond any doubt it was him.'

'I take it the national database has been searched?' said Elliot.

'Yes,' said Dylan.

'What's that?' said Sandra.

'The national database?'

She nodded.

'The national database was established back in 1995 and continues to grow by the day. It is populated by samples recovered from crime scenes and taken from police suspects, although data for those not charged, or found not guilty is deleted. At the moment there is no match on the national database, which means that the killer may not have been arrested previously, or it is possible if he has been arrested, for some reason his DNA wasn't taken – but it should have. The DNA sample we have will be routinely checked against new samples being added from across the country and as I said earlier, every male we come across during this enquiry will be asked to provide a DNA sample.'

'How do you collect a sample of DNA?'

'They swab the mouth,' said Elliot.

'You do what?'

'A swab is a bit like a cotton bud but it's twice as big,' said Dylan.

'What do you do if anyone refuses to give a sample?'

Elliot took hold of Sandra's hand again.

'If someone refuses then they become more of an interest to us. We'll dig deeper, and if need be we'll arrest them but, we can only do that if we have sufficient evidence to arrest them.'

'So if someone has been arrested they can't refuse to give you a sample?'

'No, and there are other ways and means by which we can obtain a DNA sample... Let's just say you can be assured that nobody is going to escape the net Sandra.' Dylan shuffled to the edge of his seat and spoke directly to Patti's mum. 'Look if there is anything at all you don't understand or, want to know then please ask either Jaene,' he said, glancing in the direction of the

FLO, 'or myself. If we don't know the answer we'll find out for you. Now, for the sake of repeating myself, what the DNA profile means to us, in this investigation, is that we can eliminate people without a shadow of doubt very quickly and easily. That is invaluable to us right now.'

'And when you find him, you'll let us know?' Sandra's eyes were awash with tears.

'Of course. And, will you do something for us?' asked Dylan.

Sandra nodded her head. 'Anything.' The tears flowed down her cheeks and she brushed them away with a tissue that until then had been concealed up the sleeve of her cardigan.

'Don't listen to rumours. They're unhelpful, could be hurtful and can be very misleading. Like I say, just ask one of us.'

Saying his farewells and giving his thanks to Jaene Dylan left the house and walked briskly down the path towards the large horse chestnut tree under which he'd parked his car. Checking his mobile phone en route he saw four missed calls from Vicky. With car keys in hand he turned at the door to see the dark, scaly plates on the bark of the tree that showed him its age. He looked up to see hairless, stout twigs and down to see spiky green casings, palmate leaves and red-brown conkers surrounding his feet. Stooping down he picked up a large conker – the child in him returning for a split second. 'The first recorded conker game was on the Isle of Wight in 1848,' he heard Jen whisper in his ear, as smiling, he sat down behind the wheel.

\*\*\*

'I wonder if Stuart Sykes has told his parents he was arrested yesterday, and if so what for?' said Vicky following Dylan into his office. She carried a notebook and pen in her hand.

Dylan took off his suit jacket, put it on the back of his chair and slid behind his desk. He switched on his computer and searched his messages for updates. 'Doubtful: did Shelagh charge him?'

'Yeah, and then bailed him.' She sat down on the chair opposite him with a thump.

'Good, now the Court's involved they can ask for background checks, and make sure he gets treatment.'

'I just hope the magistrates don't give him community service, in the park,' Vicky raised her brows.

Dylan flicked nonchalantly through his in-tray – half listening to Vicky's chatter. There was an internal email from Jaene Booth. Her enquiry for Sandra and Elliot regarding the patio doors, which were on central lock at the time of checking by the search team, was not unusual. They were both aware that the doors had not been bolted for several months since Patti had lost her key and couldn't gain entry to the house via the front door. 'So, did she enter the house that way the day of the murder? And did someone come home with her on that occasion?'

Vicky continued. 'Anyway, if his DNA's a match his parents will know soon enough what their little angel's been up to – especially when we arrive at the door to arrest him, and start turning the house upside down. Do you think they have any idea what he's like?'

'Probably not; as a parent we've just got to hope and pray that the time we spend teaching them right from wrong is not in vain. CCTV puts a stop to the hassle we used to get to from parents these days – thank god.'

'The camera never lies...'

'No, it doesn't.' Dylan stopped for a moment and was thoughtful. 'My dad was a keen amateur photographer. His favourite saying was, 'A camera is a mirror with a memory...'

Vicky carried on regardless. 'Maybe Sykes parents should see the body cam footage from the arresting officers. The magistrates will be shown it and what a shock they'll get when they see even the presence of the cops didn't deter him.'

'Mmm... People's perversions, addictions, whatever you choose to call it, are the driving force in their lives – nothing else matters other than where they're going to get their next fix. We'll know soon enough now whether Sykes is our killer. If he isn't we move on but one thing for sure, whatever happens this time I'm certain we haven't heard the last of him.'

Vicky put her pen to her lips. 'Pity castration isn't legal.'

'It's still early days. But, that said we need to identify an arrest team for when we get a hit, to enable us to strike immediately.'

'Consider it done.' Vicky showed Dylan her perfectly neat, white set of teeth. 'And I'm making one in with Donna shortly to interview, and take DNA from Patti's gym teacher, Mister David Bale.'

'Is he coming into the nick?'

'Supposed to be, if he's recovered from yesterday's dental emergency.'

Dylan chortled. 'What's you betting he turns up in a tracksuit and trainers?'

'Me and Donna, we're banking on shorts. Apparently, he's a bit of a looker.'

'Ah, so that's the reason for joining Donna in the interview?'

Vicky caught the teasing glint in Dylan's eye. 'And sending Ned off elsewhere,' she grinned. 'Well, it'll make a change from the usual. I don't think half of our customers have heard of deodorant, and in the confines of that small interview it's remarkable I'm not a size zero.'

'Yeah, well don't you be wearing those rose tinted glasses when you interview him, and make sure you do get his DNA.'

Vicky blushed before smirking. 'As if.'

Patti's coach, Michael Parks and David Bale would hopefully give them a better understanding of the type of girl Patti was and help build her profile. Dylan encouraged those at the next briefing. 'I want to feel the ghost of Patti sat beside me, taking me through her daily routine. Each person you speak to brings us closer to knowing Patti, and her contacts. I want names. Although we are clearing the ground beneath our feet we also need to be aware of the wider search. Whoever did this heinous crime cannot stay out of the net – not if we are structured, and that structure is airtight.'

There was silence for a heartbeat. Dylan continued. 'Have we got an update on her laptop, the service provider of her mobile phone?'

Ned was slouched over the desk. His chin rested on his hands. 'No boss.'

'Why not? They could be holding crucial information.' Dylan's voice was raised. 'It's a murder enquiry for god's sake. Ask them what's taking them so long?' Tiredness caused the impatience that was rearing its head. 'Do they need to work more hours?'

Ned shrugged his shoulders. 'Dunno.'

'Find out then! If we need to allocated some overtime, we'll do it.'

The detective sat up with a grunt. 'Yes boss.'

Moments after the briefing the incident room was cleared, to a rustling of paper, a murmuring of voices, a banging of draws, chairs against desks and a slamming of doors. There was nothing like Dylan's raised voice to motivate the team. He used this weapon infrequently but always to good effect. He settled behind his desk with a contended smile on his face. The warm afternoon autumnal sun on his back. He felt surprisingly relaxed. Quiet time in an incident room was unheard of so he took the opportunity to revisit the murder scene footage that David Funk had taken, on the day of the murder, at the scene of the crime.

Dylan's initial visit at the murder scene was as much about preserving the scene as getting a feel for the surroundings. 'See how she lived and you'll see how she died.' The words of his mentor Inspector Peter Reginald Stonestreet rang in his ear. At that point he had been under pressure to get the enquiry up and running. Now, undisturbed he scrutinised the scene. Was there anything he had overlooked? Like watching a movie the second time around was he about to notice things he wasn't aware of at the time?

Momentum was building with each action completed. Which in turn led to another enquiry required to be conducted. Thoughts popped into his head as the footage took him back into the house where the murder took place. There was an outstanding enquiry by the house-to-house team who were asking the neighbours for information with regard to seeing Patti that day. He wrote himself a note to see if that task had now been completed.

His eyes focused on the screen once more, his pen hovered over his notepad. More questions to note:-

1. What clothes had Patti been wearing on the morning of her murder? Was it the clothing that they found folded up, near her body? Or had she changed at school, changed at home, and if so where were the clothes she had been wearing that morning, including her knickers?

2. Did Patti have a locker at school? He was sure Nev Duke's team would have checked but, he needed to know.

3. Was it possible Patti was caught on CCTV en route to school, at school?

4. Her normal route to school was past the Spar shop? Did she walk that fateful day? Did she use the bus? Did she get a lift?

The answers to these questions would confirm whether her routine was compromised and in turn who she had spent time with her that fateful day. Corroboration, information by those known to be with her had been actioned.

5. Her swimming bag found at the foot of the stairs. Could anyone confirm if the complete kit was inside?

6. Patti's fingernails and toenails were painted when she was found. Were they painted by Patti or someone else?

Dylan was more than aware this was the very basic information that the incident room should know, and if they did, then he hadn't been updated? If however this information was not known then it would be a matter of priority that the questions were answered. His head was buzzing, trying as he may to absorb all the information being played on the screen before him.

Dylan's phone rang and absentmindedly he picked it up, without taking his eyes off the footage. 'Dylan,' he snapped.

'How's it going?' Jen's voice held a spring in it.

'We're making progress, but not as fast as I'd like.' Dylan paused the footage, put down his pen and sat back in his chair. He ran his fingers through his hair and gave a tired sigh.

'Well, you've got to admit that you're not the most patient person when it comes to waiting for the information to come in to catch a criminal, are you?'

Dylan smile was wide. She knew him well. 'Kettle calling pot black comes to mind.' Dylan laughed. 'Now, when it comes to moving house...'

'That's different,' she said almost apologetically. 'In fact that's why I'm ringing. The guy I've found to do the building work wants to meet at the house. I can go this afternoon after work – what about you?'

'Ah... That might be difficult. The roof and windows have got to be our priority. Can you cope?'

DS Vicky Hardacre and DC Donna Frost sat behind a waist-high table in the small interview room, opposite Patti's gym teacher David Bale. The fact that he was dressed down in a dark blue tracksuit raised a smile to Vicky's face. Mr Bale was clean-shaven, his aftershave excessive. A fine and perfectly symmetrical bone structure was complemented by his perfectly even tanned skin.

She recalled her crush on her history teacher and it made her cringe at the recollection of bumping into him at the supermarket and seeing how he had aged.

DC Frost introduced them and thanked him for coming in to speak to them. 'I hope you're feeling better than you did yesterday, the swelling on your face appears to have reduced considerably if what DC Granger told us was true?'

'Yes, thank you it is.' The blush that accompanied the modest smile on the face of the silver fox made him appear more manly somehow.

'So let's start with when you last saw Patti?'

'It was the morning of the day her body was found. She often does split shift training as part of her gymnastic regime, before and after school.'

'Did she fancy you?' Vicky asked.

'I don't think so.' David turned away his blush deepening.

'We are told by her friends she was the teacher's pet, your pet. Is that true?'

'I encouraged her, like I do all my students, especially those who want to work. They are few and far between.'

'Patti was no ordinary gym student though was she?'

'No, she was an exceptional young lady with a work ethic far beyond her years.'

'She had a Coach who specialises in the specific gymnastic training regime didn't she? Didn't you think that was punishing enough without you encouraging her to do extra-curricular activities?'

'I didn't mean to push her... she was good, she was a future star and I was proud of her and what she had achieved.'

'Patti was also a very attractive girl, mature, like you say for her age. Were you a little bit flattered by the attention she gave you?'

David Bale shook his head, the smile on his face widened. 'Look, I know what you're getting at but in my line of work I'm surrounded by girls bouncing about in their T-shirts and shorts every day. Some flirt with me, it's an occupational hazard. If I let it affect me then there is no way I could do my job.'

'Have you ever been involved with the police?' said Donna.

'Look I don't like what you're suggesting but you're certainly on the wrong track. I'm gay. Because of the way the questioning is heading I think I better put the record straight.' The words fell from his lips and Vicky's demeanour changed.

'Did Patti know?'

'Probably, I don't deny it but then again I don't advertise my sexuality, do you?'

'But you said girls flirt with you?' said Donna.

'Young or old, sadly they think they can change me.'

'Patti's friends, boyfriends can you help with names?'

'She trained with a couple of local footballers Ivan Sinclair and Phil Moody but they're good lads. I can't see either of them resorting to murder.'

'You'll have heard the saying "a wolf in sheep's clothing"?'

David silently nodded.

'Patti was raped and strangled, possibly by someone who knew her, possibly someone you know.' Vicky stood. 'Luckily we have DNA evidence which enables us to eliminate people by taking a sample from them.'

'From me? Seriously?'

'This is a murder enquiry Mr Bale. We don't joke.'

'But I've told you. I'm not interested.'

'We deal in evidence, not sexual preference.'

David Bale slammed his palms down on the table. 'I haven't got time for all this.' Standing his eyes met Vicky's.

The ripping open of the package Vicky lifted from the table sounded loud to her ears as her granite gaze held his. 'It takes seconds to take a swab.'

A confused look at Donna who was still seated was followed by a nervous laugh. 'It really isn't necessary.'

'That's where you're wrong. It is necessary.'

A stamp of his foot on the floor and the pushing back of his chair with some force made Vicky jump. 'I disagree. I'd like to speak to the man in charge.'

'Well, he's working. I'll see if he has the time and wishes to speak to you,' said Donna as she pushed her chair away from the table and rose slowly from her seat. 'He's a very busy man. If you had nothing to hide there would be no reason for you not to take the test. It would be nice to think that because you knew Patti and liked her so much you'd gladly give your support to us who are trying our very best to find her killer.'

# Chapter Ten

The briefing room had been used all day for an emergency planning tabletop exercise. There was no escaping the stench of stale sweat as they entered for the debrief.

'So, did he take the test?' said Dylan.

'Our Donna can be very persuasive when she wants to be.' Vicky nudged her partner playfully.

'And your gut feeling?'

'If it's him I'll bare my arse on the Town Hall steps,' said Vicky.

Seats all taken. Ned was stood on the periphery of the group with his back to the wall. 'Now that I'd like to see.'

Vicky raised her voice as the team settled themselves. 'Talking of tossers, have we got a result on Sykes DNA yet DC Granger?'

Ned strained his neck over those sitting on the corner of the desks in front of him. 'Not yet, otherwise you'd know about it.'

'Patti's nails were painted. Do you know if she did that herself Jaene?' asked Dylan.

'I don't know sir, but I'll find out.'

The door opened and CSI David Funk entered the room. He held up his hand to catch Dylan's attention. 'Just back from Forensic. They've found a small amount of skin from the index fingernail scrapings on Patti's right hand.'

'And do we know if the DNA profile matches the one on the vaginal swab?'

'It does.'

*\*\*\**

Vicky walked in Dylan's office with coffee, eyes bright, papers in hand. 'Patti's mobile data is in.'

Dylan reached out for the paperwork she offered him. Laying the documents on his desk he studied them closely. 'There's clearly a pattern of usage.'

'Most likely because she's in school. They'll have the pictures for us by debrief I'm told.'

'I think the easiest way to analyse the content is by using an Anacapa chart. That'll show us at a glance what calls were made to who, and when, as well as their duration.'

'I agree. There's nothing's jumping out at me from these sheets.'

'I want every number identifying and the owner of that mobile spoken to.' Dylan looked across at Vicky. 'Any knowledge of CCTV seized?'

She shook her head.

'Damn. I was hoping for conformation of what she was wearing en route home and if there was anyone with her, or following her.'

'I'll have a word with the others in the incident room.' Vicky got up to leave as Dylan's telephone rang. He picked up. She turned to watch him, his eyes still on her.

'Sykes, he's not a match,' he said, putting the phone back on its receiver.

Vicky screwed up her face. 'Bugger!'

***

With Vicky, his deputy at his side at the front of the room full of his team of police officers and civilian staff he commenced with the debrief.

'Ladies and gents as you are aware two excellent suspects have now been successfully eliminated from the enquiry, thanks to the DNA profile we achieved from the vaginal swab taken at Patti's post-mortem. Now we also have the results from nail scraping taken from Patti at her post-mortem, which have also proved successful in giving us a DNA profile. That profile is identical to the first.'

Vicky's input was a resume of the interview with David Bale, his initial reluctance to provide a DNA sample and his reasoning.

Dylan reinforced to the team, 'We know our suspect is male. No matter what excuses, bizarre or otherwise any male who comes into the enquiry gives us, we require a sample. The simplest way for them, and us, is for them to take the test. The bottom line is the only way any male will be eliminated from the enquiry now is by their DNA.'

DS Nev Duke spoke to the team about the enquiries at the school. 'Letters have been sent out to the parents of all male pupils from the teacher overseeing the procedure explaining the need for their corporation and assistance to eliminate anyone who knew Patti from the enquiry. It is too early to tell what the response will be but leaflets showing what the swab test entails is attached. It has also been reinforced that samples taken will be destroyed after they have been checked against the DNA profile we have.'

'Did Patti have a locker?' Dylan crossed the question off his list.

'No sir, there is not enough floor space in the school to house a locker for each pupil, therefore students are given lockers on a need basis, rather than ad hoc.'

'Patti's Coach, Malcolm Parkes, it has been confirmed was out of the area at the time of her death but has offered his assistance in providing us with names of her known acquaintants. His DNA will be taken as a matter of routine,' said Nev.

'I also need to remind you at this stage that if you come across a suspect who has died since the incident we require their DNA. If you are unable to get this for any reason we should get DNA from a member of the family to see if there is any similarity to the known profile. Jim Duggan the Coroner's Officer has been briefed and he will flag up the deaths of all males since the day of the murder and will continue to do so, until we catch the killer.' Dylan's smile was a satisfied one. 'Our killer won't escape, even if he dies.'

It was Sergeant Simon Clegg's time to give his update. He was sat at the back of the room. 'House to house enquiries have resulted in us been given the names of two young lads who'd been dropping leaflets in the area. We don't have an exact date or time for this and no one can say if they were in the area on the day of Patti's death so, they are actioned to be housed and seen as a priority.'

'I want every male resident on Burford Avenue now subjected to a DNA test,' said Dylan, his eyes seeking out the search teams sergeant. 'What are the immediate neighbours like? Neighbours from hell, or do they all get on?'

Simon stood. 'One householder believes she saw Patti shortly before she was murdered. She also believes she was with someone wearing a hoodie. She is an elderly lady who lives on the opposite side of the road and on her own admission she tells us she sits at her window daily, watching the world go by. But,' Sergeant Clegg was hesitant, 'She is the only person that mentions this... Vicky, I believe you have made arrangements to see her?'

Vicky nodded.

'Also of interest is a lad who has been seen hanging about Burford Avenue. He has approached two different members of the house-to-house team asking questions about what they are doing there, and wanting to know what's happening. He told us initially his name was Robbie Williams, until I took him on one side to have a quiet word.'

'As you do...' said Vicky.

'Yes, as you do,' said Simon. 'This time he told me his name was Elvis, Elvis Cooper. I thought he was taking the piss but I was able to confirm, over the radio that an Elvis Cooper did indeed live at the address he gave us. He is going to be seen at his home address and we'll take a sample from him at that time.'

The debrief was concluded. It was dark outside. Dylan walked back along the corridor to his office. He was thoughtful. He knew as soon as he put one suspect to bed another would rear their head. He was tiring but grateful they had secured the DNA profile because the enquiry was highlighting excellent suspects, all who would have needed more looking at should they not have had it. He walked down the steps from the floor where the briefing room was situated. On the ground floor there were no windows in the internal corridor – just closed doors. It was colder down at that level. He shivered, rubbing his arms that were covered by his shirt sleeves. As he walked through the incident room he saw the skeleton staff that manned the offices at night. He could hear his phone ringing from within his office. It was still ringing when he reached it.

'Cracker Craze from the front counter sir. I have a young man here who says he wishes to speak to a member of the investigation team. He wants to confess to murder.'

'How does he seem?' Dylan caught the sight of Vicky who was preparing to leave for the night.

'Calm, very calm.'

'I'll get someone to come up to see him.' Dylan walked slowly out into the incident room. Vicky was delving into her handbag trying to locate something it seemed. 'Fancy coming down to see a guy at the office who says he wants to confess to murder?' She looked up.

'Sounds interesting. Does he have a name?'

'Not that I know yet.'

Stood alone in the reception area of Harrowfield Police Station was a pale-faced youth sat on a bench that was screwed down to the floor with thick metal bars. He was dressed in a dark blue hoodie, the same colour as his jeans.

The officers ushered him into an interview room where they could speak to him privately.

Dylan introduced them both, 'I'm Detective Inspector Jack Dylan heading the murder enquiry and this is my deputy Detective Sergeant Vicky Hardacre. We have been told by our colleague at reception that you want to speak to us in respect of a murder?'

The youth with froggy green eyes sat in the wooden slatted chair that was bolted to the floor, at the other side of the desk from where Dylan and Vicky sat.

'Yeah, it were me,' he said fiddling with the toggles on his top. 'I did the crime.'

There was a pregnant pause. 'Did what crime?' asked Dylan.

Again there was silence.

'I know what you're thinking, but it were me. I keep seeing her face so I had to come in to confess.'

'What's your name?'

'Elvis?'

'Elvis Cooper?' said Vicky.

Elvis stopped. He looked at Vicky with his unblinking, weird green eyes. 'Yeah, you're good,' he said. He turned to face Dylan. 'She's good.'

'You've been talking to some of the uniformed officers who were making enquiries on Burford Avenue haven't you? Didn't you also tell them you were called Robbie Williams?'

'How did you know that?' Elvis swallowed hard. 'Okay, so I lied, that's till this giant of a guy grabbed me round the neck and threatened me. And, even when I told him my right name he still didn't chuffin' believe me. Wanker!'

'How old are you Elvis?' Vicky's brows furrowed.

'Nineteen.'

'Moving forward, we need to take a swab from you. Vicky inserted her hands into the plastic gloves. She stood. Removed the swab from the packaging.

Elvis only had eyes for Vicky. He noticed tiny details, like the wrinkles around her eyes, and the red dry patches down the side of her nose. His lip trembled, the feeling spread up his arm, and slowly through his body.

Vicky stifled a giggle. 'I promise. It doesn't hurt,' she said in a kindly way.

'You want to put that earbud inside my gob?' said Elvis opening his mouth, at Vicky's request. She rolled the swab up and down, in circles, against the inside of his cheek before removing it. He watched her with interest as she open the vial by twisting off the cap, popped the used swab inside and sealed the vial's cap shut.

'Now,' she said sitting back opposite him. She rolled off her gloves. 'You said you wanted to confess to a crime?' Vicky read Elvis the caution.

'Now, tell us what you've done,' she said.

Elvis's eyes fluttered. He shuffled around in his seat. 'I did the girl in. Her that was in the papers.'

'Okay, but I need you to tell me from the very beginning, exactly how you did it?'

He looked at both the officers' perplexed faces, as if he was expected to give an account of his actions by way of a detailed confession. 'I smashed her head in,' he said.

'When? When did you do it?' Vicky continued as Elvis was directing his responses at her.

Elvis looked up into the corner of the room. His smile revealed his crooked, yellowing teeth. His attention returned to Vicky. 'I followed her.' A slow grin spread across his face, an eyebrow raised, his lips tightened. He turned his head back to the camera and ran his fingers through the hair above his ear and he feasted his eyes on the camera he had found there, once more.

'Where did you follow her?'

'Home.'

'Where from?'

'School.'

'What she was wearing?'

'What she always wears,' he said with a glint in his eye. 'I used to go t'same school as her, didn't I?'

'Okay then, so you followed her, then what?'

'I followed her. I were talking to her... She didn't answer me. She got to the door and tried to shut me out. That's when I did it.'

'Have you ever been in trouble with the police before?' asked Dylan.

Elvis recoiled in his chair. 'Just stealing mainly.'

'Mainly? What does that mean?'

'I got told off for having sex with a girl.'

Dylan sat up straight, tucked his tie inside his jacket and leant in towards the table.

'Told off, you mean you were given a caution? Was the girl under sixteen?'

'Yeah, but it weren't my fault. She told me she were sixteen.'

'Is that it?'

'Well, I were once cautioned for burglary.'

'Is that it?'

Elvis nodded his head. 'Think so.' He frowned. 'I can't think of ought else I got caught for.'

'Do you work?'

He sat up, puffed out his chest. 'I'm doing work experience and my boss says I'm good.'

'What're you doing?'

'Digging graves.'

'And, do you enjoy your work? Is that something you'd like to do full-time?' said Vicky.

Elvis looked directly into her eyes. His flabby face was suddenly suffused with purple, spittle formed at the edges of his mouth. 'Dead bodies don't frighten me. Do they frighten you?'

'Can you explain to us how you knew she was dead?' said Dylan.

'I've seen lots of dead bodies – up close and personal.'

\*\*\*

'What does the tier three course tell you? Keep an open mind and don't always accept the first thing that they tell you,' said Vicky as she followed in Dylan's footsteps down the corridor to the incident room.

'And we have a DNA profile that will prove he didn't do it,' said Dylan. 'Wasting police time is a serious offence. Get hold of his care worker and get them to come in to have a chat with us.

'It's a sad state of affairs when you're got to admit to committing murder to be institutionalised, to feel as if you belong. Years ago he'd have been sent to the gallows based on that admission, and the murderer would be free to murder again.'

'On a positive note, it's one less person to eliminate as we have his DNA. Which I'm certain will come back negative.'

'That sure? By your own standards then you'll be baring your arse if it's him?'

'Not a problem,' said Dylan.

# Chapter Eleven

The results from Forensic came back in a slow stream, all negative. Now added to the 'not him list' was Malcolm Parkes, Patti's coach, and as expected Elvis Cooper.

On another positive note the purchase of The Station House was going through, and the building work required to make it habitable agreed. Jen had been the driving force and Dylan knew her well enough to know she was never more content than with a project on the go, and this was some project. The old house would be a long time in making as comfortable as their present home. The rooms were smaller, there were no luxuries such as en suites, the heating wasn't instant, no gas, a septic tank but if his mum and dad could manage to live in it happily with five young children, then he was sure they could too.

When work allowed, instead of reading bedtime stories to Maisy, Dylan had taken to reminiscing about his life at the house. Never before had Jen seen Maisy so eager to climb the stairs to bed. However true those stories were, as funny as Dylan relayed them, Jen didn't know. There were many nooks and crannies for Jen and Maisy to yet explore and often Maisy would come home from a site visit with a treasure to behold for her daddy; an old orange coloured railway ticket for a pram, a piece of crockery, a rusty tin she'd found laying around in the grounds, in the hope she'd found a boyhood token for Dylan to come up with a tale for.

The moon ended an eighteen-hour shift for Dylan and with Jen and Maisy up early and out of the house the next morning Dylan found himself home alone and eager to make his planned late shift that day result in a productive morning. Today he would go back to the house – the estate agent's diary permitting. Mystifyingly, he didn't feel a connection to the building nor the euphoria that Jen did about the move. Should he?

Dylan was pleasantly surprised that the present owner had begun to remove the clutter from the old station yard, which made the driveway to the house easier to access. He parked his car under the thirty-metre tall English Oak where under its open canopy forest floor flowers grew in the spring, and where he also knew a few budgerigars had found their final resting place. He stepped out of his vehicle directly onto a blanket of shed dry, brown leaves and a scattering of acorns – the tree was indeed over twenty-five years old to his knowledge. He stood momentarily, slammed the car door and looked skywards as an exodus of birds caused more leaves to fall on him, like confetti. The woodpecker holes where he had a memory of bats roosting could be seen. And the log the tree had given up to his dad one Christmas for the table decoration, Mum adorned with mistletoe and holly, showed him its stump. He felt a stirring inside him. There was silence, real silence. A few steps, when he scuffled the leaves in a childlike fashion and he found himself standing under the wrap around porch. This time he was encouraged inside by the low sun on his back. The worn key had been easily recognisable to him when the estate agent handed it over. Its curvature, decoration and size made it unique for the lock his father had fitted. Could this be the one he carried in his school satchel? The door's heaviness, and no doubt the rust on the hinges brought about resistance on it's opening but nothing that a little nudge with a fisted hand didn't rectify. Due to Natalie being off sick, it was trusting of the owners to allow him access alone, when the house sale had not yet completed and he was grateful for the time they afforded him alone in the property. The house smelt of what it was, an old damp shell where human life had been extinct for some time, and day had turned to night without anything other than insects in occupancy. It was much darker within and he felt compelled to switch on the light that miraculously worked instantly this time round. The bulb in the centre of the room dangled on a wire from the ceiling that splayed a paltry glow on the faded yellow wallpaper peeling away from the wall in places. He shivered, his eyes drawn to the open fireplace and the logs that lay in its hearth, beckoning to be lit. There was something about that fireplace... Dylan's faded memory wouldn't fully form in his mind. Looking down he saw a familiar grip shaped dent in the wood – was the old tin bath below? Excitedly he knelt down and touched it hesitating, before hoisting the connected planks that made a door. A grave-sized vault was revealed but the bath had gone. Dylan scoffed at himself for being sentimental but nonetheless felt a slight tinge of sadness.

The stairs were steeper, narrower than his younger self remembered, the years in between spinning faster and faster with every step he took until finally he reached the top. His bedroom window gave him the light he needed and he walked towards it as though pulled by some magnetic force. Dylan stood at the door, his hand on the door jamb casting his eyes upwards to see a handful of nails embedded uselessly therein. The old paint felt brittle to his touch but there was no getting out of this room unheard if the door was shut as well he knew, the wood swelled it tight in the winter, and it rattled with the wind in the summer – hence why him and his brothers, on the odd occasion had had to shimmy up and down the drainpipe outside into the ginnel below. Dylan chuckled at the thought of his backside hitting the stone flags and of the risk assessments he now had to do, and the protective gear his officers had to wear, just to walk up a ladder.

The sun's rays announced the window dirty. However, such was their strength they managed to light up the corner of the room where a nylon carpet had been torn from the grippers and the disintegrated foam backing had resorted to crumbling dust beneath. Too many times to recall, Dylan had hurriedly brushed fallen crumbs into that corner to hide them from his mother's prying eyes. The brother's treasure, a packet of wafers purchased at the Ice cream van, because they were longer in eating than an ice cream. Spread out on the bedroom floor back then was a rag rug he and his siblings had painstakingly made, on dark winter nights in front of the open fire, whilst listening to the wireless. 'The devil makes work for idle hands,' their mother would say throwing hooks, mismatched strands of material and a hessian sack the boys' way. There was no chance of idle hands in this house; Dylan was sniggering at the thought when his eyes caught the remnants of tyres that they'd cut in half and filled with bulbs in front of the shed outside. Under dad's army coat they had laid on their bed, all three brothers huddled to keep warm. Here was where Dylan's love of storytelling was born. In the absence of a blank piece of paper, an old station ledger and a coveted pencil had to do. He looked behind the bedroom door and there was the cupboard where his treasured possessions had been kept. Once more he was drawn to open up a memory, but the cupboard was bare. This time there was a moment not of just sadness but of disappointed. He had nothing substantial to hold onto from his youth, not like Jen and her keepsakes. Sentimentality for objects didn't sit well with Dylan – he was obviously more like his dad than he cared to admit. But was he also unintentionally going to starve Maisy of the past – or was he trying to protect her, like his dad had done with him from the horrors of man's inhumanity to man? Joe, never spoke about his time in Burma and the war.

'Look back not forward,' Dylan heard his dad say timely in his ear – so there was no surprise that nothing was left of his for Dylan to find. How strange it was for someone who didn't talk about the past to have such a passion for photography, Dylan thought. To capture a moment in time, as he knew he had done, for the future and then not to leave it for them to savour. Dylan looked around, trying desperately to remember where his dad had developed the photographs he took. He remembered the strings of pictures, clipped to the old washing line with pegs above a sink. He knew it was in this house. He was puzzled as he counted the rooms. There was a bedroom where his mother and father had slept, a room that was his younger sister's and that left only the room that he was in – the boys' room? Was his mind playing tricks on him, as was the light?

\*\*\*

'No luck with the CCTV?' Dylan's frustration was tangible.

'I'd have liked to think we'd have a sighting of her going or returning from school – its over a mile,' said DC Wormald. 'But as yet, absolutely nothing sir.'

'The images from her mobile – make sure we identify, trace, interview and eliminate all the males. I want to know what relationship they had with Patti, and who they hang around with.'

'Yes, sir,' said Andy.

Vicky was unusually quiet, even studious as she flicked through the images. 'Cor, who's the hunk on the photo she sent Gail and

Debbie? He shouldn't be hard to find?' said Vicky, with a wink of an eye in Donna's direction.

Dylan shook his head. 'Andy, see who we've got to assist in identifying him, regulars at the pool and any others from the complex that may know Patti.'

'Do you not think it might be beneficial for the house to house team to look at the logistics of us having a couple of officers sat at the reception area, requesting DNA from the males who enter?' said Vicky.

'That's a good idea.'

'And, Donna and I, we can do the follow-ups.' Vicky's smile was from ear to ear. 'I bagsy the hunk...' Vicky took a can of Coke out of her bag and sprung its tab.

'Vicky...' Dylan made a long low growling sound.

The detective sergeant shrugged her shoulders as she put the can to her lips. 'What've I said now? Come on boss, there has to be some perks to this goddamn job.'

'There was some suggestion in Gail's statement that her older brother Michael Carpenter asked Patti out on a date and she turned him down. He might be worthy of a visit?' said Andy.

'Absolutely, write up an action for someone to see and eliminate,' said Dylan. 'And an update on the would-be window cleaning, leaflet droppers, needs to be done.'

'We also need to house and eliminate the lad seen by the elderly lady, the one wearing the hoodie. I've a feeling that could be Elvis, who has admitted to following her home,' said Vicky. 'We know he didn't murder her, but that part of his story might be true.'

'And it could have been somebody else. Somebody we haven't eliminated. We've still a lot of ground beneath our feet to clear before we move on.'

'Do we know if the house to house team have managed to complete all their callbacks on Burford Avenue?' Vicky asked.

'I'll get Sergeant Scott in the incident room to do a review for us, for debrief.'

\*\*\*

Jen lifted the bolt-hole to the loft and tentatively hoisted herself up to sit with her legs dangling towards the hallway. It was dark, and warm. The previous owners had installed a fluorescent bar light affording her to see where they had boarded; beam to beam. Maisy's nursery furniture and early toys around her, she slowly started to take them one by one to the landing below. Eventually it was done. The shiny boards empty. As she reached to switch off the light and pull over the door a twinkle caught her eye. Puzzled, and with the object out of reach she pulled herself up into the loft. Standing was doable down the apex but she had to go on her hands and knees to get to the bags that were arranged haphazard to her left. Then a memory came to her... the last time she had been here she was putting out of sight all that was her fallen world – how unexpected was it then to lose her mum to a tragic accident after her initial shock that she may not have children, and her fiancé Shaun had abandoned her for another? She sat staring at the packages, contemplating her life now, the light flickered and distracted her for one moment. She heard a thump and recognised it to be Max dropping to the floor on the landing below. He moaned before resting his head, she presumed on her slippers she'd abandoned at the bottom of the ladder. Things that made no sense to her flooded into her head as she pulled a carrier bag to her – the sound of the sea, the smell of her mothers' perfume, Dylan's smile when they'd met – that had stirred her heart she thought forever numb.

She couldn't shake the feeling that her heart was made of stone as she dragged the heavy box towards her and was tempted to push it back and leave it where it was – in the dark place it belonged. Max whimpered down below at her descending. She placed the carrier bag and box against the landing wall. The rain battered against the window and the night was drawing in. She closed the curtains. A quick look at her watch told her it was time to pick Maisy up from Chantal's. Tempting as it was to discard the packages at the local tip on the way, for one bright second she saw a strand of yellow wool hair sticking out of the bag. She ripped the cardboard away, catching a nail as she did so. She plunged her hand in to find a handful of sea glass and driftwood. Then she pulled Mo the rag doll to her and hugged her tight. A tear quite unexpectedly ran down her cheek and it stalled at her lip. The taste of salt was on her fingers. At that moment she knew there were memories in those boxes that she would be foolish not to keep and she realised that the process of going through them would have to be done – but not now.

***

Vicky walked into Dylan's office to the sounds of the police sirens in the yard outside. 'I've a name for the hunk! He's Trevor Thomas, twenty-four years, Flat Sixteen, The Heights – occupation prison officer, works shifts and I've got a contact number.'

Thomas stood with a box of Yorkshire Tea suspended in the air half an hour later. 'Sugar,' he said, a smile on his round, pleasant face.

Dylan knew the floor plan of Trevor Thomas's house by heart. He had been tasked to organise the dawn raid on a previous tenant. When his team gained entry to make the arrest on the known drugs baron he was ready for them – but not as Dylan had imagined. For sat in a chair with a piece of wood pressed against the trigger of a shotgun – its handle to the floor between his feet, the criminal had shot himself in the mouth on their entry. Dylan looked down at his feet to see the blood running through the grout on the floor tiles.

Thomas wore a ring on his little finger. On the kitchen window sill in a gold-rimmed, porcelain tray was a hair bobble, a plastic bracelet, a small purse and a sampler of perfume. On the worktops large tubs of vitamins, workout supplements and a bowl of fruit. Through double doors that connected the kitchen to the dining room area a multi-gym could be seen. On the walls were floor-to-ceiling mirrors.

Hot drinks made, Thomas carried them on a tray, past the sunbed in the hallway to a lounge that was bare to the walls with a couple of leather sofas, a large coffee table and a wide screen TV. This was no stereotypical bachelor pad.

Seated, Dylan explained the reason for their visit.

'But why would you come to see me?'

'Did you not know Patti?'

'I don't think so.' Thomas was sat on the edge of his seat, his elbow on the chair arm. He stroked his chin. 'I saw her picture on the news. It didn't ring any bells.'

'She has a picture of you on her mobile, posing,' said Vicky.

Thomas's shoulder-length hair partly obscured his eyes until he threw his head back laughing. 'I'm always posing. There's no law against that is there?'

'A young girl is dead, raped and strangled. She has a picture of you, in your trunks posing, and what we're asking you is why?'

There was an awkward pause.

'Okay, I'm sorry. I know this is serious. I'm not being flippant or awkward, promise.' Thomas shrugged his shoulders. 'I just don't know why she should have that picture on her phone that's all.'

The following pause felt like a statement. Dylan and Vicky waited.

'Look I'm not trying to be clever.' Thomas threw his feet up onto the coffee table and laid back into the cushions. 'I go swimming, I speak to a lot of people, mostly girls I admit but I honestly don't recall her. Is there any particular reason that I should?'

'Perhaps this might help you remember?' Dylan slid a photograph of Patti's across the coffee table and turned it round to face him. When he sat and picked it up both officers watched his face for a reaction, but there was none.

His eyes found Dylan's face, and then moved to rest on Vicky. 'Sorry, that doesn't help either. I'm not saying I haven't spoke to the girl – I could easily have, in passing. But, I wouldn't know her from Adam if I passed her in the street and I definitely don't know her by name. As for my picture on her phone... I didn't pose for it for her. She may however have taken it when I was posing for someone else?'

Thomas showed them his diary when asked about his whereabouts on the date of Patti's murder. 'I was working at the prison on that day.' He pointed to the entry. 'And as you can see from this I was down for a twelve hour shift.'

'It would make our life easier if we could just do a DNA swab to rule you out.' Dylan said.

'But on that date I was behind bars, literally! Surely that rules me out? You're way off the mark if you think it's me that killed her?'

Dylan's eyes narrowed. 'You know and I know even people serving a sentence, behind bars, go out on day release. Some clock in and out daily. Some "lifers" have supervised trips to the seaside.'

'And even have driving lessons at a cost to us... Check with the prison, they'll tell you I was there all day.'

'Wherever you work it doesn't mean to say you couldn't nip out for half an hour, we need you to take the test please.'

'Look, it wasn't me. I've told you where I was and you're going to have to accept my word for it.'

'We are eliminating all males from this enquiry by means of their DNA, with DNA we can eliminate you very quickly which will save us, and yourself time in the long run. Let's face it, the last thing you want is us making enquiries at the prison and people knowing that a dead young girl has a picture of you, in your trunks, on her mobile phone. You and I know what the rumour squad is like in the job.' Vicky stood and opened the seal on the swab test kit.

'But it isn't me!'

'Good, then let's take the swab so we can all get on with our day.' Vicky raised an eyebrow invitingly.

His demeanour softened. 'Okay, okay. Take the test if you must.' Thomas's mouth opened wide, but his eyes were not completely shut. Vicky brushed up against his shoulder to be met by his sour-smelling breath that made her gag. She stepped back involuntary, hitting her head on the wall light. A dry rattle from Dylan's throat told her he was laughing, and she swabbed the inside of one cheek, then the other as quickly as she could. When she had finished he rewarded her with a flash of his pearly white teeth.

Minutes later, at the door Trevor Thomas pressed his card into her hand. 'My phone number. Call me,' he said. 'We'll go for a drink. I'd like to get to know you better.' His eyes closed completely now as he held her hand longer than necessary to shake it.

'So what do you think about Mr Adonis now?' Dylan, ahead of her opened the car doors. Vicky threw her bag on the back seat and sat next to him in the passenger side. He saw the disappointment on her face. 'Please,' she said tearing up his card and throwing it in the ashtray.

A wide grin spread across her face as she turned to look at Dylan. 'He obviously has taste though.'

Dylan frowned. 'Did you get the vibe he might be our man?'

Vicky's smile quickly fell from her face. 'No, although if he's taking steroids in his bid to have a superhuman body he must be a little crazy. Who knows what he might be capable of?'

'Perhaps you should take him up on that date.'

'Not on your Nelly!' she said.

***

By the time Dylan and Vicky got back to the police station, the water sat in puddles in the back yard. Darkness had fallen like a curtain and the bright lights of the incident room shone like beacons to show them the way.

Vicky's slamming of the incident room door behind her made heads turn. She giggled. 'Ha ha! That woke you lot up didn't it?' Ned's face showed her he was not impressed. The room was warm, she took off her coat and popped it behind her chair. Ned Granger put his hand towards the ceiling and stretched, moaning as he did so. He yawned, his mouth opening so wide it looked like a chasm.

'What've you got for me?' said Dylan.

Nev Duke walked towards them. 'I've got Patti for you – walking past the Esso garage on the pavement beyond the small brick boundary wall.' He had everyone's attention.

'Alone?' said Dylan.

'There are people walking in front of her, but no one with, or immediately behind her.'

'Can we see what she's wearing?'

'Yes, it shows her clearly in her shorts and T-shirt, and she's carrying a bag.'

'Have we got a time?'

'According to the recording the time is ten past one.'

'Verify that the timer on the CCTV camera is accurate and get me stills of the people around her. We'll appeal for them to come forward as potential witnesses.'

\*\*\*

In socked feet Dylan crept into the bedroom. With a thump, his shoes fell to the floor accidentally coming to rest with a bang against the skirting board. His shoulders rose and he stopped, waiting for some sign of Jen waking – there was none. He threw his clothes over the wicker chair. Ten minutes later he turned off the shower. The steam encased him for a moment or two. His mood was jubilant at the turn of events and his mind would not cease to ask questions.

What about Patti's computer? Had the technical team managed to get any information from it and if so what did it tell them about her?

The call he had put into the Tech team had resulted in him having to leave a message requesting an update. He could feel impatience rising within him. The window of time during which physical evidence was usually found at the beginning of an enquiry was diminishing by the day – and he knew it.

# Chapter Twelve

Six o'clock the next morning Dylan snuck out of the bedroom onto the landing, and as he walked past Jen's memory boxes, for the first time he felt a real longing for corroboration of his childhood. Carrying his footwear and with light-footed steps he made his way down the stairs. No one stirred, other than Max who greeted him at the bottom with a raisin of a sleepy eye and a slow wag of his tail. When Dylan passed the Golden Retriever and walked down the corridor the dog rose slowly and with a little moan stretched out his arthritic back leg, which gave away his ageing. However, once up on his feet he sprightly padded across the kitchen, towards the back door. Dylan let him outside into the garden whilst he hurriedly, collected his briefcase and top coat. He opened a cupboard, the shelves were bare apart from two mugs and Maisy's cup, three dinner plates, bowls and side plates. He opened the drawer to find three knives, forks and spoons. He turned to the table and underneath he saw the sealed boxes – he afforded his morning face a smile. Jen was organised as always.

Dylan put his arm in the sleeve of his overcoat as the front door slammed behind him. He lifted his gloves to his lips, held one between his teeth and put his fingers one by one in the other, on his way to the car. He could see his breath before him. It was still dark. Winter was coming there was no doubt – he shivered, as he turned the fan of the heater on full.

\*\*\*

In his office he stood at the window, under which folders were lined up on the floor, his hands on the radiator, thinking. The window shutters were open to the outside world, one that was awakening with speed as the clock struck seven-thirty. He suddenly felt very warm. He undid his coat. Vicky appeared at the door, two mugs in her hand. She smiled and yawned at the same time.

'We need to check the sex offenders' register and make sure all those registered have had their DNA checked against our profile,' Dylan said briskly, as he slipped into his chair behind the desk.

'It should have already been done,' she replied.

'I know that, but I want to be absolutely sure. We don't want anyone slipping under, over, through the net.' He picked up the mug she had placed on his desk and took a gulp of strong, hot, coffee. 'Are there any recent, recorded incidents at the swimming baths that are a cause for concern?'

Vicky sat opposite him with her mug nestled in her lap. 'Just one that's been brought to our attention.

'Tell me more.'

'On more than one occasion there has been verbal complaints about a man making inappropriate suggestive comments to girls in the pool, which appears to have progressed to him touching others. He's been spoken to by the management who have a record of this happening and action taken apparently. The fact that they felt the need to advise him about his behaviour concerns me.'

'Why haven't they banned him, or at the very least reported it to us?'

'He denies it.'

'Do we have a name?'

'A Malcolm Roberts, he's thirty years old.'

'Any pre-cons?'

Vicky shook her head, 'Nope.'

'Do we know if he knows Patti?'

'There's a suggestion he may do, but that's all it is, a suggestion.'

'He's a prime target for a DNA swab.'

'Absolutely, I'll get Andy and Ned on it today.'

Dylan drained his mug and handed it over to Vicky as she stood. 'Swimming baths always seem to attract 'em don't they?'

'They do.' Dylan sighed. 'When I were a lad, I remember Brelland baths had changing rooms around the edge of the pool. The saloon doors were hardly private. Kids used to run around pushing the doors open and then diving back into the water.' A chuckle escaped from Dylan's lips.

Vicky cocked an eyebrow at Dylan. 'Sounds like someone's speaking from experience?'

'You're joking. I was too busy keeping away from the cockroaches that had fallen in the water.'

'Really? There were cockroaches at the swimming baths?'

Dylan nodded his head. 'There were.'

\*\*\*

It was lunchtime and Dylan watched as his officers sat at their desks eating their meal. Detective Sergeant Nev Duke was no different, eating and working at the same time. He was a thinker, not a joker and never tried to be anything other than serious when he talked about the enquiry. In total contrast to Ned Granger sitting opposite him. To be fair to Ned he was totally committed to finding the killer, but he also made it known that he liked the overtime because it paid for next year's holiday, a new car or some other treat. The job also allowed Ned to live the life of a single man in some respects – using the excuse of the enquiry to work late, or go to the pub. Whilst they all enjoyed the extra money, something that the rank of Inspector or above didn't get – the long hours, and snacks on the hoof instead of sitting down to a warm meal, wasn't good for their health and well-being.

As a matter of routine Dylan had arranged for Sergeant Toft in the incident room to monitor the hours that officers worked along with their individual workloads. Any concerns he had highlighted and sent to Dylan so he could speak directly with the officer, and suggest to them that they take some time off. If they didn't do it voluntarily Dylan would instruct them to do so.

Dylan saw a strand of hair fall across Vicky's face, she tucked it behind her ear as she and Andy updated him later that afternoon, it softened her face. She looked tired.

'Roberts hasn't been to the swimming baths since Patti's murder,' said Andy. 'We do have his address which was recorded at the baths on the application form for his annual subscription. Flat 4, The Elms.'

Vicky yawned.

'Keeping you up are we?'

'No,' Vicky's eyes snapped open. She smoothed her hair with the palm of her hand. 'According to Si the house-to-house team have done enquiries at this address, but failed to get a response.

However, one of the neighbours did appear because of the loudness of the knocking and she told them that she believed Roberts had gone away, and that he was expected back at the weekend. His council flat overlooks the entrance to Bartlett's Academy for girls would you believe?'

Pen in hand Dylan doodled on the corner of his blotting pad – the face of another stick character. 'You've obviously marked his card on the strength of the incidents at the swimming pool. He's no convictions so there can be no objections about where he lives as far as the council are concerned.'

There was a brief pause in which time Dylan had given his stick character arms and legs. 'You're right, as usual. There's no other intelligence on him.'

'On the positive, by the weekend he should be back and then we'll set about eliminating him,' said Andy.

Dylan's eyes were flat. 'Thank god we have a DNA profile, otherwise we'd be struggling to eliminate some of these suspects quickly, and easily.'

'Before I joined the police, I honestly didn't realise there were so many weird and wonderful people out there.'

'You don't have to look far Vicky, there are a few that work here.'

'Who are we to judge,' said Andy.

Dylan slapped the palms of his hands on his desk. 'Exactly!'

As if a bell was needed to end the meeting Dylan's phone rang. He snapped it up.

'Dylan.'

'Force Control sir, Sergeant Paul from the Road Incident Investigation Team has asked me to inform you that one of your incident room vehicles have been in collision with another vehicle, a short time ago.'

'Anyone hurt?' Dylan interrupted, his eyes finding Vicky's.

'No, damage only. The driver of the offending vehicle, a Skoda, apparently pulled straight out of a junction and ran into the side of the police vehicle. It's believed the driver was using his mobile phone at the time, and he's also failed a breathalyser. He's under arrest.'

'And the officer driving the CID car?'

'Detective Sergeant Toft who has also been subjected to a breath test and failed; he's also been arrested. Both are en route to Harrowfield cells.'

'Thank you for the call and tell Sergeant Paul from me I'm grateful for the heads up.' Dylan sighed aloud. 'Bloody hell! As if we haven't enough to deal with.' He sat back in his chair. 'Toft was driving the CID car along a road apparently, doing nothing untoward. When a Skoda rams into the passenger side of the car. Fortunately no one was hurt.'

There was an audible sigh of relief.

'Thank god,' said Vicky.

Dylan shook his head. 'The driver of the Skoda failed the breathalyser and so did Toft. They're both on the way to the cells. Of all the people, I would never have said Toft would drink and drive.'

Vicky's jaw dropped. 'I thought he didn't drink? He's never once joined us for a quick one, after work.'

'If he's over the limit... ' said Andy.

'He's off the enquiry – that's Force policy. Nip down to the cells Vicky will you, see what you find out. It'll look less obvious if you go instead of me.'

# Chapter Thirteen

Vicky approached the Custody Suite. She stood at the gated doors at the bottom of the stairs that led from the first floor landing, and pressed the bell. There was a loud buzzing noise and the gates opened as if of their own free will, and closed behind her with a clang. The Custody Sergeant sat in a hunched position facing her from where he sat at his computer terminal behind the desk. He had a wrinkled brow and questioning eyes and when he spoke his breath smelt of his last cigarette, there was yellow staining on his teeth, her stomach turned.

'Vicky,' the over gregarious police officer said, with the beer belly she knew was hidden below the counter. He pursed his lips. 'Toft, he's a hell of a lucky guy. Just blown another test supervised by the duty Inspector and he's below the level.'

Vicky's eyes lit up. 'So, he's clear?'

'He's clear and relatively unscathed. Hadn't had a drink since last night he says whilst celebrating his birthday with a nice meal and a couple of bottles of red with his wife.'

Vicky blew out a long slow breath. 'It must have been a good wine.'

Footsteps could be heard approaching from the corridor beyond the wall partition. Detective Sergeant Toft appeared, his face pale, the top button of his shirt undone. He was tieless. Not surprisingly, not only had he been in a road traffic accident but also his job, livelihood and pension had been on the line.

Vicky held her arm out and put it around Toft's shoulders. 'Come on mate, let's go and grab a coffee you look as though you need it.'

He shook his head disbelievingly, 'What a bloody nightmare.'

'Take the positive from it. It's over, and you've survived.'

He rubbed his side. 'Barely! Tell you what, the side airbag activated and it nearly gave me a heart attack.'

The coffee was hot, strong and sweet. Toft pulled a face when he tasted it, and Vicky encouraged him to drink. 'I don't know how in god's name the road side test showed positive.' His eyebrows knitted together. 'I knew, no way was I over the limit but I wasn't going to argue with Traffic especially when it was Leech.'

'Leech?' Vicky's voice rose. 'Geez, you were lucky. He's already got two detectives scalps under his belt this year, to my knowledge. Maybe he was looking for a hat-trick? What a twat!'

'I honestly had no idea what I drank last night would even register.'

'Put it behind you – you've done nothing wrong. The guy that ran into you is in high water mind. I'm told he was three times over.'

While Vicky went to report back to Dylan, Toft took himself off to the rest room. He stood at the sink and checked his face out in the mirror above. Without averting his eyes he turned on the tap, and with trembling hands he let cold water run over the inside of his wrists. When the sink was full he dipped his head and threw cold water up into his face. Running his fingers over the swollen, freshly bruised cheekbone he continued to dab his face dry with a paper towel. His pale lips were slightly open. 'For goodness sake pull yourself together man,' he said, as his body shook, his stomach churned and all went black.

***

'Second breath test at the station which we know is more accurate was done under the watchful eye of the duty Inspector,' Vicky told Dylan. 'He was under. No further action will be taken. It was Leech, he's a fucking twat.'

Dylan's face was serious. 'He might be a twat but, Leech doesn't force people to drink and drive. He's only doing is job.'

'You know, I know, everyone else knows he revels in bagging a detective just as much as a footballer would enjoy scoring the winning goal at Wembley. The little short-arse pillock thinks people are frightened of him.'

'Is that it?' Dylan said, raising his eyebrows. 'I'll come and have a word with him in a minute.' Dylan looked through the glass in his office door and out into the incident room. He frowned. 'Where did he go?'

Andy could be seen running towards the desk. He picked up the phone. His demeanour made Dylan stand and make his way into the office with Vicky close behind him.

'Ambulance please,' he heard Andy say. 'Harrowfield Police Station. Man collapsed in the station after an RTA earlier today.'

\*\*\*

'Twenty-eight days from finding the house to completing – would you believe it?' Jen waved the letter from the solicitor in front of Dylan.

'We've got our date then?'

Jen's excitement was infectious and Dylan lifted her up into his arms. He twirled her around the kitchen, much to Maisy's amusement.

His face turned from happy to worried. 'To be hoped the builders can do the remedial work before we move in.'

Jen looked smug. 'Don't worry. I've got it in hand.'

Dylan pulled the knot of his tie, opened the top button of his shirt and sat down on the nearest chair. Maisy jumped straight on his lap. 'Well, what can I say Maisy Moo,' he said bouncing her up and down. 'It looks like we're moving!' The little girl giggled, spontaneously dropping a kiss on his cheek.

\*\*\*

Dylan woke at 5 am the next morning. The house was quiet. Jen lay beside him, softly snoring. Instead of putting on his suit which was waiting for him to step into, he reached for his jeans and jumper and carried his thick socks and his boots down stairs,. He picked up Max's collar and lead and ushered a bewildered, but willing Retriever out of the door. The wind was so cold it nipped at his face and he pulled the sleeves of his coat over his hands and zipped his collar up to his chin. He opened the car door and Max instantly, jumped in.

The walk around the playing fields allowed him to pass the scene of the crime. He slowed down – but only slightly, willing himself to look long enough, hard enough to find a clue he needed in the surrounding houses. Patti's house itself, its garden or its driveway where the family's car was parked once more. There was nothing untoward.

'Toft's got a neck brace and it looks like he might be off for a while.' Not the news Dylan wanted to hear when he walked in the station. 'I've let PC Leech know that if he didn't record the incident yesterday as an injury accident, it should be. As he passed his chair Dylan gave Andy a nudge. 'My office now.'

Vicky raised her eyebrows at Andy as they followed Dylan in. He turned on the lights.

'So we're a car and a man down. It could have been a hell of a lot worse.' Dylan offered them a seat with a wave of his hand.

'I want you to remind all officers at the briefings today that no one is above the law, and drinking at night could mean there is still alcohol in the bloodstream the next day.'

Vicky nodded.

'Andy,' he said, as he took his seat behind his desk and pushed the button to fire up his computer. 'Am I right in thinking you've got your sergeants exam?'

'Yes sir.'

'I'll okay it with personnel but as from now, you're acting-up mate.'

'Acting Sergeant Andy Wormald – I like the sound of that,' said Vicky patting the surprised detective on the back. Shoulders back Andy strode out of Dylan's office a foot taller. Dylan knew that feeling well. The feeling when hard work had been recognised and a boss had faith in you. He had no doubt Andy was 'a safe pair of hands' and would do him proud.

Dylan looked across at the paperwork in his overflowing in-tray. Hand atop the stack, and below he carried it the short distance to his desk. One hand lay on the middle of the three piles he had achieved a few minutes later. The paperwork now in order of priority – at the top the enquiry's budget update from HQ. He held a pen as a thinking prop and looked up and through the pane of glass in his office door at the busy incident room beyond, his thoughts fighting for supremacy. The clock above the door ticked away the minutes to the morning briefing. As he looked down the eyes of young Patti Heinz stared back at him, her picture tucked in the corner of his blotter – as if he needed a reminder how anyone could put a price tag on finding her killer. But that was the reality of it, he sighed.

The smell of toasted bread snuck into his office before he saw Emily carrying the plate. Each team member bringing their drinks to the table. He got up to join them.

'Batches, a dozen at a time of male pupils DNA swabs are being sent to Forensic for analysis,' said Nev. The enthusiasm to catch the killer of Patti Heinz carried Dylan on a wave of positivity. 'What more could be done?' he asked himself as he looked at each officer, with his own enquiry agenda.

The faces of those in the briefing upturned to the knocking at the door and Dave Craze from the front office entered.

'Sorry to interrupt sir but I've got a Malcolm Roberts at the front counter, apparently his neighbour told him we've been looking for him?'

***

The noticeable things about Malcolm Roberts were his height, his receding coloured hair and his half-moon spectacles. He dressed in a racing green pullover over an off-white open-necked shirt and baggy at the knee, corduroy trousers. He was clean-shaven and looked a tad older than his thirty years.

Detective Sergeant Hardacre introduced herself and DC Donna Frost to him, in an interview room, near to the front counter of Harrowfield Police Station. Door closed, all seated, Vicky proceeded to explain to him about the investigation into Patti's murder.

Roberts spoke slowly, 'I'm at a loss as to why you and your colleague should wish to speak to me? My neighbour informed me that you were banging on my door with such force that it caused her to go outside to see what was going on.'

Vicky had a knack of avoiding a question as much as she was good at closed questions to avoid yes/no answers. Donna let her continue.

'Did you know Patti Heinz?' Without any hesitation she held up a photograph of the young girl for Roberts to see.

Roberts showed his bottom lip. 'Mmm...' His face held a frown. 'She looks familiar.'

'A regular at the baths where you swim.' The detectives watched his face intently as he appeared to calculate Vicky's words.

'She was?' Roberts pulled away, his body stiffened and he crossed his arms.

Vicky's interest was evident as she leant across the desk. 'So do you, or do you not recognise her?' she pressed on; holding the picture still, at eye level.

Roberts shrugged his shoulders. 'I can't be sure. I see a lot of people at the baths. They look totally different when their hair is wet and they're dressed in swimming attire.'

'Well, luckily we have gained a DNA profile of her killer which means we can eliminate people very quickly from this enquiry and hence why we are speaking to, and taking a sample from, any male she might know or have come into contact with.'

Roberts lifted his chin. 'Ah, so because I'm a male and go to the local swimming baths where she frequented, you need to take a swab from inside my mouth. Is that what you're saying?'

Vicky nodded. 'Yes, that's about it, in a nutshell.'

'And what would be done with the aforesaid sample after it's been checked against the DNA profile?'

'It will be destroyed. Unless you consent for it to go onto the national database,' said Donna.

'I am of the opinion that I'd like mine to be destroyed after it has been checked. And, I would like you to inform me when that has been done. Now, shall we proceed?'

As Donna stepped forward with the swab in hand, Mr Roberts flinched. He shook his head in small jerky movements showing her the raised palm of his hand. 'Bear with me,' he said. 'I hate people invading my space.' At the second attempt the sample was taken. 'Can I ask you Mr Roberts,' said Vicky, as Donna removed the swab from his mouth and proceeded to do the paperwork. 'I understand that you were advised by the management at the swimming baths as to inappropriate behaviour towards others, is that right?'

'Yes, it is. I told some children off for misbehaving in the showers. They were running around whipping each other with wet towels. The next thing I know they were making scurrilous allegations of indecency, laughing and calling me names. And that is why I don't frequent the swimming baths these days.'

'Did you explain to management?'

He looked decidedly sad. 'Of course I did. But they said they had a duty of care, therefore had to advise me.' When he continued his voice rose. 'Advise me?' I daren't even speak to a child these days, even if they're crying, or hurt.' His head tilted, this way and that. 'Everyone is suspicious; and of course it doesn't help that I'm a childless, single man that chooses to live alone... Sadly that means I'm considered, by some, to be a threat to children.'

'I think parents are protective because they are more aware, due to the media, of what could happen. Patti was a child, she and her parents should have been able to assume she was safe in her home though, and we will do everything in our power to catch her murderer.'

'Absolutely.' Roberts looked at his watch. 'I'm sorry, are we going to be much longer? I am due at work in ten minutes.'

The DNA sample paperwork signed, and protective tube sealed Donna initialled her exhibit and sealed the bag.

'We're just about finished here,' said Vicky as she stood. 'As a matter of interest what is it you do Mr Roberts?'

'I work at the Central Library. I'm busy cataloguing archived material at the moment. It's very interesting work, albeit a little lonely at times.'

'Well Donna, what do you think of him?' said Vicky as she closed the door after him and followed the detective down the corridor that led back to the incident room.

'He should get out more.' She turned and held the exhibit aloft. 'Do you think it's going to come back positive?'

Vicky screwed up her nose. 'Nah.'

***

The briefing had concluded and Dylan was back in his office a mug of coffee in his hand when they returned. 'There is still some obvious suspects in the enquiry to speak to and eliminate,' he said. 'Patti's friend Gail Carpenter's older brother still has to be seen, and the leaflet droppers before we widen the search.'

'Mark Carpenter, he's next on my list,' said Donna.

'Good. How did it go with Roberts?'

'He's a bit odd – a stereotypical indecency man if ever I saw one,' she giggled. 'But, having spoken to him I don't think it's him,' said Vicky.

'He didn't hesitate to give us a sample. Lives on his own and works on his own at the library. I think he's just lonely,' said Donna.

'Central Library,' said Dylan.

The detectives nodded.

'Central library is temporarily situated in the council building next to the school - Patti's school.'

# Chapter Fourteen

Dylan noted Vicky gesticulating with her middle finger at Ned. The office was in uproar at some comical quip he had made. Laughter lines clustered around DS Mike Scott's eyes and mouth, which were evident when he arrived at Dylan's door. When he stepped over the threshold his face was serious.

'I thought you'd like to know we've just had a complaint come into the Safeguarding Unit from a Missus Anita Carson, 7, Bentley Grange. Their house, it's within a five mile radius of your murder scene.'

He had Dylan's attention. 'Go on.'

'In brief, she says her fourteen year old daughter Beverley is alleging that she was followed home from a friends house last night. Her daughter refuses to go to school this morning. Hence why it's come through to us. I've got a couple of officers on their way to see what the score is.'

'Any background we're aware of?'

'Nothing, apparently mum caught her still in bed this morning when she got home.'

Dylan's eyebrows rose. 'She works nights?'

'She works shifts.'

'And this morning is the first time her daughter has told anyone?'

'It would appear so.'

'Which school's she at?'

'Same as Patti Heinz.'

'Nev Duke has good liaisons at the school, he'll probably be able to quickly get you more background information via his contacts. Have a word will you?'

\*\*\*

Patti Heinz bedroom door hadn't been opened since the day the police had finished their search. Her bed was still unmade from the young girl's hurried departure on the day of her death. Patti's curtains were pulled across the window haphazardly, as they had always been since Patti had begun to draw them back herself, her mum had said.

Jaene Booth prepared to enter Patti's room behind Sandra. Patti's mum's hand laboured on the doorknob, turned and saw the place where the staining of Patti's blood had been, on the carpet. She looked up to the ceiling and took a deep breath. Jaene put a hand on hers to steady her ward. Patti's towelling bathrobe hung on a hook behind the door and it made a swishing sound against the wardrobe when the door was opened wide. Her Unicorn patterned pyjamas lay where she had stepped out of them, next to her dressing table. Sandra picked them up as if in slow motion and smoothed them out on the bed before folding them neatly and putting them under the pillow. Quickly she straightened the bottom sheet and pulled the duvet cover up over the pillow before plumping up the cushion that would lay atop – and she did so in silence. Next she chose to walk around the soft rug and swept her fingers over trinkets on her window still. She stopped at the little music box and opened it. The ballerina staggered to an upright position and the room was full of the music from Swan Lake. Even though Sandra had her back to Jaene she saw the drooping of her head to her chest, and heard a soft whimpering. A ghost of a hand, like spiders' legs running up her back made her shudder. Sandra turned to the family liaison officer and smiled sadly, her shoulders slumping with the weight of regret. 'Why?' she said in a velvet tone. She didn't even realise, it seemed, she was crying as the tears tumbled down her cheeks unchecked.

\*\*\*

In the hours, days since Patti's murder the ground beneath the detectives feet had been cleared as much as physically possible. Tens of people had been located, eliminated, swabbed and interviewed within the capability of the dedicated team, at Dylan's disposal. Hundreds of telephone calls had been made, meetings, briefings, debriefs held daily, door-to-door enquiries done, a DNA profile found, but the murderer remained elusive.

Dylan's phone rang. 'Boss, Mike, it's been brought to our attention that Beverley has been bunking off school lately.'

'Do we have a reason?'

'No, but her older brother has confirmed that she was late in last night. She's given us a vague description of her follower, a five foot eight male, wearing a dark hoodie. Beverley tells us that she had to run into a garden and hide in a Wendy house, in fear for her life, when she heard his quickening foot steps behind her, and smelt the alcohol on his breath.'

Dylan sucked in a breath. 'He got that close? Is there an alleged assault?'

'No, not an assault and her brother appeared as surprised as mum at her allegation. He says he berated her for being late from the bottom of the stairs when he heard her footsteps on the stairs following the slamming of the front door. But then he heard nothing more.'

'Your thoughts?'

'I don't know... There's obviously a rabbit off. At present my officers are driving around the area with Beverley and her mum and we are checking out the location of the Wendy house she talks about.'

'Is there anything that makes you think it's linked to Patti's murder?'

'No, there is no definite link at the moment other than she's about Patti's age and goes to the same school.'

'We'll continue to investigate the two incidents independently unless we obtain that link, otherwise we could end up creating a monster of an enquiry, and that doesn't help solve either.'

As Dylan put down the phone Vicky stuck her head around his door. 'Mark Carpenter's going back to his barracks today. I told him I'm on my way to speak to him before he leaves.'

Dylan stood up, grabbed his car keys from his desk drawer and his jacket from behind his chair. 'I'm coming with you,' he called to her retreating figure.

\*\*\*

There was nothing notable about the skinny, small-framed, nineteen-year-old Mark Carpenter other than he was dressed in army uniform.

'I don't know why you'd want to speak to me about Patti Heinz. She was just my little sister's mate,' he said.

'We heard you asked her out?' Vicky followed the swaggering young man into the lounge at his invitation. Carpenter stood, hands deep in his khaki trouser pockets, shoulders back, in front of the fireplace. His gaze less assertive when it found Dylan's.

'Look, you know how it is. She spent a lot of time here during the summer and I guess... well you know, I probably did ask her out. But she said no and I moved on, and now, well I've grown up a lot since then.' Carpenter nodded to his kit bag that stood by the door.

'There was quite an age gap. You're nineteen and she was what, fourteen?'

Carpenter grinned. 'Yeah, I know but there's a ten year age gap between my mum and dad. I never gave it a thought at the time. Anyway, Patti was very mature for her age.'

'We'll need to take a DNA sample from you to eliminate you from the enquiry.' Vicky delved into her bag.

'Not a problem,' he said walking towards her.

'You said you'd moved on?' said Dylan. 'In terms of relationships too?'

Carpenter sat down in the chair, his mouth was open wide. He made an ahhhing noise and nodded his head in small, jerky movements.

'Yes,' he said wiping his mouth with the tissue Vicky gave him. 'I'm in a new relationship.'

'And what do they call this lucky lady then?' said Vicky with a wink of her eye.

Mark Carpenter blushed slightly. 'Ah... it's early days. I'd rather not say if it's all the same to you,' he said with a tone that told them, that line of enquiry was over.

\*\*\*

Jen watched Maisy run down the path into the child minder's arms. Chantal picked her up and together they waved. She had left home later than usual because the estate agent had required her to do the viewing on their house. By the time Jen reached the police station the car park was full and there was no hiding the fact that she was late from her boss, Avril Summerfield-Preston due to the clocking-in machine. No doubt she would have to work an extra day this month to make up for all the time she had had to take off lately. Jen could feel herself growing warm. She loosened the scarf around her neck and unbuttoned her coat. Sweat beads appeared on her brow and she brushed aside a lank fringe. Her mind was chasing around things she needed to do, and not to forget as she parked the car eventually, on the main road. The quickest way to get to the clocking-in machine now was via reception at the front counter. Her hands were shaking as she locked the car and she threw the keys in her handbag that she swung over her shoulder. She ran, 'less haste, more speed,' she muttered, her heart racing.

The doors of the police station opened automatically, welcoming her. The rush of warm air, and a loud ranting man met her, but her focus was the digital coded access keypad on the adjacent door. Taking long strides and avoiding any distractions she had to admit that her direct route was not free. She stood directly behind a young woman who was sobbing hysterically, the man Jen had heard from outside was the one giving her a tirade of abuse. Jen was stopped in her tracks as the man grabbed the woman by her throat. The front office staff looked on helpless from behind the counter and rang for assistance as he threw her against the wall.

Dylan was looking forward to a day off. The investigation was feeling flat, or was that just him knowing that whilst the taking of the DNA samples was necessary the process reminded him of a conveyer belt. He didn't want his team to rely solely on the DNA process, he wanted his team to be out interviewing people, questioning their behaviour, questioning their whereabouts at the time of the murder, and then the DNA would tell them if their instincts were right about the individual in their net. He was the man in charge and his job was to keep moral high, even if his own slipped on occasions. Sooner or later they would net the killer.

***

It took three uniformed police officers to lock him up.

'Jack it's only me. Don't panic. I'm making a statement about an assault. I didn't want it to come as a shock if you read about it on screen.' Jen said, looking into PCSO Fawad Ali's blue eyes. There was something unbelievably odd about blue eyes in his young, handsome Indian face. She leant heavily into the PCSO who had taken care of her, trying desperately to focus on what she was saying.

Dylan abruptness brought her back in the moment. 'Who got assaulted?'

'I'm okay. I've just got a bit of bruise on my head...' She heard her voice trail off, and his in the distance.

Dylan felt an abdominal pain as it someone had punched him in the stomach. 'What?' his authoritative voice rose. 'Where are you?'

Jen coughed uncontrollably, her eyes watering and questioning. 'Where are we?' she mouthed to Fawad.

The PCSO took the phone. 'Patrol office sir.'

'I'm on my way.' Dylan slammed the phone down and to raised eyebrows, he strode through the incident room without saying a word. The office door slammed behind him. His pace quickened on the corridor and he took the steps two at a time, his heart pounding. Dylan heard Jen coughing before he opened the door. Then he saw her face, pale and grey, a cut to her cheekbone, a glass of water to her lips. Dylan cringed. His finger hovered over the wound. Jen swayed instinctively away and Dylan and Fawad reached out to stop her tumbling sideways from the chair. Jen's coughing worsened.

'Pepper spray sir,' Fawad said, by way of an apology. 'I'll get us all a warm drink, shall I?'

'Nothing for me thanks.' He sat down close to Jen, scrutinising her cut at close quarters. 'You're going to have one hell of a shiner.' Are you sure you're okay?' he said reaching for her hand and squeezing it tight.

His presence and the grip of his large, warm hand were comforting. 'I think so,' she said with a lopsided smile. 'It's the first time I've been headbutted.'

'Deliberate?'

'Oh, yes, he knew exactly what he was doing.' Jen shuddered. 'I won't forget them staring, blood shot eyes and that laugh.'

'He's locked up?'

'I guess so.'

'Do we know why he attacked you?'

'I think he'd been taking something, or he'd been drinking. A woman was with him. He was shouting at her. She was trying to complain about him as I recall. He grabbed her by the throat and that's the last I remember, apart from two large red piercing eyes, and the raucous laugh.'

'We know that the usual drugs and drink fuelled pathetic excuse is going to be used then, don't we? Do you need to go the hospital?'

'No, no, I'm fine honestly.'

Fawad walked back into the room. The colour in Jen's face had returned and albeit a red mark and a slight cut to her cheekbone there didn't appear to be anything else to suggest the altercation.

'I'll leave you to get on with your statement,' Dylan said. He put his hand on Jen's shoulder and laid a kiss on her forehead. 'Let me know when you're finished.'


Dylan's rank and knowledge of procedure felt very important to him as he headed back to his office via the Bridewell. He wanted to know who the lowlife was who attacked women.

'Kenny Foley, twenty-eight years from number 1, Armitage Road.' The Custody Sergeant turned the screen of his computer towards Dylan. That was a name and a face Dylan would remember.

'I dealt with Foley for a wounding a couple of years back. He's one of our homegrown pieces of shit. They should lock him up and throw away the bloody key once and for all,' said Vicky as they headed to briefing. 'But, we know that's not going to happen, don't we?' Vicky put her hand to her rumbling stomach. She appeared thoughtful. 'Does it bother you when they top themselves in prison?'

'Does it hell. Apart from the massive enquiry it causes us.'

She sniggered. 'And but think of the money it save us, the taxpayer? I'd give 'em a noose when they arrived if I was a prison officer.'

Dylan put his hand out to open the door and turned to her, 'You can't say that.'

The door of the briefing room sprung open. 'Too late, just did. I'll get coffee.'

The detectives stood at the coffee machine. Vicky picked up a mug and poured from the jug. She handed it to Dylan. He spooned sugar into the steaming liquid and stirred vigorously.

# Chapter Fifteen

The house was clean as a whistle. Jen had spent all day cleaning it, best she could when in the throngs of moving house. 'Look for the positive,' Dylan always said. And the positive today was that the altercation had resulted in her having the day off work and her card was not marked for being late.

Maisy tucked up in bed she collected the cleaning materials that she had been using together in a bucket and carried them downstairs. As she passed the radiator in the hallway she ran her duster, she carried in her hand over it. She hummed softly to herself. This house was very different from The Station House, for one it had a roof with no holes that let in the rain and the wind. The thought made her smile.

It was dark outside and with no call from Dylan Jen climbed in the shower. Rubbing soap into her body she was lost in the moment, rubbing and cleansing every spot over and over again until shampoo seeped into the abrasion on her face and, reminded her of the foul creature who had caused it.

Max's eyelids flickered once, twice and then opened wide when he heard her footsteps on the stairs. Jen's slippers scuffed on the kitchen floor, echoing off the bare walls as she stepped out of the hallway. Droplets of water ran down her back from her wet, loose hair. She patted the dog's head in passing and Max stretched his limbs out upon his padded dog bed that lay next to the radiator. From where she stood with her back to the oven she couldn't see the colour of the far wall in the dining room, so high were the cardboard, packing boxes piled.

'You're going to get such a shock mate,' she said to Max as she got a scented candle from the cupboard and peeled away its wrapper. 'There's no radiators in the kitchen at the new house – in fact there isn't a kitchen as such, not yet anyway,' she said, chuckling at his cock-eared reaction to the tone in her voice.

Jen picked up the candle. The clock struck ten and Max immediately sat up. His yawn was audible. She opened the back door at his begging and instantly the draught blew the candle out. Her shoulders dropped. There was no point relighting it she decided as fatigue came upon her. When Max returned from the garden Jen shut the door with her foot and turned the key in the lock.

That night as she kissed Maisy's sleeping head she felt a surge of love and excitement. Her young daughter smelt of soap, and her bedding of fabric softener. Jen had an urge to climb in beside her rather than face the cold bed she could see awaiting her. Her eyes were drawn through the door to her keepsake box that stood at the entrance to their bedroom and all of a sudden the move to The Station House, the next stage on her life's journey, felt very real. She collected the box as she passed and popped it at her side of the bed for opening.

Quickly and effortlessly she slipped out of her dressing gown, most unusual of her, leaving it where it fell, and jumped up on the bed.

When Dylan arrived home he found her nestled between two pillows surrounded by bits and pieces of her childhood, so seemingly insignificant, yet each an important facet of her life. He lay beside her and she gently held the conch shell to his ear. 'Can you hear the sea?'

He nodded.

She giggled.

'When I was little and couldn't sleep, because I said I couldn't hear the sea. Mum found the shell to appease me.'

'And did it do the trick.'

'It certainly did.'

Dylan picked up what looked like a piece of stone from it's resting place on a bed of cotton wool. 'And this?'

'Ah, now that's my most prized possession, my first fossil hunting trip on Compton beach I found this tooth which scientists believe belonged to a previously unknown carnivorous dinosaur. In fact an early relative of Tyrannosaurus Rex we were reliably told by a scientist who wanted to borrow it for a year and put it in a museum - I wasn't having any of it though.' When the smile dropped from her lips she looked thoughtful. 'It opened my mind to the vastness of creation and what had been living on our Island millenniums ago. She took the tooth from Dylan and popped it back in the cufflink box her father had given to her for its safe keeping. Next she plucked out a pearl neckless that her grandfather had given her grandmother. Jen gave a little laugh. 'Grandma always thought it worth a fortune. She held it carefully in the palm of her hand and stroked the flaking varnish upon the pearls. 'It was priceless to her, and very precious to me.'

Dylan didn't need to ask Jen questions about her early life. It was all in the box. 'You want tangible evidence of my childhood? It's here in abundance!'

'Do you know something?'

'What?' said Jen. A glow about her face when she turned to look at him. He kissed her on her lips.

'I've never been the jealous sort.' Dylan raised his arm to allow her to lay her head upon his chest. 'But, do you know I am jealous that your parents shared their past with you, and you have it to share with our children.'

It was true she knew little about Dylan's family – and so did he.

'Tell me about your childhood, your brothers and sisters?'

As always Dylan brushed her questions off in a carefree way. 'There's nothing to tell. I haven't seen any of the gang for years.'

Jen frowned. 'Doesn't that bother you?'

He smiled. 'It's not that I don't care. We've just never been a family who live in each other's pockets.'

'What was it like when you were all small? Did you all play together? Did you all eat together around the table? Did you have turkey and pull crackers on Christmas Day?'

'I guess we must have done. I remember Dad once cutting a log from the tree outside The Station house for our Christmas table decoration.' There was silence and when Jen looked up at him she half expected him to be asleep but, his eyes were open and staring at the ceiling, thoughtfully, as if straining to recall. 'Our Charlie kept chickens,' he said. 'I remember him wringing their necks, and mum plucking the feathers out on the dining room table. He was quite the entrepreneur our Charlie. Our Ronnie, he was the studious one. He taught himself to play the guitar, was in a band

and he owned a scooter. Now our Kirsty,' he chuckled. 'I remember her asleep in a drawer – she was born there...'

'No way!' Jen's eyes were wide. 'Did you sleep in a drawer?'

Dylan shrugged his shoulders. 'Probably, when I was a baby. I think we all must have. And what if I did, it didn't do me any harm did it? Our Dawn, she's the baby. The last time I saw her she was drunk at an office party I got called to, and with her tear-stained face, she was still really pretty.'

'What do you say we invite them all round to the house, when it's finished?'

Dylan didn't want to pour cold water on her dreams, this was her fantasy to bring his family altogether again, after all wasn't it?

# Chapter Sixteen

Dylan arrived at work. It was seven-thirty. Immediately he logged onto his computer and instantly began working his way through the homicide database. He was eager for any scrap of information that gave him a new line of enquiry. 'Any news on the leaflet droppers? I assumed not as there was no update from you last night.'

Vicky was typing. She didn't look up. 'Nothing to report. It was half-eleven before we finished and there didn't seem much point in ringing you to say nothing at silly time of night.'

'Why so late?'

'The guys work as bartenders, to pay the rent. Neither of their interviews brought about areas of concern. Their stories were consistent. Both admit to handing out leaflets on Burford Avenue for their new joint enterprise, and we took their DNA. Neither of them admit to knowing Patti.'

'They're touting for window cleaning business in the area?'

'Yes, and they're adamant they didn't put a leaflet through the letter box of Colonial House on the day of the murder; they were doing even house numbers, not odd.'

Dylan's smile was forced as he raised his eyes from the computer screen. 'And there's nothing new on the box this morning.'

'Could have told you that.' Vicky sighed. 'What next?' Her eyes met Dylan's stubborn gaze.

'We carry on doing what we're doing.'

The Force's internal post had been delivered and sorted by admin, and was piled high in the tray on the corner of his desk. He gave the documents a brief scan as to their priority, and made a start.

'Why the long face?' said Vicky when she brought coffee back with her into the office ten minutes later.

'You'd think the officer running a murder enquiry would be left out of everyday, mundane issues wouldn't you?'

'You would, but they're not.'

'No,' Dylan held up a variety of paperwork. 'Then there's the paper trail for the murder, and the stream of requests for various updates. Just so they can monitor performance from headquarters. I wouldn't care but everything is computerised, so the information they're seeking has already been gathered and recorded. They could save a bloody rainforest, never mind a bucket full of money if they only took time to access it. Dylan's phone rang. He snatched it up. 'Dylan,' he snapped.

Vicky spun on her heel and snuck out of the office, closing the office door behind her.


Although it was one of the great highs of an investigation, to get DNA evidence, it meant others expectations for a quick lock-up were high. Dylan more than most knew that, that wasn't always the case, unless the offender was already on a database. In this instance the offender was proving illusive. The net was widening. The only definite result was that Patti's murderer was a male.

'Good news from Forensic today, I hope?' said Dylan on hearing Maggie Jones voice on the end of the line.

'Not the news you were hoping for I'm afraid. We have an anomaly with a sample that's been submitted to us in a batch.'

'An anomaly? In what way?'

'The problem isn't getting DNA from the piece of chewing gum. But, that the label identifies it to belonging to an Ivan Sinclair.' Maggie paused. 'And, the DNA is that of a female.'

Dylan felt his body stiffen and his teeth clench. 'A female? So, what you're telling me is that this Ivan Sinclair, he's trying to pull a fast one?'

'I'm not saying anything, I don't know how he features in the murder enquiry.'

'He doesn't feature, until now. Thank you for that, we'll put him under the microscope.'

'Vicky!' Dylan hollered, whilst still in the process of putting down the phone and writing down the reference number Maggie had given him.


According to the incident room database Ivan Sinclair was a fifteen year old. He attended St Martin's, Patti's school. On screen

143

it also showed Dylan, by means of a Marker, that his DNA sample was to be taken from a piece of chewing gum, which he handed to officers.

The brief write-up stated: Ivan knows the deceased Patti Heinz from school. He wasn't obstructive, but stated his parents were against him giving a DNA sample. Therefore, he gave the officers the piece of chewing gum in an attempt to comply with both parents, and the police request.

Whilst that seemed reasonable to the reader; perhaps even helpful of the pupil in question, Ivan hadn't given his own DNA. No doubt he assumed that he could pass on someone else's DNA to eliminate himself. However, by using a girl's spent chewing gum he had made it very easy for the laboratory to identify the deception. If however he had used another male pupils spent chewing gum to deceive, it may not have been discovered until the police had gained two identical samples submitted from two different people.

'Why go to that extent, if he's nothing to hide?' said Vicky.

Ned's grin suggested that he suspected some sly trickery.

Nev Duke appeared surprised. 'I know about this. The officer who interviewed him asked me if it was okay, and I told them that we wanted his DNA and I didn't care how he got it. The officer said he had the chewing gum in his hand so it looked to them like he had just taken it out of his mouth. They were impressed how cunning he was in trying to help us without compromising his promise to his parents. The crafty bastard.' Nev whistled through his teeth.

Dylan raised an eyebrow. 'I wonder if the girl knew what she was doing by giving him her chewed gum?' He paused for a second. 'Can you found out if he's in school today for me?'

'Will do, and his address will be in the system boss.'

Vicky's eyes glistened with excitement. 'How stupid! He can't be that chuffin' bright if he thought he could pass a girl's DNA off as his.'

'But not daft enough to not have thought out how he could get away with giving us a DNA sample, and yet not physically have it taken by us.'

Vicky's eyes were wide. 'Could he be our killer?'

Dylan smiled in anticipation over the information that Nev fed them. 'The plot thickens,' Nev said. 'This young lad is no longer a pupil at St Martin's. Apparently, according to staff, his family are in the process of relocating to a different area.'

'Do we have a forwarding address?'

'The school secretary is on a course, and would you believe that no one else can obtain the information for us, in her absence?'

Dylan nodded. 'Yes, I would. Okay, the address that we have on screen is 12, Flaxby Court.'

'And, I'm told he presently represents the county at swimming. They might be able to help us.'

Dylan and Vicky found themselves sat in traffic at the point on the main road to Brelland where the steep craggy rocks dropped dramatically through deep dark woods onto Waterford Road. Beyond, the view to Norland was stunning.

'I checked to see if Sinclair features on the list of names we've been supplied from the baths,' said Vicky. The paperwork for their visit to the Sinclair's home was on her lap.

Dylan glanced across in her direction at the turn of the wheel to the left. 'And?'

'And, he's on it.'

'Interesting, he knows Patti from school; swimming is a shared hobby. I guess he is also aware he is relocating with the family, and he gives us a duff sample for DNA elimination to Patti's murder. So, where was he when she was murdered, that's what I want to know?'

'Do you think he knew the implications that a girl's DNA would have on the test results?'

'He probably didn't think.'

'I wonder if his parents saw the form that the school sent out for consent to be given, for DNA to be taken? Maybe, their refusal was a lie?'

'And, you and I know you don't need to lie if you've done nothing wrong. He's done one thing for us. He's put himself forward as a suspect.'

Vicky's eyes narrowed. 'I wonder if there's any history between him and Patti?'

Dylan pulled the blue unmarked CID car in front Flaxby Court.

'It's less than five miles from Patti's home. Let's go,' he said, swinging the car door open wide.

'Let's hope if they've moved, the new occupants have a forwarding address.'

The detectives' door slamming was in unison. A couple of young lads sat on their bikes at the opposite side of the road, one foot on the pavement, surveying the visitors.

'Twitchy arses at three o'clock,' Vicky spoke out of the corner of her mouth.

'Rozzers!' they shouted as if they were listening in. Dylan stepped forward. Vicky followed closed behind. The exodus of young kids from the block of flats was like a spooked flock of birds taking flight from a tree.

'Why aren't they in school?' she said with an air of annoyance. Her mobile rang and she took it from her jacket pocket. 'DS Hardacre, what do you want?'

'Indeed,' said Dylan, with a lopsided smile. He opened the door to the foyer, allowing his colleague to walk before him.

'I'm with Dylan now...' Dylan turned at the sound of his name.' His eyes found Vicky's. 'Go on Mike, I'll repeat,' she said. She listened intently. 'So, Beverley Carson has admitted to the officers that she was late home because she was with her boyfriend who her mother disapproves of – hence the cock and bull story about being followed?'

Dylan nodded his understanding. Vicky raised her eyes to the ceiling. 'And have you warned her about wasting police time?' Dylan heard Vicky say as he considered which button to press for the lift to take them to the third floor.

Vicky found herself being propelled into the small, shabby lift. They stood, facing the door, in silence as it closed. The stench of urine was foul. Vicky balked. 'Apparently, Mike says that when he visited the owners of the house, where she allegedly hid in the Wendy house in their garden they told him they had found a condom in the garden, and on inspection of the Wendy house they seized some used tissues. He's on his way back to the Carson's.'

Dylan bent down, pointing his finger towards the list indicating what floor flat twelve was situated. 'Is Rozzers the current term used for us now?' Dylan pressed the button for the third floor and standing upright readied himself for the jolt.

'Rozzer, filth, pig, copper, old Bill, plod... Depends what they're watching on the box.'

With no immediate movement he looked up at the light monitors above the door, which still read Ground Floor. The mechanical movement they heard wasn't the lift moving but the doors opening. A short, elderly lady with a hunched back, long green raincoat and holding a walking stick, limped towards them. Her head was covered in grey, tight curls, hidden mostly with a see-through Rainmate that was tied under her wizened chin. When she upturned her face she had a waxy pallor. Deep farrows ran from her nose to the angles of her determined mouth.

The detectives each took a polite step to the side and the exhausted face of the lady looked grateful.

After a few moments Vicky broke the silence. 'I don't think it's working. What floor are you going to?' she said to the old lady, as they waited.

'Eleventh, 'ere let me 'ave a look,' she said impatiently pushing Dylan out of the way with the sweep of her scrawny hand. Battering the console with a fist she stood back. The force of the jolt when it came wasn't expected by Dylan, or Vicky. The old woman smiled a satisfied smile and winked a weary eye at Dylan. 'You've either got it or you 'aven't dear. And, I've still got it.'

Vicky and Dylan alighted at the third floor. The old woman screwed up her toothless face. 'Good luck,' she said as her parting gift.

The softest of sounds bounced off the glossy white walls as the detectives strode out in unison along the corridor, chuckling.

'I'm going to be like that when I get old,' said Vicky.

Dylan gave her a sideways look. 'What do you mean when?'

Every few feet there were fire doors that closed slowly and silently behind them, until they shut with a bang as they reached the next.

'Well, there's a light on, so that may suggest someone's in?' said Vicky when Dylan gave a firm knock at No. 12. She took a pace backwards half expecting the glass to shatter as it rattled in its warped, wooden frame.

Dylan cocked his head towards the door. There was no response and no sound from within. He tried again.

'You win some, you lose some.' Vicky turned on her heels. 'Let's try a neighbour.'

The neighbour's door was already slightly ajar, secured by a link on a chain. It opened slowly to reveal a tall young man with a flat, red, round face that went with his extra large body. 'If you're looking for 'er next door you're in luck,' he puffed and panted. 'Missus Sinclair's just pulled up outside in 'er car.' The door was closed before they had chance to thank him.

Mrs Sinclair obviously had 'the knack' with the elevator button because no sooner had they walked back to stand at the Sinclair's door a harassed looking woman with a supermarket carrier bag over her arm, and a key in her hand, hurried towards them.

'What do you want?' she said looking them up and down. 'If you're after money you might as well go now.' She attempted to put her key in the lock with a shaking hand that bore three rings, a large sapphire, a loop of pearls, and a circle of plain gold, without making eye contact with either officer.

Dylan took a step towards her, 'Detective Inspector Jack Dylan and Detective Sergeant Hardacre.' The officers held up their warrant cards. 'Mrs Sinclair?'

The woman stopped as the door opened, her head turned towards them and sunken eyes appeared from under the brim of her hood. She withdrew the key. Her nostrils flared and her voice quivered. 'Has there been an accident?'

'No, nothing like that... It's a routine call,' said Vicky.

Having had her question answered to her satisfaction it seemed, the woman quickly entered the flat and turned, attempting as she did so to close the door behind her. Dylan put his size ten foot over the threshold. 'We are making enquiries into the murder of schoolgirl Patti Heinz. I'm sure you'll have heard about the case?'

Mrs Sinclair's hooded eyes opened wide. 'You'd best come in.' A flash of recognition leapt into her eyes. 'That's why you look familiar,' she said to Dylan. Busily, she collected discarded clothes that lay strewn in a haphazard fashion, upon the mismatched sofa and chairs. 'I've seen you on the news. Sit down.'

Sat in a chair surrounded by packing boxes, her once pale face had regained a healthier colour but still showed lines of strain, and her eyes had not completely lost their look of anxiety. 'What brings you here?'

'I don't know if you're aware but we're in the process of taking DNA samples from all males that knew Patti, and of course this includes the students at St Martin's school.'

'Yes, the letter they sent out explaining it was... interesting.'

'So you got it?'

Mrs Sinclair nodded.

'You have a son Ivan, yes?' said Vicky. 'Were you against him giving a sample?'

Mrs Sinclair looked perplexed. 'No, why should I be?'

'Your son Ivan, is he in?' said Dylan.

Mrs Sinclair rolled her eyes. 'He's never in. He's a teenager isn't he? Why?'

Vicky spoke briskly. 'Ivan told our officers at the school that his parents didn't consent to him having his DNA taken. Why do you think he'd do that?'

She shook her head. 'I don't understand. We discussed it. He knew it was to help find the young girl's killer.'

'The samples help us eliminate people, which saves us a vast amount of time on follow-up enquiries such as this. Instead of allowing us to swab him Ivan gave the officers some chewing gum, in the knowledge that we could get a DNA sample from it.'

'Can you get a sample from chewing gum?'

Vicky nodded.

'So?'

'So, the chewing gum that your son gave us showed the DNA of a girl. That looks to us like he is for some reason trying to bypass the system.'

Mrs Sinclair sat twisting her hands into her skirt. She tried hard to control her tears. 'I don't understand,' she repeated over and over again, her gaze fixed on Vicky's face was disbelieving. Her eyes narrowed. 'The stupid idiot, what was he thinking?' The officers' faces were lacking in emotion.

'No, no, you're not thinking he could be the murderer?' Her hand immediately went to her mouth. 'Oh my god...' Her voiced quivered, '...you do don't you? You think it's Ivan?'

# Chapter Seventeen

'We've got a date to move in?' Jen said, hugging the news that the estate agents had informed her of. She dialled Dylan's number to receive the recorded message that he was unable to take her call. Disappointment felt heavy in her stomach. There was little time to inform everyone and instruct the builders – work needed to be done as soon as possible. Like an excited child Jen opened the cupboard where she kept all the household documents and commenced listing the people who needed to be informed.

***

Ivan Sinclair's stomach must have been rumbling to bring him home as his mother anticipated.

On hearing his key in the lock she stood and immediately the hooded youngster, with jeans that found difficulty staying up on his skinny waist, entered the sitting room, she slapped him across his face.

Ivan reeled sideways, such was the force. Dragging his headphones over his unkempt, curly mop of hair he tumbled into the wall. 'What the fuck was that for?' He frantically rubbed his ear. 'You can't do that! I'll report you to childline'

'See these people here?' she said grabbing him by the scruff of the neck. They're two senior detectives and they want to speak to you.' She shook her head and hissed through her teeth. 'What the hell have you done?'

'Nothing! I swear.'

Mrs Sinclair prodded her son hard in the chest with an extended finger. 'You're a liar!' she screeched into his face as she pushed him into the chair. 'Now sit there and answer their questions. Do you hear?'

Dylan slid to the edge of his seat. He leant towards Ivan. 'We know you knew Patti Heinz. Have you any idea why we're here?'

'No,' he said sulkily, avoiding eye contact.

'Did you provide a DNA sample at school?' continued Dylan.

'Yeah, course I did. Like everyone else.'

'Not quite like the others was it?' Dylan spoke in a hushed tone.

Ivan shrugged his shoulders. 'You can get DNA from chewing gum, the copper said.'

'You can. But, there was a slight problem in this instance because the chewing gum wasn't yours.'

'It was, I gave it to him.'

'I'm not denying you gave it to him, but you hadn't chewed it had you?'

Again Ivan shrugged his shoulders.

A little bit of annoyance crept into Dylan's voice. 'Shall we stop messing about? The DNA from the chewing gum was from a female.'

Ivan's lips turned up at the corners. His freckled face turned an impressive shade of crimson.

'We're investigating the rape and brutal murder of a young girl.' Dylan's eyes were piercing, like cold steel. 'Do you think this is a game?'

Ivan's mood changed as his staring eyes filled with tears. He pressed his lips to gather tightly.

'In your own time,' Dylan said softly. 'Tell us what happened.'

The fear of what she might hear was great, but Mrs Sinclair just wanted it over. With clasped hands, and beseeching eyes she looked at Ivan aghast.

Ivan lifted his head to his mother's face and burst into tears. 'I'm sorry Mum, I'm so sorry. I don't know how it happened. I kissed her for the first time that morning. It was the first time. We'd been seeing each other but she was frightened to tell her parents about us... We arranged to meet later that day, but she never showed up. I was upset. I thought she'd changed her mind.'

Immediately everyone fell silent. Ivan must have felt all eyes on him as he looked from Dylan to Vicky and his eyes rested upon his mother. But it wasn't me. I've done nothing wrong. I wouldn't hurt her. I promise I wouldn't. You've got to believe me Mum.'

Mrs Sinclair tears were as much from shock, as relief. She dropped to her knees in front of him and took the teenager's hands in hers.

'So, you're telling us, you didn't see her after that kiss?' said Vicky, her face and voice expressionless.

Ivan vigorously shook his head. 'It was only the next day at school that I heard she'd been... she was dead. Why would someone want to hurt her mum, Patti was so kind and good...' His eyes were pleading.

Vicky's forehead wrinkled into a frown. 'That's what we're trying to find out Ivan. If, what you say is true then explain to us why would you use chewing gum belonging to someone else to try and eliminate yourself from the enquiry?'

Ivan gritted his chattering teeth. 'Because everyone was saying that the boys were being tested, because the police knew she had been killed by a boy, and I'd kissed her, and I thought you might think it was me because you'd know I kissed her.' His fears were genuine, there was no doubt.

'So, you thought because you'd kissed her, your DNA would turn up and we'd think you were the murderer?' suggested Dylan.

Ivan nodded his head. 'Yes, I looked it up on Google and it said you could get DNA from saliva. I panicked. I grabbed the chewing gum Lucy Portman stuck under the desk in history when Mr Greaves was threatening anyone chewing got detention. Will I go to prison?'

'If what you say is true, no. But, wasting police time is a serious offence,' said Vicky.

Ivan gave her an apologetic shrug and hung his head in shame. 'I'm sorry. I told Danny Briggs what I'd done. You can ask him, he knows how scared I was.'

Vicky reached into her bag and retrieved a DNA testing kit. 'We will. But what we need to do first is to swab your mouth.'

'Are you accusing Ivan of lying?' said Mrs Sinclair.

Dylan smiled slightly. 'We have seen many guilty person shed crocodile tears. And, there are those who are not averse to fabricating the truth for their own purpose. That's why we deal with the facts Mrs Sinclair, and hard evidence. If your son is innocent then the evidence will clear him of any wrongdoing. The DNA test is as much for us, as for him.'

Ivan flinched. A flash of panic crossed his wide open eyes. He turned to his mother.

Vicky broke the seal on the container and took out the swab. She asked Ivan to open his mouth, and proceeded to swab the back of his throat. 'I'm sure your mates will have told you this doesn't hurt one bit,' she said.

'The person who killed Patti had full sex with her,' said Dylan as Vicky put the swab into Ivan's mouth. 'He didn't just kiss her. And, what he did to her was not with her consent. Do you understand what I'm saying?'

Vicky placed the swab in the container and wrote on the label.

'Yes,' he said, swallowing hard. 'You mean the person who killed her, raped her don't you? I swear on my life I only kissed her.'

Dylan stood. 'You do realise that you could have ended up being locked up for what you did, don't you? Consider yourself very fortunate. Your DNA sample will now be checked against the DNA gleaned from Patti and at the scene. If it's not a match you won't hear from us again – not for this anyway.'

Mrs Sinclair escorted Dylan and Vicky to the door. 'If he wants to go to the funeral, will it be all right for him to go?'

'I'm sure it will.' Vicky put her hand on Mrs Sinclair's arm. 'Take care. I hope the move goes well. I'll be in touch when the sample comes back from Forensic.'

The neighbouring doors along the corridor were open, with their occupants stood in a group, casually smoking and talking, as the detectives left. Their reasons for being there blatantly obvious.

Mrs Sinclair slammed the door shut. She put her back to the closed door and leant heavily against it. The sooner they left this godforsaken place the better.

'Rozzers!' The shout went up as the detectives left the building. A swarm of kids on bikes rode round and around them. Some headed for the hills. 'Been in there a long time mate,' one young lad called out. 'Thought we might 'ave to come in an 'elp y'out!'

'Watched yourself young 'un otherwise I'll 'ave y'guts for garters!' Vicky shouted.

The young lad pulled a face. 'Garters? What's garters Missus?'

Vicky sat in the passenger seat of the CID car. She secured her belt as Dylan started the engine and steered the car away from the kerb. He took a look in his rear view mirror to see a line of youngsters jeering.

'Cheeky blighters,' Vicky said under her breath, wiping a tired hand around her face. She pointed to an insect that had found it's way onto the inside of the windscreen. 'God forbid, is that a louse?'

Dylan looked sideways, 'It's not a louse, it's got wings.'

She swatted it promptly with her notebook. 'Well, whatever it was it's dead now. Did you know in Shakespeare's day they'd have called us bluebottles?'

'The colour of the watchmen's uniforms, makes perfect sense to me. And, then of course Peeler and Bobby after Sir Robert Peel, the founder of the Metropolitan Police in 1828.'

'In the eighteenth century, Esclop was in fashion,' said Vicky.

'Esclop? I've never heard that one before,' said Dylan, giving her a sideways glance.

'It's Police backwards, although it was pronounced as slop.'

'I can imagine... So, the most mysterious of those and probably the earliest used is Rozzer?'

'I guess that's a variation on Robert, again from Sir Robert Peel.' Vicky appeared thoughtful. 'I'm confident Ivan Sinclair didn't kill Patti,' she said after a while. 'Can you imagine kissing a girl and then she's murdered just hours later? I can understand his panic, can't you?'

'Ah, ah!' Dylan wagged a finger at his colleague as he steered the car into the police station yard.

'I know, never assume.'

'We eliminate by means of DNA. I agree, it seems very unlikely that it's him but we can't be one hundred per cent sure until the sample is checked.'

'I know, but it's not him, is it?'

'Who knows, he managed to come up with a plan to sidestep the sample taking and he also lied to us about his parents not wanting him to have it taken. So, if he was panicking, he was still of sound mind.'

'So, are you saying that you think it could be him?'

Dylan showed his teeth when he smiled. 'I'm not saying that at all. What I am saying is, that it is highly unlikely, but you know and I know that this job is full of surprises and that's why we rely on factual, irrefutable evidence - don't we?'

'Do you remember your first kiss?'

'No.'

'I do. Me and Timmy Taylor both had braces so my first kiss was more like a bump situation. Awkward... You don't remember, honestly?'

'You mean Timmy and I, and no, I don't remember,' he said as he turned off the engine and reached into the back of the car for his raincoat. Dylan's face looked weary, like a defendant in an interview who has answered the same question many times before.

'Whatever,' said Vicky with a wink of her eye. 'It was embarrassing right?'

The incident room was filling up. The debrief soon to begin. Dylan spoke to Acting Detective Sergeant Andy Wormald and Detective Sergeant Nev Duke with regard to updates in his absence, prior to the meeting.

Vicky sat at her desk, picked up a black ballpoint pen and wrote up the results of their enquiries with ease and little effort. The swab was marked up with its unique number and added to the next batch of samples to go to the laboratory. This enabled it to be cross referenced with anything other to do with suspect Ivan Sinclair. Now all they could do was wait. The list of people who had been eliminated from the enquiry was growing, but she didn't feel despondent – the killer couldn't hide forever.

*** 

There had been days of continuous rain and Jen prayed it would stop before the removal men arrived. Max circled the boxes, huffing and a puffing before dropping to the floor in the most unusual of places, wherever there was significant space for him to squeeze his large Retriever frame. 'Moving home is enough to send even the most laid back of dogs into a spin,' said Sam, the vet when Jen had called in to update his records.

Dylan was quieter than usual, apart from the few expletives when he banged his head on the bedrooms sloping roof. Methodical, as always, he stacked the next batch of heavy boxes Jen couldn't lift downstairs into the hallway no matter what time he arrived home at night, what time he left in a morning and how many hours he had worked during the day. 'It'll make it easier for the removal men,' he said, feeling guilty for the little time he could spend helping to achieve their goal but when the job was running he had no alternative but to run with it.

As instructed by the vet to keep Max in as much of his routine as possible, Jen picked up the dog's lead and set out across the fields in her weatherproof coat and wellington boots. Not only could Max not seem to rest until his body was exhausted but, she too was feeling the angst of moving house.

The sky was a blanket of grey autumnal clouds. Yellow leaves piled high against dry stone walls of field boundaries. Max showed her the way. She stretched her legs over wooden stiles and wandered along wet country lanes as she followed him, the aroma of decay was everywhere. The wind started to pick up as she headed along Burford Avenue. The leaves on the trees fell like confetti around her. And when she neared Colonial House the Acer tree appeared to be shedding its leaves like drops of blood. The fog began to roll in between the hills on either side of the Pennines as she headed home the grim and sombre wind swirled around her in almost a frenzy – the mouth of winter was moaning.

\*\*\*

'Force Control Sir, you are shown on our records as the on-call negotiator is that correct?'

Dylan looked from the table he had set for dinner, to the calendar on the kitchen wall, wiping the sweat from his brow. 'Hold on, yes I'd forgotten I said I'd cover until seven o'clock this evening.'

'Uniform are requesting your attendance at Rayburn House, Brelland. We've a man in breach of a court order not to contact his estranged girlfriend, who appears to have grabbed her outside the flats where she is now living. He's armed with what is described by officers at the scene as a large knife. I am told they have him cornered, and we have a stand-off situation. He's threatening to kill her if the officers don't back off.'

'Get Traffic to pick me up and blue-light me to the scene will you please?'

'Will do sir, and we'll update you, as and when, with any developments whilst you're en route.'

There were spots of rain in the wind and Jen pulled on the drawstring of her hood and held it tight under her chin. Max walked protectively by her side. At last she could see the welcoming lights of home directly ahead and already she felt warmer.

A police car passed her, too fast for her to see who was driving. The lights atop blue, revolving, flashing beacons. Her stomach flipped as it always did on seeing an emergency vehicle proceeding at speed. 'Whilst others run away from danger the emergency services run to it,' she signed. 'I wonder which poor soul will be going into the unknown tonight,' she thought, to see the car broadside Dylan's car on the driveway, and Dylan step out of their front door.

With no thought other than being able to say goodbye, Jen ran towards the car. Max barked his excitement as her welly-clad feet moved as quick as they could carry her. Dylan saw her coming, he wound down the window as the car reversed. 'Urgent negotiating job, I'll be back as soon as I can,' he said. 'I've peeled the veg and the meat is in the oven.' Dylan's face was red and flushed, his hair still damp from the shower. She turned on her heels to watch them go. The tail lights were already fading into the distance. In a blink of an eye the white Range Rover was gone over the brow of the hill.

Dylan's hand firmly gripped the door handle.

'Rayburn House boss I'm told.' His uniformed driver spoke, his concentration firmly on the road ahead.

Dylan swayed too and fro with the contour of the road. 'That's correct.'

The sirens wailed and the blue lights flashed as the vehicle headed down the high street. Traffic lights ahead and his driver slowed the car down to expertly weave the vehicle in between the stopped cars. The vehicles immediately in front of them parted as they approached, but there was always one who either didn't hear the siren or wouldn't move. Dylan looked across at his driver and gripped the door handle tighter, bracing himself for what he knew was to come. As if he had read his driver's mind the car swung to the other side of the road, whilst picking up speed. Dylan wasn't concerned. He was confident of the driver's ability. As they continued, the carriageway was clear; the speedometer dial showed

Dylan one hundred miles per hour. Someone's life was in jeopardy and they both knew that the sooner they got to them, the better chance they had to ensure it was saved.

On arrival at their destination the driver pulled their vehicle alongside the beat cars. Dylan had only been in the police vehicle for ten minutes, for what would normally have been for him a forty-minute journey.

'I'll hang about boss, just in case I can be of use,' the driver said, turning off the engine.

Dylan's mind was focused on a small group of officers near shrubbery at the right side of the toughened glass, steel door of the high-rise flats he knew as Rayburn House.

'Fucking get back, or she fuckin' gets it do you hear?' He heard the shrill cry of a woman.

Dylan climbed out of the car and walked in the direction of the commotion. He spoke with Inspector Stonestreet who was in charge. The older man, at one time Dylan's mentor, spoke in a lowered voice. 'I've a fast dog car en route.'

'What've we got?'

'Twenty-eight year old by the name of Kenny Foley, given bail after assaulting his ex girlfriend. His bail conditions are such that he shouldn't be anywhere near here, let alone contact Becky Morris.'

'And, he's ignored it?'

Stonestreet nodded. 'He's come straight round here from court and waited for her to come home, grabbed her before she entered the building and has now got her at knifepoint.' Reginald Stonestreet screwed up his face. He's a bad bastard.

Dylan's eyes were fixed on the unfolding incident.

'He's got a knife, says he's going to kill her if we don't back off. And, I think he would. He's that type. He wouldn't worry about the consequences.'

'It's the bloke that headbutted Jen in the front office at the nick.'

'Personal then?' said Stonestreet, his eyes wide.

Dylan put on his stab-proof vest in silence. 'I'll start talking to him. In the meantime, get two officers with full-length riot shields at either side of me. If I can't get him to release her then we'll do the old squash routine, hopefully trapping Foley with the weapon, outside the shield. When the dog comes, get the dog man to keep it on the lead. I might need an aggressive dog to use as a distraction if we have to strike.'

'Will do. Good luck, you'll need it with this one – he listens to no one.'

Becky dared to look sideways, only to be drawn tighter into Foley's hold. He smelt of booze and sweat, his face scabby and unshaven. His focus was on the small group of officers stood yards from the hostage taker and his hostage. Her vision blurred and panic grew in her throat as she started to breathe in rapid, shallow gasps. She pulled away from Foley as his hands moved up from her waist to her breasts. She gave a cry at the roughness of his grip, twisted her head round when he relaxed the knife from her neck, and sunk her teeth into his upper arm. The jarring impact against the stone wall took her breath and deprived her of that instance where she could have run to the safety of the waiting officers. Dylan watched from the periphery. He spoke quietly to an officer preparing for him to keep a step behind, to pass information to Inspector Stonestreet should any action be required. Foley's wail of fury allowed Dylan to take two large steps forward, approximately ten feet from the hostage taker and his hostage.

Dylan stood where he had stopped, confidently relaxed. He looked Kenny Foley straight in the eyes without blinking. 'Kenny, I'm DI Jack Dylan,' he said in an amiable tone. 'I'm here to help sort out this mess. Becky,' he called, 'you okay?'

Foley's eyes sent the message of violence, rage, defiance. 'She fucking won't be if you come any nearer, and neither will you. Fuck off!'

The hostage taker had the pale, trembling Becky by the hair. Her head pulled back as far as her exposed neck would stretch. The blade of the knife to her jugular, her spindly legs shaking so that she occasionally lost balance.

Dylan held his gaze without moving, without tensing, without flinching. 'Kenny you know the routine. We aren't going anywhere. So, why not just put the knife down and let her go. We can sort this out.' The detective was conscious of Bite, the police dog, straining on his leash behind him. Bite barked, snarled, pulling frantically to be set free.

Foley appeared agitated, nervous. He looked about him as if he was about to run, but there was no escaping from Bite.

'What, so you bastards can spray me? I'm not stupid. You've got near enough once, you're not getting close enough again. You can watch me kill her... Or you can leave us to talk – your call?'

Becky shrank back from the venom in his voice. Foley's snarl was as menacing as the dogs. His gums red, his teeth grinding. 'Your call!' he yelled again.

'Why do you need the knife to talk to Becky?'

'To make sure she listens.' He took the blade from her neck, and waved it in the air.

Dylan gave the nod for the two officers with the riot shields to come stand by his side. 'Just put the knife down Kenny, let's try and sort this out.'

Foley shook his head. 'She's coming with me, dead or alive.'

Becky, without the restraint of the blade to her neck gave a little cry at his tugging of her hair. The point of the knife went instantly back at her throat. His breaths became deeper and louder and she squirmed as his wet lips brushed her cheek. Becky's looked directly at Dylan, her lips parted in her bloodless face. Foley drew his lips back on his long front teeth in a fixed snarl and growled like a dog.

'But don't you see Kenny, the decision to be with you has got to be hers? If she doesn't come to you of her own free will, she'll run away every chance she gets.'

Foley's eyes were round and staring. He appeared to be thinking. Then he raised his stubbly chin at Dylan. 'What's them toy soldiers doing with them shields? Tell 'em to back off.'

'They're here for my protection.'

'Yeah, well, if any of you step any closer she'll get it. If I'm going to prison, I might as well make it for something worthwhile.'

The German Shepherd snarled, growled, his lips vibrating as he barked incessantly at the hostage takers words as if he understood.

Dylan remained calm. 'Don't talk like that Kenny. We can sort it out. Nobody needs to get hurt.'

'Get that fucking dog away from me.' Foley started to hop from foot to foot, but at least the knife was away from Becky's throat. 'I'm losing my fucking patience,' he raged. The veins on his neck were ugly and bulging.

'If I do, will you talk to me? See if we can find a way out of this?'

Bite was up on his hind legs, barking, snarling, sniffing the air for his prey.

'I'll kill her.' The blade was back at Becky's throat. Foley's eyes on the dog and its handler allowed Dylan and the two officers to take a step closer to him.

'Are you all right Becky?' Dylan called. Becky had presence of mind to blink her eyelids twice in quick succession.

'Of course she's fucking all right. I haven't fucking touched her yet 'ave I?' Foley lunged forward with the knife. 'But, I'm gonna kill you bastards.' Foley's biting of his bottom lip was so hard that it drew blood.

'We aren't moving Kenny so you might as well let her go,' said Dylan.

With no warning other than Foley seeing the blood from his mouth drip on his forearm, he violently pushed Becky to the floor, and raised the knife above his shoulders throwing his head back. A guttural howl emanated from the depths of his lungs. Becky was on her hands and knees.

'Now!' shouted Dylan. The officers armed with shields pushed forward at speed, trapping Foley against the wall. Dylan felt the spittle from Foley's mouth hit his face, his reflexes made him blink at the sudden feeling of droplets falling onto his skin.

As anticipated by Dylan, the hostage taker wasn't fully covered by the armour. In a blind rage accompanied by an energy surge, Foley's anger, pent-up emotions, fear, erupted as one and he kicked out hard. It was so hard his shoe came off. Becky screamed for Foley to stop. The sound of grunts and groans assaulting her ears.

'If I can't have her nobody else is gonna,' he hissed, spitting blood, pulling, kicking at the officers, until Dylan with equal determination screwed his hand into a tight fist, drew his arm back, reached over the safeguards and punched Foley as hard as he could on the nose. The bone crunched. Foley flew backwards into the glass with an almighty thud. Immediately, his grip loosened on the knife, which dropped with a clatter onto the stone flags. Dylan kicked it with the tip of his shoe and it skidded across the bloodied floor. Winded, the officers squashed Foley hard against the wall and brought him down to the ground. But the hostage taker was not giving up his face swelling, blood oozing from his nose and mouth he squirmed beneath the transparent buffer and pushed back at the officers with the strength of a caged animal fighting to be free.

Once down, back-up ran forward to assist in his restraint. Becky held her hands to her ears, to drown out the noise from Foley's abusive mouth. He was handcuffed, his legs fastened around his jogging bottoms to stop him kicking out. Becky sat on the small wall to the side, her head in her hands whimpering; her heart pounded. She leant forward, dropping to the floor in a faint – bruising evident in her face that was fast becoming the size of a balloon.

'We need help, here!' came a cry from the officer attending to her.

The knife was collected and Kenny, his face a red ruin, with dark sheets of blood flowing steadily from his split lip and rubbled nose was carried to the waiting Police van screaming at the officers. The prisoner was tossed into the transit van for transportation to the cells.

'They'll throw the book at him this time. Kidnap, threats to kill, assault for starters,' said Stonestreet.

Dylan splayed his fingers, his knuckles cracked, red and swollen, Foley's blood splattered on the white cuff of his shirt.

'You better get that seen to,' said Stonestreet.

\*\*\*

'Haven't you heard the saying, 'Back a dog into a corner...?' said the traffic officer when Dylan climbed in beside him. 'I'll call in A&E en route. They'll check that over.' His face held a frown.

Dylan could feel his hand stiffening. He grimaced. 'You're probably right.'

The clean-shaven traffic officers looked young, fresh, smart.

'I've not seen a negotiator at work that close before, sir. A few words, and smack. You showed him whose boss.' He smacked a fist in the palm of his hand. A look of respect crossed his face.

'Well, it's supposed to be about listening and talking, and nobody is supposed to get hurt.' Dylan pulled a face.

'I prefer it the way you did it Basher.' He cocked his head in Dylan's direction as he started the vehicle.

'Now where did you hear that nickname?' said Dylan, genuinely interested.

'My dad, Barry "Razor" Sharpe? You got a cold case of his cleared up, long after he retired. It nearly saw him off, the Tina Walker murder?'

Dylan nodded.

'I was at uni at the time but I was inspired. Made me want to be a police officer, and here I am.'

'Really?' A surprised smile crossed his face. 'Why Traffic instead of CID?'

'Boys and cars eh? There's time for me to jump ship yet.'

'From Traffic to CID?' Dylan raised an eyebrow and with a fleeting glance at his epaulettes, noted his collar number. 'I'll look out for you then PC 4038,' he said.

'Bob to my friends,' he said lifting his hand off the steering wheel to acknowledge the uniformed police officer waving them on.

Dylan's mind was elsewhere – appreciating all that was around him. The way the sky seemed more blue, the grass greener, the way he always did after a negotiating incident. He never took things for granted, he never had since becoming a police officer.

The police radio gave the officers constant updates on divisional incidents and when the traffic officer heard that the dual carriageway was blocked due to a road traffic accident, and his colleagues were dealing Bob located a narrow meandering lane through waist-high dry stone walls, that led them directly to the hospital's door.

'Dad died, soon after it was solved,' Bob said, as he pulled up outside the hospital entrance. 'Mum always said that job would see him off and in essence it did.'

'I'm sorry,' said Dylan, and he meant it.

Bob's melancholy was short lived. He held in his hands a large pot of tea that had been instantly brought to him the moment he arrived, and he flirted with the hospital staff unashamedly as ice packs were wrapped around Dylan's hand.

Dylan winced.

'It might be painful to begin with but it reduces the swelling and inflammation,' said the nurse. With little fuss she elevated his hand above the level of his heart.

Dylan's X-rays showed a fracture to the knuckle bone. The nurse produced some painkillers. 'You can't drive.' She bound the injured site to the adjacent finger. 'That'll keep the knuckles straight,' she said in a satisfied way.

'How long will it take to heel?'

'About two to three weeks.'

'Can you still work?' said Bob as he drove Dylan to work.

'Not much choice with a murderer to catch, but my worry is that we're also moving house.'

Dylan walked through the incident room and as he did so the noise in the office changed. The computer keyboards started to clatter more and desk draws banged louder. Voices came and went in wave the nearer he got to his office door. The sound of laughter from the kitchenette was raucous. He put his hand to his forehead.

'Hey, I thought you were day-off?' Vicky said with a quizzical stare as he passed her desk. She slid back her chair, rose and followed him into his office. 'I heard you were called out. Stuck for words were you?' Her voice was loud. He screwed up his eyes as he turned on his heels to face her.

Dylan's legs felt weak, he looked helplessly boyish. 'I think I'd better take you home,' she said.

\*\*\*

Hand trembling, Dylan let himself into the house with his front door key. The curtains had not been drawn and through the lounge window he could see Jen laid asleep, Max at her side. The television created shafts of brilliance in the otherwise darkened room. The dog's tail tapped slowly and gently against the sofa, his eyes and ears raised but he didn't get up. An empty wine glass stood on the edge of the coffee table next to an empty glass. There was a HOME magazine on the chair. Dylan paused at the door considering her reaction to his bandages. He put his finger to his lips. 'Best let her sleep,' he whispered to the dog.

Dylan sat quietly at the dining room table. It was laid just as he had left it, with the exception of the bottle of wine that had then been unopened in the cooler, and a glass.

Jen's hair framed her pale face. She rubbed her eye with a fisted hand. Her clothes were crumpled.

'Are you okay?' he said.

Her eyes widened. 'More's the point, are you?'

'I am now. I will be.' Dylan looked deadbeat. This was no time to give him a hard time, remind him that his health came first so, instead she walked towards him, knelt down at his feet and put her hand to his arm. 'Can I get you anything? Have you eaten?'

Jen stood listening to the sound of a quick splash wash, and his opening of drawers. She cleared the table swiftly and prepared him a tray; warmed him some soup and a bread roll. Whatever had happened he needed fuel in his belly.

***

'What on earth?' said Jen when Dylan walked into the kitchen early the next morning. He carried his tie, and looked at her questioningly. No words were spoken as he stood before her, bent his head and proceeded to lift his collar with one hand. His eyes looked up to the ceiling while Jen knotted his tie. She put the palm of her hand to his chest when she had finished, tapped it gently, and looked up into his white face. He planted a kiss on the end of her nose.

'I guess there is no point in me asking you to take the day off?' Dylan gave her a wane smile. Just then there was a tap at the door. Maisy burst into the room and straight into Jen's arms, squealing at the top of her voice. Chantall followed close behind carrying Maisy's overnight bag. At that moment Dylan's mobile phone rang, he turned and walked briskly into the dining room to take the call. The women exchanged glances both watching Dylan through the half glass doors. Chantall lifted an eyebrow at Jen. 'Good night?' she said with a little smile on her lips. The expression on Chantall's face changed on seeing Dylan's bandaged hand as he opened the doors and re-entered the kitchen. He picked up his briefcase. Jen shook her head gently at Chantall, her face gave nothing away. He walked towards Jen, kissed her on the cheek and tasting the salt from her tears, he drew back – his face pained. He kissed Maisy, thanked Chantall for looking after their daughter, said goodbye and was gone.

Maisy wound her arms around her mother's neck. 'Don't ask,' Jen said over her daughter's shoulder. She sat Maisy at the table with her crayons and colouring book and sat down next to Chantall. Feeling a lump in her throat, tears sprang into her eyes but she didn't wipe them away immediately, half hoping that Chantall would not see them as she responded to the little girl's pleas for her to help. Chantall got up, filled the kettle and got two cups out of the cupboard. Jen was thankful for her friend's intuition. She stared round at the empty shelves and walls and back at the packing boxes as Chantall busily prepared the drinks. She brought the hot beverages over and handed a mug to Jen who in turn looked up into her friend's face that was full of concern.

'There is no way on God's earth that Dylan is going to be fit to help with the move. I've got to do something.'

Chantall's smile was reassuring, as was her warm hand on hers. 'I'll help.'

Jen looked her up and down, from top to toe. Chantall was always dressed immaculately, groomed and made up. Then she looked down at herself and despaired. 'I doubt us two will be much use lugging furniture around, do you?' Max's ears shot up at that very moment, and he ran to the front door growling, to be met by leaflets being thrust into the letter box with force. The dog barked frantically, leaping up and down incessantly at the door handle. Jen frowned, 'Must be someone new,' she said. 'He's not usually like this.' Jen shouted at him to cease but his abnormal behaviour didn't stop. There was a thud as he backed into the waist high set of drawers that was just big enough to house at its top, the telephone. Calling repeatedly at Max, Jen hurried down the hallway, dragged Max away, picked up the post, put the table back in its place and stood the phone on top, scolding the dog all the while for his bad behaviour. Fallen from one of the drawers was a small book and as it lay opened on the floor she could see it had Dylan's handwriting inside. A sparkle appeared in her eyes as she looked up from reading the words.

'That look, I've seen it before Jennifer Jones,' Chantall said as she walked back in the kitchen. 'What is it?'

'I have a plan.'

'I knew it.'

'Tell me more,' she said eagerly.

***

Dylan scanned his computer – one particular prisoner's information he read, over again. Surprisingly, he felt rather calm.

'Good job you've got another to pick up a coffee cup,' said Vicky nodding in the direction of his bandages, 'otherwise you'd be buggered.'

Dylan nodded but didn't take his eyes off the screen. When he spoke a few moments later it was in a slow drawl, 'Yeah, I can sympathise with David now. But...' He turned the computer screen to face her and lay back in his chair, an audible sigh coming from his lips, 'it was worth it to lay one on that bastard.'

'Has Foley made a complaint of assault against you yet?'

Dylan afforded himself a chuckle as he sat up. 'I don't deny I hit him. I hit him as hard as I bloody could.' His tone changed. 'But, in my defence, your Honour, I only used as much force as was necessary to disarm him.'

'The twat deserved it,' she said raising her eyebrows and shrugging her shoulders.

The morning briefing was interspersed with sarcastic comments from the jovial team.

'Boss, is it true you've had your ACAB tattoos removed?' said Ned.

'Not all coppers are bastards,' Vicky said clipping him around the head. 'Just some...'

'We'll call you Mr Punch from now on, shall we sir?' said Nev.

Dylan chuckled at their reaction, put his chin to his chest and shook his head. When the tormenting ceased, he stood tall. 'If you lot worked half as hard as you did at taking the mick, this murder would be solved,' he growled, but his lips were still turned upwards at the corners, and the smile reached his eyes.

The assembled walked out of the briefing room in single file, each with a fisted hand above their heads. Some had handkerchiefs wrapped around their hands, others with paper tissues. Ned held a tea towel. 'The police force really is a job like no other,' he said.

## Chapter Eighteen

Sitting in his office Dylan drummed his fingers on the desk, rhythmically soothing his frustration. Vicky had been gone no more than ten minutes when he heard her feminine throaty laugh emanating from the outer CID office. When he looked sideways at the tapping on his door he could see through the glass that she was carrying something. When she opened his door the smell told him that it was a warm meat pie. He smiled at her appreciatively when he handed him a small, brown, paper bag. Invited, she slid into the chair opposite him and adjusted the position of the remaining bit of sandwich that she held between her fingers, before popping it in her mouth.

'If the Chief Super saw you eating outside he'd have a dicky fit,' said Dylan.

'Yeah, well there's no fear of that because he'd have to come out of his office. Not all of us have the privileged of a dinner hour, or a secretary to go out to get our lunch. So?' She looked at him, and continued to look at him, in silence, her eyebrows raised.

'What?' he said, catching the warm gravy that ran from the side of his mouth, with the handkerchief he retrieved from his trouser pocket.

'Who's the next front runner?' Vicky pointed to the gravy on Dylan's chin and he instantly dabbed it with his finger. 'This enquiry feels like the Grand National – just when we think we've a good suspect, the DNA results stop us at the next hurdle.'

'I agree, I really hoped information from Patti's laptop and mobile phone would reveal something, anything. A contact we didn't know about, a secret liaison she'd been having?' He screwed the empty paper bag up into a ball and threw it across the room, straight into the waste bin. 'Not only is that not the case, but they tell me she hardly ever used either.'

Vicky eyes were down as she peeled the paper from a bar of chocolate. 'What no social media?' she said opening her mouth and placing a square of chocolate on her tongue.

He shook his head. 'No, absolutely nothing,' he shrugged his shoulders. 'I guess she didn't have time. Has the CCTV enquiries brought anymore actions to be pursued?' Dylan continued. 'Is there CCTV that still needs viewing?'

At the shaking of her head Dylan groaned in despair. He ran his hands through his hair, and then cradled his head in exasperation, as he placed his elbows onto the cool surface of the desk. 'We need to review the house-to-house enquiries in that area. Have all the callbacks been done? If not I want to know why not? Basically,' he said placing the palm of his hand flat down on the desk before him, 'I want to know we have cleared the ground beneath our feet, and left no stone unturned before we move on.'

'Guess we're lucky we have the DNA because if not the review team would be all over us like flies on a big, steaming, turd loaf.'

'A what?'

Vicky chuckled. 'I went out with an American once, that's what he used to say...'

Dylan slid a piece of paper over the desk towards her and threw her a pen. She caught it with ease, clicked her tongue and winked an eye.

'I want the house-to-house pro-forma's reviewed. Any occupant known to us, I want to know about. Did we ask the right questions to get the answers we need?' Dylan said matter-of-factly.

'Would it be worth doing house-to-house again? Someone might remember something that they didn't, when they were initially seen. Maybe some people were in shock at the time they were interviewed? After all, they had just been made aware that a murder had taken place on the street where they live.'

Dylan looked straight passed her to the CID office, through the half glass door.

'Maybe...' His eyes found hers. 'Check we have taken DNA samples from all those who reside on Burford Avenue, or were known to have been in the area at the time. I want to know there are none outstanding. I also want each and every resident to be asked to revisit the day of the murder in their mind and ask themselves, "Was there anything, absolutely anything, that they remember now, that wasn't passed on to us at the time?" I'm considering a reconstruction of her route she took that day – what do you think?'

Vicky nodded in the affirmative with a blink of the eye and a swift nod of her head. Her pen was still poised.

'For now we have the mobile police incident unit parked on Burford Avenue and we have a small group of officers staffing it?'

'We do.'

'One officer present at all times as a public liaison, and others I want to systematically visit the households again. Ask Sarah Dodsworth to arrange for the Mounted Section to walk the streets in the area. You never know, it's amazing how many people come out to stroke a police horse and speak to an officer on horseback, but won't speak to an officer in uniform on the street.'

'Good plan,' Vicky said, enthusiastically.

'High profile, high visibility and a good photo opportunity for the media to keep Patti's murder headline news.'

Dylan picked up the phone, the sign to Vicky that their conversation had finished.

'Nev,' she heard him say as she left the room. 'I'd like a meet today to review where we are with the mass DNA sampling at the school.'

***

'Hello Charlie, I'm Jen, Dylan's wife.' Jen's hand trembled slightly, whether because of the cold, slight fear of the stranger who was her brother-in-law, or from excitement she was unsure. 'Thank you for coming to the rescue.' Charlie's face held the same effortless smile as his younger brother. Underlying in his warm handshake was the same energy too.

'I'm so excited to hear you and Dylan have bought the old place. Oh, and to meet you at last, of course.' He hung his head, and his hair fell over his eyes, giving him a look of boyish vulnerability.

Smiling broadly Jen stood at the peeling front door, with the key in her hand and listened to Dylan's brother's tales of their youthful antics. 'More often than not we spent our childhood outside rather than in,' he said, and she could understand why.

'What child would stay indoors with a railway on their doorstep, trees begging to be climbed and all at the gateway to acres of moorland?' She could barely take her eyes off Charlie as he chatted, so alike her husband in his looks, and mannerisms.

Hearing Jen talk about their plans Charlie was as enthusiastic as if the project was his own, and the love and respect for his younger brother was apparent. Building being his line of work, he shared her vision for the renovation that others, it was apparent, didn't see. He looked up and down the driveway, out towards the garden to the fields beyond, and turning towards the house from the floor to the roof of the building before them. 'This house... Tell me, what was my brother thinking when he took it on?' he said in wonderment before returning his attention to Jen.

Jen's cheeks flushed. 'That was sort of my fault...' she hunched her shoulders and grimaced. 'He wasn't sure. Then, someone else put in a bid and if he hadn't made an instant decisions we would have lost it.' Jen's head dropped to one side. 'He knew how much I loved it. And, as usual he's working too hard, never at home and well once he has the bit between his teeth, there is no letting go... hence why I need your help.'

'That sounds like our Dylan. He had two paper rounds a day when he was thirteen, and as small and skinny as he was, he never welched on his turn at digging the garden over for our potatoes and veg. I kept chickens which ensured a bountiful Christmas, and meant we always had eggs.' He turned his head to look up the path. 'Is he meeting us here?'

Jen looked at him. 'I...'

'He doesn't know you called me does he?' he said with a raise of an eyebrow.

She shook her head.

'May I?' he said, as he took the key and placed it in the lock.

'It's one of those houses that beckons you inside... and hugs you...' she said following him. The house was cold, dark and smelt of damp.

'You're really moving in here tomorrow?' he said. Jen nodded her head.

Jen watched Charlie's eyes fill with the wonder of a child on an adventure as he walked around, pointing out the original features, the unusual curve of the stairs, 'Dad was a dab hand at joinery...' Dylan's brother made no mention of the tree growing through the window in one of the bedrooms or the damp rising up the walls from the floor. But, what he did do was write down in his workbook what needed to be done. 'We worked hard,' he said,

171

standing for a moment, looking over the overgrown vegetable patch. He rested his hand on the window frame. 'It was no easy life being one of five children, with dad working shifts or away, and mum trying to do her best by us all. We all slept in a drawer as babes in arms.'

'Dylan hasn't any photographs of you as children. I guess men aren't as sentimental...'

'Oh, I don't know about that. Our Ronnie – have you met our Ronnie?' Jen shook her head. 'You will tomorrow. He has Dad's medals, and his army papers,' he said with a grin as Jen followed him down the stairs. 'Joe was a keen photographer you know.'

'So Dylan said. But, what I can't understand is why there isn't more photographs, or a family album? Do you think Ronnie will come and help us?'

Charlie seemed to be thinking about what she had said. 'We'll all help,' he smiled. 'We might not live in each other's pockets but we're there for each other. I want you to remember that.'

Jen gave a sigh of relief. Again, Charlie looked thoughtful. 'You're right. None of us, as far as I know, have photographs baring the mandatory school snap.' He stopped and turned. Jen saw the mark of weariness that resembled Dylan's. Suddenly he hurried down the remaining steps. His eyes when he turned were wide. 'That's it! That's the room that's missing – Dad's darkroom!'

Charlie's steps were long as he strode out of the front door. From the hallway she saw him pass each window as he paced the outside. When he returned his face held a puzzled expression. 'I remember the room as plain as day, but for the life in me I can't remember where it was in the house... and there isn't floor space for it to be hidden.'

'Could there be a cellar?' Jen frowned. 'But if so, where's the steps or the door?'

Charlie banged on the walls of each room from left to right.

'What are you doing?' she asked as he reached the utility room, which housed the butler sink with the skirted, checked curtain below on a wire. He had his ear turned to the wall. The sound his knocking made wasn't like the noise on the other walls.

'It's a timber stud wall,' he said.

Jen's heart missed a beat. 'What are you saying?'

'It's a stud wall, covered in plasterboard, therefore it isn't load-bearing.' Their eyes met.

'I think I might have found it.'

***

The mobile police incident unit was paying dividends. The team had already been informed that on the afternoon of Patti's murder was the day the local Brelland and surrounding homeless charity were collecting the bags that had been left out on the kerb edge. Surprisingly this hadn't been mentioned by any person who they had interviewed previously.

The BASH team member could be an important witness, and if the driver on that day were a male then a DNA sample would be required; enquiries were made a priority. Two others had come forward to say that on the afternoon of the murder they had received deliveries of orders from Internet purchases – again this information hadn't been shared previously as it was thought irrelevant. Enquiries to trace the delivery people were a priority.

The incident room office door opened and shut, and moments later Dylan could hear Vicky taking her frustrations out on Ned. 'I don't know why we bother?'

'With what?'

'All that media attention! Not one of those bloody drivers came forward to say they were on Burford Avenue on that day. It's a bastard murder enquiry for Christ sake!' She slammed the lid down on the Xerox machine and the regular hum of the copier machine drowned out Ned's reply.

'They'd know they'd been on Burford Avenue, and if they weren't sure of the date you'd think they'd check their diary wouldn't you?' Vicky eyed him from where she sat.

Ned shrugged his shoulders.

'I want them finding and interviewing,' she said as she turned her head and typed the action required into the computer.'

Ned yawned.

'You still here?' she snapped, when she looked up a few minutes later.

Ned grunted and groaned as he stood, put on his coat and collected his keys from his drawer. Two minutes later he was out of the door.

Tracing the driver of a vehicle belonging to a charity never proved easy. In most instances drivers were volunteers and the working hours ad hoc due to availability. In total there were four volunteers who did the collecting and to be seen. Luckily, David Funk, the CSI was a fundraiser for the charity and therefore he had contact details of those involved.

In respect of the two deliveries from items purchased via the Internet, with the assistance of the householder and the providing companies, two local distributors were identified. The buzz had returned to the incident room with potential witness to see who the officers knew had been in the immediate area at the time.

'I want them seen today,' Dylan told Vicky. 'Jen and I are moving house tomorrow.'

Vicky's expression told him he'd be lucky, but Dylan's stance was adamant. 'It's achievable,' he said in away that she knew was non negotiable.

Dylan waited patiently. The news from David Funk that there were no hits on the latest batch of DNA samples submitted to Forensic, including that from Ivan Sinclair was a blow, but not unexpected.

'I'll break the news to everyone at the debrief,' said Dylan.

At debrief four charity volunteer drivers had been seen. Two retired men, and two middle-aged women. The men had willing given DNA samples to the officers who spoke to them and the volunteer coordinator had confirmed that Brenda and Grace had been doing the collections that day which had resulted in a visit to Burford Avenue. But as there was nothing deemed as out of the ordinary at nine o'clock in the morning neither woman thought about speaking to the police.

'At least we've cleared more ground beneath our feet,' said Acting Detective Sergeant Andy Wormald who sat next to Dylan. Detective Sergeant Nev Duke was keen to report his team's update.

'We've seen two distribution service providers. Luckily for us at the first the owner, manager and his drivers were in for a meeting when we called, all the males in attendance gave us DNA samples a couple more have been seen at home and we've now got theirs too.'

'Good. Anything Ned?' said Dylan

'I spoke to the other identified distributor. A single working mum who is otherwise employed to distribute Internet stock from her place in Union Street. She's only recently taken on the extra work to make ends meet. She is out and about most days in the local area. A signature is required for each parcel delivered. Oddly, she doesn't recall going to Burford Avenue recently, but she definitely didn't rule it out.'

'No wonder you were ages! So, basically she couldn't help?' said Vicky.

'No, but she seemed shocked and apologetic.' Ned grinned broadly. 'There's more...'

'I should bloody hope so!'

'Following the route she uses all the time, Burford Avenue would have been one of the first drop offs of the day, so it would have been around nine o'clock if she had been dropping parcels off in that area on that day, hours before Patti returned home.'

'Before we close the meeting,' Dylan looked left and right at his Detective Sergeants, all whom sat facing the incident team personnel. 'I am taking a few days off. We're moving house...' As the words left his mouth there was a knock at the door. David Funk stood and opened the door. Rachael, the young police officer who had protected the Patti Heinz murder scene stood in the doorway. The pair shared a knowing look and she a shy smile before she continued to speak. 'Sir, sorry to interrupt. There's an urgent telephone call for you in the incident room – from headquarters control. They want to speak to you immediately.'

Dylan looked to the sea of tired, expectant faces before him. They all knew what that meant... as did he. Did he, have the staff from the existing enquiry available to deal with another major incident? No, but he needed a few to assist with the basics, and get whatever incident it was off the ground.

'Vicky, come with me, Ned, Donna, Emily, David don't go anywhere until you hear from me.'

*** 

The bin store at Shroggs Grove housing complex was cordoned off with police tape. Rain, sleet, snow and hail that had fallen while he was en route had left the ground sodden.

Dylan flashed his warrant card at the uniformed police officer who logged him in at the outer cordon. Immediately after he lifted the police tape to allow Dylan to go under, and up the churned-up grass verge where the rest of them stood. It was dark but the fact it was icy cold didn't deter the locals, dressed for the weather, gathering.

The senior officer on site beckoned Dylan out of earshot. 'A female, sir, stuffed behind the bins. Paramedics have attended and pronounced life extinct. Is there anything else you want me to do?' Lee Ambler was an ex detective and Dylan was glad to see him on site.

'I understand the waste collectors found the body, have you got their details? We'll need statements.'

'Done sir.'

'And the nearby bins, they've not been emptied?

'No, they're still in situ. I've ensured that the inner cordon has secured the immediate area around the body for you, and the outer as you can see won't allow even prying eyes. CSI and supervisor are en route and they have been informed that we need screening and possibly an inflatable tent.'

'What else can you tell me?' said Dylan who busied himself by pulling on his protective clothing.

'The deceased is a young woman, possibly mid twenties. Waste collectors saw the body behind the bins and immediately contacted us and the ambulance. Paramedics attended shortly after us and confirmed her dead, left their details and told us they will prepare the necessary statements. Apart from pronouncing her dead the paramedics also tell us that she has a severe injury to the back of her head.'

'Once CSI are fit we'll take a look. Well, done with the cordon by the way,' Dylan said over his shoulder as he headed towards the inner cordon.

'Thanks sir.'

The lifeless corpse was dressed in dark coloured leggings that were arranged in such a way they showed the left cheek of her bottom. There was a deep graze to her exposed hip that was covered in a mixture of dried blood, grit and dirt. Her upper body clothing that was pulled up under her arms revealed a red, lacy bra; the lower part of her breast visible. Her shoulder-length, brown hair strewn across her face was matted with blood. Dried, blood-streaked fluid traces showed signs of travelling from both ear and nose. A closer inspection revealed part of her skull sunk inward from the trauma, which suggested she had been hit with a heavy object.

Senior CSI Sarah Jarvis hung over the body taking photographs. The 360 degree angle camera was working away on the tripod, being monitored by CSI Karen Ebdon. What was apparent was the different shutter speed noises. David Funk stood back for a moment and let the younger CSIs, covered from top to toe in white paper suits do the necessary.

'As the photographer, it is not up to us to determine the relevance of the injury, or item, but to document it,' said David who stood at Dylan's side. 'We must remain impartial and non-judgemental in order to maintain the highest level of service and photograph the scene in order to show the body prior to it being moved. I wonder how many irrelevant images we collect in a year?'

'And a tiny fragment of something you preserve, or an image you take can be the very piece that proves a case for us,' said Dylan.

David looked pleased. 'Looking at her clothing and the grazing it suggests to me she was dragged into her present position behind the wheelie bin. She's received one hell of a blow to her head which would have had immediate effect, so what we have here may just be the dump-site.'

Vicky, suited and booted walked in to the inner cordon. 'Good grief, I can see my breath,' she said pulling her mask over her nose and mouth. 'Her eyes looked dull and sad. Not only as the poor kid ended her days at the hands of a killer, but to be dumped like garbage is shit.'

'Satisfied you guys have done everything you need to do?' said Dylan to David. David nodded.

A plastic body sheet was laid on the ground next to the body, and the victim was rolled very slowly onto it.

The girl's eyes were closed. Her cheek was badly grazed, smeared with blood and there was a mixture of grit, mud and the slime found from the remnants of decayed, rotting food.

'Rigor, rigid. Mortis, dead,' Vicky mumbled. The girl wore no jewellery that could be seen, except for a small metallic stud in her left nostril, and in her ear. 'No, ID, no coat and her clothing's dry. How far, and from where has she travelled?'

'With some luck we may find out sooner rather than later. My initial thoughts are that we remove her to the mortuary and keep this immediate area protected, including the bins and their contents. I want you to arrange to have them fingerprinted in case our attacker moved them to get her in that position. A search will tell us if the murderer has done us a favour and dumped the weapon in one of these bins.' Dylan looked around. 'We won't know that until we get in touch with Operational Support to ask for a POLSA search team. I also want a house-to-house on Shroggs Grove before we cast our net wider. David, can we get a head shot of the girls face, she looks asleep doesn't she? We may have to consider using that to identify her.'

The clicking noise from the camera shutter was immediate. 'Not a problem boss,' he said.

'Also we need the CCTV database checking. See if this location is covered, and any routes to the area. Call Raj. She'll deputise; we'll run on HOLMES. Tell her to set up the incident room next to Patti's, and that way I can keep a foot in both camps. Anyone got anything else before we move on?'

'Who's exhibits boss?'

Dylan turned to Donna. 'Can you pick this one up?'

'Absolutely.'

'Okay, phase one, arrange for the young woman to be moved to the mortuary and I'll request two teams from ops support. Check the Mispers, it could be we have someone reported missing from home that fits her description. I'll speak to the Coroner's Officer see when we can get a Home Office pathologist to carry out the PM.'

When he did so the response was quick. Arrangements were made for eight o'clock. A press appeal was drafted, maybe someone would come forward and report her missing.

Limited details were used:-

'A murder enquiry is underway after the discovery of a body behind wheelie bins in Shroggs Grove earlier today. The person was fully clothed and had suffered a severe head injury. She is slim, white, has shoulder-length light brown hair and is dressed in black leggings and a pale blue, knitted jumper. She also has a small silver coloured ball nose stud in her left nostril, and likewise in her ear. A post-mortem will be carried out tomorrow to ascertain the exact cause of her death. DI Jack Dylan leading the investigation said, "I am not convinced that this young lady was killed in the location she was found. I appeal to anyone who may know her, or may have seen a person fitting her description recently to please contact us. Anyone with any information shouldn't hesitate to contact us in confidence.""

Dylan eyes looked skyward. 'Oh god, we're moving house tomorrow,' he said out loud.

Vicky looked at her watch. 'Correction sir, you're moving house today...'

\*\*\*

Dylan put his briefcase down at the kitchen door. Exhausted he shook off his jacket, unbuttoned the top button of his shirt, and loosened his tie. He switched on the light, dropped his newspaper-clad fish and chips onto the kitchen table and as if on autopilot walked to the sink and filled the kettle. Opening the cupboard door only showed him they were bare. Dylan looked around him at the moving boxes taped up and labelled 'KITCHEN' in big, bold, black lettering. He noticed a lone glass on the draining board, rinsed it out and filled it with ice cold water from the tap. The window bereft of curtains, meant he stared directly out onto the back garden but it stared back at him like hollow eyes. He put the glass to his lips, his head back and he drank heartily before reaching out to the cutlery drawer to find it empty also; all the homely comforts packed away. He left the glass next to the fish and chip paper and turned to the fridge, but there was no can of beer that he sought, only half a pint of milk and a bottle of wine. His hand hovered over the milk, he looked over his shoulder, attempting to locate a jar of coffee. There was none to be seen. So, he grabbed the wine bottle by the neck and collecting his supper en route he carried them both into the lounge. There was one chair in the living room that was devoid of clutter – obvious to him the seat Jen had been using earlier as Maisy's bedtime story book still sat on its arm. The answering phone blinked next to a pile of papers and mail, he didn't touch them but left them lying in wait for tomorrow, today, this morning, when Jen woke, the removal men would arrive and Dylan would have left for work. He stood from the chair sometime later, his stomach full, his head reeling, nearly pitching himself onto the floor. He grabbed at the coffee table, upset the empty bottle and it fell with a thud to the carpet. He made his way unsteadily to the door and grabbing hold of the foot of the banister pulled himself up the stair steps.

Jen rolled over and spoke in a hushed tone when Dylan slid into bed next to her. 'I heard the news... Are they trying to see you off?'

Dylan's head facing the ceiling sank into the soft, cool pillow. Immediately his eyes closed. The breath that emerged from his body was by way of a long, low sigh.

Jen propped herself up on one elbow. Overwhelmed to see his dark, sunken eyes and the tautness of his face, highlighted by the moon that shone through the window, she frowned down at him. 'How much more are you going to let them dump on you before you collapse? Are you trying to kill yourself?' she said in a hushed tone, through gritted teeth.

His droopy eyelids flew open at a noise outside and he watched the shadows from a car's headlights dance on the ceiling. 'I don't think that's in the role profile,' he said after a moment or two.

'I bet it isn't. Because, they don't want it to be public knowledge how few of you are holding the fort.' Jen sat up, punched her pillow, and turned to face him, her cheek and ear sinking into her pillow.

'Maybe so.' Dylan closed his eyes and for a moment he slept to be woken when he stretched and his leg cramped. He sat up with a jolt, threw his legs out of bed and bent down to rub his thigh vigorously.

'The likes of Hugo Watkins... They sit in their bloody ivory towers and let others do the work for them. He was telling someone in the office today he had never been to a mortuary or given evidence in a Crown Court! How can it be right for a Chief Superintendent to say that?'

'There are some good bosses Jen, you know that, they're not all like him.'

'But you can count them on one bloody hand.'

Jen rolled out of bed and headed for the bathroom.

Dylan opened his eyes and turned his head to face her. 'Apart from that what's annoying you?' He said when she returned.

'Avril Summerfield-Preston had the great pleasure announcing today that she's heard the government are planning to tax the lump sum, therefore reducing the police pension by a substantial amount. She says it's a plan to make officers retire sooner than they intended.'

'Really? Well, Beaky will know.' Dylan smiled a wry smile. 'I had heard a rumour. But I'm told we won't lose out over time.'

'Sadly time is something that no one is guaranteed...'

'I guess sleeping with the boss means she finds out a lot more than the hierarchy intend. Pity she doesn't know when to keep her mouth shut.' Dylan put his hand up to his face and stifled a yawn.

'You know what they say. Give them enough rope...'

'Well, at least you wouldn't be called out to that.'

Dylan's frown was visible.

'Sorry.' Jen's apology was hardly heartfelt. 'Will you be able to take time off for the move now?

'Yes, of course,' he said, his eyebrows knotted together. 'The others can hold it together for one day.'

'Good,' she said, a contented smile on her face. 'Because I have a surprise for you.'

'You have?' he said snuggling up behind her.

Dylan's sleep was fitful and he felt drowsy on waking when night turned to day. He vividly remembered waking and writing down a thought or two and he turned his head on the pillow to see the luminous Post-it notes he kept by the side of the bed littering the floor. Jen was snoring softly at his side. Tentatively, he rose, bending over to pick up his notes on his way to the bathroom. Some notes were readable others not, just as some were obvious procedure, others made no sense at all.

# Chapter Nineteen

Dylan's eyes snapped open. He looked at his phone to see there were no messages. He breathed a sigh of relief and set his phone down, then laid his head down on the pillow. Dozing until daylight he heard his phone vibrate and it startled him. Jen stirred beside him. He placed his hand gently on her shoulder, reassuring her as he would a child. She moaned contentedly. He accepted the call.

'I've a young lad in the front office sir. He's telling me he hasn't seen his girlfriend for two days and he thinks she might be the girl who was found yesterday,' said Dave Cracker Craze.

Dylan gently, so as not to disturb Jen, threw his legs over the side of the bed and pulled a pair of socks from the radiator with one hand. 'Can you inform DS Raj, and tell her I'm on my way.'

Jen's eyes flew open to see Dylan staring at her, knowing with certainty that she wouldn't be pleased. 'No,' she shook her head repeatedly. 'Please tell me this is a joke?'

'Sorry, I have to go.'

\*\*\*

Dylan and Raj sat in a warm, windowless interview room at Harrowfield Police Station, opposite a giant of a man who had given a birth date, which led them to believe he was twenty-seven years old. He had broad, muscular shoulders, the sturdy hands of a manual worker; grit under his fingernails and calluses on his knuckles. His shoulder-length hair was curly and his jaw line framed by an unruly beard. For five minutes he sat perfectly still, and didn't speak a word. It was hard to tell if he was scared, drugged, shy, in shock or drunk, although there was no smell of alcohol. He was casually dressed in jeans and a T-shirt that displayed a myriad of small holes to its front.

Raj introduced both herself and Dylan and, although he looked at her briefly when she spoke, it appeared to take him a while to process what she had said. Eventually, he replied eventually with his name.

'Alan Sanderson.'

There appeared to be a sudden change in his demeanour once she used his name in her questioning and DS Raj grasped the opportunity to move on. 'And your address?'

'Flat Four, Wingate Heights.'

DS Raj gave Alan her best reassuring smile when he afforded her a brief glance. 'We understand the reason for you coming to the police station is that you think the dead girl, found yesterday, may be your girlfriend. What makes you think that?'

Alan tapped his foot rhythmically on the linoleum floor. He held his right hand in a fist that he rested on the table that sat in between him and the detectives, and this is where his concentration lay. 'Julie and me, we had a row,' he said raising his dark brown eyes, to meet hers. The emotions he had experienced began creeping back, making it difficult for him to keep his voice from cracking. 'I think she's been seeing somebody.' He wrung his hands. 'No,' he said shaking his head briefly. 'I know she has.' He looked from Raj to Dylan. 'I confronted her. She stormed out.' His voice lowered. 'And she didn't come back.' Unblinking for a moment or two he appeared to hold his breath. He stared passed the officers to the blank wall beyond. He cleared his throat. His face crumpled. Tears sprang into his eyes and his gaze shifted to his hands that were clamped between his legs in a prayer like position. 'I waited, and waited for her to return. I had hope because she hadn't taken any of her things. But, her car is gone...' Emotions overwhelmed him and fighting them only appeared to make it worse.

'What's Julie's surname?' asked Raj.

He took his time in answering. Fighting tears, he swallowed hard. 'Dixon, Julie Ann Dixon.'

'And the car, what make is it?'

Alan's eyebrows knitted together. 'It's a Morris, Mini Classic.'

'Do you know the registration number?'

He closed his eyes briefly, screwed up his face and shook his head slightly. He was hesitant. 'Fifty six H.A.C.'

'Can you describe Julie to me Alan?' said Raj, softly.

The description that followed satisfied Dylan that the dead woman he had seen, was being described through the eyes of someone one who knew her well. Dylan placed the headshot photograph on the table and rotated it to face her boyfriend, Alan flinched and his face looked pained.

'Is this Julie?' Dylan asked.

Head down Alan licked his pale, dry lips. As if in slow motion his jaw dropped, his mouth moved but no words came from within. He brought a hand up to his forehead and tucked a stray tendril of hair behind his ear. His eyes didn't leave the image before him. Eventually, he nodded his head faintly, sighed deeply, lifted his head slightly and briefly shut his eyes so the officers couldn't see them. Tears tumbled down his cheeks. He wiped them away with the flat of his hand. The officers gave him a moment to compose himself.

'I knew it. I knew she was dead,' he sobbed. 'Can you tell if she suffered?' Alan's mouth remained open, his face gravely pale, his body braced in anticipation as he stared into Dylan's eyes.

Dylan's eyebrows furrowed briefly, then his body relaxed and he hunched over. Looking down at the photograph he rubbed its corner between his finger and thumb. 'She was hit on the back of her head with something hard,' he said, 'I am told that Julie would have died instantly.'

'Why?' he said, his words barely a whisper. 'Why?'

'That's our job to find out,' said Dylan.

Alan threw himself back in the chair. Put his hands up to cover his face. 'I wish I hadn't come,' he said through his sobs. 'I didn't want it to be her.' He inhaled deeply through his nostrils, and at last the relief of the exhalation.

'There is a lot of questions we need to ask you but firstly we need to search the flat.'

Adam's expression hardened but his eyes were accepting. 'Of course.'

***

Police search advisor Sergeant Simon Clegg made a primary search of the flat Alan and Julie had shared, and within the hour a full POLSA trained search team were waiting for the instruction to go in.

DI Jack Dylan stepped under the outer cordon crime scene tape. He climbed the littered stairs to the third-floor two at a time, sidestepping the takeaway boxes, waste paper, empty bottles and cans. The stench of urine, stains of which ran down the walls, was overpowering. He rummaged in his pocket, retrieved a mint and popped it into his mouth.

'Detective Inspector Dylan,' he said, flashing his warrant card at Rachael the uniformed police officer who stood guarding the door. There was something different about the young girl but he couldn't figure out what – maybe the beaming smile. The door was ajar the handle hanging, limp. His eyes followed the direction of his pointed finger to a room at the end of a dark, narrow hallway.

'Looks like you've had an unwelcome visitor mate,' said Ned, to Alan. Alan's face held the makings of a smile. 'No,' he said. 'This is how it is.' The detective at the scene's role was to watch Alan Sanderson closely. He remained their prime suspect. One of the reasons for this preliminary visit was to see if there was any evidence of a struggle. Had this the marks of a crime scene? If there had been a struggle however, it would have been hard to tell. Dylan looked and listened, as he walked around the flat alone. Alan chatted to Ned about Julie's family – his earlier reserve apparently forgotten. David Funk stood with Dylan in the lounge, quietly observing all they surveyed.

'Always time to stand and stare,' Dylan said to the CSI. David's eyes were drawn to a dark brown runner that ran the entire length of the room, and the wooden floor it rested upon. He gave Dylan a knowing look, and a nod. Dylan's eyes followed him as he proceeded to chemically test the floor coverings.

'Blood?' Dylan's voice was a whisper. David nodded his head. Standing perfectly still, taking in all that was around him Dylan noticed a lone bare screw in the wall at head height, which suggested to him that that something had been removed. David busily swabbed the floor. When the runner was lifted there was apparent heavy staining on the floorboards and it appeared that there had been some attempt to clean the area. Again, a swab was taken and the chemicals used to test the sample showed that blood was present. Dylan sneezed heartily as they entered the kitchen. 'Bleach,' he said by way of an apology. 'Can't do with the stuff.'

The kitchen by contrast to the rest of the house was spotlessly clean.

'I'm a chef,' said Alan by was of an explanation for the way the kitchen was presented and Ned's obvious surprise. He pulled his T-shirt from his torso at the waist, '...hence these holes where I am permanently rubbing up against the counter – ask Jamie Oliver, it happens to him all the time.' He walked away and Ned followed. David opened the cupboard under the sink. Stuffed behind cleaning products he plucked out a wet, dirty, blood stained cloth. David beckoned Dylan.

'I think I have enough,' Dylan said gravely as he stepped back into the hallway. Alan and Ned turned on hearing Dylan's footsteps approach them from behind 'We've found blood on the floor and carpet runner. Underneath the runner there appears to have been an attempt to try to clean it up. A blood-stained cloth has been located under the kitchen sink. A check will be made to see if this is Julie's blood. Tell me, did your argument with Julie result in her being injured enough to bleed?'

Alan's face looked shocked. 'No, no way!' Dylan could see the whites of his eyes. 'I've never hit a woman in my life.' He held up his right hand, which was clenched in a tight fist for Dylan to see. 'If I had she wouldn't have lived to tell...'

'Nobody else lives here?' said Dylan.

Alan swayed, and steadied himself with his hand flat to the wall. 'I don't believe this...' His head bent forward, he made throaty gurgling noises before falling to his knees. 'This can't be happening,' he said, hand to his chest as he fought for his breath.

Dylan reached down and held Alan Sanderson by the scruff of the neck. 'Alan Sanderson I am arresting you on suspicion of murder...'

'What? You've got it wrong.' Alan sobbed as he was handcuffed and removed from the flat to the police car, to be transported by a marked police car to Harrowfield Bridewell, to be detained.

'The flat,' said Dylan to David and Simon, '...it needs going over with a fine tooth comb. Find me evidence to show she was murdered here.' His head turned this way and that. 'And I suppose telling you to find me the murder weapon too, is too much to ask?'

Simon gave Dylan a lopsided smile. 'We'll do our best.'

Dylan gave David a pat on his back before turning his attention to DS Raj.

'Can I leave it with you to get the house-to-house team from Ops Support to visit the occupants of the other flats; interview them, see what they can tell us, and circulate the details of her vehicle. If we can find that it'd be helpful.'

Raj nodded towards the door.

'I'll have to go. I should've been at the mortuary for her post-mortem ten minutes ago,' Dylan said checking his watch. 'We'll meet after to exchange notes,' were his parting words.

Dylan started the car, turned on the hands free facility and dialled the incident room to ensure that there had been an exhibits officer nominated for the mortuary and another CSI other than David had been booked to attend.

Everyone was present at the mortuary when he arrived. DC Donna Frost was the first to greet him and as he stepped into his coveralls she tugged at his sleeve. 'They've found a donor card at the flat, sir.'

'Have you informed the Coroner's Officer?'

'Yes.'

'He'll speak to the Coroner, but sadly I doubt very much considering the length of time, that her organs would be of any use. It's also vital that this examination goes ahead to ascertain her cause of death... Not only that but she will have to be kept for a future defence examination, even if a suspect isn't found within the next few weeks or so. Who's her next of kin, is it known?'

'I'm told her mother sir. We are trying to trace her.'

At that moment the thin, five foot nine, grey bearded, ex police officer, now Coroner's Officer walked into the room where Dylan was putting on his theatre gown. Geoff Painter looked gaunt. He slicked back his thick silver hair, which drew more attention to his long, thin face. 'The Coroner will make reference to her wishes at the inquest. However, the post-mortem is to go ahead.' He put on his head covering and pulled his mask up to rest on the bridge of his nose as he followed Dylan and Donna into the mortuary theatre.

The pathologist was an accomplished middle-aged man by the name of William Townsend, whose demand of military-like discipline, and haughty manner proceeded him from those previously under his command in the army health care team. It was said that the doctor had survived a severe leg wound in Afghanistan, and indeed he walked with a stiff knee. Stood by his side was one of his students from the university where he taught. The student had just failed the spelling of syphilis and Dr Townsend rewarded her with one of his withering glares. A bead of sweat slid from the student's forehead and down the side of her pretty face. He stood at the far side of the aesthetically pleasing, slim pedestal, stainless steel autopsy table and continued his brutal questioning with what looked like savage glee. Embarrassing the young student was unnecessary in Dylan's eyes and he tried to detract the doctor's attention by announcing his presence and offering to introduce his staff, and following that he outlined the circumstances surrounding the discovery of the dead body of the young woman laid out on the table before them. The student threw Dylan a grateful look for his chivalrous attempt to save her further torture. Townsend hobbled around the table. The dead girl's clothing was removed item by item, each being bagged and tagged by the exhibits officer. Each exhibit numbered and a police exhibit label attached for future reference. Transfer of fibres was likely from outer garments so tapings were taken.

'We believe the body to be that of a Julie Dixon, although a positive identification needs yet to be made,' Dylan said. Townsend snuggled alongside the table. As he did so he spoke into a hand-held voice recorder externally examining the naked body with a general description, ethnicity, sex, age, hair colour and length, whilst looking for distinguishing features such as birthmarks, old scar tissue, moles. Bending slightly he could see that the body block had been correctly situated enabling the dead young woman's arms and neck to fall backwards, whilst stretching and pushing the chest upwards to make it easier for him to cut it open. Photographs of bruising noticed to the left side of her face and arms were taken.

'We think that we also might have found the murder scene. Within the last hour the boyfriend has been arrested on suspicion of her murder. Although he strenuously denies it and any knowledge of the blood found in their flat,' said the senior police officer.

He turned to the student. 'Miss Case, what would I be looking for now?' he said, collecting several insects, bugs and leaves and placing them in containers. There was no evidence of animals scavenging on the body, although Dylan was aware that smaller animals may have got to some of the soft tissue.

Kate Case's voice wobbled. 'Evidence, such as residue, flakes of paint or any other material that could be collected from the external surfaces of the body sir.'

Dr Townsend pursed his lips and nodded his head. 'If I was to use an ultraviolet light in a post-mortem when would I use it?' Again his question was directed at his student.

'Now sir.'

His eyes narrowed and there was a sense he was waiting for more. His nostrils widened on a deep breath.

Kate's gloved hand went to her chest, and her eye lashes flickered. 'To search the body surface for any evidence not easily visible to the naked eye. If it was believed that there may be any significant residue on the hands, for instance gunpowder, a separate bag would have been put around each hand and taped around the wrist.'

'What samples should I take at this time?'

'Fingernail and under nail scrapings, hair, foreign and pubic in cases of suspected sexual assault.'

'Good,' Dr Townsend said. His shoulders visibly relaxed and on turning his head he nodded to the mortuary assistant indicating that he was about to start the internal examination.

Dylan sucked hard on the strong mint that had been resting on the roof of his mouth. As his sinuses cleared he smelt the aroma of a menthol vapour rub and he knew that it was a practice others used around the entrance of their nostrils, as a shield against death's stench.

The pathologist made a large, deep Y-shaped incision, starting at the top of each shoulder, meeting at the lower part of the sternum and continued down to the pelvic bone making the mandatory diversion to the left side of the naval.

He stopped, once more he spoke directly to Kate Case. 'Why would I choose this method over a T-shaped incision or a single vertical cut?'

Kate stood straight and spoke with more confidence. 'Essential in cases of suspected strangulation, sir.'

His eyes opened wide and he continued without comment, peeling back the slab of skin, unveiling the mustard-coloured layer of fat and the pink and purplish viscera underneath. He opened the chest cavity and removed the organs in one block. 'When would I adopt this method as the norm?' Dr Townsend asked Kate.

'During the autopsies of infants this method is used most of the time, sir.'

Townsend nodded. 'Generally, in an adult where the cause of death is unknown I would remove the organs one by one checking for?'

'Abnormalities or disease, sir,' said Kate.

A series of cuts were made, along the vertebral column and the organs were detached and pulled out in one piece. They were weighed and sliced for examination, the pathologist looking all the while for clues suggesting foul play, discolouration of tissue, other bruising and wounds. Tissue samples were collected and retained as the clicking of the CSI's camera continued to record every action.

The examination of the head injury Julie Dixon had sustained was thorough and included the taking of numerous photographs. Her head was shaved and revealed a large depressed wound, almost twenty-five centimetres square. It was apparent that this injury had shattered her skull.

Townsend stood with his bloodied, gloved hands aloft whilst the body block that was previously used to elevate the chest was moved, to elevate the head and enable the brain to be examined. An incision was made from behind ear to ear, over the crown of the head.

'You won't notice that when it's sewn up and the head is rested on a pillow for the viewing of her body by the family,' said Townsend. He pulled the scalp away from the skull in two flaps. The front flap going over the face, remaining secured by the tip of the nose. The final act of cutting into the top of the skull with a circular bladed saw created a cap that was pulled off, exposing the brain to be observed in situ. It was covered in blood.

At the end of the post-mortem Dr Townsend lowered his mask. His eyes were red rimmed. Dylan noticed his voice and manner had changed towards Kate Case as his respect for her grew.

'What makes a good pathologist Case,' William Townsend said.

'I think a crucial attribute of a good pathologist is a strong visual memory and a talent for pattern recognition.'

'Mmm...'

'And, you're favourite pathology textbook?'

'Robbins sir, Kaplan sucks, it focuses too much on detail.'

A smile escaped his lips. 'Well done!' he said, 'Well done indeed.'

Kate Case's eyes were wide. Townsend turned to face Dylan. 'I've taken all the relevant samples you will require. Cause of death, blunt instrument trauma to the skull causing massive damage. She would have been rendered unconscious immediately, and died shortly after. Something the size of a lump hammer would be of the right size and weight, in my opinion.'

'Not an injury she could have sustained from a fall?' said Dylan.

'Certainly not.'

'Then I thank you. Once her mum has been traced we can go ahead with a formal identification.'

William Townsend walked down the corridor. Kate Case hurriedly followed him. 'Sir, sir, sir,' Dylan heard her say. Eventually he stopped at the office door and turned. 'The mark on her right breast, do you think that it could have possibly been a bite?' Townsend dismissed her question with a wave of his hand as he turned and walked through the office door, letting it shut on his student. She took a step backwards, squeezed her eyes shut and pressed the palms of her hands against her eyelids. Dylan shrugged his shoulders, and smiled at her face that looked skywards, her muttering not audible. When she heard Dylan's tittering down the corridor she looked and saw him point in the direction Townsend had gone. 'Go on,' he said. 'You don't seem to be the type to give up that easy.'

The searches and examination at Julie Dixon's flat that she had shared with her boyfriend Alan Sanderson continued Dylan was told on his return to Harrowfield Police Station; as were the examination in and around the wheelie bins where her body had been found, and the location of her vehicle was still outstanding.

DS's Raj and Andy Wormald had completed the first interview with Alan Sanderson for the murder of his girlfriend, on his arrival at the station. Dylan was told Sanderson's solicitor was Janet Munroe who had listened intently to what the officers had to say and made notes throughout the interview. Not once did she interrupt them. To allow Ms Munroe further consultation with her client the officers joined Dylan in his office. The Detective Inspector's stern face greeted the two rather grim and pensive-faced detectives.

'The results of the post-mortem confirmed to us that Julie Dixon died from a blow to her head. We are looking for some object the size and weight of a lump hammer,' Dylan said. 'What's he saying?'

'He tells us that he last saw his girlfriend around six o'clock on the morning she went missing. He admits they argued. He thought she'd been seeing someone behind his back and was fearful she was about to leave him,' said Raj.

'But, he denied that he knew about the blood in the flat or any knowledge of the bloodied cloth that was found under the sink,' said Andy firmly.

'When she didn't come home that night he says, he thought she might have gone to stay at her mother's,' said Raj.

Dylan leant a little forward. 'Had she done that before?'

Raj frowned. She shook her head slightly. 'No, he said not.'

'When he watched the news, he said he just knew instinctively it was his girlfriend who had been found dead.'

'Which is when he came to the police station.'

'Yes, the last thing he expected was to be locked up.'

'Any previous convictions?'

'No, he's of good character; works twelve hour shifts, seven till seven at the dye works.'

'So, what's your initial thoughts now you've spoken to him?'

Raj raised her eyebrows. 'Well, there's no doubt he's genuinely very upset.' She stopped and grimaced. 'But, we've seen it all before and they could be crocodile tears. It's too soon to tell.'

'What do you think Andy?'

'We haven't got under his ribs yet. Once we start asking searching questions, who knows, we might see another side of him.'

Dylan sighed. 'You're going into a second interview shortly and I'm considering the storage of the exhibits.' He raised a pointed finger. 'One, we have to consider the items seized from the area where she was found as the dump site and two, other items seized from the house. We must avoid any chance of contamination, thereby negating the inference at a future Court case.

The phone was ringing in the outside office, as if someone was refusing to accept that there was nobody there to take the call. Raj stood, opened the office door and headed towards it. 'I'll put whoever it is out of their misery shall I?' she said to Ned who, headphones removed at her hurried appearance from the bosses office, threw his arms in the air.

'Do I have to do everything?' he cried.

Raj scowled at him as she proceeded to pick up. 'Make yourself useful and put the kettle on,' she snapped. Ned slid off his chair and dragged his feet across the floor, hoisting his baggy trousers up by the belt. He mumbled through his teeth. 'I'm supposed to be listening to the transcript... Put a broom up my arse and I'll sweep up on my way...'

Raj was sat back in Dylan's office when Ned brought in the coffee. 'Julie Dixon's car has been located at Ogden I've just been told,' he said. 'To all intents and purpose it appears to have been driven nose first into the reservoir. But, as luck would have it, it's only two-thirds submerged and the rear end of the car, is visible. If it was someone's intention to sink it fully, they've failed miserably.'

Dylan stood and whipped a cup from the tray Ned was holding. He took a mouthful of the hot beverage and grimaced at its bitterness. 'Ned, get your coat,' he said, swallowing hard. 'We're off fishing.'

Ned pulled a face but unquestioningly he put the tray down on Dylan's desk, and left the room.

Dylan turned to Raj and Andy. 'At least the vehicle isn't a burnt out shell. Are uniform in attendance?'

Raj nodded. 'Stoneywood Motors have been called to recover it, and officers from the Marine Unit are on en route.'

Dylan put on his suit jacket and shrugged an arm into his all weather overcoat. 'Ned,' he shouted, seeing him talking to the typist. 'Get a move on!' Dylan scowled as he walked past Ned's desk in the CID office, where the DC was now exchanging arrangements for a drink after work.

'You'll need your weatherproofs,' Dylan said, his face like stone. 'I'll see you at the car.'

As Ned leant in to whisper in the typist's ear he turned towards Dylan, and lifted his chin by way of acknowledgement. A few minutes later the DC emerged from the CID office door smiling broadly and carrying a lightweight jacket stuffed under his arm. Dylan shook his head, started the car engine and rolled the vehicle alongside Ned who had stopped to answer his mobile phone. 'Get in,' he said abruptly. The detective constable did as he was told and pocketed his phone. With a nod of his head Dylan pointed at his cotton jacket. 'What the hell's that, and where's your boots?'

'It'll be reet,' Ned said with a lopsided grin. 'I'm from Yorkshire!'

Dylan's jaw muscles tightened. 'You'll catch your bloody death,' he said.

***

Ogden Water car park was positioned high above the beauty spot, from where the public were rewarded with magnificent views of the woodland trails and waterside paths. From the confines of the car Dylan could see the wind ruffling the water in the thirty-four acre reservoir that was enclosed by woodland, with open moor beyond. He was unusually quiet, appearing to Ned to be in a world of his own. The detective constable was grateful for Dylan's distraction, and respected his silence knowing police protocol would be running through his head. Should anything go wrong with this procedure there was only one place the blame would fall, and that was at the senior detective's feet. Dylan was instantly aware of the grouping of the police recovery personnel. As Dylan and Ned simultaneously opened the car doors to alight their car the noise of the recovery vehicle's engine in the distance, roared to life. Its distinctive sound at the positioning of the lorry loader crane being guided into place, for the recovery of the casualty vehicle could be heard very loud and clear. The two detectives crossed the shingled car park, their footwear making a crunching sound on the gravel-sized stones. The blue and white 'do not cross' crime scene tape signified the nature reserve's entrance and exit to the locality could be seen happily flapping this way and that, in the cool breeze that came off the water. A blur of movement on the sun kissed water drew Dylan's attention to the Marine Unit. The rear transit van doors were wide open and their personnel unloaded their equipment at the water's edge expediently. From the shingled ridged car park the two detectives ambled downwards, over tree stumps and fallen branches in their path through the dense part of the wood. The sight of a woodpecker drilling the damp ground for worms caught Dylan's keen eye. Two grey squirrels ran across his path and directly up a tree, at which point he had an overwhelming urge to voice what he'd seen, as he would if he'd been with Jen and Maisy. Instead he kept his head down and navigated the damp, dark, woodchip path that was surrounded by tall trees that filtered the light. A drip of cold water dropped on his head and ran down his neck making him shiver. He took his gloves out of his pocket and pulling them on his cold hands and he continued to walk briskly in front of a cursing Ned as he stumbled and slid his way towards the reservoir. The temperature dropped noticeably as they descended nearer to the water's edge. The woodland birds could be heard long before they were seen. Twigs snapped and drier leaves crackled under foot. Once through the woods that surrounded the large body of water the detectives came across a wooden stile. The ground surrounding it was wet and boggy. Dylan trudged through the mud and over the stile knowing there had been shoes, socks and dignity lost here before. He knew Ogden Water and its surrounding moorland well. From child-to-man it had been a regular haunt of his, and his siblings. A place of peace and quiet as he grew; a haven to visit, to think and reflect. As a youngster he recalled trudging over the moors from The Station House in ill-fitting wellington boots that chaffed his legs, for he never wore socks. He tapped his pocket as he walked towards the circus and half expected a bottle of water and a jam sandwich to be there, as it was in those days.

Dylan found CSI David Funk at the top of the slipway suited and booted for the job in hand, and the elements. Here it was all shadow and light – the result of the cold wind that blew off the water, through the surrounding trees. This cordoned-off scene was a hive of activity. Everyone working as one in a well-rehearsed recovery in a timely fashion. He was aware, as were the others that they were losing light fast. Three police officers stood in the shallow, murky waters talking to a colleague who was submerged to his shoulders. The diver had his face mask firmly in place, looking to all intent and purpose like a seal, due to his professional attire. Quickly he confirmed to all those present that he could see no one inside the vehicle.

All eyes were diverted as a shout went up, and a hand of another diver flayed near to the vehicle. 'No airbags required,' he called. Dylan looked down to the yellow lift bags that would remain on dry land.

The winch line from the recovery vehicle was attached to the casualty vehicle. Slowly it was winched back to shore. On doing so water spewed from every gap, hole, vent, crack, cavity and groove. CSI David Funk took picture, after picture as the vehicle slowly approached dry land. Once placed upon the slide bed, the four wheels were strapped down. A diver tried to open the rear van doors, which he found to be unlocked. He opened them wide. Inside were two packages both wrapped in a grey plastic bags. The driver continued to traverse the outside of the vehicle. He opened the driver's door, and then the passenger's. Again, he confirmed that it was beyond doubt that anyone had been trapped inside the vehicle when it had been driven into the water. What Dylan did see, and was of interest to him as he looked through the windows of the van was an engineer's lump hammer, with a hardwood handle, in the passenger side footwell.

It appeared to Dylan that David Funk saw the tool at the same time as he. Their eyes met. 'Photograph and seize the hammer and the parcels.' Dylan said without hesitation. 'I'll see you with them back at the nick.'

David nodded. 'Yes sir.'

The six foot six recovery vehicle driver dressed in navy blue overalls stomped through the mud towards Dylan. The squelching sound of his heavy, steel toe-capped boots became louder and louder the nearer he approached them on the concrete slipway.

'Good job George,' said Dylan raising his voice over the sound of the vehicle's engine.

George looked over his shoulder as the blue tarpaulin was placed over the van. The number plates were covered with black tape.

George stood directly in front of Dylan. 'Aye and a bit quicker than last time. A submerged car, in five metres of water, fingertip search; took us two days to recover the vehicle. Do you remember?'

'I remember it well. Hence why I came prepared this time,' Dylan said pulling his thick wool coat around him and glancing down at his boots.

George nodded his head towards Ned who was limping towards them in his bare feet, carrying his sodden shoes. 'You could have warned him. He'll catch his bloody death.'

'I told him. And if he rings in sick tomorrow I'll be dragging him into work by his ears.'

Ned's feet were covered in mud. His trousers rolled up to the knee. His cheeks were white in an unshaven face; his nose red, his eyes watering. He shook his head in seeming confusion about how to form the words. 'Everyone knows you can't catch a cold by being cold.' His tut was followed by one sneeze, two, three.

George shook his head slowly from side to side. 'Sneezing three times amounts to pneumonia in my gran's book,' he teased, with the wink of an eye.

Dylan chuckled. 'Can you take the vehicle to the Collision Investigation Unit? I need it drying out so we can get it forensically examined as soon as possible.'

At the calling of him by his aide George shook Dylan's hand, turned quickly on his heels and walked away at a pace. 'Will do. Give me a shout if you need anything else,' he shouted.

Ned's attention was on the neatly tarpaulin wrapped car. He had a puzzled look upon his cold-worn face – as if he were finding it hard to think straight. 'Highly likely it was used to transport Julie Dixon's body, don't you think?' Dylan could hear the detective's teeth chattering.

There was a lot of banging and slamming of doors. The men turned to see the Unit's transit van being reloaded with their equipment.

'Highly likely, as you well know DC Granger is not good enough, we need hard evidence,' said Dylan lifting his hand in acknowledgement of those leaving the scene.

Ned stumbled putting one cold foot in front of the other precariously as they ambled back into the woods. At the woodland side of the stile he replaced his socks and shoes and climbed upwards behind Dylan, towards the car park. Several times Dylan caught him rubbing his hands together, snivelling or wiping his eyes with the cuff of his sleeve. 'If you ask me I think she was killed in the flat, transported to the dump site by her killer in the van, and then the killer attempted to get rid of it so we've no evidence to prove what took place.'

'Maybe, but what puzzles me is why the killer didn't leave her in the vehicle if the plan was to drive it in the reservoir in the first place?' said Dylan when they reached the car.

'It's obvious!' said Ned with a raise of his eyebrows. 'Something happened to make him panic. Wouldn't we all if we had a corpse in the back of our vehicle?'

\*\*\*

The removal van stuttered at the steepness of the driveway that led from The Station House, just as the sun was going down. The driver tooted its horn, and him and his crew smiled and waved at the children happily playing on the tree swing that Uncle Charlie had made. Dylan's youngest sister Dawn, always the tomboy, stood at the front door and whistled a high pitched whistle through her teeth, beckoning the children to return to the house. Ronnie nudged Charlie who in an attempt to secure a new pane of glass to the front window had kneaded the putty into a pliable lump and was presently rolling it into precise pencil-sized strips, when the children ran past.

'Remind you of anyone?' he said with a smile on his ruddy face at the two eldest elbowed each other for prime position.

Jen tottered down the stair steps, squinting up into the singular light bulb that hung from an old knotted flex in the middle of the hallway ceiling. She dropped the empty box she was carrying onto the floor and proceeded to flatten it with a determined foot. Wiping her brow with the back of her hand she stopped on hearing the thudding of footsteps running down the ginnel, which led between The Station House and the outbuildings. Maisy was the first of the girls to rushed through the front door giggling as if she was fit to burst. Her wellington boots covered in mud, she carried a rusty, red bucket and spade in her hand. Her trousers were ripped at the knee, her arms open wide to her mother. Max in tow was wagging his tail with such excitement that his entire rear end was gyrating. Oval eyed, ears down he stared at the little girl as he jumped around, making short high-pitched little barks. The collective noise grew to a crescendo, and then whimpered out to a silence as the three girls stopped, breathless, arms secured tightly around Jen's legs and waist. Max not to be left out nudged and muzzled instead. Jen put her hand on her daughter's head and picked from her hair a white feather – tears sprung to her eyes. She held it tightly between her finger and thumb. 'Mum,' she said softly. Maisy looked up, her eyes bright, her chubby hands and smiling face smudged with dirt.

Ronnie followed the leaner Charlie out of the lounge. He held a putty knife high in his hand. 'All secure for now,' he said with a smile. He stood perfectly still, sighed and with eyes staring he looked up to the ceiling and surveyed all around him. 'By 'eck lass,' he said his eyes settling upon her face. 'I never thought I'd see the day that we'd be together again in this house.' His arms swept the line of the next generations of the Dylan clan who continued to fuss around the youngest, Maisy who was sat in the middle of the floor.

Kirsty appeared at the door of the dining room. In full make-up, a mop cap covering her shiny chestnut hair. She held the handle of a broom looking as if she had just stepped off the set of Upstairs Downstairs. In contrast, curly-haired Dawn was make-up free, wore khaki trousers, her shirt sleeves rolled up at the elbows and she had a scarf tired around her head, like a land girl.

'Well, most people would have fussed about the damp and baulked over the roof, never mind about the decay. I've got to hand it to you for tackling the old place Jen. When's our Dylan due home?' she said.

Jen shrugged her shoulders, a tired, accepting smile upon her face. 'Your guess is as good as mine but there's one thing for sure he's going to be shocked to see you guys,' she grinned.

Kirsty nodded towards the white feather still in Jen's hand. 'You believe in angels,' she said matter-of-fact.

Jen smiled 'I do,' she said, her face assuming a dreamy expression. She looked at her sister-in-law closely.

'I collected them in a jam jar when I was a child.' She smiled with a faraway look in her eyes.

A shuffle of boots and six foot, balding Ronnie put his dusty hand around Jen's shoulder and gave it a hearty squeeze. 'We might not be a family who lives in each other's pockets lass but we're alas here for each other, just you remember that.'

Jen swallowed the lump that had appeared in her throat. She looked across at Charlie. 'And I can't thank you enough,' she said softly. 'If it hadn't been for you... Well, I don't know what we'd have done. How're you doing with that stud wall?' she said quickly in an attempt to rein in her emotions.

Ronnie looked across at his brother, who in turn looked over his shoulder towards the kitchen door. 'We're ready to break through.'

Jen's eyes were wide. 'Can we wait for Dylan?'

\*\*\*

DS Raj walked into the interview room behind Janet Munroe, Alan Sanderson and A/DS Andy Wormald. With some persuasion the heavy fire door closed slowly behind her, and she secured it shut. Andy sat down next to the recording machine and looked up to check the video camera was working. Raj positioned herself next to him, opposite the prisoner and his solicitor. The small, soundproofed room was quiet, its occupants silent and still, critical for the recording quality but challenging to obtain due to the proximity of other rooms in the police station. The force issue, abuse-resisting furniture was adequate but not comfortable by any stretch of the imagination. After relevant formalities were concluded, including everyone introducing themselves for the requirement of voice recognition, the interview commenced.

'You are probably aware that enquiries are continuing whilst you are in custody.'

The wide-set eyes of the prisoner were round and staring and showed no expression, and the skin on his face looked to be stretched tight, and without emotion.

'I can confirm to you that Julie died from a single blow to the back of her head. We also know that where she was found, is not where she was killed,' said Raj.

The prisoner's eyes were wide open, transfixed – cold and dead.

'You are aware that we found blood on the floor in the hallway of your flat, and on a cloth, in a cupboard beneath the sink in the kitchen of your home? Further examination of the flat shows blood splashings on the hallway wall. Tests on that blood are being carried out, and your flat that you shared with Julie is now under intense scrutiny. We are told that it is highly likely this is where Julie was attacked. Is there something you're not sharing with us Alan?'

Alan Sanderson's face was a white mask. His eyes were on Raj's lips.

'Do you understand what Detective Sergeant Rajinder Uppal is saying to you?' said Andy.

Sanderson cast a bewildered look at Andy. 'I told you,' he said in his low, hypnotic monotone voice. 'She was absolutely fine when I last saw her. I would never, ever hurt her, I couldn't. I told you we argued. I was sure she was seeing someone else.' He shrugged his shoulders helplessly, put his head down and shook it from side to side. 'She denied it, but she was.' His head dropped lower and he stared at his hands. 'She had this bite,' his eyes looked upwards. 'On her left… her left breast.' He swallowed. 'And, I know I didn't do it.'

Andy looked at Sanderson with renewed interest. 'So, you were angry, really angry, that's understandable. Did you lose your temper?'

Sanderson closed his eyes and shook his lowered head again. His voice petered out to a whisper. 'No, no, I didn't hurt her. I loved her.'

Andy readjusted his relaxed seating position to sit up right. He leant forward and duly rested his forearms on the table. 'Just you and Julie live at the flat don't you?' said Andy, his lips forming a straight line.

Sanderson looked up, his staring eyes narrowed. 'I've already told you that.'

Andy put his hands flat on the table. 'Okay, we deal in facts. And the facts tell us that someone has attempted to clean blood up from the floor in the hallway of your flat; where we believe your girlfriend was attacked. She was found dead elsewhere but there is no sign of a break in. What do you expect us to think?'

Sanderson's face crumpled. 'It wasn't me. I swear on my mother's life, it wasn't me,' he cried.

'My problem is believing that if it was a stranger who had killed Julie, creating such a blood bath in your house why would they bother cleaning up afterwards and removing her body?' Andy pushed.

Sanderson threw his arms up in the air. 'How am I suppose to know? You're the bloody detective!'

'We know Julie wasn't killed where she was found, but that's what someone may have been trying to have us believe,' said Raj.

'How many times do I have to say it? It wasn't me. Why don't you believe me?'

Raj cleared her throat. Her arms were crossed loosely on her lap. 'Alan, do you know the area around Shroggs Grove?'

Sanderson signed deeply. 'Yes, one of my schoolmates lived there. We played football most Saturdays in Shroggs Park.'

Andy's eyes narrowed, watching for any indications in his body language that he was lying. Raj continued the line of questioning.

'Do you know Ogden Reservoir?'

Sanderson's face was sombre. 'Yeah, of course I do. If you've been to the flat you'll have seen pictures of me and Julie walking over Pendle Hill from Driver Height. We'd always stop at the kissing gate...' Emotion got the better of him and he swallowed as a lone tear fell onto his cheek. He wiped it away with the cuff of his sleeve.

'You see, Julie's vehicle has been pulled out of the reservoir today.'

Sanderson's eyes showed more than a hint of disbelief. 'No, no way!' He looked confused. 'And you think I would do that? Why would I?' His hysterical laugh turned into uncontrollable crying. Janet Munroe raised a hand.

'I think its time for a break,' she said with a look of concern for her client on her face. She offered him a tissue.

***

The incident room was buzzing with police personnel offering their theories. Everyone was under pressure to complete their personal task in hand, to achieve the shared goal – the conviction of a murderer. CSI Sarah Jarvis, senior at Flat 4, Wingate Heights, the home of the deceased Julie Dixon and her boyfriend Alan Sanderson opened the debrief. 'Based on our findings sir, I am confident that Flat 4 is where Julie was attacked. The samples of blood we took from hallway floor were sufficient to have soaked through the rug. I am confident that this will also match Julie's DNA profile. On the ceiling, and on the walls, we have not only found splashes of blood but also minute bits of flesh. The pattern of the evidence follows the action of the attacker striking the victim and then pulling the weapon back above his, or her head intending to strike again. In this case, there was no need to render a second blow. One blow had been sufficient to kill her. We have found traces of blood on a damp cloth, secreted in the cupboard beneath kitchen sink, and further traces of blood have been found in the U-bend of the same. I have no doubt someone has attempted to clean up after the event, but not sufficiently to conceal what took place.'

Dylan thanked the CSI. 'And I believe the scene is still sealed should we need to revisit?'

Jarv nodded her head.

Dylan turned to Raj and Andy. 'What's Alan Sanderson saying in interview?'

Raj took the lead, 'Well he's talking to us, which is a step in the right direction. Whether he's telling us the truth, only time will tell. He tells us he works long hours, twelve-hour shifts, and although the money's good Julie didn't like being home alone. In recent weeks she's been helping a friend out, which apparently she enjoyed, and this meant she has become less needy. He swears he has no knowledge of the blood in the flat and denies the cleaning up. He is adamant that the last time he saw Julie was on the morning of the day she was murdered at approximately half past six, before he went to work. He claims that they argued due to the fact he believed she was seeing someone else.'

'And has he any evidence to substantiate that?' said Dylan.

'No, and she denied it. But, he says he saw a bite mark on her left breast.' Raj raised her eyebrows.

'And he hadn't done that to her?'

Raj shook her head. 'He says not sir.'

Dylan turned a few pages over in his notebook, scribbled a few words and when he looked up. He was still frowning. 'That's interesting because no bite mark to her breast was recorded in the pathologist's report. We'll have her body re-examined as a matter of urgency.'

'Sanderson admits knowing his way around Shroggs. Ogden Water was a place of interest to him and her.'

Dylan sighed and turned towards Andy. 'Your thoughts?'

'In all the interviews he hasn't changed his story and, you know what, I actually believe him sir. But I'd be interested to see if we found her blood on his clothing... He has a valid excuse for it being on the soles of his shoes because he admits walking over the rug after she went missing.'

Dylan was thoughtful. 'What's your take on him Raj?'

'Honestly? I'm not sure. If he did kill her in anger, carry her body from the flat to her vehicle, dump her behind the wheelie bins then go onto drive her vehicle in the reservoir, wouldn't we expect to find wet shoes, damp clothes etcetera in his possession?' Raj screwed up her face. 'And, would he come and report her missing so quickly after the event?'

'Why would he not leave her in her vehicle?' said Donna.

'Exactly! And whilst all the evidence we have available to us points to him, some things just don't add up,' said Raj.

David Funk put his head around the door, 'Can I come in sir?' he said.

Dylan eagerly beckoned him. 'Have you got an update?'

'I do, yes sir,' he said. 'The parcels in the back of Julie's vehicle contained drugs. In one we found two blue Tesla pills, a new blend of dangerously strong MDMA tablets that's so potent Gary Warner tells me I'd need a self-driving car to get me home safely after taking a hit, assuming that nothing worse happens to me first.

The other, hash disguised as tea. Regional Crime are getting the necessary tests done on both, but his initial reaction considering the packaging is that they are linked to their target dealer.'

Dylan sat back in his chair. 'Dealing on the Darknet?'

'Drugs in the post – bought with Bitcoin, the latest way to pay cash over the Internet. Yes, I believe that's what RCS are looking at.'

'Okay, so in the first instance we need to get a twelve hour extension for Sanderson's detention. Second, I want us to look into both Julie and Alan's backgrounds, relations and friends. Thirdly, we need to visit his place of work. Fourthly, some of you may not be aware but in the footwell, on the passenger side of Julie's van we also found a lump hammer. This could be our murder weapon and as you just heard David also took possession of a couple of undelivered packages that were in the back of vehicle.'

'Where's the vehicle now sir?' said Donna.

Dylan lifted his arm, pulled his shirt sleeve back and squinted at his watch. 'Right now, it should be on a vehicle skate at CIU so that it can be moved around easier once the recovery guys have left.'

Donna nodded. 'And once it's dried out we can examine it properly.'

'Yes.' Dylan turned his attention to Raj. 'I hear what you're saying about there being no wet clothing to be found at the flat...'

'And, if the murderer drove the vehicle into the reservoir, and the lump hammer is the murder weapon wouldn't you think that he, or she would have thrown it into the middle of the reservoir knowing the sinking van had failed to submerge?' Raj frowned.

'Valid point. But, we're sat here with a relatively clear mind, trying to make sense of the actions of a person who might have been in a blind panic, attempting to get rid of evidence as quickly as possible, and maybe worried about being caught. Hindsight is a wonderful thing,' said Jarv.

'Although he has given himself a motive, if he did believe like he said that she had been seeing someone. Do you think he knew about the drugs?'

Dylan slapped the palm of his hand down on his desk. 'Okay, it's late. I'm certain Gary will be in touch re the RCS drugs enquiry as soon as he has anything to discuss with me. In the meantime continue with priority enquiries, and I'll call the Coroner's Officer to get the pathologist to revisit Julie's body to confirm or negate what Sanderson is saying about the bite.'

'If there are marks on her breast then presumably it reinforces his motive,' said Donna.

'Mmm... Leave off interviewing him further until we have more to put to him.' A shrewd light entered Dylan's tired eyes. 'Raj, just out of interest see if the automatic number plate recognition system picked up her vehicle on the day she went missing.'

# Chapter Twenty

Dylan put his key into The Station House door lock, under the cover of darkness, with the ease of someone who had done it a thousand times before. He pushed it open as quietly as he could, but he knew somehow it would squeak anyway. Startled by a familiar low-pitched roar, 'like the sound of the ocean' in a conch shell, he glanced over his shoulder into the still, starless, night sky. Above his head he saw a horde of bats fluttering, like butterflies. Hearing the tiny, flicking sound of their wings brushing against other bats and against the walls of the surrounding buildings, he stood perfectly still, head up with his back to the door and closed his eyes trying to search his mind for answers... When he opened his eyes a few moments later it was quiet and there was no moon coming through the clouds. Now he could hear little unseen creatures rustling around in the leaf litter, and then came the expected hooting of the owls. Dylan turned, stepped over the threshold and shut the door slowly, behind him. He entered the kitchen. But, not being privy to the whereabouts of the crockery and cutlery he fumbled around in a cupboard or two, and then gave up on making himself a warm drink. Instead he opened the fridge door and tugged out a can of lager from the pack of four. Dylan stood at the sink with a furrowed brow, pulled the ring-pull and put the open can to his craving mouth. He swallowed its contents in one making tears appear in his eyes. He burped and drew his hand across his mouth. Setting the empty can down on the drainer, he crept up the stairs in a zombie-like fashion, stumbled into the bedroom and kicked off his shoes at the side of the bed.

'Where have you been?' Jen said sleepily as she watched him step out of his trousers. He put his finger to his lips and lifted the duvet gently. Sneaking under the covers he felt Jen's warm body open up to him. His feet were freezing cold and Jen gave a little squeal, which brought a little smile to his face.

'I'm sorry I wasn't here to help. Did the move go okay?' Dylan's eyelids were quick to close.

'There is so much to tell you. Charlie, your brother, he brought Ronnie, Kirsty, Dawn and the kids to help, and Maisy had the time of her life... And, the room that your dad used for his photography, you know the one that you thought was missing? Well, Charlie and Ronnie think that maybe it's in the kitchen behind the stud wall. That, they say should offer space under the staircase...' She stopped to feel Dylan's soft, regular breathing on her face and knew that they were the breaths of a man who was fast asleep. How much he had heard she was unsure.

\*\*\*

'You're in early!' said a jovial Vicky. 'Wet the bed?'

'Funny,' said Dylan showing her his deadpan face.

In return Vicky showed him her bottom lip. 'Want a cuppa?'

'If its black and strong,' he said. 'Truth is there's only one place I want to be, and that's unpacking boxes with Jen but that's not going to happen with two ongoing murder enquiries is it?' Dylan stopped with his hand on the handle of his office door. A moment later he turned and spoke in a softer voice. 'I thought the sooner I was here, the sooner I'd get home. With a bit of luck before Maisy goes to bed tonight.'

Vicky walked towards the kitchen, holding the papers she held aloft in her hand. 'You mean you couldn't face seeing the disappointment on Jen's face when she woke up and you informed her you were coming to work today?' she called out from the kitchenette.

'Something like that,' he said vanishing into his office.

Vicky pushed open Dylan's door, precariously carrying two steaming mugs of coffee. The papers she had been carrying now under her arm. Dylan was flicking through the paperwork that had been left on his desk by the night crew, waiting for his computer to boot up, when Raj walked in. 'What have you got for me?' he said without looking up.

Vicky acknowledged Raj, slid Dylan's mug across his desk and took a seat.

'Search teams have completed their task around the area where Julie Dixon's body was found. The exterior of the wheelie bins have been fingerprinted, and a few partial marks lifted.' Raj had Dylan's full attention. 'Only time will tell if they are of any relevance.'

'According to this...,' he said holding up the piece of paper containing the forensic report he had been reading. 'The bins have been emptied and their contents sifted – there was nothing of significance.'

'According to Simon Clegg when the bins were moved there were drag marks visible on the ground signifying Julie's body had been pulled behind the bins, by another. Everything's been photographed and recorded so that nothing has been left to second guess,' said Raj.

Dylan turned his attention to Vicky. 'I'm conscious I haven't been in all the meetings regarding Patti's murder in the last few days. I need to sit with you and review the lines of enquiry to satisfy myself the investigation is still on track.'

'There's nothing startling.' She leant forward and handed him the paperwork she'd been carrying. I've had the HOLMES team do an audit of existing enquires and review the priority on them, for you.' Vicky stopped, cocked her head and scowled. 'The mortuary? Something happened that I don't know about?'

Raj shook her head. 'No, we just want to be present when Julie Dixon's body is re-examined in relation to the bite marks on her left breast that Alan Sanderson talks about in interview.'

*\*\**

Dr William Townsend used a large magnifying glass and bright lights on the notable area of breast tissue, to confirm on the second examination, that the oval shaped mark, that was hardly noteworthy the first time.

'What am I looking for Case?' he said to Kate who was again at his side.

'A representative pattern left in an object or tissue by the dental structures of an animal or human – a bite mark, by definition sir.'

He remained bent over the body peering closely at the further discolouration of the skin. 'You're good Case, very good.'

'Thing is I don't want to miss any opportunity to nail her killer,' whispered Dylan.

Was Alan Sanderson speaking the truth? Could he be responsible for the bite mark, and to try to protect his innocence be making up this cock and bull story? Dylan had no way of knowing.

'It just seems too good to be true. If we can identify the person who bit her...' His eyes lit up. 'Get hold of Sanderson's dental records.' Dylan said to Raj as they pulled out of the hospital car park. 'And, get his prints checked as a matter of urgency against the partial marks that have been lifted from the bins in Shroggs Grove.'

'And if any turn out to be his. Then that would be the final nail in his coffin with all the other circumstantial evidence?'

'Exactly,' he said. 'I want the team out chasing up results and, I'll look forward to the debrief to see how they fare. If we're going to charge Alan Sanderson with Julie Dixon's murder then I want to be able to show, beyond any doubt, that the murderer could have been him, and him alone.'

\*\*\*

The building of a new supermarket in Harrowfield was causing major traffic congestion on the main route into town. As they approached the roundabout that took them to the police station Dylan saw several red tailgates. Suddenly, the traffic came to a standstill. Raj was distracted, talking to her son on her mobile phone; no he couldn't go out to play football before he did his homework, he had an exam tomorrow. Dylan allowed himself a half-smile, relaxed back into his seat and tapped his fingers on the steering wheel to the beat of the music, waiting patiently for the traffic to move on. Light drizzle became heavy raindrops peppering the windscreen. A few minutes later the rain hammered on the roof. Raj struggled to hear her son and eventually, put down the phone with a look of satisfaction on her face, as Dylan turned the windscreen wipers to work faster. 'Someone up there likes me,' she said turning her big brown eyes skywards. 'Thank you!' The traffic coming in the opposite direction stopped, started, crawled and suddenly stopped again. Dylan turned to look out of his driver's window to see sat opposite him, in a black BMW a man whose face he recognised. Their eyes met. Instantly the man turned away and edged his car forward. Dylan looked puzzled.

'The man in the car to my right,' he said to Raj. 'Do you recognise him?'

Raj shook her head. 'No,' she said matter-of-fact as the sound of sirens blared loudly, and blue lights flickered in the distance.

'Once a copper, always a copper eh?' Dylan's mind still continued to search for the man's name as he pulled the car towards the pavement to allow the traffic cars and motorcycle outriders to pass. He went through all the letters of the alphabet hoping that it might provide a spark, but sadly the prompt aid that he had used as a child, didn't work this time.

'Why've we got the circus out?' Dylan asked as he entered the CID office.

'Planned drugs operation that's ended up on our patch apparently, sir. Gary Warner from the Regional Crime Squad is waiting to see you.'

\*\*\*

Julie's Dixon's vehicle had dried out sufficiently for the crime scene investigators to have another look inside. On the floor, in the back of the vehicle they found a clear trail of what appeared to them to be blood. The area was photographed and samples taken.

The lump hammer, found in the footwell was already on its way to be forensically examined. Immediately the exhibits officer could see that the parcels were addressed to two different people. Each address written in a different hand. Another night drying out in the garage for the vehicle and Dylan was told that they would then be able to look for fingerprints, lift fibres and swab for DNA. Dylan wasn't one to be fobbed off with negative comments; 'It's been in the water so it's unlikely we'll get anything...' would be immediately challenged with; 'You don't know till you've tried.' He had known success with blood traces, good enough to be used as evidence, in a court of law, found on clothing washed in a washing machine.

'The packages are addressed to different addresses other than Julie's. They're unopened so I wonder why they're in her possession? Do you think they've been nicked,' said Ned at the briefing.

'Nicked from where, the post office?' scoffed Vicky.

'No, off of people's doorsteps you fool. You know how lackadaisical some folk are, and Posties aren't an exception to the rule.'

'Perhaps the reason for them being in Julie's vehicle is something to ask Sanderson about in the next interview?' said Raj.

Dylan's next question was met with blank expressions. 'Have we fingerprinted them do you know? And has anyone visited the addresses on the parcels?'

'They're recorded as being in our possession so they're on the system. But, as far as I know there have been no actions raised to visit the addresses.'

'And perhaps we should see what's in parcels?' Andy suggested.

'Okay,' said Dylan. 'So, first let's find out who and where they are addressed to, secondly get the exterior of the packages fingerprinted if we haven't already done so, thirdly open them to see what's inside and fourth visit the addresses, see who the occupiers are and what they have to say about them. Of course Raj, it's definitely something else to speak to Sanderson about.'

'There's no doubt we will have to go for extended detention at Court with Sanderson sir, to allow us to get some more time added to his detention clock so we can question him further. Unless of course you think we should charge him on the strength of what evidence we've already got?' said Andy.

'No, I'm holding off charging him for now. I've tasked the pathologist with trying to give me a time of death for Julie Dixon. If Sanderson was at work, his shift being twelve hour, I am very aware that what the pathologist maybe able to tell us could show us that it couldn't have been him that killed his girlfriend – even if all the evidence, at this moment in time, points in his direction. Let me know the time we'll need to go before the Court to get his extension, then we'll call the Magistrates Clerk.'

They're gonna love us if it's after hours, and it's likely to be...' Dylan sighed and looked up at the clock.

'Even if Sanderson was supposedly at work that doesn't prove anything though does it? He wouldn't be the first, and he won't be the last to sneak out of work to commit a murder now, would he?' said Ned.

'All we can do at this moment in time is gather evidence which will hopefully at some point tell us what took place. I take it we've done all the usual background checks on him? Made the usual enquiries regarding his normal working hours, time off, a friend at work he might confide in?'

Raj looked across at Andy and he nodded, 'Yes sir.'

'And I need confirmation that we have his DNA and that Forensic have identified the blood on the cloth we believe was used to clean up at the flat, before we decide what to do next.'

***

Dylan's heart felt heavy as he looked out of his office window to see the day turn to night. 'Aband,' he said with an air of acceptance.

'What's that?' Vicky said, her excited voice broke into his thoughts and he turned sharply to see her eyes shining brightly. 'Aband? It's a German word that means the afternoon turning into night.'

'Get you! I didn't know you could speak German?'

'I can't. Our German teacher used to say it a lot when he gave us detention.'

The younger detective considered his face. 'Why so sad? We're making headway aren't we?'

'Just thinking that there's not a cat in hell's chance I'm going to be tucking Maisy up in her bed again tonight. Did you want something?'

Vicky's eyes shone brightly. 'Gary Warner left these papers for you with Rachael when we were in debrief,' she said handing him a file from an outstretched hand. 'Apparently someone that we have a mutual interest in is back on our patch.'

'Malcolm Reynolds,' he said, staring at the mugshot picture attached by way of a paperclip. 'That's who it was...'

'THE Malcolm Reynolds; Gary told Rachael that they've spoken to DI Giles, Hendon CID in relation to Reynolds being outstanding in connection with the murder of our former colleague, and your deputy Detective Sergeant Larry Banks. As much as I didn't like the slimeball, he didn't deserve to die.'

'Maybe this time we'll see him caught not only for the death of a colleague but also for all those deaths he caused by distributing drugs...' Dylan appeared reflective.

'We almost had him when Jen's stepbrother got involved with the distribution of drugs a few years ago. But, he's rose so high in the network to a place where the bastard was able to give us the slip.'

'I wonder if he's back to see his daughter Gemma?'

'According to Rachael, Gary said that they had visited Malcolm's mother-in-law and spoken to her and her husband but they told him that neither they, nor Gemma have seen hide nor hair of him since he absconded from the prison.'

Dylan looked puzzled. 'Why would he risk coming back into this country, this area, if it isn't to see his daughter? What could be more important than your own flesh and blood?'

***.

Alan Sanderson's fingerprints were not found to be any of those lifted from the wheelie bins, where Julie's body had been found. Dylan was told that the marks were not good enough to search on the database. But, they were sufficient to be checked against a suspect.

'The blood in the van, in the hallway, and on the cloth is confirmed as Julie's,' said Jarv.

A faint muttering amongst her audience grew louder and louder, abruptly ceasing when Dylan raised his hand.

'However,' Jarv continued. 'What is interesting, is that on the bloodied cloth they've found someone else's DNA.'

There was a sharp collective intake of breath.

'Has it been checked against Sanderson's?' said Dylan.

The team were on the edge of their seats.

Jarv nodded. 'It has... And it isn't his.'

From the collective exhalation of breath and their body language, it appeared that most had convinced themselves that Alan Sanderson's guilt was a certainty.

'On the wooden handle of the lump hammer they found minute traces of Julie's DNA.' Dylan paused. When he continued he spoke to the team as a whole. 'So, we now know where Julie was killed, and how she was transported to the dump site. What we don't know is who attempted the clean up, put her in the vehicle and transported her to the Shroggs Grove, or drove her vehicle into the reservoir?'

'On the parcels,' said Donna. 'I've two names and addresses for you sir; one is a M.R Unwin, 15 New Road, Sibden and the other a C.A. Parker, 23, Bridge Terrace, Tandem Bridge. I have spoken briefly to both, and they categorically deny ordering anything.'

Dylan's eyes scanned the room. 'Not surprising since they contained drugs. We'll leave that enquiry in the capable hands of Gary Warner and his team.'

'On the positive for us, this is where it gets interesting though because both these items were actually sent to the home of a Lucy Waldon, who lives at 9, Union Street, Harrowfield. She is apparently one of a number of approved local Internet distributors. Which basically means she gets parcels delivered to her and it's her job to deliver them to the relevant addresses in her area, within the specified timescale. So, it is a mystery in itself why Julie Dixon would have them in her vehicle.'

'Does Lucy Waldon know Julie Dixon?' asked Dylan.

'I don't know. I visited Union Street just before debrief but there was no response, so I was planning to go back tomorrow morning early doors, to see if I can catch her in.'

'Have you checked our systems to see if there are any reports of parcels being stolen?'

'I have yes, but nothing similar is outstanding sir.'

Dylan appraised Donna. 'Treat the visit to 9, Union Street as a priority and take DC Granger with you. 'It's important that we catch up with Ms Waldon first thing.'

Being at the end of the line where the senior officers sat facing the rest of the team Raj had to lean forward to lean forward to see Dylan when she spoke. 'It appears sir that Alan Sanderson hasn't taken any time off work, according to his manager. However, he had confided in his work colleague, Barry Winter that he thought Julie was seeing someone; he told him he had no idea who it was.'

'So again, the information is consistent with what Sanderson has been telling us in interview isn't it?'

Ned was slumped in his seat, his usual sitting position, but he looking troubled. 'It doesn't mean to say that he's not involved though does it?'

'No, it doesn't but we've got to look at the evidence on the bloodied cloth which suggests Sanderson wasn't the one who attempted to clean up the blood at their flat, so we need to know who did?' said Raj.

'He could have had an accomplice?'

'He could. Or, it maybe that she was seeing someone behind his back as he suspected,' said Donna. 'And that person could have been in the flat with Julie.'

'We need to dig deeper into Julie's background. Let's speak to neighbours to see what they know Raj. Ask them if they've seen another man other than Sanderson there.' Dylan stroked his chin. 'Do we know if she has a mobile?'

Raj made notes. 'No, and when her mum identified the body she didn't have a phone number for her, according to Geoff Painter the Coroner's Officer.'

'And we haven't located one, as yet,' said Andy Wormald.

'After your next interview with Sanderson Raj, Andy, I'll make a decision about our next move. At the moment, I'll be honest with you I'm leaning towards bailing him.'

'Bail? Really sir?' said Raj.

'Unless you can find me more evidence to keep him, yes. The evidence we have so far suggests to me that someone else is involved. Does he have any noteworthy friends? Who visits him? Let's see what he can tell us...'

***

The next interview was a difficult one for the detectives. Raj and Andy trawled through Sanderson's relationship with Julie Dixon.

'I can't remember the last time we had anyone around to the flat,' he said. 'It just doesn't happen. I work all hours. I don't have time for friends... Anything else... Me and Julie, we just have each other. That's how it is.'

Forty-five minutes later the interview concluded. A flash of understanding crossed Dylan's face when the detectives related Sanderson's explanation to the team. 'I can relate to that...' he said.

Ned and Vicky exchanged a look. 'You can?' said Ned.'

'Absolutely I can,' said Dylan.

Raj folded her arms, she sat back in her chair. 'Me too. I believe him. When we questioned him about Lucy Waldon, he told us she was someone that Julie used to work with. He doesn't have anything good to say about her. What he did say is that she was a user. She got Julie to help her deliver parcels that she was paid to do.'

'So, we now have a possible link with the parcels recovered in the back of the vehicle.' Dylan paused and cleared his throat. 'If we bail him has he somewhere to stay?'

'Yes, for the foreseeable future he can stay at his father's address. Returning to the flat doesn't appeal to him,' said Raj.

Dylan considered her words. He took a long breath and blew it out slowly. He looked directly into Raj's eyes. 'Bail him.'

'Bail him?'

Dylan nodded. 'I don't think he is the person we're looking for.'

'Really?' was the collective whisper. 'Has the boss lost the plot?' Dylan ignored it. He was in charge. It was his decision, and if it turned out that Sanderson was the murderer, he knew his credibility amongst the detectives would be shattered.

The night was closing in as he closed his policy book having recorded his reasonings for bailing Sanderson. As Dylan drove down the dark, winding, narrow road that led to The Station House he felt the need to turn up the volume on his radio and let the noise fill his head. The autumn air was still and strangely warm. He pulled up outside the house and when he turned the radio off, the doubts were still there. He leant his head back on the headrest and closed his eyes. The white noise was louder to his ears than the music. 'Should I have bailed him?' he asked himself again, and again as he turned his head to see the dim night light from Maisy's bedroom windowsill flickering though her curtains. By the time he stepped out onto the asphalt and felt the camber of the driveway beneath his shoes, walked up the path and turned the key in the door he had convinced himself that although it was a difficult decision to make, it was a necessary one, and the warm glow of the log burning fire that greeted him inside the house encouraged him to look forward not back.

Tonight was family time and silently, as he passed the bottom of the stairs to hang his coat up under them he observed the space under the stairs that was concealed. No matter what Jen said, there was no way there was enough room in that void to represent his memories of his Dad's workroom. It must have been another house they had lived in – Jen's fantasy was just that, a fantasy. But they'd knock the stud wall down in the kitchen anyway, to satisfy Jen and the family and to give them extra space in the kitchen.

# Chapter Twenty-One

DS Nev Duke stood on the doorstep of 9, Union Street and knocked on the door. He put his hand into the inside pocket of his raincoat and pulled out his warrant card. Ned Granger stood beside him on the pavement holding a handkerchief to his face, his head went back and he sneezed, once, twice, three times and blew his nose hard. Nev scowled, leant forward and turned his ear to the door. He listened for a moment or two sure he heard a chair scrape back on the floor within. He knocked louder this time. Above them they heard the opening of a window. A man popped his head out of the neighbouring house. He leant heavily on the windowsill. 'Why can't you fucking sneak about like they do on the telly, some of us are trying to sleep,' he shouted before slamming the window shut. A moment or two later the door opened, on a security chain, and peering out was a scraggy, short-haired female, her face contorted with distaste.

'Lucy, Lucy Waldon, Detective Sergeant Nev Duke said holding up his warrant card. He pointed to Ned, 'And this is Detective Constable Granger, from Harrowfield CID.' Ned pushed aside the lapel on his jacket, fumbled in the inside packet of his suit jacket, pulled out his warrant card and also held it up for her to see. 'Can we come in?'

'What do you want?' Lucy Waldon leant forward and her eyes searched left and right to make sure no one was watching.

'We need to talk to you about a murder.'

Lucy stared at Nev for what seem like an age. 'A murder? I don't know anything about a murder.'

'Do you know Julie Dixon?'

The young girl nodded her head, her expression one of confusion. 'But, I don't understand Julie wouldn't murder anyone.'

'She won't now,' said Ned.

'Fuck. No!' Lucy said, ushering them quickly inside.

The officers wiped their shoes on a threadbare doormat and walked along the hallway, passed a bundle of coats that hung on a bank of hooks on the wall, a pram, boxes, bags and other clutter.

A toddler sat up to the table in a high chair, playing with toys on the food tray. He looked at the detectives with interest then with one jerky sweep of his hand he knocked his bricks to the floor and started to cry. The young woman took a deep breath, picked them up and put them back on the tray. 'Mattie, no!' she said, showing him a pointed finger. 'That's naughty.' The little boy wriggled, squealed and remained eye contact with Lucy when he picked up a brick between finger and thumb and dropped it to the floor. Ned bent down and picked it up. Lucy turned towards the work surface, picked up the kettle and again to the sink to fill it. 'Please, sit down,' she said indicating to the chairs that surrounded the circular pine table. 'Do you want a brew?'

Whilst the kettle boiled she sat on the chair next to the little boy and gave him a feeding cup that was already on the kitchen table. He drank from it eagerly. Nev relayed the reason for their visit.

Her eyes filled with tears. 'I don't understand. How do you think I can help?'

'We need to build a picture of Julie, and her recent movements,' said Nev.

Lucy's face appeared vacant.

'For instance. Did she help you deliver parcels?' Ned asked. He turned to the little boy and pulled a face. The little boy rewarded him with a giggle.

'Yes – how'd you know that?' Lucy's face was one of surprise.

Ned raised his eyebrows and gave a toothy grin to Mattie. 'Because we're policemen, and we know everything,' he said.

Lucy scoffed. 'Yeah, whatever.' The kettle switched itself off. She stood walked briskly to the worktop, took three mugs from the mug tree, put a tea bag in each and poured boiling water atop. 'I get parcels delivered en bloc, and my job is to deliver them. I need all the money I can get as a single parent.'

Ned spooned sugar into the drinking vessel she put before him on the table. 'So, how's Julie involved?'

'Occasionally I have other work and the parcels have to be delivered in a timely fashion.' Lucy said using air quotes with her index fingers for the words timely fashion. She turned to collect the other two mugs from the worktop.

'What other work do you do?' said Nev.

'I work at the Palma Club. I'm a pole dancer,' she said over her shoulder.

Ned stopped blowing raspberries at Mattie – his eyes wide. 'Close your mouth,' Nev whispered.

'It's not that well paid but the tips make it worth it,' Lucy said on her return to the table. 'I usually work in the evening but sometimes they need me at lunchtime for private functions.'

Mattie threw the feeding cup and started to scream, quietening the moment Lucy lifted him from his highchair.

'There are two parcels that were in the back of her vehicle,' said Nev. When Lucy turned towards him, he thought he saw a glimpse of fear pass across her face; her cheeks were flushed.

'They weren't delivered?' Mattie started to cry. She rocked him in her arms. His eyes closed instantly.

'No, but don't worry they're safe,' said Ned.

'We're going to need to take your fingerprints and DNA so that if any Forensics are found on the parcels we can eliminate you – I guess you'll have handled them?'

The young child jerked at her sudden movement, waved his arms and legs and screamed. 'Yes, I would have... I guess.' She stood. Mattie was inconsolable. 'He's tired. I won't be a minute,' she said, walking towards the door. 'He needs to go down for his nap.'

The detectives could hear Lucy's footsteps on the stairs. The little boys intermittent crying suddenly stopped, all was quiet. Ned leant across the table. 'A bloody real life pole dancer eh? I'll have to look out for her next time I'm at the Palma,' he said with a wink of an eye.

'You'll never learn will you. One day that lass of yours will kick you out once and for all.'

'Nah,' he said leaning back in his chair. 'She loves me.'

Lucy closed the bedroom door behind her. Still holding the knob, she rested her forehead on the top of her sleeping son's head. Panic swept through her. The top man, Malcolm Reynolds had visited them at the club, and now she found out her friend who she'd implicated in this whole sorry mess was dead. What was she going to do? She laid Mattie down in his cot, tucked his fluffy rabbit under his arm, stuck in his dummy and went to the bedside table. Her hands hovered over the blue tablets in her drawer. Mattie turned, and cried once. Hurriedly, she popped a whole tablet in her mouth and swallowed it down with spittle. She took a deep breath, closed her eyes and counted to ten. Soon the drugs would start to take effect and she knew from experience that she would, with the help of the ecstasy, be able to ride this one out.

'There's a rumour flying around that Julie had been seeing someone, other than her partner Alan Sanderson. Have you heard anything?' said Nev when she returned.

'No, no way, she wouldn't do that, she adores him,' she said with an emphatic shake of her head as she passed him. She had intense butterflies sensation in her stomach. Lucy didn't sit down but busied herself loading the washing machine. Her hair began to tingle.

'Why don't you come and sit down,' said Nev. 'You don't need to do that right now, you've just had a shock.' Unhearing, she threw toys in the direction of the toy box. Next she pointed to the mugs on the table. 'Have you finished?' she asked, and waited for a nod of the head before she attempted to collect them. Eventually she had the three mugs on the fingers of one hand and she carried them to the sink where she proceeded to run them under the tap. She lay them upside down on the drainer. When she turned to face the detectives she noticed there was a glow around the artificial light and the colours began to pop. She suppressed a dry heave and leant on the worktop for support.

Nev stood and walked towards her, his hand outstretched. 'Lucy we're going to need a statement from you,' he said. 'Could you please come and sit down?'

Lucy side stepped him, opened the fridge door and poured herself a glass of cold grapefruit juice. She sat down opposite the men, still clutching the glass. It was apparent to their trained eyes that her pupils were dilated. Nev looked at Ned concern on his face.

'When will Julie's funeral take place?' Lucy's voice was shaky.

'Not for a while yet,' said Nev.

'Was she in pain... you know before she died?' she asked, her eyes wide and staring. The words that Nev had written on the paper in front of her were especially dark and bold.

'She was hit over the head. We are told by the pathologist that she would have died instantly.'

'Poor Julie,' she said putting a hand to her mouth. 'Why would anyone do that to her?' Lucy dropped her hand slowly to hover over her heart and gasped.

Nev reached out to touch her clammy hand. 'Lucy. Lucy. Lucy. Talk to me Lucy,'

\*\*\*

Dylan was stood over the street map that was laid out on a table, looking at the distance between Julie's home address, where her body was dumped and Ogden Reservoir where her car was found. A complex web of possible routes had been identified and were highlighted, but the chances of finding CCTV or speed cameras was down to two major roads, due to the rural locality of the reservoir.

'Her car is quite distinctive. If it travelled either of the routes we should be able to pick it up at some point during the period of time our intelligence tells us it would've been mobile,' said Raj.

Vicky stuck her head around the CID office door. 'I'm ready when you are to update you in relation to Patti Gordon's murder, boss.'

Dylan turned to Raj. 'I'll be next door if you need me.'

\*\*\*

With her legs crossed, cup of coffee in one hand and a biscuit in the other, Vicky Hardacre sat in the comfort of a visitors' chair, around the little round table, tapping the toe of her brown leather boot on the carpet-tiled floor as she waited for Dylan to emerge from his meeting. She hoped that he would be pleased with the way she had proceeded with the murder enquiry in his forced absence, and although there was no one in custody yet, the ground beneath their feet had been covered and she and her team were ready to move on to the next phase of her action plan, with his approval.

The room was quiet and warm, as was intended for more intimate meetings and she quickly found herself relaxing, so when Dylan opened the door she jumped, reached out for the file she had brought with her and pushed his coffee mug across the table to where he sat with his back to the door, looking tired, but also pleased with himself. He leant back in the chair and pulled his tie loose. 'Thanks,' he said as he picked up his drink and threw the policy book, and his mobile phone in the middle of the table. 'So, what've you got for me?'

'The swabbing at Patti's School is to extend to the lower year, with your permission? And, I'd like to extend house-to-house and swabbing to the surrounding areas.'

Dylan nodded. 'While we have the ability to put people in or out of the enquiry en bloc at the school let's do it. However, you'll need to check with Operational Support to look at the logistics of the wider aspects of house-to-house and swabbing – they'll have their limitations. Nothing more from the CCTV footage we've collected is there?' Vicky shook her head before continuing to ask Dylan questions on her list. She wrote copious notes in her notebook.

'You've done good.' Dylan said with a smile when she concluded.

Vicky cringed, 'You might not say that when you look at these,' she said offering him the overtime cards. He bowed his head at the pile of cards that sat on his lap and ran his fingers through his hair as he counted up the hours. 'How anyone can budget for hours needed to be worked on a murder enquiry is beyond me?' One by one he scribbled his initials in the appropriate box for the each officer to be paid, until his ringing phone had him reach for it and on listening to the caller at the other end the colour drained from his face.

# Chapter Twenty-Two

Dylan gazed out of the kitchen window watching a robin tug at a worm in the rockery. He called Jen and Maisy over to see, from where they sat eating their breakfast by the coal fire. When Maisy came running he scooped her up into his arms. Her leg that had been closest to the fire felt hot to his touch.

'Is he eating spaghetti?' Maisy asked enthusiastically, she shivered and Dylan stretched her slipper socks up over her knees.

'It certainly looks that way, and it'll make him big and strong if he eats up all his breakfast. Have you eaten yours?' Jen asked, peering over Maisy's head towards the table.

Dylan put her down on the floor and she ran back to the table and climbed up on the chair, eager to get back to the warmth of the fire, and her porridge.

'Not for giving up is it Jack?' Jen spoke, bewitched by the red-breasted robin struggling with its food. 'Remind you of anyone?'

They shared a knowing look. A smile crossed Dylan's face. 'He's probably a reincarnated detective focused on keeping hold of his prey,' he said playfully.

Jen shivered and pulled her dressing gown around her. 'I never thought I'd say this but I don't half miss the central heating at our old house.'

Dylan turned his back on the window and drained his coffee cup. 'Softy Southerners are urged not to travel unless necessary as snow, ice and blizzards approach,' he said in a silly voice, stopping for effect before he continued. 'Northerners – you'll need your big coat.' His laugh was infectious and seeing her parents laughing made Maisy chuckle. Dylan walked over to the fire and put a finger under Maisy's chin, he spoke softly to her. 'Do you know, when I was a little boy I slept in the bedroom where you sleep now, and it was so cold in winter that when I woke up in the morning there was ice on the inside of the window.'

'Go on with you,' Jen teased.

'It's true!'

Although Jen wore her slippers she could feel the cold striking up through the floor. Dylan put his pot in the sink. 'I for one can't wait to rip up this lino,' she said, her eyes looking downwards. At her feet lay a white feather. She bent down and picked it up. She looked at Dylan and raised her eyebrows. 'Your Kirsty believes in white feathers too.'

Dylan scoffed. 'Figures,' he said, as Max ran to the door and began barking. Suddenly a bundle of letters, tied with string, came flying through the letter box and landed with a 'plop' on the doormat. Maisy jumped down and ran to the door, hastily bringing the post to her parents. So excited was she, she tripped and landed in a heap at Dylan's feet. All was silent for one moment, before the piercing scream. Jen scooped her up into her arms. Dylan stooped down to rip up the raised piece of floor covering. 'It's no good,' he said ripping up more and more, as it cracked and crumbled at his touch. 'We're going to have to take this lot up.' He nodded towards the far wall. 'At the same time as we knock that down.'

'Charlie's got a team coming to start on the roof and Ronnie said he'll be here early tomorrow morning.'

Dylan looked at his watch. 'I'd better be off but with a bit of luck, I'll be here to help.'

Jen smiled, Dylan bent his head to Maisy and pursed his lips, his eyebrows were furrowed.

'Ouch,' he said, 'I think Mummy might have a plaster somewhere? Dylan looked around at the unpacked boxes and Maisy followed his gaze.

'Thanks,' Jen said rolling her eyes. Dylan kissed Jen on the cheek.

'See you later alligator,' he said to Maisy as he shrugged into his overcoat.

A smile crossed her tear stained face. 'In a while crocodile,' she replied shyly. Dylan waved a hand, unlocked the door and let himself out into the yard, now shrouded with a dense, rolling fog. Quickly he closed the door behind him to keep the warmth within.

*** 

The black limousine eased away from the back door of the Palma Club on its way to the airport. A slight, young woman in a bright orange boobtube and a short black skirt stood at the bottom of the metal fire escape in her six-inch heels, ensuring her neckerchief covered the marks made by the studded, leather collar. Her younger malnourished friend sat three steps up in her stocking feet, stroking the red chaffing on her inner thighs. She looked up at the sound of the car approaching, clutched the tattered remains of her clothes to her and looked at the older woman beseechingly, until she passed her the joint – it was her turn to draw on the spliff they'd earned. Together they strained to see passed the tinted rear windows, hoping to catch a glimpse of the big man himself. Malcolm Reynolds looked straight ahead. He loved the feeling of power he got from being driven in the back of the car; his driver satisfied with his payment.

***

Vicky picked up Dylan's phone, just as she saw him pull into his car parking space directly under the office window. She beckoned him in. 'Forensic on the landline,' she called when he entered the building. Dylan bustled into his office, briefcase in one hand, post in the other. The phone receiver was lying on his desk. Still wearing his outer coat he sat behind his desk. 'Jack Dylan,' he said.

'I've news on the Julie Dixon murder.'

Dylan picked up a pen. 'Go on.'

'We've checked Lucy Waldon's DNA profile against the packaging from the two parcels found in the deceased car. Was she a friend of Julie Dixon do you know?'

'Yes, why?'

'There are some markers that are strikingly similar to samples we have lifted from the parcels, and the bloodied cloth that was found at the flat. Do you know if she has any relatives that are connected to your investigation?'

'I am only aware of a child living with her. Her little boy had to be taken into care when she took a drug overdose. There has been no mention of other family at the house.'

'Some of the markers are not quite fifty per cent but I suggest you priorities male siblings for DNA sampling.'

'Really?' Vicky walked in the office with a hot drink. He signalled her to take a seat. His eyes held hers as she sat. 'So, for clarity, what you're saying to me is that the DNA profile you have on the sample from the bloodied cloth we found under the sink, and on the parcel is male, and so similar to Lucy Waldon's that it is likely to belong to a male sibling?'

'In simple terms, yes!'

Dylan could feel his pulse racing. 'I appreciate the call.'

'I look forward to receiving priority samples, or hearing from you when you locate any of her family.'

The line went dead. There was a knock at the door and Gary Warner opened it.

'You might be interested to know sir, that I've just been informed the foil that the drugs were wrapped in, in a parcel you recovered from Julie Dixon's car gives us a link to our target in your area.'

'Malcolm Reynolds by any chance?'

'The one and only.' Gary closed the door and sat down next to Vicky. 'If Forensic haven't a match then we know it's someone who isn't already recorded on our systems, nor had their DNA taken.'

The optimism was tangible at the morning briefing. All personnel in attendance to hear what the detective sergeant from the Regional Crime Squad had to say.

'That's what they do, isn't it?' said Dylan. 'Enrol kids, with no previous, to be their mules.'

'They pick them up and take them to school in their big fancy cars – make them feel like somebody. Treat them as one of the gang; buy them anything they want – and the kids think it's all for free. Remember the kids they target are usually from care homes, or excluded from mainstream education. When the drugs syndicate decide, they put them to work. Children as young as twelve are involved in this particular operation and Malcolm Reynolds is reputed to be the main player in this area, he knows well. We have already uncovered these kids travelling long distances, from coast to coast, delivering drugs in shoe boxes, pills in bags. We call it country lines; the children call it going country. It's a new kind of organised crime that is unreported and unrecorded but our research suggests it runs into thousands of youngsters. These kids are being groomed right under our noses, to run drugs. Sadly, as you know the drugs market has reinvented itself you'll have heard of the Darknet, basically eBay for drugs.

Ninety-eight per cent of a test purchase order will get to us via the post in a couple of days, and they are also using the Internet parcel distribution service too. Bitcoin is the cash currency, which cuts out the middle man and a trace.'

'I think we need to speak to Lucy Waldon again as soon as possible. This is a giant step in the investigation allowing enquires at last to become streamlined and focused. Raj, Andy, I want to see you in my office after this meeting. I want you to visit Lucy Waldon. I want to know about the men in her life and who might have handled the parcels. Be subtle in your approach, we don't want to rattle anybody's cage just yet.'

Gary nodded. 'The boss is right. She doesn't need to know the same sample was found on the bloodied cloth, at this time. The last thing we want her to do is warn someone either directly, or indirectly of the results from Forensic, and ultimately our suspicions.'

'So we're okay to mention to Lucy that a male's DNA has been found on the parcels and use that as a reason for the revisit?' Andy asked.

'Yes, just go with the unusual elimination stuff. You might want to speak to Nev and Ned about their visit, but I want to know your views after you meet with her.'

***

Detective Sergeant Rajinder Uppal and Acting Detective Sergeant Andy Wormald got no response from their knocking at the door of 9, Union Street and decided to look for Lucy Waldon at her place of work. It was lunchtime as they pulled up across the road from the Palma Club, on Venn Street. At either side of the illuminated entrance stood two large boxed plants and in the middle, blocking the entrance, a seven-foot tall, bald man with a sloping forehead wearing a black suit, white shirt and a dickie bow tie. A barbed wire tattoo could clearly be seen crawling over his face.

'Have you ever seen a scarier doorman?' Raj asked as they surveyed the scene for a moment or two.

Two young girls approached the bouncer and it was obvious that after speaking to the bullet-pierced hulk they were not welcome.

Not taking their eyes off the door the detectives got out of the vehicle and walked over to the entrance, climbing the few stone steps to stand before the muscle bound man. He bowed his head and opened the doors for them. 'Good afternoon,' he said.

Andy ushered Raj inside, but she halted instantly, blocking his entry. He blinked, letting his eyes adjust to the relative darkness, sidestepped his colleague and opened the double doors into the main room of the club. Even over the throbbing bass of the rock music they could hear the murmur of voices and the jeering of the clientele. There were plenty of patrons, but not a real crowd. The doors and windows of the dimly lit room were swathed in velvet curtains of red and gold. The rosy diffused light around two small stages showed them the route to the bar. Ahead, a couple of gentlemen could be seen perched precariously on cushioned stools in front of the moderately lit bar. Their heads turned in the same direction, watching the dancers performing on and around the poles. Each man had a drink in hand and although dressed like they meant business, looked decidedly worse for wear. Raj noted six booths faced the stage. A couple were occupied with men who were being personally entertained by scantily clad lap dancers. A pile of bank notes sat upon the tables, and several could be seen in the entertainer's garter. As the detectives reached the bar, a petite, dark and delicate looking young woman appeared. She was dressed in a tight, thin, low-cut dress and it was pretty obvious to them that she wore no undergarments.

'Hello sir,' she said to Andy, a velvet tone to her voice. 'Can I get you something to help you relax?'

Raj stepped forward. 'No thanks, but you can get us the manager.' She smiled sweetly.

'I'll get him,' she said briskly, the smile dropping instantly from her overly made-up face.

She turned picked up the phone behind her and as she spoke she covered the mouthpiece. 'There's two plods here to see you,' they heard her say.

At the appearance of the man who purported to be the manager the detectives had to do a double take. Wasn't this the jacketless man who was stood at the door not five minutes ago?

'My name's Grant Marchant,' he said, his sleeve tattooed arms full of empties that he placed upon the bar. 'Can I get you a drink?'

Andy shook his head. 'No thanks, we're working on the investigation into the murder of Julie Dixon, and as a matter of routine we need to speak to one of your employees Lucy Waldon, is she about?'

'If you'd like to come this way.' Mr Marchant led them through a door in the wall that was papered in the same dark red, flock wallpaper, into a brightly lit, cold, corridor. The corridor was so narrow that they had to walk in single file. The noise of their shoes on the stone slabs echoed up to the high ceiling of the whitewashed stone walls framed by a metal spiral staircase. He stopped at a door at the foot of the stairs, took out a large old key and opened it wide.

'You won't be taking Lucy away with you will you, she's working a double shift for me?' he said as he stepped back against wall of the corridor to allow the officers to enter the office before him. He followed them in and closed the door behind him. 'Please, sit down,' he said, motioning to two old oak armchairs that were positioned either side of the large oak desk. The office looked like something out of an old nineteen-forties' detective movie.

'Hopefully not, we just need a chat with Ms Waldon for now,' said Raj.

'Good, because finding good workers this day and age is hard,' He eyed Raj up and down. 'If you ever need any extra cash here's my number,' he said taking a business card from out of his wallet and sliding it across the desk.

Andy leant forward and picked the card off the desk. 'Thanks. I'll bear that in mind, but I've got to warn you I'm not good on a pole.'

Grant Marchant looked peeved that he'd not got the reaction he had wanted from Raj. He picked up the phone and asked whoever answered to get Lucy to his office immediately.

# Chapter Twenty-Three

Lucy Waldon's skeletal frame was encased in a drab, rather shabby silk dressing gown in varying shades of red. Her feet were bare and dirt-stained with fading fuchsia paint on her nails. She apologised for her appearance, smoothed her hand down the crumpled fabric of her gown and sat on the upright wooden chair, with its back to the wall.

Raj introduced them and smiled, but she didn't return it. 'You probably want to know why we're here?'

Lucy's pale face was tear-stained. She wasn't crying, but she was trembling uncontrollably and her teeth were chattering. 'Yes.'

'We need to ask you some more questions regarding the murder of Julie Dixon.' Raj lowered her voice. 'I'm sorry we've had to come to your place of work but it is important.'

Lucy lowered her eyes and brought her hand up to her face to touch a reddish bruise on her cheekbone that reflected the colour of the blood in the skin. She shrugged her shoulders. 'It's okay.'

'The parcels that we found in Julie's vehicle have now been forensically examined and we have a DNA profile which isn't yours so, as a matter of routine we need to identify that person and eliminate them from the enquiry too. Tell me, who apart from you would have handled these parcels Lucy?'

Lucy shivered. Her face was pinched, her bottom lip quivered.

'Does anyone live with you?'

Lucy's shaking of her head was emphatic.

'Okay. Is it possible that any visitors could have touched the parcels? You see, it's just about tying up loose ends for us,' said Andy.

She shook her head again, opened her mouth as if she was going to say something, then closed it again, her teeth now clenched.

'Has anyone stayed here looking after the little one while you're at work?' suggested Raj.

'If so, you see we need to swab them too.'

Lucy was still hesitant. 'I do have the occasional visitor... Sometimes they stop over.' Lucy's eyes darted from Andy to Raj and back. 'It's not a permanent thing you understand. I don't want you telling the Social it happens regularly.' She bowed her head, closing her eyes for a moment and took a deep breath. 'I just don't understand how anyone could have touched the parcels... I keep them in the cellar away from Mattie because he'd rip the paper off. Ever since it was his birthday – he thinks all parcels are for him.' She frowned. 'And no one else has access to the cellar but me,' she said, in no more than a whisper.

'Do you know the contents of the parcels Lucy?' asked Raj.

Grant Marchant rapped at the door and opened it without being invited in, his large frame filled the doorway. Lucy gave a sudden, small, indrawn gasp of someone who'd been about to be discovered giving away a secret. 'How long is this going to take?' His question was directed at the two detectives.

'How long's a piece of string?' said Andy.

He turned to speak to Lucy. 'Misty's called in sick. 'On a downer no doubt. I need you back at work sharpish,' he looked at his watch. 'In fact you're on in five,' he said, turning on his heels and leaving them once again alone.

The office was silent. Lucy's red-rimmed eyes were wide. She sat on her hands and rocked too and fro, grinding her teeth. 'I'll be home at four o'clock, but I'm working again at six. Can we finish this then?' Periodically she bobbed her head and Raj thought it odd. 'I'm not being awkward, honest I'm not. If I lose this job I'm fucked.'

Moments after Lucy left the office Raj and Andy could hear Grant shouting his instructions from directly outside the office door. His hurried feet stomped up the steps. A moment later there was a short, shrill cry. Both detectives were wide-eyes and curious. Andy crept to the door, opened it a crack, just enough to see what was going on, on the first landing. Grant held Lucy roughly by her forearm. 'Whatever it is, sort it. Do you hear? I don't want the Rozzers sniffing around here again. Understood?' Grant hissed before forcibly pushing her away from him. 'And remember, keep your mouth shut if you know what's good for you, or you can kiss your ass goodbye.'

Jen had a fresh pot of coffee ready, knowing Charlie and Ronnie would be arriving shortly, the coffee addiction Dylan was notorious for apparently ran in the family. When it was time to knock down the stud wall they stopped and waited patiently for Dylan to arrive to help – not because his brothers needed his help but because of Jen's belief that Joe's illusive dark room was behind that wall.

'There is insufficient room under the stairs for it to be there,' Charlie had told Dylan.

'I know that, you know that,' said Dylan.

'It's a stud wall so there's something behind it,' said Kirsty.

'Yes, a sloping space that was no good to anyone, so it was boxed in probably because the person living here kept bumping their bloody head,' said Ronnie.

'Whatever,' said Dawn raising her eyebrows at her brothers. 'Just appease them,' she said throwing her head in Kirsty and Jen's direction.

The 'waiting' for Dylan day after day afforded the family time at the former Dylan home. Together Dylan's siblings, their children and Jen and Maisy had peeled yellow stained wallpaper from the upstairs walls, exposing the wet, crumbling plaster behind it for the two older men to repair. They'd rubbed the paint curls from the ceiling, and the children, not to be left out, had collectively, eyes closed lifted their cupped hands and tried to suppress their giggles whilst catching the paint shower before it fell on the hard wooden floors – sweeping up afterwards with dustpan and brush.

'I wouldn't cover these floorboards again Jen, they're the real deal,' said Ronnie going down on his haunches to run his fingertips over the plank ends that had been nailed directly to floor joists. 'Pre 1898, before the end matcher was invented.'

Now adrenaline pumped through Jen's veins at the anticipation of the night ahead. The plan that Dawn would pick up the kids from school, Kirsty would collect fish and chips on her way home from work and once Dylan arrived home the knocking down of the wall would commence. She had put so much emphasis on the discovery of the illusive dark room that it now seemed irrelevant, what had happened since buying this house had given them so much more. She looked at the space the knocking down of the wall would reveal and she knew that, it wasn't anything like the size of a room, she also knew they were going along with the idea to please her, and she loved them for it.

Whilst laying the dining table in preparation for the family meal – such as it was to be, Jen was conscious of how warn and shabby the room looked. The carpet threadbare in places, and with most of their good furniture in store it looked like a mismatch of clutter to be relinquished to a skip when the renovations were complete. The warmth of the sun that shone brightly through the south-facing window made her tug at the sun-bleached edge of the curtain as she passed. She stopped in her tracks and watched the dust particles sifting sideways about the room. Her hand turned the curtain to reveal the tatty linings. 'There's no point replacing them until the building work is finished and kitchen replaced,' she thought. The unkempt foliage that had spread to the windowsill and its suckers clinging to the bottom panes now acted like a sail to the wind. Parasitic vines, thick ivy stems and woody roots had overtaken the lawn, which might be beneficial to the wildlife but not good for the weight they put on the ailing trees in close proximity to the house. 'Maybe they'll have to come down,' she thought dipping her head to see the top of the Ash.

Maisy had been quietly playing in the lounge. It had been a good idea of Dylan's to put all her toys in the empty room with the hideous patterned carpet, and the just as hideous patterned wallpaper. Jen could hear her daughter excitedly talking, and laughing, and assumed it was Max she was playing with as he had hardly left her side since they had moved in. All of a sudden Jen heard Maisy's screech of delight then a high pitch stuttering bark that she knew meant Max thought whatever they were doing was as important as him wanting her to throw him a ball, or chasing another dog, so she hastily ran to check on them. She pushed the door open as far as it would go, stopped and stood with her mouth open wide, torn between the urge to laugh, or cry.

'Maisy, what on earth...?' Jen said, stopping instantly she saw the writing on the lower part of the wall that she had stripped of its paper. Max ran at Jen falling at her feet in a play bow but she ignored him, and as if in slow motion she walked the few steps to touch the pencilled drawing of the detailed Queensbury Railway

Line. Stick men and a lady with a pram at the station, the pale yellow, single, Brelland to Harrowfield Town ticket No. 3259 and the signature Jack Dylan, age nine.

***

'We talked earlier Lucy about the two packages that were found in Julie Dixon's vehicle and the man's DNA sample that Forensic had discovered,' said Andy sitting down in the old armchair at Lucy's home.

Lucy traversed the kitchen, putting away the shopping, dumping breakfast pots in the sink, emptying the washing machine. Finally she carried the faded washing up bowl full to the top with wet off-white, grey white, yellow white clothes, and plopped it on the end of the kitchen table in between her and Raj.

'I haven't had time to wash for two weeks,' she said pulling clothes out one by one to hang on the empty clothes airer she pulled alongside her.

'Like we said, we are not saying for a minute that the parcels, or the man whose DNA they have discovered has anything to do with Julie's murder. What we are saying is that they were in the back of her car when it was dragged from Ogden Water and we need to identify the persons whose DNA is on them to tie up our loose ends. So, back to the question we asked you earlier. Can you think of any male who may have touched the parcels whilst they were here, accidentally or otherwise?' Raj said.

Eventually, Lucy sat, head-down relentlessly picking at her fingernail until the dirt was gone and trickles of blood leeched out from under the nail bed. She looked over at Raj and put her finger in her mouth, sucking it for a moment like a baby. 'Honest to God, there has been no one here,' she said sulkily. 'My cretin of a brother would put anyone off coming round here.'

'Look, I can't officially admit to someone else delivering those parcels. It's more than my life's worth.'

'What do you mean?'

'Grant put a good word in with the top man to get me the job of distributing goods from an Internet site. It pays more money than the pole dancing – a lot more,' she scoffed. 'He also gave my brother a job to keep him off the streets, and from under my ruddy feet.'

'Do you know what's in the parcels Lucy?' said Andy.

'I guess lots of different things.' She frowned. 'I never gave it a thought. They come in all shapes and sizes.'

'We aren't interested in whether you deliver the parcels or not,' said Raj. 'Trust me, we aren't going to tell on you for getting someone else to deliver them.'

Lucy sighed deeply. She looked at the detectives with slitted eyes. 'Okay, if you're not going to grass me up, Reggie has been taking the parcels round to Julie's for me whilst he's been here. I mean, he's just dropped them off, like I do, nothing else.'

'How old is Reggie, Lucy?'

'Don't worry, he's old enough to drive. The boss paid for him to have driving lessons and he passed first time, six weeks later.' She gave a little laugh. 'God knows how. He must have given the examiner a back hander.'

'Does Reggie work at the club regular?'

'Pff! I wish. He's idle; always has been. Surprised he's still working for Marchant actually – Grant usually wants his pound of flesh, and more besides but he seems to have taken to our kid for some unknown reason. They're thick as thieves.'

'What does he do?'

Lucy shrugged her shoulders. 'Dunno really; I know he's a pain in the arse.' The detectives remained silent and she appeared to reconsider the questions. 'They bought him a uniform and he does a bit of chauffeuring... He thinks he is somebody in them big, posh cars.'

'Is he still living, with you?'

'Not since this morning he isn't,' she bent down plucked her purse from her handbag, opened it and tossed it across the table. 'He's taken everything I have bar a few coins. Thieving little bastard. What do they say? Leopards never change their spots?'

'Any idea where he might have gone?' Andy said, with urgency in his voice.

'That's what I'd like to know. Apparently he took Mum's car without asking, and she hasn't seen hide nor hair of him since.'

'Do you have a recent picture of Reggie?' said Raj.

'There's plenty on Facebook,' she said flicking through her phone.

'What's your mum's name and address? We'll need to visit her.'

'Ellen Hartley and she's at 14, Windsor Gardens.'

'Is Hartley Reggie's surname?'

'Yeah, Waldon was my married name.'

'Your brother didn't by any chance leave any of his stuff here did he, suggesting he might return?' sad Raj.

Lucy plucked a carrier bag off the floor. 'Yeah, his dirty washing. I was just about to throw it but if you're going to me mam's...'

'We can take that for you?' said Andy reaching out and grabbing the bag.

She looked bemused. 'Okay, if you're that keen.'

'It's no trouble.' Andy smiled at Lucy. 'We'll need a quick statement from you, for continuity.'

Lucy looked up at the clock. 'Will it take long?'

\*\*\*

'Bit of luck that. We'll get his DNA from the clothing, and more...' said Raj, opening the boot of car and tossing the plastic bag inside.

Andy sat behind the wheel. Put the keys in the ignition, checked his rear-view mirror, indicated and pulled out into the traffic. 'And his picture's on Facebook. Much as I hate social media I can't deny that's a gift,' he said, as he slowed the car down in front of the school gates, waved on by the lollipop man covered head to toe in a fluorescent suit. The car rolled slowly forward in the traffic.

'I think Winsor Gardens is the first right, after the school,' she said, pointing in the direction of the estate. There was a click followed by the soft tick-tock of the indicator. Suddenly, Andy turned the steering wheel and the car left the queue of traffic but the driver of the white Land Rover Discovery heading towards them in the opposite direction showed no such consideration and came to a halt right beside the roadworks blocking their intended path. The nearside door opened and a child jumped out. The driver leant across the front seat to shout something to the lollipop man, who walked over to the car. They exchanged a few words. Andy wound down his window. Other drivers honked their horns, shouted at the driver and flashed their lights, but the driver paid no heed. To add to the chaos a bus stopped behind the Land

Rover and all of a sudden the school gates opened and flooded the street with its passengers.

'Doesn't anyone walk these days?' Andy said, looking around him, his fingers tapping rhythmically, on the steering wheel.

'And would you believe that out of all these people not more than a handful have come forward offering help on the Patti Heinz enquiry.'

Ellen Hartley's council house was nestled in between other like-for-like semis. It had an overgrown garden and a hedge that spilled out onto the driveway. The house had long since lost its freshness, the walls were grey and the stones a slush white. Andy parked next to the black, rusty gate. He slammed the door with purpose, and as he strode to the pavement where Raj was alighting the vehicle he looked up towards the red tiled roof and horizontal casement windows. Mrs Hartley could be seen on the top step, leaning on the back door jamb chain smoking and flicking ash into a chipped saucer.

'Our Lucy rang me, she said you were coming,' she said as they approached. She turned and put one foot over the threshold as if she intended to go inside the house. 'Kettles just boiled – fancy a cuppa?' Ellen looked pale and tired. When she smiled her front teeth were flecked with tobacco. She ran her hand through her short black, dyed hair, putting the saucer next to the kettle, and stubbed her half smoked cigarette out with a degree of brute force. She looked at Raj questioningly. Her daughter had her chestnut-coloured eyes.

'That would be lovely thanks, one with half a sugar and Andy takes two,' Raj said. Andy stood for a moment outside taking in the scene at the back; an overgrown garden, divided symbolically, with strands of wire stretched from concrete posts. The boundary at the end of the garden was partly walled, partly open to the open fields beyond.

The two women acknowledged the detective sergeant joining them in the lounge a few moments later. Ellen rolled a cigarette from dried tobacco in an old rust spotted tin that sat on the threadbare arm of the comfy old chair she was sat in. She licked the cigarette paper, looked critically at the roll-up she'd prepared, popped one end into her mouth, flicked her lighter, inhaled too quickly, and coughed – a thin, smoker's cough. 'I hope he's not in bother, he's not a bad lad really,' she said, her cough now being a persistent ppf. Raj's eyes flew to Reggie's picture she had noted on the corner of the sideboard. 'Bad Lad, Bad Lad,' the frame read. Ellen followed her gaze and sighed. 'He's easily led, alas has been, but he's never been in trouble with the police.'

Raj flicked her shoulder-length hair, her large brown eyes found Andy's, and she knew he was thinking the same thing.

'I don't know if Lucy has explained why we need to speak to you, but we are working on the murder investigation of a young woman called Julie Dixon.'

Ellen's cigarette bobbed up and down with the movement of her lips. Unnoticed, a long section of grey ash fell onto her lap and when she suddenly sat up, it rolled onto the carpet. She rubbed it in with her slippered foot.

'Julie Dixon was helping Lucy deliver parcels. You did know Lucy delivered parcels?'

Ellen shook her head. 'Aye, Julie Dixon, poor lass, I remember her when she was younger. She used to come here on a Friday night before her and our Lucy went out on the town.'

'So, Reggie knew Julie?'

Ellen nodded her head. 'Yes, he got on with her better than he did our Lucy, until she took up with that Alan man.' She screwed up her nose. She lowered her voice. 'I think they had a bit of a thing going on but he alas denied it.'

'When we found Julie's vehicle there were some parcels in the back that hadn't been delivered. As a matter of routine the packages were checked, and it is our job to trace everyone who has had contact with them.'

'I don't understand why you should want to see our Reggie?' Ellen's eye caught the sight of ash on her trousers and she licked her finger and rubbed it in.

'Lucy has told us that Reggie took them to Julie's house on her behalf.'

Ellen's heavily plucked eyebrows moved down and knitted together in a frown. 'I see.'

'Do you know where he is?'

'I don't. I never know where he is these days.' Ellen shook her head. 'I doubt if he does either. His brain is pickled with that stuff he takes.'

'You mean drugs?'

'Aye, I mean drugs. What's this Darknet and Bitcoin, that's all I hear him talk about on the phone to his pals.'

Andy knowingly raised his eyebrows at Raj, who smiled at Ellen, who had no intention of waiting for a reply before continuing. 'He came back from our Lucy's this morning before I got up, ranting and raving he was. When I got downstairs he'd emptied my purse, and cleared off with my car. That'll teach me to stay sober enough to remember to take my handbag upstairs with me when I go to bed.' Ellen gave a little chortle before waving a flaying arm. 'Ah, he's insured and all that, so don't worry. He'll be back when the money runs out. He usually is.'

'Can you tell us the make, model and registration number of your car? Just in case we come across it?' Raj asked.

'It's a turquoise Fiat CHW 431W.'

'Does Reggie have a mobile phone by any chance?' Andy asked.

'Says it was stolen and he can't afford a new one but I'm not daft. I know he's just saying that so that I don't go on at him to give me his number and if I haven't got his number then I can't get hold of him. I've heard him talking to people when he's in his room – he's devious that one.'

# Chapter Twenty-Four

The briefing room was packed. The updates rolled in from the team. Working staff including Detective Sergeant Vicky Hardacre from the Patti Heinz murder enquiry were also included. Heads down, many notes were taken.

'In respect of the elimination of Lucy's younger brother, Reggie Hartley. We have secured worn clothing,' Andy told the group. 'This will be sent for examination and tested against anything connected with Julie Dixon.'

'And, if we get a DNA profile it will be checked immediately against the cloth used to clean up her blood in the hallway of her home and the parcels,' said Dylan. 'The information Raj and Andy obtained today also gives us a link between him, Lucy, Julie and the packages.'

'The mother's vehicle is circulated and flagged up as of interest to us here at the incident room. If the vehicle is subject to a stop and check it is highly likely that the driver will be one Reggie Hartley who needs to be eliminated from the Julie Dixon murder enquiry.'

Vicky raised her hand. 'Sir, number nine Union Street, I believe there has been an action raised on the Patti Heinz murder investigation for that address.'

'Can you check and get back to me?' Dylan said, his hopes raised.

'If so that would be an interesting link, between both investigations wouldn't it?' said Raj.

'Ah, but not unusual if the address is a delivery distribution address for Internet deliveries. In the meantime I'll speak to Maggie and let her know Hartley's clothing is en route and if she does get a DNA profile could she compare it against the unidentified profile on the Patti Heinz murder.

Dylan was about to walk out into the all but empty car park, looking forward to the night ahead with the family when Vicky called him back. Looking over his shoulder to the far side of the incident room he saw her put down her phone and stand. She ran down the walkway in between the desks. 'The database shows that there is an outstanding enquiry at number 9, Union Street regarding a delivery of a parcel to Burford Avenue.'

'Patti's home address?'

'No, across the way; apparently a note has been left by the officer asking the householder to contact the incident room, but to date no one has been in touch – hence the enquiry remaining open.'

\*\*\*

'I'm home!' Dylan called cheerily as he stepped over the threshold. He put his briefcase down, unbuttoned the top button on his shirt, loosened his tie and took off his jacket. 'Where is everyone?' he shouted, as he turned to hang up his coat behind the door. There was a rush of footsteps on the stairs, the hallway door burst open, a loud cry and the children led by Maisy ran in screaming, laughing and shrieking. 'It's a ghost! It's a ghost!' Frantically dodging each other in an effort to lose 'the ghost' they ran rings around Dylan until Maisy ran behind her daddy to catch her breath and clung to his trouser leg. She held her side as a stitch stabbed her under her ribs and, instantly dropped to the floor. The others, red faced and sweating flopped down around her giggling. Mabel the oldest, headscarf covering her hair and bed sheet draped over her shoulders 'Whoo'd' one last time before flopping down at Dylan's feet.

Jen stood in the hallway and beckoned a hesitant Dylan into the lounge. He looked directly into the blazing coal fire, its flames danced merrily in the big, wide fireplace with two mantle shelves; one high up near the ceiling and one lower down. There were green ceramic tiles on the inner side of the wood columns and on the hearth floor. The hairs on his arms stood up and goosebumps multiplied over his skin. He narrowed his eyes and scanned the dimly lit room, and in his mind's eye he saw the beautiful mahogany sideboard with the oval mirror. The piano, a soft, comfy couch and two armchairs. The vision, lovely as it was, was gone with the flick of a light switch. He was dazed for an instant as if he had woken from a dream, to see his brothers and sisters smiling back at him. At the foot of the ladder where his youngest sister Dawn stood was a stripped heap of the hideous wallpaper. She had a scraper in one hand and a wet sponge in the other. He could hardly believe his eyes. He held his breath. His heart thudded against his chest as he heard his mother chastising him, 'Wait till your father gets home,' she said, wagging her finger at him. The drawings he had done as a child were still there, as if they'd been drawn yesterday. 'That's surreal,' he said.

'Aye, and we all took the belt for that,' said Ronnie. 'Do you remember?'

Dylan nodded his head.

'Most importantly do you remember what happened next?' Charlie's grin was wide.

'We locked ourselves in the cellar...' Dylan said hesitantly, his voiced lowered '...so he couldn't find us.'

Dylan hurried back to the kitchen, rolling up his sleeves as he went, his brothers on his heels, the remainder of the family in tow. He tossed fish and chip paper from the work surface and picked up a sledgehammer he knew to be there. Raising the hammer above his head and with adrenaline-fuelled force he closed his eyes, turned his head and lifted his left arm to shield his face; an almighty thud followed, then a crash and a rain of fragments of plasterboard, broken bits of bricks and mortar flew in his direction. Dylan stepped back before subjecting the wood to hastily delivered repeat hammer blows, tripping and sliding on the uneven floor covering, at each blow. Charlie and Ronnie big enough to break his fall coughed and spluttered at his side as they, and the rest of the family watched the dust settle around them, in silence. At last the hole was big enough for him to step inside. His heart raced, and when his feet hit the floor, he reached back with his open hand. 'Torch?'

A set of voices echoed his words in the distance, he could hear the pitter-patter of footsteps that he knew to be Jen's running up the stairs. Stood, as if glued to the spot he waited for his eyes to adjust to the darkness. 'There are objects, stacked against the wall...' he said into the abyss, squinting his eyes. 'I can see silhouettes, but I can't quite see what they are... It smells like musty cardboard and paraffin.' Dylan shivered.

With the aid of torchlight a set of narrow steps leading down into the basement opened up to him. Dylan's heart raced as he was forced to tiptoe down.

'What can you see?' came a call from above a couple of minutes later.

'A dolly tub, not where Dad used to mend out shoes,' he said. 'But at Mum's mangle end.'

# Chapter Twenty-Five

'Bloody frustrating Ellen Hartley's vehicle hasn't been located,' said Vicky, pulling her chair closer to her desk.

Raj sitting opposite her played around with her computer mouse, waiting for a response. 'We can't do anymore.' Clicking a button on the mouse a few times brought up the briefing screen. 'See,' she said turning her screen around for the younger DS to see. 'His details have been flagged up again to every officer.'

Vicky yawned so hard it brought tears to her eyes. 'Do you know if there is any priority stuff back from Forensic this morning?'

The next sound told the office the systems had gone down.

'Bloody computers,' Ned said throwing down his pen on the desk from a great height. He picked up his mug, stood, stretched and headed towards the kitchen to refill it.

Raj stood, and walked towards the printer in the centre of the room and gathered the printed papers. She frowned at him as he passed.

'Well, I for one was quite happy with my pocket book.'

Vicky lifted her empty mug in Ned's direction, 'I suppose that had nothing to do with an impressionable young typist doing your work for you? Mine's two sugars,' she smiled sweetly.

Ned raised his eyebrows as he took it from her hand. 'How come you're so happy this morning?' He cocked his head to one side. 'Got laid last night?'

Vicky waved him on. 'Act your age, not your shoe size just for once can't you?' She turned to hide the little blush that she felt on her cheeks.

'How old do you think I am, seriously?' he said preening himself in front of the mirrored, glass partition.

Suddenly Dylan's door burst open, which was enough to make Ned jump a foot high. 'Call all officers and civilian personnel from both investigations back to Harrowfield incident room for an urgent briefing at twelve noon,' he said, then promptly retreated back into his office. Adrenalin pumping through his body, he could barely contain his excitement. He knew they were on the verge of solving both murders. The phone rang and Gary Warner was on the line.

'Sir, we've got intelligence that Malcolm Reynolds is due to board a flight back to Spain within the hour. I thought you'd like to know. He's under surveillance.' Dylan's ears caught the words, but his mind found it hard to accept them.

'After all this time?'

'After all this time I'm going to feel his collar, for the murder of Larry Banks and all the other people who have died because of the drugs empire he created.'

Dylan's heart was in his mouth. He looked out into the CID office in a trance-like state, to the seat where the deceased detective sergeant Larry Banks had once sat – Vicky turned around, saw him looking at her, got up and walked to wards his door. 'Can I get you a coffee?' she said. For some reason he was filled with emotion. His reply laboured. He shook his head slowly.

'No, no,' he said. 'I'm fine.'

'You sure? I think I might be able to find some chocolate biscuits?'

'No, no.' Dylan turned away and opened his desk drawer. He slid his hand to the back and retrieved an envelope. Putting it on the desk directly in front of him he stared at it, in silence, for a moment or two. As if contemplatively whether he should open it, again.

It was Vicky's turn to shake her head as she closed Dylan's office door quietly behind her. 'There's something up,' she said to Raj and Ned. 'I've only seen that look once before.'

Dylan slowly, slid his finger beneath the flap that was yellowed at its curled-up corners. As he did so he took a deep breath before he pulled out the unfolded papers. Dylan hated loose ends; unfinished business. He accepted that Liz Reynolds had been murdered as a consequence of greed, but greed by his one-time colleague and friend was still hard to stomach. How could he have been so naive to have taken DS Banks words at face value? Most probably he decided because at times a police officer has to rely on his colleagues in a life and death situation. 'The DNA's confirmed the body is that of Detective Sergeant Larry Banks of Harrowfield CID,' he read.

'And that's not all,' he heard his colleague John Benjamin say at the time as he handed him the letter from Larry's solicitor.

Dear Jack,

I crossed the line, and knowing the kind of person you are, I can't expect you to understand. I'm writing this because if I know Malcolm Reynolds, he'll be intent on revenge and won't be satisfied until he knows I have taken my last breath. Who can blame him? The drink was my downfall, I don't need to tell you that, but I do want you to know the truth. Liz was being blackmailed and needed my help. I let her down by taking the money, but believe me I honestly never thought the blackmailer would kill her. I also let you and the team down Jack I'm sorry.

Larry

P.S. You work too hard. Don't let the job ruin your life. You should work to live, not live to work.

Never again would a colleague call him Jack. From then on it was Dylan.

***

The personnel from both murder enquiries filed past Dylan's office. He heard their speculations of what might have occurred to require the urgent meeting and smiled faintly. The assembled voices grew in volume, intensity and excitement.

At twelve noon Dylan stood at the front of the team, with his detective sergeants Vicky Hardacre, Rajinder Uppal, Nev Duke and Andy Wormald sat alongside. Turning slowly in a semi-circle the Detective Inspector faced each one, seated or stood. Some wore sceptical looks. They quietened, sat back, folded their arms and leant against the wall or filing cabinets – wherever there was space. There remained a little bustling and muffled chatter as late arrivals squeezed in on the fringes. Dylan waited patiently for a few moments for silence.

'Thank you for coming in at such short notice.' Dylan's voice was serious as he spoke. 'A short time ago I had an update from Forensic.' He nodded towards David Funk who he'd identified stood at the back, by the door next to Rachael the young police officer who had been at the scene. Heads turned in his direction and he appeared shy. She touched his arm. 'Due to their excellent work they have identified the person responsible for the murder of Julie Dixon.' There was a wave of muttering, and many exchanged glances. 'Also this person has been identified by DNA as a match to the Patti Heinz murder.' An audible gasp sprung from some. 'For now, the information I am about to share with you must remain within these four walls. We can't risk the media hearing about this, just yet.' He paused. 'When the time is right I'll release a statement through Connie Seabourne in the press office.' Dylan looked around the room. It wasn't hard to find Connie in the crowd because of her light blonde hair. She smiled at his acknowledgement, felt the colour rising in her cheeks and shook a little as her stomach did a little flip-flop with excitement and nerves.

'Julie Dixon's blood was found on front of Hartley's left sock, therefore it could be suggested that he had a hole in his footwear he was wearing at the time?' said Dylan.

Ned punched the air. 'Let him try and get out of that one,' he said nudging the man sat next to him.

Dylan raised his eyebrows. 'They also gained a DNA sample from his clothing which matches the outstanding unknown DNA that was found on the cloth, under the kitchen sink.'

'So, now we can focus on finding Reggie Hartley,' said Andy.

'Yes, like DS Wormald says, obviously due to this recent information the priorities and focus of our enquires have changed and new priorities will be raised,' said Dylan. 'Now, if you haven't taken lunch yet, then please do.' Dylan looked from left to right at his detective sergeants. 'The debrief will be at six o'clock.'

The detectives sat around Dylan's desk. The lines of enquiry that required urgent pursuit were discussed. Dylan checked his mobile phone repeatedly.

'I want someone to visit the house of the occupant on Burford Avenue, we know they took a delivery via Lucy Waldon's Internet delivery network on the day of Patti's murder. First and foremost I want to know if they saw the delivery driver, and if so can they give us a description.'

'You hoping that there are some connections with the Hartleys and the Heinzs sir?' said Andy.

'Well, we know that Lucy Waldon delivered parcels for an Internet business, some we know are dodgy, and Gary Warner from regional crime is on top of the drugs aspect,' said Dylan, looking at his watch. 'Get Ellen Hartley's home and the room that Reggie occupies searched again, and at the same time let's take Lucy's home apart. I want to know everything about the family.'

Raj put pen to paper. 'We'll need to identify officers for specific tasks, once Hartley is located and arrested whilst we have time on our hands. Search, examination of vehicle, prioritising exhibits, interviewing anyone he has connections with or is in contact with,' she wrote.

Dylan looked from Raj to Vicky. 'I want you and Vicky to interview him as you both have in-depth knowledge of the independent enquiries. We'll discuss the strategic approach. Initially it is my intention to arrest him for both murders but we will start with the murder of Julie Dixon and work backwards to the murder of Patti Heinz.'

Vicky sat staring at the photo of Reggie Hartley. Suddenly she let it fall. 'You know we put the note through the door of 9, Union Street, due to the information we were given on the Patti Heinz murder, saying we wished to speak to the occupants?'

Dylan nodded. 'Lucy Waldon's home address?'

'Yes, and the address of the delivery parcel company. If Reggie Hartley was living there, he probably saw the note before she did... if she did.' Vicky's eyes were bright. 'You don't think, he thought that Julie might have named him as the person delivering the parcel to Burford Avenue do you and panicked?'

'We'll only know that if when he's caught he talks to us,' said Dylan.

'According to his mother, he got on with Julie better than his sister. Maybe he was the one Julie was seeing?'

'We have a bite mark,' said Nev.

'We do, but at this moment in time we are making assumptions and we...'

'Never assume,' was the chorus from the detective sergeants.

***

Dylan's phone was on speaker. 'Force control, Inspector Stonestreet. We have a report that the vehicle you have circulated has made off from Birch services, M62 eastbound. Unit's responding and the helicopter is en route. It is believed there is one male occupant.'

Dylan put the phone down. Vicky turned up the volume on her police radio and stood it on Dylan's desk. The team were silent.

The commentary was rapid. 'Bravo Foxtrot 42, we have sight of the vehicle ahead on the A672, Ripponden heading towards Sowerby Bridge.'

Dylan's stomach tightened. 'Don't lose it. Don't you dare bloody lose it,' he said, the ball of his right foot pressing down on the floor under his desk. The next voice they heard over the airways on the dedicated channel was Sergeant Lisa Rothwell's, the observer in the police helicopter. She had taken over the commentary from the eye in the sky, to aid the units pursuing the vehicle on the ground.

Vicky fist was a clenched ball on the chair arm that drummed to the rhythm of her beating heart. Andy's leant towards the radio, his teeth clenched.

'Where's the Stinger?' Nev hissed. 'Get the Stinger deployed.'

'Units requesting vehicle stop. Vehicle increasing speed,' Lisa informed all units.

Units ahead blocked the entrance to the Triangle turn off, ensuring the vehicle stayed on the A58.

'Stinger deployed,' came the shout. 'Vehicle continuing at speed with deflated flat tyres.'

There was a pause. The five detectives looked across the table at each other – eyes wide, breath held.

'Target vehicle off the road, crashed into the canal bridge. One male occupant out on foot, running. All units male suspect in canal attempting to evade capture.' Lisa's commentary was clear and concise. 'All units, suspect reached opposite banking. Suspect attempting to climb out. Dog handler deployed. Suspect out and running. Police dog in pursuit... Suspect detained by police dog. All units suspect detained.'

'Thank God.' Dylan's shoulders dropped as he heaved a sigh of relief. He looked up to the ceiling, leant forward and picked up the radio. 'Control,' he said, making eye contact with the others, one by one. 'Can you pass on my compliments to all involved and can we have the car back here to be searched.'

***

'Reggie Hartley has been arrested for two counts of murder and at this time is en route to Harrowfield Hospital to be treated for an ankle injury, and several dog bites that require stitches.'

'Remind the officer searching him that we need his clothing as an exhibit, wet or otherwise.'

'Why would anyone in their right mind think of running away from a police dog?' said Vicky.

'He won't do it again,' said Dylan, his smile spreading across his face. He allowed himself a chuckle.

'You're evil,' Vicky said screwing up her eyes. 'Naively, I once volunteered to help an old flame train his police dog. I put the thick protective sleeve on...'

'Are you totally stupid?'

'No, it cost him a week in Tenerife.' She giggled. 'I bruise easily, but he wasn't to know that.'

'He'd be wet, and cold too. Brrr...' Raj shivered. 'I bet it was really painful.'

'I'd be more worried about what diseases I might have picked up from the canal,' said Andy.

'Well, he's alive and in custody so Raj and Vicky will have chance to find out,' said Nev.

Dylan walked out of his office after the others. 'Anyone heard anything from Gary Warner?' His question was met by the shaking of heads.

'Inspector Stonestreet is on the phone for you sir,' said Donna.

'I'm at the scene Jack, the boot of the car is stacked with drugs. No wonder he didn't want to stop for the police, and ran when he was. My officers are instructed not to speak to him but record anything that he might say to them. And, I'll tell you now he's singing like a bloody canary.'

'He is?' Dylan smiled.

'He is. And, if what he says is true Malcolm Reynold's won't be seeing the light of day for a long time, and we'll get the bloody pole dancing club shut.'

Dylan sat down in his chair, his head in his hands. A knock came at this door. Gary Warner stood before him and nodded. No words were necessary.

'Is he here?' said Dylan. He felt a lump in his throat.

Gary nodded. 'It looks like we have just locked up one of his latest recruits a Reggie Hartley for both our murders. If that wasn't good enough, his car boot is full of drugs, and can't stop talking about Reynolds.

'Everything comes to those who wait eh? It's been a good day all round. His sister Lucy Waldon and Marchant along with others have been arrested. Now I know why we didn't find the haul at the club.'

'You think she was involved? She knew about the drugs distribution?'

Gary grimaced. 'I don't know... time will tell.'

Within the hour Dylan had heard that Hartley had complained of pains in his head, suffered a bruise to his forehead and as a matter of precaution the hospital had decided that they wanted to keep him overnight for observation. 'He has received forty-two stitches for the dog bites, and his wet clothing has been removed by the hospital staff and seized by me,' said Emily. 'His ankle is badly sprained but not broken.'

'Have we sufficient uniformed officers on duty to guard the prisoner overnight?' Dylan asked Stonestreet. 'The last thing I want is for anything to go wrong now, or the media getting into his room to take pictures of him in his hospital bed.'

Stonestreet grinned. 'It's going to be a long day tomorrow Dylan,' he said. 'Get the Chief Constable updated, send a press report and call it a day. I'm on duty till two o'clock tomorrow morning.'

Larry Banks might have let him down, there was always one bad apple – but one thing he knew for sure Reginald Stonestreet, his mentor, would never let him down. Everything he was, he owed to him, because he had taught him all he knew as a police officer, in CID.

The following hour went swiftly. He discussed with the team what required doing that evening and then he sent a short message for the information of the Chief Constable and also one to the press office that read.

'A man was arrested earlier today in connection with two recent murders of young women in Harrowfield. He is under police guard in hospital after injuring himself attempting to evade capture. Today also the long-awaited reign of local drug dealer Malcolm Reynolds, who absconded to Spain some years ago, after the discovery of Detective Sergeant Larry Banks' body was found has finally come to an end. More information to follow.' He had agreed the release with Gary Warner. Dylan picked up his phone.

'Connie?'

'Speaking.'

'I'm sending over a press release. Do me a favour will you and hold off releasing it as long as you can. I don't want to create any more problems than necessary for the hospital staff.'

'What time are you off Vicky?' asked Dylan as he shrugged on his overcoat. She peered out of the half glass door that separated Dylan's office from the CID office. 'What time's Gary off?' she said. She turned back to Dylan with a grin on her face. 'I'm happy to work over.'

Dylan shook his head. 'You never change...'

# Chapter Twenty-Six

Dylan threw the switches, and the makeshift lights Ronnie had assembled whilst he was at work, blazed into the darkness, brilliantly illuminating the galley-sized cellar. He shivered and hugged his arms. It was four am, he couldn't sleep and it was too early to go into work. The house was eerily silent. Gradually, his senses adjusted. He donned one of the headlamps Charlie had brought that enabled him hands-free to closely examine the stock on the shelves. The area was well organised, although covered with thick dust, and cobwebs. The orderly stack of tins, glassware and odds-and-ends the home to spiders and other insects, dead and alive. As he walked carefully down the aisle he passed faded, dented, plastic toys and strips of wood and metal that were leant precariously against the opposite wall. Under foot he paid particular attention to the worn flagstones underneath and particular to the mortar in between. At the point where the ceiling lowered, he was forced to dip his head. Beyond nothing more than a big black chasm that led to a tunnel stretched as far as the eye could see, and beyond. Tentatively, he walked on, the beam of his headlamp his only light. Two hands gently stroked the cold, damp walls for guidance. All of a sudden a door to his right appeared. As he stood before it his heart began to beat a little faster. He turned his head this way and that and then down at the floor for some evidence that this room had had long-term use. There was none. He blew out a breath and put his hand on the doorknob, turned it once forward and then back. His headlight showed him a furnished room. He blinked and blinked again, but once he put his foot over the threshold, he instantly knew where he was – a flaying hand to the right and he touched something cold. It tumbled to the floor, glass crashed at his feet. His shaking hand felt down the door jamb and tried again for a switch he knew instinctively was there. A long low fluorescent light flashed, juddered once, and he saw in an instant photographs pinned to string that bowed from the ceiling. Twice, a long, low trough against the wall, three times and the light lit the room, albeit dimly. He looked around him not prepared for the emotion that ran through his body.

Jen calling his name brought him to his senses and he shuffled to step back into the corridor. Shards of glass crunched beneath his feet and when he looked down his headlamp showed him a hundred or so white feathers. It brought a smile to his face.

For a while the pair stood in the half-light, speaking in soft whispers, touching and giggling at treasures they had uncovered. Finally, Dylan allowed himself to take with him one box from a cupboard on the wall. Jen took a box camera to look at in the daylight that upstairs would give them, and a couple of vinyl records. The rest would be explored as a family.

When they arrived at the top of the cellar steps Jen could see Dylan's eyes were not only red but also moist. 'You okay?' He nodded his head. Instinctively she knew he was reliving his childhood.

'I'm jealous,' she said.

'Jealous?'

'I might have a memory box, but you've got a whole memory room!' Her eyes filled with wonder as she opened up the camera. 'And look, look here, there is film in this camera, that we might be able to get developed.' Her eyes were wide. 'We can only imagine what else we might find about your past.'

Dylan sat at the dining room table. Maisy was ready for school, Jen for work. Breakfast had been made and eaten and Max had been walked.

'Any chance you might be coming in today?' she said with a twinkle in her eye.

'Mmm... I'm right behind you,' he said with a laugh as he discarded one photo for another in his hand.

'Why didn't Joe take it all with him when you moved do you think?'

Dylan looked puzzled. 'I have no idea...'

'Maybe one of the others might know?'

# Chapter Twenty-Seven

Reggie Hartley had been released from hospital and was ensconced in the cells when Dylan arrived at the station later that morning.

Vicky had disclosed to his solicitor the necessary evidence in connection with the murder of Julie Dixon. In the first instance, in fairness to Hartley the detectives prepared to talk to him first about the most recent incident.

'I have briefly spoken to my client,' said the solicitor. 'He would like me to make an official complaint about the dog handler.'

Vicky smiled sweetly. 'He's entitled.'

'He won't be dissuaded, mind you...' his solicitor grimaced, 'if you saw the bites... The dog has had his pound of flesh.'

'Is he going to talk to us?'

'I've told him he's not obliged to answer any of your questions.'

Adrenaline-fuelled, Raj walked beside Vicky down the corridor to the interview room.

'Keep an open mind, and don't always accept the first thing that he tells you,' said Vicky, as much to remind herself as her colleague. 'This interview, it feels important, I feel nervous for some reason. The things he has done makes me really mad – I hope I can keep a lid on it.'

'You can, and you will. There's method in our madness. If we have to shake hands and thank him we will.'

Vicky lifted an eyebrow and gave her a sly smile. 'I'd befriend the devil if he'd admitted to a murder he'd committed and I could get him locked up for life.'

'Remember murder takes precedence, he'll be interviewed about the drugs later. Stick with the plan. We've done our preparation. I'm ready for him not answering any of the questions we put to him, are you?'

Vicky nodded. 'As if we haven't enough pressure without Dylan watching us from the sanctuary of his office via the link to the interview room. The solicitor told me, he'd informed Hartley he's not obliged to talk to us, but we know of old that if we ask all our questions we might get a reply to some, if not all.'

Raj winked at Vicky, 'Exactly! I'll do the caution shall I?'

'Caution,' Vicky tutted. 'The most stupid thing about British law is the bloody caution.' She put on her posh voice. '"You do not have to say anything..." Then we're upset when they don't – now, that's madness!'

The interview commenced after the necessary formalities had been completed.

'Have you ever been to the home address of Julie Dixon?' said Raj.

'No reply.'

'If you have, now is the time to tell me.

Hartley sighed deeply. 'No reply.'

'Are you going to say, no reply, to everything we ask you, or are you no replying to that particular question?'

'No reply.'

'Did you have anything to do with the murder of Julie Dixon?' asked Vicky.

'No reply.'

'Okay, so you have never been to the home address of Julie Dixon, and you had nothing to do with her murder. Is that right?'

'No reply.'

Sat watching the unfolding of the interview from the confines of his office Dylan chanted under his breath. 'Come on, come on, keep pushing him,' he said gently as he bit his lip nervously.

As if hearing Dylan, Raj dropped the bombshell on his toes. 'Then can you explain why your DNA is at the scene?'

There was a long pause in the interview room. A slight rap at the window made Dylan turn his head to see David and Rachael hovering at the door. He motioned them in.

'Can we sit in boss?' said David.

'By all means,' he said.

It was apparent to Dylan by watching Hartley's body language that he didn't like the fact they continued questioning him even though he had 'no replied'. 'How naive was he?' he thought. It was very frustrating, being on the outside looking in, but it helped the

SIO to pick up on things that the interviewers didn't. He looked up at David and Rachael sitting opposite him, eyes on the screen.

Hartley lifted his head. 'Look, I didn't mean to hurt her. I lost my temper. One minute she was begging me to shag her, the next she told me she was going to drop me in it for that other girl, her that does gym stuff. I told Julie, the girl meant nothing to me, she was just a dick tease, but she wouldn't believe me. They both come onto me and then they change their bloody minds. What do you women expect?' His eyes were cold, his mouth ugly. He stared at Raj, unblinking.

Raj swallowed. 'Can we go a little slower Reggie so we can understand. Is it all right to call you Reggie?'

'Absolutely,' he said.

'Okay Reggie, do you want to tell us what happened from the beginning. Your sister Lucy has told us that you helped her out sometimes and took parcels round to Julie's, is that right?'

Hartley scoffed. 'Aye, well she thought I was helping her out but I was using her. Bloody thick she is. Why would I want to help her out if I wasn't getting something out of it? The bonus was Julie had the hots for me – begging for it she was.'

'And did Alan know about this?'

'No, what a dick, he must have been blind. I even bit her on her tits and he didn't even say owt.'

'And did Julie seem upset when you bit her?'

Hartley shrugged his shoulders. 'She likes it rough, it's a game we play.'

'Okay, so how did Julie get hurt?' said Raj.

'It were your lots fault actually. A note came through our Lucy's door asking her to contact the police about a parcel delivery.'

Vicky turned to look at Raj.

'What? What've I said?' said Hartley with a mocking laugh.

Raj frowned. 'Nothing, go on.'

'I knew our Lucy would talk to Julie, so I went around to see her and ask her not to say anything about me doing the delivery that day – that's when I saw that gymnast girl, brandishing her arse at me. She gave me the come on – I followed her home. She left the door unlocked for me to go in after her. She'd even got upstairs to get ready for me. Took her clothes off. She didn't wear knickers.'

'And then what happened?'

'I was shagging her.' Hartley's smile grew on his ugly face. 'How was I to know her bra was around her friggin' neck. She should have taken it off like I asked.'

'But you must have known...'

'She was moaning – girls moan when they're enjoying it, don't you?' He stopped for a moment, a twinkle in his eye. 'I left her lying there... That's the truth.'

'I knew it were me that had done the delivery for her that day didn't I? So I went round to her place and asked her not to say anything. I took a few drugs with me, to say thank you like. But she started acting really strange when I offered her them.' His eyes grew wide. 'Like really, really strange. She tried to run out on me. She fell instantly to the floor... there was blood all over. I had to move her. A cop car followed me from the end of her street. I panicked, changed direction over the moors and dumped her in Shroggs Grove, behind the bins, where she belonged. I dumped her car in Ogden Water. 'Your lot started it with the letter, and then I had to drug her. Just bad luck they were both accidents. '

'You raped a young schoolgirl before you strangled her and you killed Julie by smashing her head in with a hammer,' Vicky told him. 'We can prove both were deliberate acts, not accidents. Forensic evidence tells us that.'

'Yeah, well shit happens, and do you want to know something I fucking enjoyed it. The Boss is right. You women are tarts, you get everything you deserve,' he shouted and spittle sprayed from his mouth causing Raj to lean back.

'Boss,' questioned Vicky.

'Top man, Malcolm Reynolds. You'll never catch him.'

The buzzer on the tape sounded, indicating the end of the interview.

Dylan turned the screen off and smiled across at David and Rachael. 'Well, what do you think?'

'He's a monster that needs to be behind bars,' said Rachael with a look of distaste.

'They'll interview him again but my guess is he will "no reply" to everything we put to him after his solicitor has spoken to him.'

'Samples need to be taken,' said David, 'I should get off.' The couple stood. Rachael walked to wards the door.

'Thanks sir,' she said with a wave and she was gone.

'And then he'll go before the courts,' said David.

'He will indeed.' Dylan raised his eyebrow at David. 'Tell me,' he said. 'You two an item?'

David colour rose on his cheeks. 'Not much gets past you does it sir?'

Dylan grinned.

'You know, I have experienced some rather painful situations in my youth when people have reacted badly to my missing hand. I travelled, I bought nice cars, I love this job but I never thought I'd find anyone who'd love me. And then I met Rachael who was guarding the scene at Patti's murder and, I cannot honestly say I've never been happier.'

'Should I tell Jen to buy a hat?'

'Who knows, sir, who knows...'

\*\*\*

'Neither investigation has been easy and now they are one,' Dylan said at the debrief. 'Nobody expects a murder down their street, and when it does happen, the shockwaves ripple far and wide across the community. Lives have been lost and others destroyed. I want to thank each and every one of you, for our excellent work that is worthy of recognition by the Courts. When a killer strikes, what most people don't appreciate, or the perpetrator realise is that they have unleashed a relentless pursuit by dedicated officers that never ends until the offenders are caught. We will have a proper get together when Hartley is convicted, but anyone who wants a quick drink this evening, across the road, you're welcome, my shout!'

Later that evening across the road in the pub Dylan stood quietly sipping his pint at the bar. His eyes lazily scanned the room. Success was in the air, and that wasn't all as he noticed David and Rachael sat talking and laughing in the corner by the door.

'Hartley was a monster that needs to be behind bars,' Vicky said as she joined Dylan with Raj.

'For once I have to agree with her analysis of the man, if you can call him that,' added Raj.

Dylan picked up his mobile phone and typed a message to Jen. 'It's over. He's charged Miss Jones,' his name for her when they had first met at Harrowfield Police Station. 'Just standing the team a drink and then I'll be leaving one station for another. x'

'Brilliant news! When you decide to retire, you'll be busier than ever, there is so much here to be done,' she replied.

Dylan smiled a contented smile, downed his pint and ordered another. The beer as addictive as his job, for now it was anyway.

If you haven't already read them, don't forget the other titles in the DI Dylan series.

Deadly Focus
Consequences
White Lilies
Snow Kills
Reprobates
Killer Smile
When The Killing Starts

If you have enjoyed this or any of the other books in the series then please think about leaving a review on line. It means so much to us and our authors.

## Further Reading recommendations from Caffeine Nights

If you like police procedurals then you will enjoy the DS Hunter Kerr and DS Scarlett Macey series by Michael Fowler

Other great crime books from Caffeine Nights include

The Dead Can't Talk – Nick Quantrill
No Doves – Andy Boot
Suits and Bullets – Alfie Robins
Remission – Ed Chatterton
Vile City – Jennifer Lee Thomson
Body Breaker – Mike Craven
Breathe – David Ince

Check out these and other great crime and horror fiction titles from Caffeine Nights at caffeinenights.com